JC INC
NOVEL

BY JOHN CLARKSON

AND JUSTICE FOR ONE

ONE MAN'S LAW

ONE WAY OUT

NEW LOTS

REED'S PROMISE

AMONG THIEVES

BRONX REQUIEM

JOHN CLARKSON

ONE MAN'S LAW

A NOVEL OF VENGEANCE BY THE AUTHOR OF
AND JUSTICE FOR ONE

Second Edition published 2018 by JOHN CLARKSON INC.
11 Schermerhorn Street, Suite 6WB, Brooklyn, NY 11201

ISBN 978-0-9992155-0-0   softcover
ISBN 978-0-9992155-3-1   e-book

1. The main category of this book is – Crime Thriller – fiction.
2. Murder/mystery - fiction. 3. Vengeance – fiction.
4. Corruption – fiction. 5. Suspense – fiction. 6. Hawaii – fiction.
7. U.S. Military – fiction. 8. Vietnam – fiction

Cover and interior designed by Anton Khodakovsky

Printing History:
Berkley Publishing Group / June 1994

PRINTED IN THE UNITED STATES OF AMERICA

CONTENTS

No law can be sacred to me

but that of my nature.

—RALPH WALDO EMERSON

Author's Note

They say you can't go back. That's true most of the time. But with a novel you can go back and fix it, change it, try to make it the book it should have been. That's what I've done with *One Man's Law*.

This book was the second in a new series I started when I first started writing novels. I won't bore you with the publishing details except to say that my agent at the time convinced me to leave Crown Publishing and accept a deal with Putnam/Berkley to publish *One Man's Law* and the sequel. That changed everything, particularly the editor in charge of my books. Mistake number one. Also, around that time I sold the movie rights to the first book in the series to Paramount provided they let me write the screenplay. Mistake number two. Also, at the time I was running my own advertising agency. I liked the work, was good at it, and it gave me a chance to earn a good living. (In case you're wondering, publishing rarely does.) So, can't say that was a mistake. It was a necessity, but not ideal for continuing the work on the novels.

Bottom line, I was too caught up in other endeavors to make sure *One Man's Law* was published in the best form possible. It was a bloated (137K word), messy rendition of an interesting idea. This new edition is what the original should have been. Edited down to a proper 113K, now the story and themes of the book come through. *One Man's Law* tackles issues that include dealing with our county's misguided policies of war, militarism, colonialism, racism, greed, guilt, and the warrior spirit required to fight all of the above. It's ironic that in this story our beloved tough-guy protagonist, Jack Devlin, has to confront the wrongs done 20 years in the past. It took me about the same amount of time to confront and correct the mistakes I made the first time around with this book.

It was worth the effort. It gave me great pleasure to revise *One Man's Law* and turn it into a story worthy of Jack Devlin. I look forward to you sharing in that pleasure when you read it.

ACKNOWLEDGMENTS

I don't think most people know much about Hawaii beyond the usual images of beautiful beaches, destination hotels, and tourist attractions. There's more to this fascinating set of islands, including disenfranchisement, poverty, racism, and the fact that Hawaii has the largest concentration of U.S. Military bases and compounds in the country. To know about these things, you have to know the people who live there. Two people in particular helped me discover this "other" Hawaii.

When *One Man's Law* was first published, I wrote: This book could never have been written without the help of Richard McMahon who started out as my guide and ended up as my friend. He shared his knowledge of Hawaii with me, his experiences as a decorated Army officer, his companionship, and his home. That's just as true today as it was then. But now I can add that his friendship and support deepened over the years as we shared experiences, ideas, and thoughts regarding the process of writing. Thank you for all of that and more, Richard.

I'd also like to once again thank Roger Christie for giving generously of his time and sharing the power of his activist spirit. In the years since the book was first published, Roger's spirit has not only never wavered, it's grown stronger. Roger has paid the price for his beliefs and earned the accolades he deserves because of his commitment.

PROLOGUE

As dawn slowly pushed the darkness out of the cloudy sky over Pahoa-town, Billy Cranston smoked up his last bud, on the last day of his life.

He cradled a well-used wooden pipe in his right hand, sucked sharply, and inhaled deeply. He held his breath so that the sacramental smoke would seep deep into his lungs. He exhaled very slowly and sniffed back the exiting smoke, trying to capture all that the sacred herb had to give him.

He squatted coolie-style underneath a piece of weathered plywood hanging over the back of a rundown, empty wooden building sitting at the east end of a small rural village on the big island of Hawaii. Billy had slept under the flimsy shelter, wrapped in a tattered wool blanket that he carried rolled up, tied with a thick piece of twine, and slung across his broad back.

Billy settled into his plantation squat, pulled in more sacred herb, watching the small trails of smoke that rose from the little wooden pipe bowl. He watched the clouds in the dawn sky release a fine mist of tropical rain. He looked down at his worn-out boots estimating how long it would take him to hike the miles that lay ahead of him.

Billy took another toke. He had cultivated the marijuana himself, not too far from his destination, planting it according to the season and cycles of the moon. Billy Cranston considered the herb to be a sacrament, just as sacred as receiving a Catholic communion host had once been to him. That was long ago. Before his life had dwindled down to very little except pain and anguish.

The trade winds whipped through the sky, and suddenly the tropical mist turned into a steady downpour. After a few minutes of concentrating on the rain, it seemed to Billy that he could see the individual drops falling through the balmy tropical air. Big, fat, heavy drops of warm water splattering into the rubble-strewn back lot, turning the red Hawaiian earth into blood-red mud.

A mynah bird fluttered into view, landing about five yards in front of him. The funny little black bird with a bright yellow beak and bowed legs began strutting back and forth pecking at tufts of pungent molasses grass, breaking Billy's reverie.

He smacked the pipe against the palm of his hand, emptying the residue. Billy looked at his hands. They were big hands. Still strong, even though two fingers on his left hand were permanently bent inward. His hands were dirty, and Billy hated being dirty. Even though he had long ago lost his capacity to maintain a home where he could wash in a real bathroom, Billy always tried to stay clean. He leaned forward out from under the protection of the plywood overhang and held his hands in the cool Hawaiian rainfall. He rubbed them clean as best he could, then wiped them dry on the sides of his worn-out jeans.

He rubbed his face and stroked a long black beard flecked with gray that reached to his chest. He ran his fingers through his thick black hair graying at the temples, pushing it behind his ears, getting ready.

Billy Cranston had fought and survived many battles, in war and in peace, but now even the victories felt like life-sapping losses. All the struggle had somehow created a terrible downward momentum in his life. Billy Cranston felt like he was fading into something less significant than the last puff of pungent smoke that had disappeared in the rain-filled morning air. All that loss would end today. He focused on one overwhelming impulse, wondering if the last spark pushing him now came from love or hate, murder or sacrifice. He wasn't sure. The attempt to decide spiraled him to a confused moment, his life lingering in a hazy limbo of inaction. And then the feisty little mynah bird twitched, stopped, and looked at him. Stared right at him as if to ask, *why are you here? This is my world, not yours.*

So, Billy Cranston stood up, brushed off his clothes, squared his shoulders. He even lifted his chin as he stepped out into the morning rain to take back one last thing that was still his. The mynah jumped up and fluttered off, having no idea that his piercing little eye had sent Billy Cranston walking toward a terrible death.

CHAPTER 1

Devlin woke as the change in air pressure made his left ear hurt. It was his built-in airplane alarm clock. He waggled his jaw to equalize the pressure and shifted his six-feet-four-inch body stretched out in first-class seat 4A. Far enough from the kitchen and bathrooms so his sleep would be relatively undisturbed. Devlin needed sleep. In the last seven days, he'd averaged three hours' sleep for every thirty hours awake until he had finished what he had to do in New York.

The plane would be landing in San Francisco. He'd have a fifty-minute break between flights; then he'd be on to Honolulu. He looked forward to walking around the terminal until he had to board the next flight. Get his muscles moving. See how his hip was holding out after being nicked by a .38-caliber bullet.

But when he emerged from the jetway, Devlin saw a young man trying to pick someone out of the stream of passengers coming off the plan. He guessed that someone was him. Just for the hell of it, Devlin shifted behind two people in front of him, blending in, concealing himself. His movements were smooth and artful enough to hide his large body from the young man until he was almost close enough to touch him.

Devlin's sudden appearance made the young man take a full step backward.

"Are you looking for me?"

"Mr. Devlin?"

"Yes."

"Uh, Mr. Chow has to meet you here in San Francisco instead of Honolulu. He sent me to get you."

"Where is he?"

"The Mandarin Oriental Hotel. Downtown. He said you should stay the night and fly to Honolulu tomorrow."

The young man pulled an airline ticket out of the side pocket of his suit coat. "We have a new ticket for you. Same flight out tomorrow."

Devlin withdrew his ticket from his breast pocket and made the exchange. Chow's man stood where he was and stared at Devlin.

Devlin asked, "Anything else?"

"Uh, no. Is that your only luggage?"

Devlin handed a finely made carry-on bag to the young man.

"Lay on, Macduff."

The young man looked confused for a moment, then said, "Isn't it lead on?"

Devlin smiled. "Not if you work for William Chow."

#

William Chow had reserved a one-bedroom suite on the top floor of the Mandarin, a hotel that occupied the upper floors of an office building tower. The suite sat hidden in the clouds with most of San Francisco spread out beneath it. Only the Transamerica tower poked its pyramid tip high enough to share the airspace.

The suite offered sweeping views. In one direction, was a view of the bridge to Oakland. Out another window was a magnificent view of the Golden Gate. Thick clouds of fog were rolling in from the bay, covering the city beneath them. The setting sun colored the fog with tones of purple and red.

William Chow, the founder and head of Pacific Rim Security Company, stood with his hands clasped behind his back looking out the north window. He was dressed in black slacks made of very fine lightweight wool and a crisp white dress shirt made by his tailor in Hong Kong. The clothes hung perfectly on his lean, well-proportioned body. Chow was a compact man, a mix of Oriental bloodlines and Occidental manners. He was part Chinese, part Caucasian, a lineage that had blended to produce a strikingly handsome man, aging gracefully. The more years Devlin knew him, the more Chow seemed to become a unique kind of Everyman. A citizen of the East, at ease in the West, working anywhere in the world that required his attention.

Green tea had been served. The teapot rested snugly in a thickly insulated wicker basket. Devlin sat on the couch, sipping the slightly bitter brew from a fine porcelain cup, watching Chow. Waiting. On the glass end table, a manila folder rested unopened. Devlin knew it contained the information that would soon disturb the tranquility of their elegant room in the clouds. But for the moment, the folder just lay there, like a silent, unwanted guest.

Finally, Chow turned away from the window and spoke. "New York was difficult?"

"Yes."

"Your wounds?"

"More troublesome than serious."

"Good." Chow paused. "So, we have a problem."

"Yes?"

"A death. Very disturbing. Someone we know."

Devlin frowned. "Who?"

"William Edward Cranston."

"Billy Cranston?"

"Yes."

Hearing the name brought up a flood of memories. Even the smell of mortars exploding in a rotting jungle. Devlin's expression darkened. He asked, "How did he die?"

"Violently."

"Murdered?"

"Very likely."

Devlin felt a mixture of pain and anger so intense he stopped breathing for a moment. Devlin bowed his head, feeling as if the private, luxurious room in the sky made hearing this news even more offensive.

Chow continued, "We don't know the details. His father has retained the firm to find out exactly what happened."

Devlin knew that Chow had a long relationship with Billy Cranston's father, a retired Brigadier General, Jasper Cranston. Devlin had never met the father. His relationship had been with the son, had lasted less than three days, but had changed his life.

At the time Devlin met Billy Cranston, his father, Jasper, was a Lieutenant Colonel commanding an Army Intelligence battalion in Vietnam. Cranston, a Korean War veteran, was on his second tour of duty in Vietnam.

Billy Cranston, an Infantry grunt, was nearing the end of his first tour of duty in 'Nam. Fate had placed him in a series of brutal jungle battles that earned him the kind of reputation an entire Army could feed on to prove to itself that it still produced brave men. In a little under two years fighting in Vietnam, Billy had risen to the rank of sergeant first class, had won a Bronze Star, two Purple Hearts, an Army Commendation Medal, and a recommendation for the Silver Star, along with two disciplinary actions for insubordination.

Billy Cranston's style didn't fit with his commanding officer's approach, so he solved the problem by transferring Billy to Jasper Cranston's Intelligence battalion. At that time, the battalion was monitoring Viet Cong arms and supply movements by stationing two-man observation teams on secluded mountaintop areas. The teams hunkered down and hid in the jungle, counting trucks and personnel moving on the paths and roads beneath them. It was considered safer duty than most combat assignments. There was, however, the risk of being discovered. Discovery meant almost certain death.

Each team stayed in its hidden observation post for one week. After that, the teams had to be replaced, because a week alone in the jungle was about all the soldiers could take before they began to break down mentally.

Devlin had only been in the country for two months, not yet assigned to his Military Police post, but in those days MP's provided combat support. When a young Lieutenant found himself short one man, he ordered Devlin to join another soldier and replace a team positioned on a hilltop ridge, eleven miles inside Cambodia. The team consisted of Cranston's son, Billy, and another soldier, named James McNally.

Devlin and his partner, a skinny Jewish kid from Queens, New York named Ralph Axelrod, were helicoptered in along with three other teams. They were the first team to be dropped into a clearing about two miles from the observation site. It took them over two hours to hike up to the site.

Six minutes after Devlin and Axelrod arrived at the observation post, Viet Cong mortars started falling. The first mortar landed ten meters to the right of the bivouac. The second, eight meters to the left. All four soldiers knew they were bracketed, but before they could even look for cover, four more mortars exploded around them. The ground shuddered, the explosions concussed them into oblivion.

When Devlin regained consciousness, Axelrod had been turned into a blackened mound of green uniform, blood, ripped flesh, and shattered bones. McNally had lost an arm and most of the left side of his face. Billy Cranston had survived with only a large gash above his right ear. He leaned over Devlin, the right side of his face and shoulder covered in blood, trying to get Devlin to sit up. He seemed oblivious to his wound. In fact, he seemed energized by the mortar attack.

Devlin tried to sit up, but he kept falling onto his back. Billy yelled at him, "C'mon, get up. Get up before these rat bastards swarm us!"

Cranston pulled Devlin into a sitting position, then ran off to pour disinfectant powder all over the bloody, blackened area of flesh where McNally's arm had been. He tied a compress to the man's face, turned him over on his side so the dirt wouldn't grind into his wounds, all the while yelling at Devlin to get up.

By the time Devlin made it onto his hands and knees, Billy was pushing a syringe filled with a morphine solution into McNally's thigh muscle.

Devlin remained bent over on all fours and threw up. It wasn't the sight of the carnage that had made him vomit. It was the concussion he had sustained in the mortar attack.

Devlin spat out the bile and felt a big hand pat him on the back. He looked up and saw Billy Cranston's dazzling smile. He would always remember how white and perfect Cranston's teeth looked, how alive and confident his expression was, even with his face covered in blood and dirt.

Billy shouted, "Can you hear me?"

Devlin realized his hearing was just coming back and nodded.

"Good." Cranston stopped patting Devlin on the back to wrap a field dressing around his head wound.

"Let's get the fuck out of here before they make it up the hill. There's gonna be way too many of them for us to stay here and shoot it out."

Devlin nodded in response. It was about all he could do.

Billy yelled at him, "You're not hit. You're a lucky motherfucker, but you got to get moving and help me drag this guy out of here, or we're all dead."

Devlin stood up and staggered over to McNally. He wanted to hook him under the armpits and drag him away from the hilltop, but there was only one armpit left on the man. Cranston was gathering up rifles, a radio, supplies. Devlin was about to grab McNally by the collar of his shirt when Billy appeared holding a tarpaulin and a rope. He dropped them on the ground near at Devlin. "Tie him onto this."

Devlin did as he was told. Cranston finished loading up with as much ammunition and supplies as he could carry, then motioned for Devlin to follow. He staggered after Billy, dragging the tarp bearing the wounded soldier.

They made it halfway down the mountain when Cranston suddenly stopped and crouched in the jungle foliage, motioning for Devlin to do the same. He flashed Devlin his mesmerizing smile and whispered, "Now we see just how lucky you are, soldier."

Cranston smeared soil on the white bandage around his head. Devlin could barely hold still. He wanted to keep moving, but Cranston remained motionless. McNally had passed out from shock and morphine. And then Devlin saw them. North Vietnamese Army regulars. Rifles held in front of them, climbing slowly up the hill in a firing line, each soldier about twenty yards apart from the men on either side. The line extended as far to the right and left as Devlin could see.

The fear hit Devlin right behind his balls. He felt his heart pound and the strange, demeaning urge to evacuate his bowels. The intensity of it nearly overwhelmed him, but Cranston's unmoving presence steadied Devlin. Suddenly, Devlin had an intense need to have his rifle in his hands. As if Cranston could read his mind, he slowly slid the two M16 rifles off his shoulder and handed one to Devlin, whispering, "Don't fucking shoot unless I do."

Devlin gripped the rifle and nodded. He started visualizing how many of the NVA he would be able to shoot before they cut him down. A strange hot energy filled him. The insanity of combat. Billy turned and smiled at him as if he felt Devlin's heat. For a second, Devlin wondered if Billy was a brave man or a lunatic.

For a moment, it looked as if the enemy soldiers would walk past them as if these two trapped men crouching in the jungle were so dangerous they sensed they should avoid them. But then one soldier began to veer in their direction, taking a path straight toward them, and both Devlin and Billy knew they were going to be discovered. In the next instant, without a word, Cranston lay down on the jungle floor and slid forward, down the hill.

Devlin watched the jungle foliage move as Cranston made his invisible way toward the oncoming soldier. The slight noise didn't attract any attention. There were plenty of sounds coming from the other soldiers struggling up the hill.

Slowly, step by step, his back covered in jungle foliage for camouflage, the NVA soldier kept coming right at Devlin. Inside his head, Devlin screamed curses at the enemy, but the soldier kept coming, step by step. Devlin slowly shouldered his M16, blinked his eyes, and tried to track the moving soldier in his sights. Two or three more steps and Devlin was certain the NVA would see him. Suddenly the enemy soldier fell backward. For a second, Devlin thought the man had slipped and fallen. And he had. But it was because Billy Cranston had pulled his legs out from under him. Almost before the enemy hit the ground, Billy clamped his hand over the man's mouth and shoved his knife into the NVA regular's throat. Billy rolled on top of the soldier, twisting the knife, covering the gurgling sounds and spasmodic attempts to push Billy off.

Devlin eased the M16 into his lap. He couldn't believe the guts it took to pull that off. He breathed slowly and deeply, trying to come back to himself. The enemy troops were well past them when Billy popped up into view, his shirt soaked in the blood of the enemy, and motioned for Devlin to come forward.

They made it down the hill, dragging the still comatose McNally with them. They crouched under deep cover while Billy radioed for a helicopter to pull them out, but the Army air rescue told them they had to wait. Army personnel weren't supposed to be in Cambodia. How could they authorize a chopper to get people who weren't there? They told Billy to standby.

Devlin hadn't listened closely to Billy's conversation on the radio. He had made it off that goddamn mountain. It was over.

All he had to do was wait for the helicopter. Billy turned to him and smiled, "Guess what, brah?"

"What?"

"I don't think they're coming anytime soon, and we don't have time to wait."

"What?"

Billy shrugged. "We ain't supposed to be in Cambodia, dude. The assholes in charge gotta run the request up the line before they send a chopper in here. We're gonna be fucked if we wait for them to get their thumbs out of their ass. Too many NVA crawling around. C'mon. We can make it. You're a big strong lucky rookie motherfucker. You can do it."

"Make it where?"

"Other side of the border, man." And then Billy Cranston looked wide-eyed at Devlin and said, "What the fuck, it's only about twenty klicks. Just five or so klicks east of here, we'll be clear of all these fuckin' NVA, and we'll be safe as houses."

"What the hell does that mean?"

"I don't know. Heard some Brit say it. I like it. Let's go. You can do it."

And at that moment, Devlin believed he could. He didn't think about how dense the jungle was. He didn't think about dragging a dying man behind them. He didn't think about how many NVA soldiers were looking for them. Billy Cranston had that kind of effect on men.

As night came on, they stumbled through the tropical mess for almost eight hours, dragging McNally behind them. They were still alive in the morning, but McNally had died from blood loss and shock. Cranston insisted they drag the body with them. Devlin didn't argue. They wrapped the tarpaulin completely around their dead comrade and kept walking. Cranston took the lead, chopping a path through the thick forest and vines, Devlin stumbling behind him, constantly struggling to pull the dead weight of McNally's remains.

When Devlin began tripping and falling from exhaustion, Cranston hacked away with one hand and helped him pull the body with the other.

For the rest of that night, they slowly made their way toward the border. Dehydrated, without food, still hurting from the mortar attack, abandoned, Devlin almost wished the enemy would find them and shoot them, so the struggle would end. But Billy Cranston never wavered, never complained, continued to tell Devlin they would get out.

Billy kept track of their position. Kept contact on the radio in short bursts. Kept working to find a way out. And sure enough, near dawn, they received instructions to hike due east for two miles until they reached a rutted jeep trail.

Billy lied to Devlin about how long it would take. Told him how tough he was for a two-month, in-country, lucky fucking rookie ass-kicking grunt. Told him he would never be hurt again in 'Nam because he had already been through the worst. The words helped, but they weren't what kept Devlin going. They both knew it was all just a bullshit pep talk. It was that goddamn dazzling hero smile that mesmerized Devlin, kept inspiring him to put one foot in front of the other, kept him believing.

They finally reached the road. Actually, just two overgrown tire tracks in the jungle. And by what seemed like a miracle of Billy Cranston's willpower, three hours later, they heard an old, beat-up truck slowly bumping its way through the tropical forest.

Cranston stepped out, and a tiny Vietnamese man who looked to be at least eighty stopped the truck. Cranston helped Devlin lift McNally's corpse into the truck bed, he climbed in next to the driver, then helped Devlin into the front passenger seat. Devlin drank from the canteen of warm water the old man handed them. Then he slumped down, lay his head on the back of the seat, and fell into an exhausted unconscious sleep listening to Billy Cranston try to talk to the old Vietnamese driver.

When Devlin woke, they were back at battalion headquarters. He and Billy shook hands and promised to keep track of each other. Just when Devlin was about to head off and report to his squad, Billy gave him a gift that stayed with him for the rest of his life.

He said, "Jack."

It was the first time Billy had ever used his name.

"Yeah?"

"You do know that you're a warrior, Jack, don't you?"

"What do you mean?"

"You took some heavy hits up there. Had your brains rattled real good, huh? Saw one soldier blown to shit, another die. You held it together when those NVA bastards closed in, and you wanted that fucking rifle in your hands, didn't you? Didn't you?"

Devlin remained silent.

Billy nodded once and said, "You'll be okay, brah." Billy tapped his chest. "You got it in here."

Devlin never saw Billy Cranston again. It didn't matter. He'd already experienced the best of the man.

#

Devlin asked Chow, "What happened to him?"

Chow came away from the window, sat across from Devlin, and poured himself a cup of tea. He spoke in a soft voice touched with a slight British accent, a voice that never failed to lend intensity to his words.

"We're not sure. Mr. Cranston was found in a remote area in the Puna District on the Big Island of Hawaii. In an undeveloped section of the Ola'a Forest Reserve, west of a series of abandoned subdivisions that were chopped out of the rainforest years ago but never developed. By the time they found the body, it had been ravaged by feral pigs and whatever other wild animals were wandering around in there."

Devlin jerked back as if the words were a slap. "What?"

"Not an ending anyone would wish for him."

Devlin shook his head. "The man was a hero, William. How could that happen to him?"

"That's what you must find out, Jack. Cranston's father is retired now. He mustered out as a brigadier general. Jasper lives on Oahu. He asked me to investigate his son's death. I assured him Pacific Rim would devote whatever resources necessary. As you know, Jack, General Cranston and I go back many years. I told the general we would find the answers he seeks."

Chow stood up and walked back to the window, then turned and stepped toward Devlin. He remained in that position, hands at his sides, backlit by the red twilight. He was more an outline than a man. More a presence at that moment than a person.

"I know you and Billy Cranston served together."

"For all of about three days. Long enough for Billy to save my life. Long enough to see everything that was wrong with that damn war and everything that was right with Billy Cranston."

"That's why I want you to be the one investigating this."

Devlin couldn't remain seated. He stood up and turned away from Chow. He looked out the window on his side of the room. Now the blankets of purple-red rolling fog reminded him of blood and bruises and death. He waited for a few moments before he spoke.

"What do the local authorities say?"

"Very little."

"Why?"

"A reflection of how much they cared about Mr. Cranston."

"What does that mean?"

"Apparently, Billy Cranston had degenerated over the years. He was living the life of a wandering soul. Virtually homeless. He was not a person of importance to them."

"What the hell happened?"

Chow answered tersely, "I don't know."

Devlin tried to imagine Billy Cranston reduced to a homeless man wandering around a desolate rainforest in Hawaii. He simply could not.

"What about his father? What does his father say?"

"General Cranston believes his son was murdered."

"Why?"

Chow pointed to the manila folder. "Read the medical examiner's report. They estimated the body was in the rainforest about two weeks. Most of the intestinal cavity was rooted out and eaten. The rest of the soft-tissue organs were badly decomposed. However, the M.E. thinks, thinks he may have detected a nick, a cut on the periosteum covering the back rib on the left. Not the kind of cut that could have been made by an animal's tooth."

"A knife."

"Presumably."

Devlin turned away from the window and faced Chow. "It would have to have been a long knife to reach all the way to the back rib."

"Yes."

"On the left side."

"Yes."

Devlin said, "Shoved in by a right-handed person with enough force to push it almost completely through the body."

"Yes."

"And whoever did it left him out in a rainforest so that whatever animals roam around in there could feed off him?"

Chow nodded.

"And we have no idea why?"

"None."

Devlin knew it was pointless to ask any more questions, except one.

"Where do you want me to start?"

Chow picked up the manila folder from the end table and handed it to Devlin.

"Read the file. Then talk to General Cranston. After that, you decide. The organization is at your disposal. Cranston insists he has the resources to fund our investigation, but it proves to be beyond his means, I will personally reimburse the company."

"Understood."

"I'm needed in Hong Kong. Please keep me informed."

"Yes, sir."

Chow took a step toward Devlin. He held his hands clasped behind his back and bowed his head for a moment before he spoke. When he looked up, he had Devlin's full attention.

"I wish you had more time to recuperate from New York, help with your brother's convalescence, mourn your father's death. But assigning this to someone else is out of the question."

"I understand."

"Good." Chow reached out and lightly grasped Devlin's upper arm. "Please do your best, Jack."

Devlin nodded, and Chow relinquished his grip. Somehow, by simply making physical contact, Chow had added his depth of feeling to Devlin's.

And in the next instant, the meeting was over. William Chow, the only man in the world Devlin trusted enough to be his boss, picked up a small leather portfolio that had been resting on the hotel room desk and left, quietly closing the door behind him.

CHAPTER 2

Devlin avoided reading the report until the following day on the plane heading for Honolulu. He was in no hurry to immerse himself in the details of Billy Cranston's death. But now with his plane landing in a couple of hours, he couldn't put off the grim task any longer. As the big DC-10 streaked west, prolonging the fading sunset, Devlin switched on his overhead light and pulled the manila folder from the seatback pocket in front of him.

There were three pages of single-spaced notes on Pacific Rim letterhead summarizing the initial contact report with Jasper Cranston. There was a photocopy of the fifteen-page medical examiner's report on the autopsy performed in Hilo along with a copy of the report from the Puna District office of the Hilo police force – only a single page. And then there were the pictures. Twelve of them. Color. Eight by ten. Lurid. So unreal that they looked to Devlin like still frames from a cheap horror movie.

Devlin set aside the written reports and steeled himself for the photographs. Five shots had been taken in the bright outdoor light. The corpse looked like it had been propped against the base of an ohia tree, pushed onto its left side by the animals who had fed off the corpse. The area from the sternum to the abdomen was a black, ragged hole ringed with torn flesh mottled with decay. A dirty, ripped-open T-shirt ringed the rotting hole. Inside the cavity were speckled white bones – pieces of the spine, ribs, and pelvis along with clumps of black, rotting flesh, and decomposed remains of cartilage and tendons. The head bent was sideways, arms outspread. His face a frightening death mask with sunken cheeks, mouth agape, dead eyes, and dirty, matted hair. The beard reached almost all the way to the open cavity in the center of the body.

Billy Cranston had ended up a ripped-apart, emaciated wreck in a hellish Pieta pose, a tree supporting the corpse instead of a virgin mother.

The rest of the photos were garish eight-by-ten blowups of the medical examiner's 35mm shots taken indoors under the saturating glare of a strobe flash. The dead body had been cleaned up, laid out long and flat. The skin was an ashy grayish-brown with necrotic patches around the ragged hole. The long beard and hair had been shaved off; the chest split apart; the skull cap removed; the brain probed.

Devlin wondered what internal organs had been left to examine. Not many he supposed. What was left of Billy Cranston seemed as close to an abomination as Devlin had ever seen. The once vibrant, magical hero of his youth, now a torn-apart, ravaged corpse laying across a stainless-steel table. Even the once bright, gleaming teeth looked like small, dead, dingy bones.

Devlin persevered through the written reports. They added little more than to document that a tragedy had occurred but told him nothing about why, or how, or when Billy Cranston had fallen so low and met such a ruinous fate.

Devlin closed the folder and his eyes, knowing the images would haunt him. Clearly, the answers would have to start with Billy's father, General Jasper Cranston.

Flying toward the sun had elongated the day, but as the plane approach Honolulu, day turned into night. Looking down, Devlin had no sense of being in the middle of the vast Pacific Ocean. The view of the city below showed the same strings and clusters of lights poking through the darkness as the other cities Devlin had flown into.

The sameness continued as Devlin walked off the plane into the terminal. He could have been in any Mainland city. It was only when he reached the juncture where the gate area merged with the corridor leading into the main terminal that Devlin knew he'd landed on a tropical island. There was a floor. There was a roof to keep out the rain. But long sections of the corridor were open to the elements. The balmy Hawaiian air surrounded him. Even laced with jet fumes, it still felt welcoming.

Everything else about arriving fell into the usual pattern. Get the rental car. Drop his bag onto the passenger seat. Shove the rental forms in the glove compartment. Push the seat back. Adjust the mirrors. Find the switch for the headlights and drive out.

It was all very familiar and routine except for one thing. As Devlin drove north out of Honolulu, in a small office at the east end of the airport all the passenger lists for the evening's incoming Mainland flights landed on the desk of Keeko Ramon, a wiry, intense man of Portuguese descent who worked for the company that provided security at the airport. Keeko wore the standard brown uniform with a square badge on the right shirt pocket and the insignia on his left sleeve that made him look almost like a cop. But he wasn't a cop. He was another underpaid worker, just in a better uniform than most.

The acronym for the company befitted the man who owned Hawaiian Islands Security. Eddie Lihu believed whatever he wanted should rightfully be HIS. Whatever arrived on the Hawaiian Islands – tourists, consumer goods, drugs, prostitutes, whatever – Lihu's reason for living was to get his piece of anything worth something. And that started with knowing who and what came in.

So Keeko Ramon scanned the passenger lists of three airlines. His task wasn't complicated. He was looking for names that fit a certain profile: individual men or pairs, individual women, and people with names that seemed African American or Hispanic.

First, Keeko checked the coach class passengers, carefully picking out the chosen few. Then he checked first class. The name Devlin didn't stand out. It wasn't like Brown or Williams, which Keeko always assumed belonged to blacks. A single man named Brown or Williams always made the list. Devlin wasn't a Jewish name, which Keeko tended to ignore. Nor was it Hispanic. But the name Devlin belonged to a man traveling alone, flying first class, so Devlin made the list along with sixteen other names. Ramon typed them in alphabetical order with the flight numbers and faxed them to the HIS main office in Honolulu. As soon as the fax connected, Keeko headed for the coffee machine. He still had three hours left on his shift, but he'd pretty much finished his night's work.

CHAPTER 3

The drive to Cranston's house on the North Shore of Oahu took almost an hour. Devlin knew the roads. Had traveled them before, but even in the dark, he could see that the surroundings had changed. As the H2 Freeway dwindled down to the two-lane Highway 99 and farther down to the 82 Kam Highway, there were more intersections, more stoplights. Even the pineapple fields seemed smaller.

It rained on and off during the drive until he reached the small town of Haleiwa on the North Shore. Then the air stirred with a fresh breeze off the ocean and blew away the rain clouds. Devlin rolled down the windows of his rental car and slowed down to the 35-mph speed limit. The slower speed made it easier to spot the landmarks Cranston had given him: Jameson's restaurant. Sunset Beach. Foodland. They eliminated the need for a roadmap, which Devlin couldn't read while he was driving. And they relieved Devlin of trying to decipher the long Hawaiian names attached to the few road signs he was able to catch. It would take him a couple of days to re-adjust to the Hawaiian names for the various roads and towns, many of which were exactly the same names used for different roads in other towns on Hawaii's other islands.

As he drove closer to where Cranston's house was supposed to be, Devlin began looking for a long five-foot-high wall made of lava rocks on the ocean side of the road. The wall's length and height made it hard to miss. He slowed down, looking in the dark for a driveway or entrance. After about a hundred yards, he finally reached a chain-link gate on wheels about fifteen-feet wide, closing off a driveway which led to a two-car garage. After the gate, the wall continued for about another thirty feet.

Devlin pulled the car over on a grassy strip just before the gate, got out, and peered through the fence at a large house that occupied a plot of land running along the shoreline. There was a single yellow light burning near the front door.

Devlin looked around for a bell or intercom but could find neither. Nothing about Cranston's house invited entrance.

Devlin tested the rolling gate and found it latched but unlocked. He lifted the latch and rolled the gate open just wide enough to walk onto the property. Devlin rolled the gate shut behind him and had taken about ten steps toward the front door when a bullmastiff dog came running around the corner of the house, charging straight at him.

The dog had a terrifying, savage bark, which sounded as if the animal was intent on tearing Devlin's throat open. Even in the dim moonlight, Devlin could see that the charging dog had to weigh at least 150 pounds. There was no time to get back on the other side of the fence. Devlin was about to jump up on the fence to get above the beast, cursing as much at the dog as at Cranston for not warning him, when the dog skidded to halt between Devlin and the house and stood his ground. The terrifying barking turned into a steady, fearsome growl.

Devlin took two slow steps back, but the mastiff moved toward him immediately and started barking again. Devlin stopped, but the barking didn't. Devlin was ready to risk kicking the dog in the jaw to shut him up when the front door to the house opened, and Jasper Cranston stomped onto the porch yelling, "All right, Arthur, goddammit! Down!"

The dog stopped barking and dropped to the ground.

"Stay!"

The dog stayed.

"You must be Jack Devlin."

"You must be Jasper Cranston."

"Sorry about the dog. I keep him out on the property so the local mokes around here stay away from the house. I couldn't find the fucking cur to chain him up. I was gonna sit on the porch and wait for you, but I didn't want to get eaten by the goddamn mosquitoes that come out after sunset. Come on in."

Devlin considered doing some of his own barking at Cranston, but he kept his mouth shut and looked at the man standing in the glare of the yellow porch light. He had never met Jasper Cranston. He looked like the type who would get along well with a monstrous dog. Cranston was a big man. Not as tall as Devlin, but with the heaviness that muscular men take on when they age. Even with the added weight, Cranston looked fit. He had a fine, full head of close-cropped white hair and a gruff air of command that reminded Devlin of a master sergeant more than a general. Devlin would have bet there was only one retired general in the U.S. Army walking around on a peg leg like a damn pirate.

Devlin let the adrenaline rush settle down and headed for the porch. He told Cranston, "You're lucky I didn't have my gun on my hip. I might have shot that beast."

"I'm glad you didn't. I like the dog. He does his job."

Cranston extended a meaty hand, and Devlin shook it. The general spun on the tip of his peg leg and led the way into the house, asking over his shoulder, "Where's your luggage?"

"In the car."

"Come on in. We'll get it later."

Devlin followed Cranston into the well-lit interior of the house. Cranston wore a plain blue T-shirt and beige cargo shorts. His prosthesis had a plastic socket for a right-leg stump attached to what looked like the bottom half of a crutch. One side of the peg leg extended up the outside of Cranston's thigh, ending just below the hip, the other side reached mid-thigh.

Without turning around, Cranston said, "I guess you can see why I didn't feel like chasing around in the dark after Arthur. I could have put a bowl of food out, and he would've shown up pretty quick, but then he'd have had an extra meal, and I prefer he doesn't get overweight."

Devlin realized that the dog and his master had done pretty much the right thing. The house was located on a dark stretch of road, the entire back facing the beach where by law anybody could walk.

"Forget about it. You're right. It's a damn good dog. Obeys well."

"Thanks." Cranston pointed to a spot near the foyer and said, "Slip off your shoes and come on in."

Cranston's one foot was bare. Devlin felt overdressed in his long slacks, shoes, and socks. Getting the shoes off felt good.

He followed Cranston across polished floors made of deep brown koa wood. The floors were quite beautiful, as was the rest of the house. One side of the living room consisted of double-tier wall of windows and sliding glass doors that revealed a white sand beach and the Pacific Ocean not more than twenty yards away, both illuminated by silver moonlight. The ceiling in the main room peaked at twenty-five feet in the center, then tapered down to about twelve feet where it met the opposite wall made of dark wood, horizontal windows, and wooden louvers underneath. Oriental area rugs defined spaces for socializing, dining, watching television. On the left, an open kitchen space occupied a large area. Further left a hallway led to the bedrooms.

Cranston's home was open, spacious, and airy. Tradewinds off the ocean constantly streamed through the house, cooling it, and keeping the air fresh. This was an Hawaiian house. A great deal of the outside came inside.

Cranston indicated the large sectional sofa in the center of the main room and said, "Have a seat. You hungry? Want something to drink? A beer?"

"I could go for a beer."

Cranston walked to the kitchen area along the south wall and brought out two large twenty-five-ounce German beers. Cranston held two mugs in the other hand and set down everything on a coffee table in front of them. For a big man on a peg leg, he moved about easily with his hands full.

Devlin poured himself half a glass and drained most of it. Cranston filled his glass and took a long swallow. The beer was cold and very good. A strong, refreshing lager.

Cranston said, "I don't imagine you want to go over this whole thing tonight, do you?"

"Maybe. Your dog did a pretty good job of waking me up."

Cranston grunted and picked up a half-smoked cigar sitting in a large ashtray formed out of a chunk of molten lava.

"Chow told me you knew my son in Vietnam."

"Yes."

"But you weren't in my battalion."

"No. I got dragooned into surveilling a looking post with your son while I was awaiting assignment in the CIC."

Cranston grunted. "I heard that didn't go too well."

"No. It went very bad."

Cranston made another guttural noise, then said, "So you were an MP."

"Yes."

"How come?"

"I was a cop before I went in the Army."

"Why didn't you stay a cop? You could have kept your deferment."

"I didn't want to be a cop anymore."

Cranston frowned at Devlin's answer, but let it go.

"When did you go in?"

"Seventy."

"Ah, it had really turned to shit by then. Just before Billy's second tour. You hear what happened?"

"No. We didn't really keep in touch after that mess in Cambodia."

"You guys should have never fucking been there. We had no business doing half the shit that went on over there. Too many kids like Billy got ruined."

"What happened?"

"To Billy?"

"Yes."

"My son was cursed with the propensity of young men to believe they are invincible. Took all sorts of crazy risks. I thought I'd be able to keep him out of trouble under my command, but ..."

"What?"

"Just before he was scheduled to come home, the poor bastard got captured. Spent over two goddamn years in a POW hellhole before we traded him out on a prisoner exchange. It was too much. Whatever fight he had left in him was used up in that camp. They went at him hard, Mr. Devlin. Billy was never the same."

"How so?"

Cranston jammed his unlit cigar in his mouth as if to stop the words, but they still spilled out in a bitter torrent. "Aw hell, post-traumatic stress syndrome. I guess that's what they call it now. In my day, they called it shell shock. Or battle fatigue. Amounts to the same thing. You're confused, paranoid. Can't be in a room with people. Can't concentrate. Loud sounds can spin you out of control. You wake up with night sweats. Can't hold a job. I imagine someone like you who served in the Criminal Investigation Command saw a good of that."

"Yes."

Cranston chewed on his unlit cigar and grunted again. "Yeah, well, nobody much wants to hear about it anymore. Even those of us who were over there."

"Sometimes especially those of us who were there."

"I'm not ashamed of what we did, Mr. Devlin."

"Perhaps that's because you were able to avoid doing things that were shameful."

Cranston's response was to push himself up off the couch and walk into the kitchen. He pulled open a drawer and rummaged around for a box of kitchen matches to light his cigar.

"Whatever, I survived with my head in mostly the right place."

Devlin asked, "What happened to your leg?"

Instead of responding, Cranston busied himself with firing up the cigar. Then he reached into a cabinet above the kitchen sink, took out a bottle, and poured himself enough Maker's Mark bourbon to fill half of an eight-ounce tumbler. He came back into the room puffing a trail of acrid cigar smoke as he made his way across the koa wood floor. He dropped back down on the couch, took a swallow of the bourbon, and said, "Got shot stepping out of a helicopter. That's mostly what I did over there. Ride around in a fucking helicopter checking on things. Was barely out of the hatch when some big-ass-caliber bullet hit me about two inches above the ankle. Separated the right foot from my leg in one shot. They had me back on the helicopter with a tourniquet and ten milligrams of morphine injected into me so fast I hardly felt a thing.

"Aftermath was the usual mess, but the problem is the damn stump keeps going bad. About every five or six years they gotta chop off another bad piece of bone. They keep telling me the stump will last longer if I don't walk on it. Like I'm going to fucking roll around in a wheelchair. Not likely."

Devlin didn't respond.

"I don't think walking on it has a damn thing to do with it. I picked up something rotten over there I can't get rid of."

Silence fell over the two men after Cranston's speech. He took another swig of his bourbon, chased it with beer, and looked at his watch. "It's about an hour past my bedtime. I'm usually up about five or six. Except for a couple of old-man trips to the head to piss at night. If you're on Mainland time, you should be ready to knock off."

Devlin would have preferred to talk instead of sleep, but he knew he wasn't going to convince Cranston.

"All right. We'll pick this up in the morning. I'll get my bag."

When Devlin returned with is carry-on, Cranston led him down the east-wing hallway and showed him the bathroom and bedroom he could use. The bedroom had two large sliding glass doors that faced the ocean. Cranston said good night and thumped off to his bedroom.

Suddenly the house was very quiet. The sound of the waves outside became more distinct. Devlin looked at the moonlight filtering through the ironwood trees for a few moments, then turned and went into the bathroom.

#

While Devlin showered off the jet-fume travel smell that lingered on him and readied himself for bed, five-hundred yards south of Cranston's house a group of three men sat under a blue tarpaulin strung between palm trees near the beach. They were what Cranston had referred to as mokes – low-class, poor, indigenous people that were often part of the criminal underclass. Dispossessed, disgruntled, and at times dangerous.

The three mokes were sitting on a strip of beachfront land that had once been a junkyard. The land had been repossessed and cleaned up by the state. But the bureaucrats couldn't agree on what to do with the small strip of land, so the homeless had turned it into a makeshift public park and refuge. Depending on the day, families, couples, single men, small groups, even destitute tourists could all be huddled around dilapidated tents or makeshift shelters made from plastic tarps.

The three men fit in easily with the displaced locals. However, they only appeared to be unemployed. In fact, they had a job. Their job was to keep an eye on Jasper Cranston and report his activities to their boss, a former Hell's Angel named Big Daddy

Dwayne Bukowski, who ran a local gang based on the Wai'anae Coast. Bukowski, in turn, reported to Eddie Lihu. Two hours after Devlin parked his car in front of Cranston's house, a fax bearing the license plate number of his rental car appeared on Eddie Lihu's desk, joining the pile of faxes that included Keeko Ramon's fax.

Just as Devlin had been unaware of being flagged at the airport, he had no idea his visit to Cranston was also being reported. He fell asleep bathed by the cool Hawaiian night breezes and the soothing sounds of the Pacific, thinking about a wounded, angry man drinking heavily behind a big wall guarded by a big dog, while something slowly rotted inside him.

CHAPTER 4

Devlin woke the next morning with the sunrise. He sat up and looked out the double-glass doors of his room. There was a narrow, wooden deck, a strip of grass, a few ironwood trees growing out of lava rock, and twenty yards of pristine white sand leading down to a vast blue ocean, coral reef, and dawn sky.

Tradewinds pushed a patchy bank of gray clouds out to the east.

Devlin rocked to his feet, hit the bathroom, returned, and walked to his open suitcase which rested on top of a small dresser. He pulled out nylon swim trunks, a pair of shorts, a T-shirt. In thirty seconds he was dressed. The morning air was cool and fresh, but shorts and T-shirt were all the clothes he needed.

Devlin slid open the screen door and stepped barefoot onto a deck that ran the entire length of the house. Cranston sat at a table set up outside the main room of the house reading the morning paper through a battered pair of half-glasses. He motioned Devlin over and offered him a breakfast of papaya and coffee.

Devlin ate the fruit and sipped his Kona coffee while Cranston nursed a tall glass of iced fruit juice. The general picked up their conversation from the previous night.

"Might as well get through what I started to explain last night."

Devlin nodded, "Go ahead."

"You read the police and medical examiner's reports?"

"Yes."

"Nothing much there."

Devlin said, "That's not unexpected. What can you tell me the reports didn't?"

"Be more specific."

"Let's start with how Billy end up being considered a homeless bum wandering around the Big Island. Someone nobody gave a shit about."

Cranston bristled. "I gave a shit."

"Anybody else?"

"Not that I know of, besides his sister. Certainly not the police. Doesn't seem possible that he could sink so low, does it?"

"No. Not the man I knew. The man I knew was fearless, confident. Unstoppable."

"Goddamn right he was, Mr. Devlin. Men like Billy come few and far between." Cranston sipped from his glass and continued, "But that was a long time ago. And if you fall just a little bit, every day, every year, for a lot of years, you can fall very far."

Devlin nodded again and waited for the story to come. Cranston took another swallow of his drink which Devlin knew wasn't just fruit juice. He suspected gin.

"After the war, after he got out of that POW camp, he tried to get his life going. He went back to school on the Mainland, UCLA, but it didn't last long. He said he couldn't be in a room with a couple of hundred kids in a lecture hall. Couldn't breathe. When that didn't work, he went off to Santa Fe and worked as a photographer. That petered out. He lived with some Navaho woman for a while, but she left him. I think he started drinking pretty heavily at that time. And other things."

"What other things?"

"Pot for sure. Maybe peyote. Other hallucinogens. During that time, I got a letter from him you wouldn't believe. Pages of block letters, jumbled words scrawled all over the page, drawings. Bunch of blood and dirt on the thing. I thought he might have gone over the edge. I had no idea what to do. I flew out to Santa Fe to find him."

"And?"

"No luck. He was gone. I found the trailer where he'd been living. I found out his breakup with the Navaho lady had hit him hard."

"Anything else?"

"No. After that, I lost track of him."

"For how long?"

"Almost a year. He showed up here near the end of '87. His mother was still alive. She welcomed him back like nothing was wrong. Like nothing had happened. He had somehow patched himself together enough so that he could behave almost normally. He just about covered up whatever torment was going on underneath it all. I could tell he was walking a tightrope. But what the hell, his mother accepted it, so I went along with it, too. I wasn't about to stand up and say, 'Hold on there, soldier. Gotta get you checked out. Report to the base shrinks at oh-six-hundred. Get a piss test, blood test, let's see what's ticking inside there.' No. I went along with the act. About the last charitable thing I did for his mother."

"How long did he hold it together?"

"Almost nine months. He got a few odd jobs. Construction. Selling boats. Garden work. He made a run at it; I'll give him that. Goddamn guy was brave, you know, even then. Every damn day he got up, fought the demons." Cranston pointed to a section of the house in the west wing. "He lived in that last bedroom over there. We fit it up with a little kitchen and bathroom. Separate entrance. He kept up the act until his mother died. Just holding it together until she was gone. She had cancer. Billy didn't want her to die worried about him. He did it by sheer force of will, Mr. Devlin. Sometimes I'd look at him, and it seemed to me his head was splitting apart, but he got up, went to work, smiled at his mother, even came over for dinner once a week. But I know when a man is used up. It wasn't him."

"And then your wife died."

"Right. Three days after we put her in the ground, Billy left. He was on full disability benefits. He didn't have to work. He'd done what he had to do. He moved over to the Big Island. Became part of that dropout group of people that gravitated to the Puna District. Mostly around Pahoa."

"Dropout group?"

"Burned-out hippies, potheads, Vietnam vets, religious nuts. What do they call it? New Age people. Not bad people. It was either the worst place he could have picked or the best. People had been growing a lot of pot in that area for years. I knew he smoked the stuff. He said it helped calm his nerves. What the hell was I going to do? Tell him to drink instead?"

Cranston looked at Devlin for a reaction but didn't get one, so he continued. "That was in '88. I wasn't in the greatest shape myself. My military career had ended. Wife died. Goddamn stump rotting. I threw myself into finishing this house. I let Billy go and hoped for the best. He smoked his herb as he called it. He was in a place where it was plentiful. I thought he might be okay."

"Okay?"

"Mr. Devlin, by then *okay* meant being stable enough to stay out of a psycho ward."

"Any violent episodes, that kind of thing?"

"Not that I know of."

"But he was a combat veteran."

"He certainly was."

"Did you worry he might hurt himself or somebody else?"

"Maybe I did somewhere in the back of my mind. Billy proved he could fight and kill with the best of them, but he never showed any signs of violence. In fact, if I were to give you my honest opinion, I'd say every day he lived after the war he hated violence a little bit more than the day before. He was suffering inside, but I never saw him take it out on anybody but himself."

"What happened then?"

"Then good old Uncle Sam decided to fuck up Billy's life one more time. He was out there in Puna smoking his grass. Growing it, too, I'm sure. And then the state and feds decided to declare war on marijuana. The boys on top decided the marijuana business wasn't good for tourism. Unsavory. They started running these Operation Green Harvest raids. Flying in on helicopters. Conducting surveillance. Spraying crops. Arresting people. Seizing property. I don't condone trafficking in drugs. I didn't agree with Billy's smoking that shit. But what they did seemed ridiculous to me. They ran it like some half-assed military operation. They had carte blanche. State, feds, local police. Everybody jumped on it. DEA provided the money and helicopters. Whatever peace Billy had found over there was pretty much destroyed."

Devlin said, "Sitting on a tropical island with military helicopters flying around, hell, he must've felt like he was back in 'Nam."

"Even for those who were never in Vietnam, it must have felt like they were in a war zone. Next thing I knew, Billy was gone again. No contact. Nothing. I went over to see if I could find him. Pahoa is where he seemed to be based, but I couldn't track him down. The people in the town knew who he was but had no idea where he lived or how to find him. He had no house. Best I could figure he was living out in the rainforest somewhere hiding from helicopters, showing up in town once in a while for supplies and his disability check."

"How long ago was that?"

"Almost two years."

"You never located him?"

"No, I tried another angle. I figured his disability payments were being sent to the village post office in Pahoa. They came the first of the month. So, I went back on the first and waited around town for a week."

"Did he show up?"

"Yes. I saw him going into the local grocery store one morning."

"Did you speak to him?"

Cranston drained the tall glass he had been sipping.

"No."

"Why?"

"It wasn't Billy anymore. It was somebody else. Good Christ, he was like a shell of himself. He was still a big guy, you know, but wasted looking. Hair past his shoulders. Long beard. Nothing on but a pair of baggy shorts and old shirt. Worn out flip-flops on his feet. I just couldn't, I ... I don't know. It was a combination of things. I was worried if I confronted him, it might upset him too much. And I realized I didn't really know what to say to him or offer him."

Jasper Cranston looked away, staring out at the ocean, remembering the moment, but unable to speak about it.

Devlin cut to the core question.

"Do you think his marijuana dealings got him murdered?"

"I don't know. I only know he was murdered. I assume you read the medical examiner's report. What do you think?"

"It's possible."

Cranston looked at Devlin and said, "What do you call it when someone sticks a knife in a man and feeds him to the wild animals?"

"The report said a possible knife wound. As for the rest of it, I don't know if what happened to the corpse was intentional, or a consequence of leaving the body outdoors."

Cranston turned his empty glass on the table. Devlin watched him struggle with the urge to get up and refill it. Devlin waited. Cranston finally blurted out, "Well, Mr. Devlin, I need to know what happened. That's why I went to Chow. That's why I asked for help. What I want to know is if you're going to help me find the answers. Where are you on this?"

The photo of Billy Cranston's ravaged corpse flashed through Devlin's mind.

Devlin asked, "What do you mean where am I at on this?"

"Is this just another job for you? Do you give a shit? Because even if Billy wasn't my son, and I was just his commanding officer in Vietnam, he deserves better. He was a goddamn hero who gave everything he had for his country and for the men he served with. He deserves someone who cares enough to find out what happened. I realize nobody gives a shit about some wasted drifter. But Billy deserves better than that. He deserves it from me. And he deserves it from you."

Devlin nodded, meeting Cranston's gaze, but saying nothing. Cranston suddenly stood, spun on his peg leg, and headed for the kitchen with his empty glass.

Devlin turned away, working to control his anger, and saw a woman walking on in their direction a couple of hundred yards to the south. Even from that distance, Devlin could tell she was tall. She walked with an effortless long-legged stride. Cranston's exit to the kitchen gave Devlin a chance to stare at her without distraction. The closer she came, the more Devlin wanted to see.

Cranston stomped out onto the deck with a full drink, and Devlin turned back to him. Cranston sat and took a long swallow.

"You have anything to say, Mr. Devlin?"

Cranston's belligerence was more tiresome than anything else. Devlin's anger had left him. He leaned forward and said, "First of all, Mr. Cranston, let's you and I get something straight. I'm sorry for your loss. But you're not my commanding officer, you're my client. As such, you deserve a certain amount of deference and consideration. Okay, fine. But, just to be clear, I came here to find out information that would be helpful to my investigation. You've given me background information which is helpful. I thank you for that. But I don't need to be the focus of your anger. And I don't need you to question whether or not I give a shit about what happened to Billy. Your son saved my life. He changed my life. Your son was one of the few reasons serving in the stupid, cesspool of an ill-conceived and executed war that killed and ruined countless lives wasn't a complete waste. As far as I'm concerned, the fact that Billy Cranston ended up a half-eaten corpse, thrown away like a piece of garbage dumped in the middle of nowhere is just another abomination caused by that war.

"It's early in the day, so I hope you're clear-headed enough to hear what I have to say, General. I care more about Billy than you know, more than you'll ever know.

"Now, you want to know what I *don't* give a shit about? I don't give a shit about the fact that you're sitting in a place damn near close to paradise pouring booze over your pain. I don't give a shit that you're pissed off at some local cops who probably don't know the first thing about investigating a homicide to begin with. I don't give a shit about a line of politicians and lying, incompetent military brass that goes back for fucking decades. I can't go back and make those bastards pay for what they did to Billy and millions of others. I can't go back to Cambodia and find the North Vietnamese who rattled his brain with those mortars they dropped on us. Or those animals who terrorized him and tortured him in that POW camp. I can't do anything about every woman who ever left him, or every drug he took to get through another day. What I can do is find out if someone stuck a knife in him and left him bleeding in the jungle for whatever decided to feed off him. And if that's what happened, once I find them, I goddamn guarantee you I'll bring them to justice."

Jasper Cranston stared at Devlin his face expressionless. He blinked a few times and said, "Fine. Then go and do it."

Devlin stood and turned to head back to his room to pack up and leave, but the woman on the beach had veered in their direction. She was walking straight toward them, now no more than fifty feet away. Her straight, jet-black hair was pulled into a ponytail that rested on her right shoulder. She wore a black string bikini which barely covered her body. She moved with a sensuous fluidity that reminded Devlin of a thoroughbred racehorse.

She was close enough now so that Devlin could see her face, a stunning mix of Pacific Island and Caucasian bloodlines. Her skin was a flawless blend of tan, copper, and bronze. She carried a red sleeveless T-shirt. She slipped it on, as she approached. She had an intricate black and gray tattoo that started just above her right hip and extended down past her buttock and the side of her long leg. Every line was crisp and cleanly etched deep into her skin forming interlocking triangles, circles, and lines that merged into a whole greater than the parts. A tribal island tattoo that was at once very feminine and very powerful. Devlin decided it belonged exactly where it was on the body of a confident, exotic, beautiful woman.

Devlin asked, "Who is that woman?"

Still staring at his drink, Cranston said, "She's my daughter."

CHAPTER 5

As Cranston's daughter approached the deck, she checked out Devlin almost as carefully as he had her.

Cranston's gruff voice interrupted, "Meet my daughter, Mr. Devlin. Leilani Kilau Cranston."

Leilani stepped up onto the deck, extended her hand, and Devlin shook it. The fingers were long. The skin smooth. But the palm of her hand was rough, and the grip strong.

She smiled only for a moment, revealing dazzling white teeth that reminded Devlin of Billy Cranston's smile. That mesmerizing, heroic smile of Devlin's youth. The smile he would always associate with something powerful enough to save his life.

"It's Jack," he said. "Jack Devlin."

"Are you enjoying the view here on my father's lanai?"

Her half-smile communicated her full meaning to Devlin.

"I am."

Cranston said, "My daughter lives about a mile down the beach."

Devlin said, "You have a nice walk between houses."

"Yes. It's beautiful. Although I don't do it very often."

"What brings you here this morning?" asked Devlin.

"You. I wanted to hear what you two are planning to do about Billy."

Cranston interjected, "Lei, we've been over this. I told you I wanted to hire a professional to investigate this. It's not something…"

"It's not something I want to be left out of."

"I'm not leaving you out of anything for chrissake. Mr. Devlin just got here last night. I've told him what I know. He's ready to head over to the Big Island and start working."

She turned to Devlin. "What have you discussed so far?"

"That's up to your father to share with you. Not me."

"Goddammit, Lei, I'm not reporting everything I'm doing to you."

Devlin interrupted. "Why don't I try out your beach while you two discuss this? I could do with a walk myself."

Devlin stepped off the deck and headed toward the beach. He noted that the father and daughter held back until he was out of normal earshot, but Cranston's booming voice was too loud not to hear.

Devlin walked quickly away from escalating argument. Suddenly, he wanted to be far away from Cranston's house, his anger, his pain. He took off his shirt and shorts and dropped them on the sand as he approached the water.

He walked into the surf. The North Shore breezes had made the ocean a bit rough, and he had to dive into a wave before it smacked into him, but the cool blue water felt good.

He swam parallel to the beach, heading north, feeling awkward in the rough water for the first five minutes. But gradually he warmed up, and his muscles began to catch the old rhythms. The salt sting felt good on what was left of his New York cuts and scrapes. He let his mind drift. Kept working at it until he felt the heat of his salty sweat mix with the ocean. He fantasized about spending a few days eating fresh fish, walking on long beaches, swimming in the ocean, and laying in the sun, but knew that wasn't going to happen.

Devlin would have liked to avoid both Cranstons, grab his things, and leave, but when he emerged from the water, Leilani was sitting on the beach next to his clothes. She'd taken off the red T-shirt. All she had on was the black string bikini, but she sat completely at ease. Devlin was immediately wary of her. She looked angry. And he didn't feel like being the one she took it out on. If she weren't so beautiful and alluring, Devlin would have probably politely excused himself and walked back to Cranston's house.

He sat down next to her but made sure to keep several feet of empty beach between them. He faced the ocean and waited for the sun to dry him off. And for Leilani Kilau Cranston to speak.

"I can't talk to him," she said. "Maybe I can talk to you."

"About what?"

"My brother. My half-brother, Billy."

"Hmmm."

"Hmmm? What's that supposed to mean?"

She spoke with a vehemence that took Devlin by surprise. He looked at her to see how serious she was. She looked very serious.

Devlin said, "It means I have the feeling you're about to give me a hard time."

"I see."

"And, frankly, I'm not exactly in the mood for that."

"What's next? Are you the kind that yells? Or the kind that clams up and freezes someone out?"

Devlin glanced at Leilani. He ignored her questions.

"You and Billy obviously had different mothers. Were you close to him?"

The question annoyed her. "What does that have to do with this?"

"You wanted to talk about Billy, didn't you?"

Leilani paused for a moment and said, "Yes, we were very close. We lived through my father's polygamy together."

"He had two wives at the same time?"

"Not officially. Billy's mother, Edna, was his legal wife. My mother, Lili, was their live-in housekeeper. When my mother became pregnant with me, everybody knew who the father was, but Billy's mom refused to throw my mother out. We became part of the household. Billy and I grew up together under very trying circumstances. Billy meant a lot to me."

"I see."

"I doubt it."

Her flip answer was one jab too many. Devlin turned to her and shot back, "Look, I'm sorry you and your father don't get along. I'm sorry for your grief over Billy. But I'm not here to be your punching bag, or your father's."

"Don't yell at me."

Devlin raised his voice. "I'm not even close to yelling."

"Why are you so angry? Are you feeling threatened?"

"My anger level isn't the topic here. And I'm not going to spar with you about who's in charge. You are aware of what happened to your half-brother, aren't you?"

"Don't call him my half-brother. Billy was my brother."

"Fine. Your brother."

"I saw what happened to him. I identified the body."

"How much of his body did you see?"

"All of it."

"Then you should understand why I don't take what happened to your brother lightly. I don't think you should be using this tragedy to polish your assertive feminist skills. And I'm finished with proving to any of his family how strongly I feel about Billy, and what happened to him. I'm not in the mood for snide comments about it. I'm not in the mood for anybody trying to push me or pressure me on this. Not you, not your father, not anybody. If you think I'm being short with you, I apologize, but that's the way it is."

Devlin moved to stand up, but Leilani snapped, "Do not walk away from me."

Devlin turned. When she saw the look on his face, she said, "Just hear me out. I'm not playing games either. I know you fought together in that disgusting war, but you have no idea of the battles Billy and I fought together. Think about growing up in a racist community being the half-breed bastard sister to a haole brother with a father who was gone most of the time and two mothers who would barely speak to one another. Billy did more for me and protected me more than any older brother should have needed to. What happened to him is driving me crazy. I haven't had a decent night's sleep or been able to work normally since it happened. So maybe my fuse is a little short, too."

Devlin looked out at the sparkling blue ocean in front of them and calmed himself. He lifted his hands up and said, "Okay. Okay. Truce. We're on the same side."

The sun was beginning to feel hot. Devlin ran his hands through his wet hair and rubbed the cool water on his face. "Look, Ms. Cranston, anything you can tell me or anything you think will be helpful, I'd be happy to hear it. In fact, I want to hear it. But other than that, I'm not interested."

"What do you mean other than that?"

"Anything other than hearing information you think will help me find out how he died and who was responsible."

"What if I offered to help you?"

"How?"

"I know the Big Island better than you. I know that area where Billy lived. I know that scene over there. I could be helpful."

"That's not the way it works."

"No women allowed."

Devlin made sure to speak calmly, but it didn't reduce his force or emphasis. "I don't care if you're a woman or a man or a Martian. Would you ask a doctor, a woman doctor, if you could help her operate on a patient? Why do you think you can ask me to work on this?"

"I'm asking because I have to," she said quietly.

"And I'm saying no because I have to."

Devlin felt the skin on his back heating up. He flexed his shoulders and felt a film of dried sea salt pull at his skin. The drying salt wasn't the only thing that made him feel uncomfortable. Leilani had become quiet and calm. Devlin could see how upset she was. It made him want to help her. It made him attracted to her. And the fact that she was wearing very little on her spectacular body didn't help.

"Look, officially I'm working for your father. I don't report the results of my investigation to a client until the entire investigation is over. And even then, the information comes from my company, not me. But I will contact you and make sure that you're informed of everything I find out. That's the best I can offer you, no matter what your relationship to Billy.

"As far as you helping me, that's not possible. I work alone, or with other professionals associated with my company. That's how it's done."

"I see."

Leilani nodded, but Devlin had the feeling that she wasn't so much agreeing with him as making her own decision about the matter.

Devlin stood up. Leilani put her hand out for him to help her to her feet. He did, and they found themselves standing almost face-to-face for a moment. Devlin's height made that impossible with most women, but Leilani Kilau Cranston was six feet tall, and she was standing on a higher part of the beach than he was. Their eyes met. Hers were a deep, vivid brown.

Leilani said, "Thanks," and stepped back away from him. Devlin watched her brush the sand from her nearly naked rear end. She put her T-shirt back on, and Devlin did the same, then stepped into his shorts.

Helping her up had meant touching her hand again, and it prompted him to ask, "What kind of work do you do?"

"I'm a sculptor. I work with limestone mostly. And I do some plumbing part-time when I need money."

"A working woman, huh?"

"Yep. I'm stronger than a lot of men."

"I'm sure you are."

Devlin tried not to stare at Leilani. He looked past her at a local man dressed in a stained white T-shirt and old khaki pants walking on the beach in their direction. He carried a fishing rod and an empty five-gallon plastic bucket, the kind that held spackling compound. He seemed to be looking for a good place to catch dinner.

Leilani said, "I still want to tell you what I know about Billy, Mr. Devlin."

"Jack."

"Jack."

"And I want to hear it."

"When will that be?" She made sure to ask the question so there was no demand in it.

"I have to get into Honolulu today and take care of a few things. The soonest we could talk would be tonight."

"Fine. Should we talk over dinner?"

"Sure. Where?"

"I hate Honolulu."

"How about someplace halfway."

"Jameson's in Haleiwa is a little more than half-way in this direction, but it's the best food between here and Honolulu."

"Okay."

"What time would be good for you, Jack?"

"Eight o'clock."

Leilani reached out to shake hands. Devlin took her hand, and she smiled at him. "Friends?"

"That's better than enemies."

"In your case, I'm quite sure that's true. I wouldn't want to be around when that short fuse of yours runs out."

"No," said Devlin. "You wouldn't."

They finished the handshake. Devlin watched Leilani turn and walk back south on the beach. But he didn't watch for long. He didn't want her to catch him staring at her shapely rear end, particularly since he knew damn well Leilani already knew he was. He was so intent on not staring at Leilani that he hardly noticed that the local fisherman had dropped his bucket and cast his line not ten feet from where they had been talking.

CHAPTER 6

During the drive back to Honolulu in the daylight, Devlin was able to see what his night arrival had hidden from him. Much of what was built along the Kam Highway contrasted greatly with where it was built. He drove past gleaming white sand beaches, palm trees, sparkling blue water, lush tropical foliage, and walls that bordered multi-million-dollar homes. But there were also plenty of structures that were little more than shacks made of plywood sheets nailed to flimsy wooden frames; stores slapped together out of corrugated tin siding; public buildings made of unappealing concrete blocks. Many of them needed painting. Some of the houses were so weathered and worn that their plywood sheets were coming unglued.

Then there was the universal sign of poverty no matter where in the world you were – junk cars littering front yards. And since this was an island, the junk cars were joined by junk boats.

Even in paradise, hugely wealthy people had grabbed the prized shoreline, while too many others lived in cheap, decrepit housing, drove used-up cars, and scraped by on public assistance and odd jobs.

Devlin drove slowly on the two-lane road, past Sunset Beach and Waimea Beach, the famous meccas of surfing. In five months, the winter surf would be pounding the shores bringing the best in the world to compete for prize money beyond anything the locals could imagine.

Finally, Devlin past the little North Shore towns and turned onto the highway leading across the island and into Honolulu. Soon, the easy flow of cars turned into stop-and-go traffic.

Devlin finally made it to Kuhio Avenue, pulled up to the entrance of an underground garage, and was greeted by the ageless Winston Chan. Devlin hadn't seen him in two years, but Chan greeted him as if they had been together yesterday. Mr. Chan was the custodian of the high-rise building owned by Pacific Rim. The top floor condominium was reserved for guests and employees. Chan spoke the peculiar pidgin English endemic to the Islands and combined it with constant bowing and grinning. Nothing in Chan's greeting annoyed Devlin because he knew it was an act. In a heartbeat, Winston Chan could change from a bowing, scraping old-school coolie into a formidable, quick-moving, armed guard capable of defending Pacific Rim's property.

Chan could usually be found sitting on an old barstool behind a podium placed near the underground garage entrance wearing a short-sleeve shirt and dark pants.

"Oh, Mr. Devlin" Chan nodded as he jumped off his stool. "You back, huh, you back now. How long you stay, huh?"

Devlin unfolded himself from the rental car and stood in front of Chan, watching the continuous bobbing up and down that conveyed Chan's attention and respect. Devlin, of course, went along with the Chinese-coolie-servant act, but he knew that Chan had a .25 caliber Beretta stuck in the back pocket of his black pants and his squinting eyes missed nothing. He also knew that Chan's rickety podium held a panel of control buttons that would bring down steel gates that sealed off the underground garage. Once Chan pressed the right button, not even a speeding car could crash in or out. Nor could anyone call an elevator or open a ground-floor door unless Chan allowed it.

"Hey, Chan," Devlin said. "Hold still for a second and let me look at you."

Chan stood ramrod straight. Devlin patted him on the shoulder and shook his hand. "How's your family?"

"Family all tip-top. Wife's undying bitch of a mother okay. Kids okay."

"How many kids you got now, Chan?"

"Oh, still same number. Same same. Six. Half dozen, huh?"

"No more since I last saw you?"

Chan laughed, "Still fucky fucky with wife, but no more kids come out. Good for me, hey?"

"No. Good for your wife."

Devlin reached in and lifted his carry-on bag from the backseat of the car. "Is the apartment ready?"

Chan handed Devlin a single key on a ring and told him, "I park car. Apartment is ready. Code box set for today's date plus six for each number. Okay?"

"Same as your kids."

"Yeah, yeah," bobbed Chan. "Half-dozen. Half-dozen."

Devlin nodded, checked the date on his watch, and headed for the elevator.

He rode up to the twenty-fourth floor. At the apartment door, he unlocked the cover to the key box and punched in the correct numbers. The locks clicked open and released the apartment's reinforced front door.

Devlin stepped into an air-conditioned fortress that overlooked the clutter of hotels and shops that bordering Waikiki Beach.

The condo had large glass windows on the south and east sides. Out the south windows, Devlin could see Fort DeRussy's open expanse and the jumble of hotels that almost completely blocked off any view of the ocean. To the east, he looked over the Ala Moana Shopping Center toward Pearl Harbor and downtown Honolulu.

He unpacked, checked in with Mrs. Banks at the Pacific Rim office on Bishop Street, ordered food, and make an appointment at the Prince Hawaiian Shooting Club on Kalakaua Avenue. The club catered to tourists but did, in fact, have a well-appointed shooting range. Devlin reserved a quiet booth away from the Japanese tourists happily plunking .22-caliber shots from pistols, rifles, and revolvers equipped with laser-sites that made it almost impossible to miss the target.

Devlin let himself into the secure room in the back of the condo with the same code numbers and picked out the weapons he wanted to have adjusted to his specifications: a 9mm SIG-Sauer P226 which he liked because it was a virtually failure-proof gun and carried a full fifteen-round clip. A small Beretta 21A Bobcat for a backup. It held seven rounds of .25 caliber bullets, plus one in the chamber, but weighed just under twelve ounces. And three alternatives to the SIG-Sauer: a .45-caliber Caspian Arms Commander, a 9mm Browning Hi-Power Double Action, and a 9mm Heckler & Koch P7.

The Caspian Arms gun made him wish his customized Caspian wasn't in the evidence locker at the NYPD. Even though it would take far too much gunsmithing to match the Caspian he was trying to replace, he still wanted to have it in his arsenal. The Heckler & Koch P7 was another solidly built German gun that differed from the SIG in its rather unique squeeze-cocking system. The third possibility was one of his old standby favorites: the venerable Browning. It had plenty of fire-power. He loved its smooth action. And liked how the gun felt in his hand.

He packed the weapons in a foam-lined case, selected the ammunition for each gun, and left for the firing range.

After firing two hundred rounds and carefully discussing his preferences with the resident gunsmith, Devlin left the range satisfied that the weapons would be set to his specification. He'd arrange with Chan to have them picked up and brought to the apartment.

His next stop was the Pacific Rim office on Bishop Street in downtown Honolulu.

Edith Banks, the administrator of Mr. Chow's most important Pacific Rim office, was expecting him.

Mrs. Banks was just under five feet tall, hovering eternally around the age of sixty, and made of solid steel. The best word to describe Mrs. Banks was – proper.

She ignored the usual laid-back attire of the Islands. She never appeared in the office wearing anything other than one of her size six business suits, dark hose, and sensible shoes. Proper in her speech and behavior, proper in her work, Devlin knew that when he entered her office, the correct gun permits and licenses would be properly filled out, with the exact serial numbers of the weapons he had chosen.

Mrs. Banks's husband had retired to a life of golf, gin and tonics, and other leisurely pursuits. Edith would work until the day she died. Probably with a Pall Mall burning nearby as she sat ramrod straight behind her uncluttered walnut executive desk.

Devlin entered her office and smiled at her. She nodded at him and allowed only a quick grin.

"Mr. Devlin. Welcome back. I'm very sorry for your loss."

"Thank you, Ma'am."

"And your brother is recovering well?"

"He is."

"I'm glad to hear that. Why don't you have a seat while we go over the forms?"

Devlin would never sit in front of Mrs. Banks until invited. And now he did, in a chair positioned so his knees pressed into the face of her walnut desk. It was as close as he was going to get to Edith Banks.

Meeting with Mrs. Banks was not something Devlin had to do. He appeared in person out of respect for a woman who was a master at what she did. There was no other individual in the world that Devlin could depend on more in any situation, than Edith Banks.

She slid over the state license forms and gun permit papers.

Devlin signed his name in the right spots and slid the forms back to her. Mrs. Banks folded and placed them into a pre-addressed envelope.

"I'll have your temporary permits delivered to the condo tomorrow."

Without the permits, there was no way Devlin could legally carry the selected weapons in the state of Hawaii, and there was no way Edith Banks would let him.

"What else can I do for you, Mr. Devlin?"

"How about we run down to Waikiki, take the elevator to the top of the Sheraton, throw back a few Banana daiquiris in the Hano Hano Room, and watch the sunset over Diamond Head?"

"Thank you, but I already have plans for tonight."

"Canasta?"

"No, Mr. Sophisticated-International-Man-of-the-World, tonight is bridge. Come, Mr. Devlin, I haven't got all day."

"All right. I don't know everything I may need. It's possible I'll know a bit more after tonight, but for now, I'd like you to go into your files and see if you can find me a contact on the Hilo police force, preferably someone familiar with the Billy Cranston case."

Mrs. Banks made notes on a legal pad without looking up at Devlin.

"Anything else?"

"I need to get in touch with the Samoan. I'll need tickets to Hilo tomorrow around two, a car in Hilo, and a place to stay in Pahoa."

"Pahoa?"

"Yes."

"Do you want public or private lodging?"

"Both. Find me something in town, and a private house within a couple of miles or so."

"As for Mr. Mafa, I'm sure you know that he stays with various relatives on the North Shore. I have a number for him, but he takes his time answering."

"Ah, yes, the unfettered nature of the primitive island native."

"Something like that."

"Put out the word I'm looking for him. If he doesn't call in, I'll find him myself."

"I'll messenger over your ticket, car rental information, lodging information, and so on to Mr. Chan by tomorrow morning."

"Thank you, Mrs. Banks. You do know that none of us could do this without you."

"Yes. I know. But thank you, it's very nice of you to say so."

"You're welcome."

"Jack?"

"Yes, ma'am."

"I understand that Mr. Chow has put some personal pressure on you over this matter. Please be careful."

"Edith, I've come to the realization that they're all personal. Every single one of them."

Mrs. Banks looked at Devlin and thought about that. After a few moments, she seemed to agree, with a quick blink of her eyes and a swift, imperceptible nod.

"Yes," she said. "Well, be careful."

"I will."

Devlin pushed back from the desk and left the office. His knee-caps felt slightly numb from pressing against the front of Edith Banks's desk.

CHAPTER 7

While Devlin and Edith Banks met in Honolulu, Eddie Lihu sat at a large desk in his well-appointed home office on his ranch east of the Waimea Valley near the North Shore of Oahu trying to decide what to do about somebody called Jack Devlin.

The name had shown up on one of Keeko Ramon's report. And it matched the person who had rented a car at the airport and parked that car in front of Jasper Cranston's house.

Lihu also knew that Jack Devlin had spent the night and morning at Cranston's house, and that he was going to meet with a woman for dinner tonight at Jameson's restaurant.

Lihu did not know who the hell Jack Devlin was. For the last two hours, both Lihu and a lawyer he had on retainer named Eric Engle had tried to find information on Jack Devlin without success. That in itself made Eddie Lihu conclude whoever Jack Devlin was, he was trouble.

Eddie Lihu contemplating trouble was not a pretty sight. Lihu had a flat nose, small eyes, and thick, wormy lips on a face that looked like it had been hit with a frying pan when he was an infant. Lihu was a big man, almost six five, and morbidly obese. But Lihu never let any of that stop him from relentlessly pursuing his twin goals – power and money.

The key to Lihu's success came while working as a lowly baggage handler for a small, inter-island airline when he realized most everything had to be imported to and between the Hawaiian Islands.

From that moment on, he single-mindedly set out to gain control of local airlines, shipping fleets, trucking companies, even taxi and car rental agencies. Lihu never stopped working, was completely ruthless, and never made much of a distinction between legal and illegal goods other than the fact that illegal goods were much more profitable. Lihu's companies transported fuel, water, food, liquor, furniture, auto parts, electronics, clothing, construction materials, pharmaceuticals, anything that could be moved, right along with illegal goods – into and between the islands.

For twenty-three years, Lihu had been building his empire, and now he sat behind a massive wooden desk in his home office, head bowed resting on triple chins, fat lips pursed, thinking. He checked the calendar on his wall for the tenth time. He needed six, seven days at the most to complete his most profitable venture to date.

One goddamn week to wind things up, and now this.

Lihu's bodyguard, a six-foot-six, three-hundred-pound former Hell's Angel named Charlie, sat on a big leather couch on the other side of the office. Charlie didn't usually speak much, but right now he knew by Lihu's expression he shouldn't even move. The boss was angry. Charlie knew Eddie Lihu was angry because Lihu sweat when he was angry or tense. Even in the air-conditioned office, Lihu exuded an acrid body odor that even the expensive cologne he always wore couldn't cover up.

Lihu raised his enormous head, looked up at the ceiling for five seconds, which momentarily pulled smooth the rolls of his multiple chins until he pitched forward and swiveled his chair toward Charlie.

Charlie sat up straighter. Lihu had come to a decision.

Lihu rumbled, "You're going to meet with Bukowski. Call him if you have to find where he is, but no talking on the phone."

"Right."

"You're going to give him a message."

"Yes?"

"Tell him it's about the guy he told me is going to be at a restaurant tonight."

"Okay."

"I want Bukowski to arrange it so this guy gets beat up real good. And robbed. Whatever they take off this guy, he gives to you. Wallet, whatever."

"Okay. How beat up?"

"Enough to put him in the hospital, but not enough to kill him. I don't need no more dead people. Should look like some local assholes beat the shit out of a tourist."

"Got it."

"You talk to Bukowski in person. No phones."

Charlie repeated, "No phones."

CHAPTER 8

On the drive back to the North Shore, Devlin wondered if whatever Leilani Cranston had to tell him was going to be worth the trip. He smiled ruefully, knowing he'd make the drive just for the chance to see her in clothes.

As he turned off the H2 Freeway and headed toward the coast, Devlin thought about how he would describe Leilani. Maori? Polynesian? Southwest American Indian? She could probably pass for all of those descriptors except for her perfect, thin, elegant nose.

Devlin had been with beautiful women who used their looks to glide through life without bothering to develop much of a persona. It seemed to Devlin that Leilani's beauty had the opposite effect on her. It seemed that the attention she attracted had forced her to develop a strong, independent personality. In one short meeting, she had been intense, prickly, assertive as well as seductive, alluring, sensual, and calm.

The restaurant loomed up ahead on Devlin's right, and he stopped thinking about Leilani. On this section of the North Shore, there was only the restaurant on one side of the road and an empty stretch of beach on the other side. Outdoor spotlights illuminated the restaurant's sign, and two six-foot Tiki torches burned at the entrance to the parking lot.

Devlin pulled into the lot and circled twice without finding an empty spot. He drove back out onto the road, turned right, continued for about a hundred feet, and pulled into a small beachfront lot.

A sign said, No Parking After Sunset. He parked and stepped out of the car and into the balmy night air. There was just a hint of the day's sunset left. A nearly full moon was rising out of the dark ocean. He watched the silver moonlight create a gleaming path on the water under the fast-moving clouds overhead. He took a moment to listen to the faint whoosh of waves and breathe in the mixture of tropical flowers accented by the salty tang of the ocean. The balmy Hawaiian air surrounded him. He stood savoring the experience, then turned and walked toward the restaurant.

Devlin had changed from his Mainland clothes into a pair of lightweight unconstructed linen pants and a white Armani polo shirt. His morning in the sun had renewed his month-old Cayman Island tan a bit. He didn't mind looking a little less like a pale-skinned haole tourist.

An athletic blonde hostess who gave Devlin the impression she'd spent the afternoon surfing greeted him with a smile. She wore white shorts, a pink tank top, and nothing else except a deep island tan. Devlin made sure to maintain eye contact. He still hadn't adjusted to how much skin was casually on display in the Islands.

"Good evening, sir, do you have a reservation?"

"No," he said. "I don't. Do you have room for two somewhere?"

The young girl didn't need to look at her reservation book to know she was going to disappoint the tall, interesting man she would have liked to accommodate.

"Oh, I'm so sorry," she said. "We don't have anything until ten-thirty. You didn't make a reservation?"

"Wait a second. Check if you have something for Cranston at eight."

The girl looked at her list and said, "Yes. Here it is. Your party is already seated."

Devlin smiled and followed her upstairs to a table next to a large corner window. Leilani sat in the chair facing the room, a glass of white wine in front of her. She wore a simple, light-green cotton shirt and faded jeans. Her thick black hair was held back by a large pink coral comb, revealing more of her long neck than he had seen on the beach. A single candle flickered in front of her bringing out the highlights in her copper-colored skin. She looked up as Devlin entered the room, and he noticed that she had on just a touch of pale lipstick.

Leilani flashed a quick smile that revealed her dazzling white teeth, then suppressed it so she wouldn't appear overly friendly.

The hostess pointed out Devlin's seat and made a quick exit.

Devlin sat down. His knee bumped into Leilani's under the table, and they both shifted their long legs to accommodate each other. He had a beautiful ocean view on his right, but that wasn't going to distract him from looking at Leilani Cranston.

"Thanks for making the reservation. I never even thought of it."

"You have to live here to know that Wednesday is a busy night. They run a special to fill up the place."

"What's that?"

"The second entrée is half price. Encourages couples."

"Or big single eaters."

"Yes, I suppose so. There are a lot of big boys around here that could easily polish off a couple of main courses. I could see you doing that."

Devlin slapped a hand on his flat belly. "Are you implying I'm overweight?"

"Are you fishing for a compliment?"

"Of course."

"Don't worry. You're one of the few men I've seen who has a body as good as mine."

Devlin said, "Interesting way of putting that."

Leilani shrugged. "Let's face it. These bodies are the luck of the gene pool. I just try to take care of mine and use it as much as possible."

Devlin picked up his menu and said, "You're succeeding."

They busied themselves with ordering food and wine. When that was done, Leilani asked, "Where should I start?"

"Start with whatever you think might be helpful. Whatever might explain what happened."

Leilani nodded once and began. First, she talked about how tough it was growing up. The problems she and Billy faced. How close they had become. Then how terrible she felt about Billy's war experience. The helplessness she felt when he was a POW. The frustration she felt when Billy began to deteriorate. She told him that she had stood by and watched her father try to solve Billy's problems, and that when Jasper asked her to stay out of it, to let him handle it, she had acquiesced. And now, she told him, she regretted stepping back and acceding to her father. It hadn't helped Billy, and it didn't do her father any good. Jasper had a hard time after Vietnam, and it hadn't gotten any better.

As Leilani continued, Devlin became increasingly annoyed. Instead of hearing information that might help him, he worried he was listening to a long pitch leading to a request he didn't want to hear.

While she talked, Devlin fell into his old Secret Service habit of clocking the room. Checking the diners. The exits. The staff. He half-listened but focused his attention on Leilani because he enjoyed looking at her. He even enjoyed watching her elegant bronze hands use a knife and fork. He began to think maybe Chow should have sent a therapist to the Cranstons instead of him.

Leilani's virtual monologue was, in fact, quite poignant. Her brother's death had obviously affected her deeply. She struggled with the relationship with her father. But Devlin doubted any of that would help him find out what happened to her brother.

He noticed that there were now several empty parking spots in the restaurant lot. He interrupted Leilani and said, "Sorry, I parked in a lot that said no parking after sunset. I don't want to get towed or something. You mind if I bring it over here?"

Leilani was a little surprised by Devlin's request, but said, "Uh, sure. Okay. Go ahead."

"How about you order some coffee, and I'll be right back."

Devlin left the table and walked outside, relieved to get a break and a breath of fresh air.

Devlin couldn't understand why Leilani's input disturbed him so much. In was more than it being so one-sided. As he walked out into the dark Hawaiian night and a moment to himself, he realized why. He simply did not want to hear what the Cranstons were saying about Billy Cranston. They were talking about a hero of his youth. Even if he had idolized Billy out of youthful naivete, it was Billy Cranston who had shown him how to act in the face of fear. Who turned to him and told him he had what it took. It was Billy Cranston who told him he was a warrior and that he would be okay. And now most of what he was hearing might mean that Billy had simply gone down so far that one day he walked into a desolate spot, all alone, and gave up. What if this case amounted to just another Vietnam vet with PTSD who abused drugs and got involved with a bunch of lowlife criminals? What if the dazzling American hero who saved his life ended up in a stupid dispute over a patch of marijuana, and someone got pissed off enough to stick a knife in him and walk away?

"Shit."

Devlin told himself, whatever happened, you're going to find out. So stop mooning around over Billy's exotic half-sister, go back in that restaurant, and hear her out. If it sounds like she knows something you can use, get it out of her. If not, cut loose and figure it out yourself.

Devlin walked across the two-lane road toward the beachfront parking lot, and any concerns he had about the Cranstons evaporated. He saw two men standing near the back of his car. A rusted-out Chevy van was parked ten feet to the left of his rental. There were no other cars in the lot and nobody else. A single floodlight mounted on a wooden pole at the corner of the lot cast everything in dim light and shadows.

The two men stood staring at Devlin. They were both big, surly, menacing Island men, the kind who were accustomed to getting their way because they scared the shit out of people

The bigger of the two wore only a pair of dirty, baggy shorts...no shoes, no shirt. His heavy arms and thick legs were decorated with a ratty assortment of tattoos. He looked at Devlin with heavy-lidded eyes, holding a two-foot crowbar in his right hand. The kind with a chisel end and curved swan neck for pulling nails.

His partner, in a filthy denim shirt and cut-off jeans, had long dirty hair, a scraggly beard, a pockmarked face, and a hunting knife with a six-inch blade in his right hand.

Devlin stopped about eight feet in front of them. The long-haired thug with the knife took a few steps to Devlin's left, trying to flank him.

The shirtless guy with the crowbar said, "Why you park your car here, you dumb fucking haole?"

The one with the knife said, "Gonna cost you a lot a money, asshole."

Devlin stood where he was, looking to his left for a moment, and then back at Crowbar.

Crowbar said, "What the fuck you lookin' at, dumbass?"

Devlin didn't have a gun. He didn't have any weapons. But he knew where he was going to get one.

He said to the bigger assailant in front of him and said, "Get away from my car asshole, before I shove that crowbar up your ass."

For a second, Crowbar seemed confused, but in the next instant, he raised the iron bar overhead and sprang at Devlin, yelling a curse. Devlin timed his response almost perfectly. He stood his ground and snapped a simple, devastating front kick with everything he had straight at Crowbar's chest. The big man's momentum meeting the force of Devlin's kick created an enormous impact. His feet flew out from under him, he fell back hard and slammed the back of his head into the parking lot asphalt.

The knife wielder came at Devlin, but Devlin was already moving to get the crowbar. The knife came slicing towards Devlin's face, but he twisted away from the blade as he bent down to grab the curved head of the crowbar. In one fluid motion, he pulled it out of the first attacker's hand and swung it at the knife wielder, catching him on the shoulder, knocking him back. Then he whipped the crowbar in the opposite direction and smacked the first attacker in his forehead, cracking his skull, and then to make sure he wasn't going to get up, brought the heavy bar down on the top of the big man's knee, shattering the kneecap.

Devlin turned to face the knife fighter, who switched the knife to his left hand, still wincing from the blow to his right shoulder. Devlin adjusted his grip on the crowbar, thinking about his days studying Iaido, angling to slap the crowbar on the knife wielder's wrist, anticipating the sound of the bone cracking when he heard the van's engine revving up. Suddenly, the driver shoved the van into gear and aimed it at Devlin.

Tires squealing, the van fishtailing toward him, Devlin overhanded the crowbar at the windshield and dove to his right. The driver instinctively turned away from the crowbar and smacked into the second attacker. Devlin hit the ground, hearing the sickening sound of a muffled crack and a scream as the van banged into his attacker.

Devlin rolled, sprang to his feet, as the back wheel of the van run over the knife wielder's leg.

Devlin winced at the sound of bones breaking.

He ran for his car, but by the time he got in, started the engine, and made it out of the parking lot, the tail lights of the van were far in the distance. Devlin floored the accelerator and gripped the wheel. The moon had disappeared behind a cloud bank, and there were no lights along the two-lane road. Devlin couldn't see much of anything but the taillights of the truck. At 75 mph, he was closing in on the tail lights when the van disappeared around a curve.

Devlin held his speed as he came around the curve, nearly sending his car into a slide. Up ahead, he saw the van turn off the road, its taillights bouncing as the van plowed through a field on the outskirts of Haleiwa.

Devlin braked, turned, and slid onto a rutted road. The rental car bounced and bucked over the humps and holes. Devlin could barely see the road, much less the van's tail lights, and had to slow down to stay in control. His car jounced around a bend and Devlin's headlight illuminated the Chevy van shut down, lights off. Devlin braked furiously. He was too close. The rental car banged into the back of the abandoned van. The car's airbag exploded into Devlin. By the time Devlin shoved the deflated bag out of his way and got out of the car, the driver of the van was nowhere in sight. Devlin looked around and saw a few houses about five-hundred yards to his left. In the other direction, back toward Haleiwa, there was a field, a few trees, and then nothing in sight but darkness. Devlin saw no movement, heard nothing but the engine of his car. Even if he'd known where to look for the driver, he hadn't gotten a good enough look at him to identify him.

Devlin peered inside the van. The ignition lock on the steering wheel was broken, a screwdriver jammed into it to turn on the ignition.

Stolen.

Devlin stepped back, thinking it could have been a coincidence that some local tough guys happened to see a rental car in an isolated parking lot and decided to take advantage of the opportunity. It could have been a coincidence that they looked like the type of low-echelon criminals who could get into a dispute over a marijuana crop and stick a knife in someone. But Devlin didn't believe in coincidences. Somebody had set those two on him. The only reason had to be because of his connection to Jasper Cranston. And his daughter.

But how did they know he was connected to Cranston? And that he would be at that restaurant?

Devlin jumped into his car and raced back toward the restaurant to warn Leilani and find out if she knew anything that could answer his questions. But as he approached Haleiwa, he saw flashing red and blue lights. The cops had already closed off the main road into town. Eight cars ahead of him were stopped at the roadblock. Devlin pounded the steering wheel, made a U-turn, and drove away. He looked at his watch. Almost ten o'clock. Past Cranston's bedtime. He'd have to wake him up.

#

Back at the restaurant, Leilani was so angry and embarrassed that her hand shook as she signed the restaurant bill. She couldn't believe Devlin had abandoned her with some bullshit excuse and left her with the fucking check. Worse, she hadn't had enough cash, so she'd had to use an already overdrawn credit card and sit with a forced smile hoping the waitress didn't come back and tell her the card had been rejected.

Somehow the charge went through. Leilani wrote in a tip and scribbled her signature, stood up, and walked out of the restaurant staring straight ahead, convinced that everyone was looking at her because they all knew her dinner date had walked out on her.

As soon as Leilani made it outside, she began quietly cursing Jack Devlin. She cursed him thoroughly and completely. And she cursed herself for letting another man try to tell her what she could and couldn't do. And she vowed never to let it happen again. Her anger blinded her to everything except her resolve. She saw a police car and ambulance in the small beachfront parking lot down the road, but never even thought of connecting them to Devlin. She assumed it was another car accident, the kind that happened all the time on the dark North Shore roads. Her only thought was – she was going to do what she had to do, and to goddamn fucking hell with Jack Devlin and anybody who tried to stop her.

CHAPTER 9

Devlin stopped at a local gas station on Kamehameha Highway and called Cranston. The phone rang six times, and the answering machine kicked in.

Devlin thought, just as well. Won't have to waste time trying to explain anything.

"General, this is Jack Devlin. Sorry to call you at this late hour. Please do me a favor and call your daughter as soon as possible. Tell her to get in touch with me. I need to speak to her."

Devlin left the number for the Pacific Rim office and hung up. He didn't have time to waste. He wanted to be on the Big Island tomorrow. Which meant he had to find Tuulima Mafa, tonight.

Devlin pushed the battered rental car as hard as he could, pulled into the Chinatown district of Honolulu, and parked on Hotel Street. He knew Tuli could be working in any number of places, but he doubted the big man would bother with most of the sleazier strip clubs and sex clubs. Not unless a friend needed his help. Devlin preferred to go straight to the best place to locate him, which unfortunately also happened to be the worst place a haole could enter – a Samoan bar called YC3 located on Ala'pahi Street. Unfortunately, Samoans and alcohol did not mix well, but Devlin was racing the clock, so he steeled himself and walked into the bar.

There were only five men in the bar, but it was full. Dangerously full. Four of the five were Samoan. Devlin estimated their average weight to be three hundred pounds. The fifth man was a skinny

Filipino who seemed lost in the bulk that surrounded him. The bartender was a woman, also Samoan, also quite large.

Devlin smiled politely, edged his way to a small opening at the bar, and ordered a beer. In Devlin's experience, if a Samoan was drinking, it was usually beer. Lots of it.

He smiled and asked the woman tending bar if she knew Tuli, and where he might find him.

She smiled back at Devlin, revealing a missing front tooth. She seemed amused that a haole had appeared in her bar. Devlin hoped she continued to be amused and smiled back.

"Tuli?"

"Yes," said Devlin. "Tuulima Mafa."

"Yeah, yeah, I know Tuli. I think he working at Hubba Hubba sometime. I don't know about tonight. Maybe tonight, ioe i?"

"Thanks. If you see him, tell him Jack Devlin is looking for him, and he should call Mrs. Banks. He knows the number. Can you tell him for me?"

"Sure, sure."

She smiled her missing-tooth smile, Devlin took a swig of his beer to be polite, handed her a ten-dollar bill, and thanked her. He turned from the door, careful to avoid eye contact with any of the big men staring at him, particularly one guy standing next to the jukebox glaring at him. The guy was big enough to make the jukebox look small.

Devlin walked back to Hotel Street, passing a pair of worn-out hookers standing on a dimly lit corner, and headed for the Hubba Hubba club. It was a decrepit strip joint that had been an attraction on Hotel Street for decades but was long past its heyday. Mounted on the outside wall of the club were framed black-and-white photos of strippers who, judging by their outfits, must have performed sometime in the fifties.

A female junkie dressed in tight-fitting jeans and a clinging white sweater that showed she was braless sat huddled in an empty alcove near the entrance to the club. She looked at Devlin as he passed. She wasn't able to come out of her stupor fast enough to proposition him. Welcome to Hotel Street, thought Devlin.

He stepped into the club. A mass of neon lights and a miasma of stale beer, cigarette smoke, and Pine-Sol greeted him. The place looked like a Budweiser salesman had convinced the Hubba Hubba owners that the club should be a showcase for signage left over from years of failed promotions.

The front area had logos, clocks, bottles, and slogans all in neon, not all of which were fully lit. Everything in the club seemed old and dirty: the furniture, the floor, even the guy who appeared to be in charge.

Devlin glanced at the rectangular bar to his right and walked past four young men playing pool. They were in good shape, had short hair, and clean clothes. Devlin assumed they were soldiers on a night out.

He continued to the main part of the club. A large room dominated by a long runway surrounded by a ring of chairs. Tables with chairs filled the rest of the room. Devlin thought about the hundreds, perhaps thousands, of women who had stripped on that runway over the years.

On this night, an enthusiastic, middle-aged brunette strutted up and down the runway dressed in a shabby bolero outfit. An upbeat version of a song that matched her outfit blared out of a worn-out sound system. Devlin was baffled to see almost every seat around the runway occupied. He knew Honolulu had plenty of well-lit, clean places with dozens of genuinely striking young women, completely naked, young, friendly, and enthusiastic. Why would these guys pick this place? Why would anybody? The booze must be a hell of a lot cheaper, thought Devlin.

Devlin stood for a moment trying to determine any need for a bouncer in this depressing place when a squat, beefy man in his sixties came up to him and told him in a raspy voice, "Hey, buddy, either take a seat and buy a drink or move on. No standing there."

Devlin looked down at the unpleasant man. He had a pug face. His head was covered with a patchy gray stubble of hair that almost matched the scraggly stubble on his face. His teeth were rotting; he had sour body odor and bad breath. And he spat when he talked. Devlin had felt a bit of spittle land on his chin when the pug-faced man yelled at him.

Devlin put aside his anger and disgust and kept his voice even. "Listen," he said, "I'm looking for a guy I was told works here as a bouncer, Tuulima Mafa. Tuli. I have a job for him. Do you know if he's working here tonight?"

"Hey," said the pug, "did you fuckin' hear me or not? Either buy a drink or get the fuck out."

Devlin's patience evaporated. He stuck his face right down into the manager's ugly mug, even though he had to endure his stale breath and shot back, "Hey, drop the goddamn tough guy act, old man. It doesn't work anymore. I asked you a question, politely."

The manager clenched his beefy fist and took a step back.

Devlin barked, "Don't raise your goddamn hands to me unless you want your arms broken. If you see Tuli Mafa, you tell him Jack Devlin is looking for him. You got it? If I find out you didn't tell him, I'll come back and put your ugly face through a wall. You got that?"

The manager put his hand down, but he had more craziness in him than Devlin had figured on. He started screaming. "Get out of here, you fuck. I'll have you broken in two, you big bastard. You piece of shit. Get the fuck out of here."

Devlin waved him off and turned away from the vicious, used-up man. He headed out of the bar, wanting to be out of there. Off Hotel Street. Away from this part of town. He'd find Tuli in the morning.

He headed back to his car around the corner, unlocked the door, and got in just as a man big enough to be a sumo wrestler rounded the corner. The pug-faced manager from the Hubba

Hubba club shuffled along behind the giant. The big man looked as if he had been roused from either sleep or a meal and was not happy about it. The angry monster was so big, Devlin thought he might actually be a second-rate Japanese sumo, but as he rumbled closer, Devlin decided he was either Samoan or Tongan. One of the big breed.

Devlin's rental car was jammed into the parking space. He knew he'd never maneuver it out in time. He hit the steering wheel of the car with the side of his fist, wishing he had knocked out that nasty old prick back in the bar. Now he really wanted to punch him. Unfortunately, there was a giant in the way.

Devlin looked around for a weapon. There was a promotional tourist magazine the car rental company had placed on the passenger seat of the car. Devlin grabbed it and rolled the magazine into a tight cylinder as the giant reached the car. The man was so big that his belly blocked the entire view out the driver's side window.

He was close enough now for Devlin to decide he was definitely Samoan. The Samoan boomed, "Get out, muddafucker."

Devlin had just about finished rolling the magazine into a tight cylinder when the big man pulled open the car door and shoved it back so far and so fast that both hinges cracked. But that wasn't good enough. The Samoan pushed the door until it was almost flat against the front fender.

"Jesus Christ," yelled Devlin.

The Samoan turned to grab Devlin, but with the door out of his way, Devlin pivoted and kicked the heel of his right shoe into the Samoan's left kneecap. It only succeeded in making the Samoan grunt and take a step back. Devlin came out of his seat bent into a crouch and shoved the end of the tightly rolled-up magazine into the Samoan's crotch, but the man's belly was so huge that the end of the improvised weapon didn't penetrate anywhere near his testicles. All it did, even with Devlin's full force behind it, was make the giant grunt again.

Devlin rammed his left shoulder into the Samoan's chest, knocking him back two more steps. Then he tried to jam the newspaper into his attacker's throat, but the blow didn't penetrate past the fat under his chin. The Samoan forearmed Devlin's shoulder and knocked him back against the car. Devlin decided this was as close to fighting a grizzly bear he would ever experience.

The big man closed in on him with arms open wide to grab any part of Devlin he could, but Devlin was too quick. He slid under the massive left arm and came up slightly behind the Samoan. Devlin gripped the magazine with both hands and drove it into the Samoan's left kidney with all his strength. This time the Samoan's grunt sounded more like a moan. Devlin had finally done something that hurt. He did it three more times before the Samoan reared back and knocked Devlin away with a backhand blow that caught him on the other shoulder.

Devlin staggered backward into the old man from the Hubba Hubba club who grabbed him in a bear hug. The attack from behind was bad enough. The stench on the old man made it unconscionable.

Devlin exploded. He dropped the magazine, grabbed the man's right wrist, pulled it down breaking the bear hug, stepped left, turning and twisting the arm behind the old man. He pulled the arm up into a hammerlock, and as the bar manager bent forward, Devlin grabbed the pug-faced bastard around the neck and applied a crushing chokehold.

The Samoan couldn't quite figure out how to get to Devlin with Devlin holding the manager in front of him. Grabbing at Devlin's arm, choking, the manager kicked backward and hit Devlin's shin with the heel of his shoe. That was it. Devlin rammed manager's arm up behind his back and tore a ligament in the nasty, old bastard's shoulder.

The man howled in pain. Devlin shoved him away, sending him skidding face-first into the dirty street landing in front of the Samoan. Devlin had had enough. He crouched in front of the Samoan and snarled at him, "Get the fuck away from me or I'll kill you, you son of a bitch. You hear me? I'll fucking kill you."

The Samoan blinked at Devlin twice, dropped his hands, turned, and walked away. Devlin could hardly believe it, but he knew he'd meant what he'd said and figured the Samoan must have figured it wasn't worth finding out.

Devlin turned around to get back in his car and saw the real reason the Samoan had left. Tuulima Mafa was standing behind him with a bug-eyed expression.

"Oh, brudda," said Tuli, "you one tough guy, man."

"What the hell!?" yelled Devlin.

Tuli started laughing a big, booming, disarming laugh. A laugh big enough to match his enormous body. Tuli was Samoan, too. Not as large as the bear who had come out of the Hubba Hubba, but large enough to be a presence wherever he stood. A natural force to be reckoned with. Six-five. Two hundred eighty-five pounds. But unlike many of his Samoan brethren, Tuli was not overly fat. His weight was mostly muscle and bone. Tuulima Mafa was the closest thing to an indestructible human fighting machine that Jack Devlin had ever met. In between fights, Tuli was pretty much a happy, smiling man who thought most everything in life was either made for fun or just plain funny.

Suddenly Devlin felt foolish about thinking his fierceness had scared away the fighter from the bar.

"Are you working in this shit-bag part of town?" Devlin demanded.

"Not that shithole Hubba Hubba. Who told you Tuli working there?"

"The bartender at YC3."

"Yeah, Flower. She call me."

"Where?"

"At the Black Orchid, man. Tuli don't work no shitty old strip joints."

"Why'd she tell me you worked at Hubba Hubba?"

"She not gonna tell some haole stranger where to find me. What's a matter with you, Jacky? You can't figure that out? Come down here and get in big trouble without Tuli?"

Tuli started his big, booming laugh again. Devlin yelled at him, "Did you see what that son of a bitch did to my car?"

This made Tuli laugh even harder. Tears rolled down his big face. It was too much. Devlin started laughing, too.

Tuli waved his big paw. "Ah, we fix 'em up, man."

Tuli, still laughing, walked over, and pulled the door away from the front fender, and then bulldozed it back into position, leaving enough room for Devlin to get in.

Then he walked over to the manager from the Hubba Hubba, who was up on one knee, holding his shoulder, cursing and moaning. Tuli's smile disappeared. He grabbed the man by the back of his neck and lifted him to his feet. He slapped his face to get his attention. "Hey, you some tough guy, huh? You make trouble for my friend, Jack, huh?" He slapped the man again, this time making both nostrils bleed. "Huh?" yelled Tuli.

The manager grunted out an answer, "He fucked up my shoulder."

"You lucky he just fuck up your shoulder. He one real tough guy, brudda, not like you. I saw you put hands on him. Asshole."

Tuli dragged him over to a building and pushed him hard against the wall. He pawed the man's body until he found a small Charter Arms revolver.

Tuli looked at the gun with disgust. "Good thing you don't use this. Goddamn good thing."

Tuli held the gun upside down by the handle and smashed it into the brick wall next to the manager's head. He kept at it until the revolver was bent and broken. Then he shoved the ruined gun down the front of the man's pants.

He put his enormous face an inch from the man's and said, "You fuck with us, mister, I break you up like your baby gun." He punched him once and broke two of the man's ribs.

The manager almost passed out with pain, but Tuli held him up against the wall.

"Now, you remember, or I come back and punch you a lot of times." Tuli nodded solemnly at the bar manager. "I break you up big time, shithead."

Tuli let the Hubba Hubba club manager drop to the sidewalk, turned, and climbed into Devlin's car, just about fitting into the passenger seat. Devlin was in the driver's seat trying to pull the door shut without much success.

The Samoan started chuckling and laughing again, telling Devlin, "Jacky man, you get this car at the airport?"

"I don't know where they got it," said Devlin, as he tightened his seat-belt harness.

"It's rented, yeah?"

"Yes."

"You take out all the insurance, Jacky-man?"

"The company rented it."

"No problem then. Give this piece of shit to Mister Chan. He get you another one. What kine job you got for Tuli? When we start?"

"Now."

Tuli clapped his hands once. "Goddamn right. We go see the Chief tomorrow."

"First thing in the morning. You're staying with me tonight at the condo."

"Okay with me. You got any beer up there?"

"Probably."

"How come you shouting at Tuli? You mad at me?"

"I'm not mad at you. I'm shouting because this fucking door won't close, and the wind is blowing in my ear."

Tuli started laughing again.

Devlin said, "It's not funny," which predictably made Tuulima Mafa laugh harder.

CHAPTER 10

By midnight, Eddie Lihu knew something had gone wrong. He sat at the same

desk where he had given instructions to his bodyguard Charlie, who by now should have been standing in his office handing him whatever had been in the pockets of Jack Devlin and reporting on how much damage Bukowski's thugs had done to him. Neither had happened.

Lihu looked at his watch again. Dinner had been at eight. Clearly, they didn't take care of the guy before dinner. So, ten, ten-thirty, even if dinner had lasted until eleven, even if they'd confronted him with the woman near the restaurant, he should have known by now.

At 12:20 A.M. Lihu's phone finally rang.

Lihu picked up the phone and said, "Yeah?" Then he listened without saying anything beyond an occasional grunt at the bad news. One man with shattered kneecap and a concussion. Another in the hospital with a list of injuries too long for Lihu to be interested in hearing, injuries sustained after having apparently been run over by the idiot who was supposed to be driving their getaway car. Stupid, fucking Bukowski thugs.

Lihu finally interrupted. "Enough. Tell Bukowski to find the driver. Fast. Then he brings the fucking driver here. You stay on it until that's done."

Lihu hung up.

Obviously, Cranston had called in a professional. This had to stop, now. There could be nothing that prevented Lihu from doing what he needed to do in the next week.

Lihu picked up his phone.

Eric Engle made sure to answer on the first ring.

Lihu's voice rumbled, "Listen carefully."

Engle did just that.

#

Devlin rose with the sun. He took a slow jog on the beach parallel to Fort DeRussy Beach Park, mostly to see if the wound incurred in New York when a bullet clipped the top of his hip was going to bother him. The only discomfort came from the tear in his skin that hadn't completely healed. Maybe a bit more time in the salt water would help.

When he returned, Chan had delivered his weapons from the gunsmith and laid out four topographical maps of Hawaii's Puna District on the condo's dining room table. Chan had positioned the four maps so they became one very detailed map of the southeastern section of Hawaii.

The four maps covered the town of Pahoa and the rainforest areas to the west and northwest where they had found Billy's body.

While Tuli slept in the second bedroom, Devlin sipped his morning coffee and studied the topo maps. They'd found Billy Cranston's body about ten miles north of Pahoa in an area that appeared to be inaccessible except on foot. Devlin assumed there were fire trails and hiking paths cutting through the forest reserve. Devlin knew that when marijuana growing had thrived on the Islands years ago, this area in the Puna district had been used by growers. They would drive in bags of fertilizer, plants, and equipment on the various hidden trails, then carry in the material a few miles on their backs to isolated areas where they could grow their crops without much fear of being discovered.

The maps showed the body had been found in an area where Billy could have been raising marijuana. But the police report hadn't mentioned the presence of any marijuana growing there. Which raised the possibility that he had been stabbed someplace nearby, and the body transported. But how? It would have been difficult to move a body in that rainforest.

The maps raised as many questions as they answered. Devlin knew he'd never what he needed to know unless he hiked into the site.

#

By 10:00 A.M., Devlin and Tuli were in the new rental car, a dark blue Chevy Impala, Chan had delivered to the condo heading toward a small residential area called Kane'ilo Point on the Wai'anae coast, the west coast of Oahu. Tuli sat smiling in the passenger seat, window open, his huge arm hanging outside the car as if it were giving the auto a big hug.

Wai'anae was home to many of the island's poorest people, and also some of Oahu's most beautiful, sunniest beaches.

Devlin's last bit of business on Oahu was to meet with Tuli's Samoan chief, the leader of his clan – Aseososo Sua, who was also Tuli's uncle.

It was more than just a courtesy call. Without the chief's permission, Tuli would not agree to work for Pacific Rim. Tuli didn't work only for himself. He worked for his clan. His family and relatives profited by Tuli's efforts, as he did by theirs. In order for Tuli to work for Devlin, Devlin had to have the approval of the chief.

Devlin hadn't seen Aseososo Sua for years but remembered him as if it had been yesterday. Sua was an exceptionally handsome man. Tall, strongly built, but not massive. The chief had classic Polynesian features, thick, gleaming jet-black hair that even at the age of sixty showed not even a hint of gray.

Sua was one of the most formidable men Devlin had ever met.

And, one of the calmest and most peaceful. Devlin didn't mind taking the time to visit the chief. On the contrary, he valued the opportunity to sit with Chief Aseososo Sua.

Tuli and Devlin pulled into the driveway of a one-story, neatly kept house. It was a more substantial structure than most in the neighborhood. It had a brick base and wood siding. It was a house befitting a chief.

They were greeted at the door by Tuli's auntie. As usual, there was a gaggle of round-bellied, boisterous kids running around, dressed in nothing but shorts. Two women in their early twenties sat in the large central room sewing the hem of a long gauzy curtain. Two older women were preparing food in the kitchen. Devlin assumed there were more people in other parts of the house. He knew that by Samoan tradition any relative of the chief's, no matter how young or old, no matter how far removed, could come to this home and stay as long as he or she wished, sharing freely in whatever the clan had to offer. Those who worked would pool their money. Those who didn't would maintain the home for the family members who were earning a paycheck. And those who did neither would still be accepted for as long as the chief deemed their presence acceptable.

Devlin and Tuli were led out to the lanai behind the house. The chief sat stolidly in a wicker chair, in a small garden area. He wore a tank top and shorts that revealed the bottom half of a dense, charcoal-colored tattoo, the pe'a. It covered his body from just above the hips to just below the knees. It was a formal decoration, designed and applied according to strict tradition by the official tattooist of Aseososo's village. By now there were many bastardized forms of the pe'a. But Aseososo's was the real thing. The mark of a genuine Samoan chief.

Aseososo smiled and nodded when he saw Devlin, but he did not stand. Tuli stood waiting respectfully in the doorway that led out to the lanai, while Devlin approached the chief.

Aseososo extended his hand to Devlin's, and they shook. The chief motioned for Devlin to sit on a small bench placed next to him and began to speak. Although he spoke softly, there was something about the timbre and pitch of the chief's voice that made it resonate into Devlin's body as much as into his ears. Most of the time the chief spoke without looking at Devlin as if Devlin had come to sit beside him and take instructions. Aseososo had assumed the role of a "speaking chief," laying out the oral tradition, giving the law by spoken word in the same way it had been passed down for generations in his clan. What he spoke about wasn't as important to Devlin as how he spoke.

Only occasionally would Aseososo look at Devlin, to gauge Devlin's agreement or to emphasize a point. By looking straight ahead, rather than at Devlin, the chief was also able to address Tuli. It lent a solemnity to the words because it emphasized that the chief was speaking the law, not just speaking. The content of his speech was clear – Tuli's working with Devlin was linked to an obligation to his clan, the 'aiga'. The meaning of his words, however, carried a deeper message. The chief was communicating to Devlin and Tuli that nothing they would do in the coming days would be done without effects that would resonate far beyond them.

After the formal speech and Devlin's indication that he understood the chief, Aseososo smiled and shook Devlin's hand. Then he inclined his head toward Devlin and spoke in a very different manner. Now Aseososo was a businessman. He emphasized that all Tuli's earnings would be sent directly to the family bank account. He asked Devlin to explain once again how Tuli would be covered in case of death or accident. Devlin outlined how Pacific Rim operatives could not be covered by insurance companies because of the nature of their jobs, but that a fund had been set up out of each operative's earnings and the company's profits. In case of death or accident, Tuli would be covered up to the amount of one million dollars, which would be paid to the family either as needed to cover medical expenses or over a ten-year period in case of death.

The chief nodded. They shook hands once more, and their formal meeting concluded.

The meeting had given Devlin a calm sense of renewal and resolve. It felt like an antidote to the confusion, pain, and angst emanating from the Cranston family. It allowed Devlin to return to himself, to return to his accustomed way of operating in the moment according to the events around him, letting his actions reveal his next move. Devlin was experienced enough and mature enough to know the value of spiritual power. Now, something else, something intangible would influence his actions. In the Islands, they called it mana. And Devlin believed mana flow through Aseososo. Devlin also believed that what had just transpired had taken place so that the mana could flow into him.

And now, Aseososo Sua took on his third persona. That of a comrade. Now he stood, rising to his full height, which almost equaled Devlin's. His face lit up in a broad, handsome smile, and he clapped a big hand on Devlin's shoulder and said, "Okay, now we get everyone together for dinner, and we guys have kava tonight, hey?"

It took Devlin five minutes of firm but polite refusing to decline the chief's invitation to a kava ceremony. Devlin had participated once before, and it had taken him two days to recover from the mind-numbing effect that hours and hours of kava drinking produced. It was their way of honoring a guest. And the event was truly unforgettable, but this time Devlin explained to Chief Sua that too much time had already been lost and each hour that flowed past him would make the chance of success more remote.

Sua looked deeply into Devlin's eyes for a moment, then nodded, and said, "I understand."

Next were all the good-byes, the bear hugs, the alohas, and finally the family business was done. Devlin and Tuli were back in the rental car making the return drive to Waikiki. They passed several stretches of beautiful white sand beach, burning under the tropical sun.

After about fifteen minutes of driving, Devlin said, "Let's you and I talk now."

He pulled over near a stretch of beach. He felt like he needed to have his feet in the sand and surf. Neither man said anything until they were walking side by side on the firmly packed sand, the gentle waves washing over their feet.

Devlin and Tuli made an impressive pair. At six-foot-four Devlin was almost as tall as Tuli, but Tuli outweighed him by fifty or sixty pounds. Devlin was big boned, muscular, with very little body fat. Tuli was huge-boned, heavily muscled, with a generous layer of bulk.

Tuli smiled at the sun, kicking the ocean surf as he walked, swinging his arms. Suddenly he said, "Chief is good people, huh?"

"He's very special," said Devlin. "Very special."

"That's why he be chief. Soon as you see Aseososo, you know Aseososo is the chief."

Devlin nodded, picturing the man's calm face, feeling his inner strength.

"So," said Tuli, "what's the plan, brudda?"

On the drive to the chief's house, Devlin had already told Tuli what he was investigating. He only had to tell Tuli once that Billy Cranston had meant a great deal to him, and Tuli accepted it without question. Now Devlin laid out the first steps.

"I'll go over to the Big Island later this afternoon. First thing, I'll talk to the police. See what information I can pick up.

"Then I'll set up in Pahoa. You come over tomorrow. Set up in the house outside town Mrs. Banks rented. You don't know me. I don't know you."

"Okay, then what?"

"I start putting pressure on whoever is behind this."

"Who's that?"

"I don't know. But whoever it is, they know I'm coming so it shouldn't be too hard to shake things up and see what crawls out."

"How do they know you comin'?"

"I'm not sure. They're probably watching Cranston's house. Somebody set a couple of local bad boys after me last night. Somebody knows."

"A couple?"

"Yeah."

"Dat ain't enough, boss."

"Well, if you include their driver, three. But he panicked and ran over one of the other two."

"Aaaii, you kidding."

"No. I chased the van, but he had too much of a lead on me. All I found was an empty van in the middle of nowhere. Looked stolen."

"Dey sound stupid, but you be careful until Tuli get over there, boss. That old Pahoa-town place got a lot of nasty boys hangin' round."

"Well, Tuli, if it gets rough, you just stand behind me wherever I go, and everyone will just back off like that guy last night."

"Who?"

"That big Samoan from the Hubba Hubba club."

"Oh, dat guy? Dat was my cousin, Fava, man."

Devlin stopped and turned to Tuli. "Your cousin?"

"Yeah, man."

"What?"

"Yeah, that was Fava."

"I thought you scared him off."

"No, nuttin scare Fava. He one tough guy. He fight everybody. He even fight me. I don't want to fight Fava. I fight Fava, I have to kill him. Break his fuckin' head open like a coconut or something. Maybe shoot him. Maybe we both have to shoot him. Fava probably take a few bullets. No, Fava and me, we don't fight. Not unless it's a real war. Some kine real big emergency."

"So, he walked away because he knew you?"

"Yeah, Fava know me. He know everybody gonna get hurt he fights with Tuli."

Tuli started to laugh again. This time Devlin didn't even smile. He just shook his head.

CHAPTER 11

Leilani's Aloha Airlines flight landed on the Big Island of Hawaii at 11:08 A.M. As usual, it was raining in Hilo.

She walked off the plane with only a backpack and a small travel bag, walked through the terminal, past the baggage areas, and down to where the airport traffic exited. She pulled out her umbrella. It was only big enough to keep her upper body dry, but Leilani didn't mind the rain at all. It would make it easier to get a ride. Of course, she could have rented a car, but she wanted to come into Pahoa-town looking as if she needed a job.

Hilo's airport wasn't very large. In five minutes, Leilani's long strides took her to the spot where cars either looped back around to return to the terminal or exited. When she spotted a car with a driver who looked okay, she motioned with her thumb and smiled. The car stopped as if a red light had flashed.

Her first ride took her into Hilo. The second to a shopping center at the intersection of Highways 11 and 130 at Kea'au. The last ride took her right into Pahoa, even though the driver, a retired schoolteacher bringing back fertilizer for his wife's garden had to drive an extra two miles to get off Highway 130, take the access road into Pahoa, then drive back out to the highway. Years ago, Highway 130 had run right through the town. But now there was a bypass that let you skirt the town and avoid slowing down.

Leilani arrived just before lunch. She asked the retired schoolteacher to let her off at the far end of town so he would pass all the places where food was served. One was a Thai restaurant. She assumed mostly family members would be working there. One was a natural food place called Paradise East where she noted that that most of the tables were occupied. The third place called Da Restaurant served burgers, pizza, and other foods that were quick and easy to prepare. From the street, it looked a bit seedy and didn't appear to be doing much business.

At the end of Main Street, Leilani thanked the retired schoolteacher and headed straight for Da Restaurant.

Walter Harrison sat at a table near the kitchen. Mid-fifties, sporting a slightly pathetic combover, Harrison had a perpetually bemused expression, and wore a pair of dingy tennis shorts and an old green Izod shirt that stretched across his ample belly. When Leilani walked in, he was lifting a large glass filled with ice, orange juice, and three ounces of Popov vodka poured from a plastic half-gallon jug. The glass never reached his lips.

Leilani stood in the doorway looking carefully at Walter. She would have bet all the money hidden in her backpack that those tennis shorts were unbuttoned under his shirt. She smiled at him, but Walter was too flummoxed by her appearance to smile back. While Walter stared at her, Leilani quickly counted the seats in the restaurant. Five tables that sat four. Three tables that sat two. Plus, the small table Walter was using as his headquarters near the kitchen. Room for twenty-six, twenty-eight in a pinch. There were only five people eating lunch. Perfect.

Walter waved a hand at her and said, "Sit anywhere." Leilani strode over to his table. Walter still had his glass in midair. When she sat down, he placed it carefully on the table.

"I'm Leilani Kilau. How's business?"

"I'm Walter Harrison. How's it look?"

"Pretty bad."

"I suppose that's an accurate albeit inadequate description of the situation."

"Inadequate?"

"Well, you fail to recognize the potential. Pleasant space. Original hardwood floor. Panoramic view of Main Street. Functioning ceiling fans. See? Short sentences. Simple adjectives. Adequate description."

"What's preventing the potential from being realized?"

Walter flashed a lopsided grin. "Ah, preventing the potential. A touch of alliteration there."

"Thank you."

"You mean, how come business stinks?"

"Yes."

"Ah, well, hhhmmm. Perhaps because I prefer to drink vodka and orange juice and read boring books on philosophy rather than seek after profits. Or perhaps because I don't pander enough to the local clientele."

"Pander?"

Walter waived a hand, "Oh, you know, jump up and pretend to be eager to serve people when they enter."

"Uh huh. How's the food?"

"Walter gave Leilani a conspiratorial look. "Well. You may have hit on something there." He winced. "It's not very good. Why do you ask?"

"I need a job."

"If I could afford to pay you, de facto, my business would be good."

"Do you own this place?"

"I own a five-year obligation. A net lease on the building. Nobody owns anything in this town. Or on this island for that matter. It's all owned by large, faceless entities of one sort or another. Corporations that once the surface is sufficiently scratched lead back to some family trust set up by the white missionaries who stole most of the Islands when nobody owned anything except a king and a few chiefs. Sort of come full circle, haven't we? Ah, yes, perhaps *that's* why potential around here isn't realized. No pride of ownership."

Leilani nodded as if she understood. "Do you have the upstairs, too?"

"If you want to use the word *have* in its broadest sense."

"Got any extra rooms up there?"

"Why?"

"How about you give me a place to sleep and food in exchange for me working here? I keep whatever tips I make. If business gets good enough, we'll talk about a salary."

"Now, here's a conversation that's taken a sudden turn. Did you actually ask to sleep under the same roof as moi?"

"In the narrowest sense of the word. You know, just sleep."

Walter smiled at that one. He was beginning to enjoy the conversation and Leilani. "Who are you? Did someone tell you I was hiring or something?"

"No. I'm just someone who wants to work."

"Simple as that? Albeit fairly unique for this part of the world."

"Yep. Simple as that."

"But why would you want to work for me?"

"I know how to cook. I know how to run a restaurant. Of the places in town that serve food, yours looks like it needs the most help."

Walter feigned a look of pain. "Oh, dear. Your offer smacks of pity."

"Not at all. I just figured I'd ask where I could make a difference."

"Why am I suspicious? Is it because you seem so forthright?"

"I don't know. I'm honest. You can tell by looking at me I'll attract business. I won't bother you if you don't bother me. I ran two restaurants when I was in college in San Francisco. I could even get you references if you want them."

"References! Is there anything more useless than friends and relatives vouching for people they're happy to be rid of? And I'll wager a goodly amount that you could turn quite a few employers into friends."

"Hey, come on. That's not fair."

Walter raised his hands and bowed his head slightly. "You're right. Quite uncalled for. Egregiously presumptive of me. But I have been the victim of feminine wiles in the past. And I assure you, you have no idea how many women in this town think they should work here and save me. I feel myself to be an easy mark."

Leilani sat back in her chair and frowned. She looked at Walter and asked slowly, "You really feel all that pressured?"

"Absolutely."

"Am I being too pushy?"

"Maybe it's just me. Where are you from?"

"Maui."

"Born there?"

"Yep. How about you?"

"I was born in Honolulu. My family is from Oahu. Came over to the Big Island when I was about twelve. Father worked in Honolulu for a long time. In shipping. Then he bought a small avocado farm over here. Played that out until he retired on the property. You don't seem like you're from the Islands."

"Why not?"

"You have the pace of the Mainland about you."

"I probably do. I went to school there."

"Oh? What did you study?"

"I got my master's in fine arts."

"An artist! I knew it. Education tells. My fears are slightly assuaged."

"A sculptor actually. I've been going at it for about eight months straight. That's why I'm a little hyper. When I get this manic, I take a couple of months off. Pick up and go somewhere. I've always heard that the Puna area was nice, so I came on over. All I really need is a place to stay. I don't eat much. I'm pretty sure I'll earn you more than you give me. That's really about all there is to it."

Walter frowned and said softly, "Puna used to be nice." He paused then asked, "So you're thinking of working here a couple of months?"

"Not sure. Why don't we give a try and see how it goes?"

"What the hell. I'd better go along with your offer before this place slides past the point of no return. Particularly since your offer does not include asking for money I don't have. If I heard you right."

"You did."

"That's the best part of your plan. Very shrewd."

Walter finally took a large sip from his screwdriver. He squinted at the pleasure the icy drink provided and looked at Leilani for a moment. Then he said in a low, conspiratorial voice, "How much work you figure you wanna put in here?"

"You serve three meals?"

"God forbid. Just lunch and dinner."

"I'll do lunch and dinner. And I'll put in a bit of time to set this place up a little better."

"I assume you're talking about cleaning."

"For starters."

Walter scrunched up his face in distaste at the thought. "Okay, here's the deal. By rights, I could ask you for half your tips. But I won't. You keep the tips, and don't count on any discussion about a salary anytime soon."

"Okay."

"There's a bedroom upstairs in the back. There's also a shower and sink back there, but no toilet. The only full bathroom is in my quarters. You'll have to use the toilet down here."

"Okay."

"I'm not accustomed to sharing a roof with anybody. Certainly not a woman."

"I'll stay out of your way."

"And I'll stay out of yours, although you will catch me gazing at you from afar."

"I can handle that."

"I'm sure you're accustomed to it. You are a very beautiful woman. There, I've said it. Now I can relax."

"Thank you."

"You're welcome. It's going to be fun watching you attract the local yokels."

"As long as they buy meals."

"Yes. Now, I can see you have lots of plans, but I'd appreciate it if you tell me before you launch into anything. I do know a thing or two about the business. Particularly when it comes to buying food and supplies around here."

"Okay."

"In your room upstairs, you can do what you want. But the rest of the place is mine, and I'm a slob, and I'm not changing. I don't want to have to clean up for any woman. And I don't want any woman cleaning up after me. You stay in your section; I'll stay in mine. If I want to drink too much and read all night, I will. I don't want to think about you up there. Okay?"

Leilani stuck out her hand and said, "Deal."

Walter withheld his handshake. "If I don't like the way it's going, you have to move on without any fuss."

Leilani kept her hand extended. "Agreed."

Walter hesitated for a moment and finally shook hands.

Leilani's grip made him pop open his eyes for a second. "Well, I guess you won't be asking me to unscrew any jars for you."

CHAPTER 12

Devlin arrived on the Big Island four hours after Leilani, just after three o'clock. By the time he strolled down to the outside baggage carousel, his suitcase had just rolled into view. He grabbed his bag, walked across the roadway to the car rental booths, picked up a white Ford Taurus, and drove to the police station in downtown Hilo to meet with the officer in charge of Billy Cranston's case: Sergeant Detective Jimmy Nishiki.

Devlin's drive into Hilo reminded him the city was a no-nonsense place that functioned more like a normal town than as a tourist destination. Hilo's almost daily doses of on-and-off rain drove most of the tourism to the west side of the island, on the dryer Kona coast.

Devlin had to wait in the lobby of the police station twenty-five minutes before Sergeant Nishiki appeared.

The cop was short, thin, with a look of perpetual annoyance. He had a typical Island mix of several bloodlines with a good dose of Japanese thrown into the blend.

With a nod instead of a hello, Nishiki motioned for Devlin to follow him. He wore the typical Hawaiian civil servant's outfit: short-sleeve white shirt, black tie, and dark slacks, with his detective shield on his belt.

He led Devlin to a cluttered cubicle office, pointed to a gray folding metal chair next to his desk, and said, "Have a seat."

The chair matched Nishiki's gray metal desk, which was covered with manila folders, two in/out baskets, and a traditional green ink-blotter desk pad with a mess of notes and papers jammed under the fake leather side panels.

Nishiki said, "How'd your woman from Pacific Rim know this is my case, and how did she get to my commanding officer?"

"I have no idea. She's good at stuff like that."

"Why is a hotshot outfit like Pacific Rim interested in a loser like Billy Cranston?"

"What do you mean by loser?"

Nishiki stared at Devlin. "So, you gonna answer my questions with a question?"

Devlin looked at Nishiki for a moment. "Any particular reason you're being an asshole, Sergeant?"

"What did you say?"

Devlin repeated himself more slowly, "Is there any particular reason you're being an asshole?"

Nishiki raised his voice, talking with the singsong Island accent Devlin found annoying.

"Who the hell you think you are? Going over my head. Calling me an asshole. Maybe you should get the hell out."

Devlin shrugged. "Okay. I'm sure Mrs. Banks can get me a few minutes with your boss. It's probably a good idea to skip wasting my time with you."

Devlin stood up. The hard metal chair had annoyed him, too.

"Sit down."

Devlin paused, sat down, and repeated his first question. "Why do you think Billy Cranston was a loser?"

Nishiki smirked. "If he wasn't no loser, what da hell he doing wandering aroun' that Pahoa-town all these years?"

"Is that what he was doing? Wandering around?"

"Looked like that."

"You mean when you asked people about him, that's what they said?"

"Yeah."

"Who'd you ask?"

"Lots a people in that town."

"Lots a people?"

"Enough."

Devlin didn't bother asking how many is enough. Instead, he asked, "Did this police department have any dealings with Billy Cranston before his death?"

"Not really."

"What does that mean? He had a couple of run-ins with you? An arrest?"

Nishiki shrugged and stopped talking.

Devlin stared at Nishiki. He stared back at Devlin. He pursed his lips. Then he made a noise like he was trying to suck a piece of food from between his front teeth. He leaned forward and said, "You think I'm gonna tell you something that ain't in my report?"

"Your report doesn't say much."

"That's 'cuz there's not much to say about it. Fact of the matter is, even if I wanted to, I don't really have much to tell you. Neither does my boss. You can ask him if you want."

Devlin nodded.

Nishiki added, "Fact of the matter is, I'm kine a curious myself what happen to dat guy."

"You don't have any idea?"

"Everybody got ideas. Not worth much."

"For instance."

"Hey what? You think I'm some kine dumb island boy here, Devlin. Anything I say to you, you gonna hang on to it, use it one way or another. Who's so interested they're sending you out there to stick your nose where it don't belong?"

"His family. Are you saying they don't have a right to want to know what happened?"

"Who's his family?"

"People who cared about him. People who know people who can help."

"What does that mean?"

Devlin leaned forward and made direct eye contact with Nishiki when he spoke. "It means, Sergeant, nobody is forgetting about Billy Cranston."

Nishiki frowned. Looked down. Shook his head. Sat back in his chair and folded his arms.

Devlin waited.

Finally, Nishiki said, "How much heat gonna be on this?"

"As much as it takes."

Devlin watched Nishiki raise his eyebrows at that. Devlin leaned forward to make sure Nishiki was uncomfortable with him getting into his personal space.

"Just so you know, Sergeant, Billy Cranston was no loser. You think Pacific Rim is a hotshot organization? You have no fucking idea what Pacific Rim is, the resources they have, or who Billy Cranston was. You want to know what the 'fact of the matter' is? Fact of the matter is, there's going to be more goddamn heat on this case than you or your boss or anybody in this building ever dreamed there would be."

Nishiki scratched the back of his neck and muttered, "Shit."

"Yeah," said Devlin. "Shit. This one could come back to haunt you, Sergeant. You can play this any way you want, but one more time, just between you and me, what do you think happened out there?"

Nishiki looked at Devlin and said, "I don't need this. Okay, fuck it. Here it is. Like I said, we don't really know what happened. There was nobody within miles of where dat guy was found. No witnesses. Nothing. Body so messed up the medical examiner comes up with nothing but some kine a bullshit guess about maybe a knife wound.

"Okay, so maybe the M.E. is right. I say to myself, maybe so.

Dis guy didn't just go out there, lay down, and die. So, what's he doin' out there? We know it's a big area for pakalolo. We know this guy been walkin' around that area smokin' herb for years. We figure he got a little patch out there. Hikes in to get it. Maybe he wandered into somebody else's patch. Or maybe somebody found his patch and Cranston caught them. Either way, things maybe got out of hand. Someone sticks him with a knife. Leaves him there. Whatever animals are wandering around out there find the dead meat and feed on him. Who knows?"

"Lot of maybes."

"Yeah. Lots."

"If someone stuck a knife in him, why not bury him? Why leave him out there like that?"

"'Cuz who wants to hang around digging a grave? Yeah, kine a nasty thing to do, leave him like that. Maybe they nasty guys. Or, like I say, maybe they just want to get the hell out of there. You ask me my theory, that's it."

"Did you find any pot growing out there?"

"Nah, but if there was, they probably pulled the plants and got 'em out of there."

"Probably."

Nishiki repeated the word. "Probably."

"So you're not sure about this wandering-into-a-patch theory."

"Not sure about anything."

"You think it might have happened elsewhere, someone drove him in there on an ATV or something to dump the body? Topo maps show some fire trails and hiking trails running through there."

"Maybe. Don't think there's any trails near where the body was."

"You don't think, or you don't know."

"Both."

Devlin suppressed the urge to smack Nishiki on the side of his head.

"Your report said a helicopter tour pilot spotted the body?"

"Yeah. Just lucky. The guy was flying his copter out to the Pu'u
O'o vent from Hilo. Just caught his eye. The clothes and the body
being a different color from all the green down there. Goddamn
tourists got more sight-seeing than they planned on, hey?"

Devlin thought for a moment, then asked, "How many police
do you have working in that area?"

"Depends. We don't have no permanent station around there.
Only a substation in Pahoa. The men use it when they need it."

"There's no police in Pahoa?"

"Not permanently. It's part of our regular patrols. Any problems, we send more men in."

"Otherwise, Pahoa is just on your regular patrols?"

"Right."

"Isn't that a little far for a patrol out of Hilo?"

"Hey, we got cops livin' all around the district. They use their
own cars. We don't all patrol out of Hilo."

Devlin nodded. "Anything else you can tell me, Sergeant?"

"Yeah. Don't cause any trouble in my district. Pahoa-town ain't
the most friendly place for outsiders. Mind your manners."

"Who's not friendly?"

"Just don't go in there trying to push people around. You find
out anything about this guy Cranston, you tell me. You required to
tell me. Anything you find out, it's my business."

"Sure. Thanks for your help, Sergeant."

Devlin stood up and left the cubicle. He didn't bother to shake
Nishiki's hand.

As Devlin walked out of the police station, a gawky man walked
up to Nishiki's desk. He had been sitting quietly in a nearby cubicle listening to Nishiki's conversation with Devlin. The man's name
was Eric Engle. The lawyer Eddie Lihu had on retainer. Engle was
forty-eight years old, and he looked like the last person in the world
to be living in Hawaii. He had pale skin, protruding front teeth, and

he was constantly pushing his thick, black-framed glasses back on his nose. Whatever clothes he wore ended up looking slightly ridiculous on him. Today he sported a stylish Hawaiian shirt and a pair of yellow Bermuda shorts. But his leather shoes and black socks made it look like Engle had missed the point entirely.

Nishiki didn't like Engle any more than he liked Devlin.

The lawyer said, "I didn't have too much of a problem with that."

"Oh?" said Nishiki.

"I will say that I wasn't comfortable about you referring to the hypothetical perpetrators as guys."

"Guys?"

"Yes. Nasty guys. Plural. How would you know there was more than one?"

"Hey, Engle. Fuck you. I gave him the line. Far as I know, that's exactly what happened to that poor son of a bitch. You go tell your boss what's going on here and leave me out of it. That guy Devlin is fucking trouble, and I don't want any part of it. You got it?"

"Correct." Engle nodded twice, stood up, and left.

CHAPTER 13

From Nishiki's office, Devlin drove to the Hilo public library. Many things in Hawaii were backwater and primitive, but its library system wasn't one of them. The state had computerized the libraries years ago.

The Hilo library was bright, cheerful, and clean. And it was well used. Devlin saw preschoolers in the children's room, retirees in the periodical room, and every age group and type in between. There were three computer stations near the old-fashioned card file boxes. He sat down at the last available computer, pressed F1, scanned the Help menu, and followed the on-screen instructions explaining how to access the library's records of newspaper articles. Devlin typed in a series of keywords: Cranston, pakalolo, marijuana, Puna, Pahoa, murder.

When a listing of newspaper articles appeared, he hit F3 and a well-worn but still functional dot matrix printer produced a list containing the titles of each article, the newspaper, date, and page numbers. He handed the list to a young girl at the reference counter. She explained where he could find hard copies of the recent newspapers and directed him to the reference room where he could find microfilm records for the older issues.

Devlin found every newspaper and every microfilm reel he was looking for. He scanned the hard copies first, then the microfiche viewing machine for the older newspapers.

There wasn't much coverage on Billy Cranston's death, so he finished everything in less than an hour. He didn't learn much more than he already knew.

There was nothing left to do in Hilo, so Devlin climbed back into the Ford and headed for Pahoa-town.

CHAPTER 14

Leilani had started working as soon as she and Walter shook hands.

She'd spruced up the restaurant, helped with the food prep, and handled the lunch service. It didn't take long for the word to spread about the new waitress at Da Restaurant. By six o'clock, the dinner crowd was twice the size as usual.

Leilani was taking an order when suddenly everything in the small restaurant came to a standstill.

She looked over toward the entrance and saw a man standing in the doorway. He was shirtless, heavily muscled, decorated with tattoos, and big enough to almost fill the doorway. He stood blocking the entrance daring anyone to say something.

Leilani was about do just that when the big man saw her looking in his direction. He looked back at her as he made a show of taking the T-shirt hanging out of his back pocket and pulling it over his muscular torso, covering most of his tattoo work. Leilani was familiar with the style. Some called it tribal. Others referred to it as Island tattoos – intricate lines and patterns based on designs first developed by Pacific natives in the 1600's.

Leilani's view shifted to his face. It was as hard to ignore as the body. The man had classic Polynesian features: broad nose, high forehead, strong chin, perfect white teeth. His jet-black hair was pulled back and bound into a tight bundle with a leather thong.

Unfortunately, his left cheekbone had somehow been crushed,

distorting that side of his face. His left eye drooped slightly in the damaged socket.

The customers in the restaurant made sure to avoid looking at the man. Despite his undeniable charisma, an air of menace pulsed around him. The man stared at Leilani with complete entitlement. She felt a nearly overwhelming urge to turn her back and head into the kitchen with her dinner order but wouldn't give him the satisfaction of forcing her to leave until she finished writing everything down on her order pad. Only then did she turn and head for the kitchen, wishing she was wearing a bra under her light cotton shirt. And that her sarong-style skirt wasn't so tightly wrapped around her hips and rear.

When she reached the kitchen, Leilani stifled her desire to ask Walter about the stranger, picked up two plates of just-cooked food, and walked back out. Walter was so busy that he never even looked up from his work. She delivered the dishes, smiled at her customers, then walked to the table where the intruder had taken a seat.

There were two other men with him. One was a short, muscular Island man. He had a flat, half-Chinese, half-South Seas, mostly-ugly face. He wore a filthy shirt with the sleeves cut off, and baggy jeans. His dark hair was wild. He looked like a giant Island troll.

The second man was a Filipino. He was the opposite of the first man. He was a wiry flyweight. He had long, silky black hair that fell past his shoulders, a trim mustache and goatee, and he was incongruously dressed in a long-sleeve rayon shirt and long dress pants, both black. The first one looked like a local bad guy. The Filipino looked evil. The scary one with the distorted face sat between them, staring at Leilani with a half-smile.

"What can I get you?" Leilani asked.

Nobody answered, but the tattooed leader of the group reached up and gently grasped the Leilani's left hand between his thumb and forefinger. It was both outrageous and intimate. Weirdly friendly and controlling.

"You're new in town," said the man. "What's your name?"

For a moment, Leilani wondered if this was some sort of hand-shake, but the man held her hand in his two-fingered grip without moving.

She answered, "Leilani."

"I'm Sam Keamoku. My friends call me Sam Kee." He nodded toward the two men sitting on either side of him. "This is Loto, and that's Angel. What's your last name?"

"Kilau."

"Good name. You didn't take the name of the haole bastard who impregnated your mother, huh?"

The comment was so outrageous that Leilani froze for an instant. But that was the only reaction she would allow Sam Kee and his friends to see. She slowly extricated her hand and wrote the number of the table on her order pad. "What would you like to eat, gentlemen?"

Kee sat back in his chair and squinted at her with his good eye. "You don't want to be friendly, you'll have to call me Mr. Kee."

"What would you like for dinner, Mr. Kee?"

"Just bring us each a glass of water. We don't want to eat here. The haole food here is shit."

Leilani turned and brought back three glasses of water. "No charge," she said.

Kee nodded at her, but she was already heading toward the kitchen.

Leilani could sense the three men smirking behind her back. She walked into the kitchen, kicked a box of empty bottles out of her way and grabbed an apron from a hook on the wall.

She wrapped the apron around her, quickly covering the body that had attracted the new business to the restaurant.

Walter stopped cutting up a chicken, looked at her, then peered out the porthole window of the kitchen's swinging door. "Ah, the barbarians have arrived."

"God, that man is disgusting."

Walter went back to his food prep and mused, "Disgusting? I guess in a certain practiced way disgusting is a part of his repertoire. However, he's more dangerous than disgusting so I wouldn't advise any attempt to point out his failings to him."

"Who is he?"

"Sam Kee. Local bad boy. General all-around psychopath."

"What's his story?"

"Well, let's see. Petty crime and intimidation executed with a cunning sort of street wisdom. He's perfected a neat game of victimizing people while claiming he's the victim. You know, the old 'They stole my island' line of bullshit. He's managed to gin up a bit of a following among the local morons. Hate has its attraction."

"Hate?"

"Yes. He spreads it and feeds off the results."

"Who does he hate?"

"Who doesn't he hate? His brand of nativist propaganda works with lots of people."

"What? The usual white man stole our islands line?"

"Exactly. It's true enough to get the right responses. Hate, resentment, discontent. Which is why as your employer I have one sincere request regarding Mr. Kee."

"What?"

"Don't piss him off. You don't have to be nice to him. Just be neutral. If he makes you angry, be wise enough to defer what I sense might be your normal response."

"My normal response?"

"Yes, something along the lines of asserting your right to do whatever it is you're doing."

"In other words, kowtow."

"No, I said be neutral."

"I don't share your tolerance for hate mongering, Walter."

Walter stopped what he was doing and said to Leilani. "You've had it from both sides, haven't you?"

"What do you mean?"

Walter said, "That chip on your shoulder came from someplace."

Leilani looked away. "Yes, when you're in-between two worlds bigotry and hate come at you from both sides. There was always somebody on the haole side who had a comment, and somebody on the native side who had theirs."

"I'm sorry, Leilani. But however bad it was being a target, I advise you to avoid being a target of Sam Kee."

"Any reason in particular?"

"I think it's better if you asked some of the women around here."

CHAPTER 15

Devlin entered the outskirts of Pahoa just before sunset. He drove past an undeveloped strip of land, crossed over a culvert bridge, and saw two hundred yards of pure, simple poverty that could have been in a dirt-poor town in the Appalachians.

He passed a falling-down two-story wooden building on his left and a strip of small, decrepit plywood shacks covered with mildewed corrugated fiberglass. Tall, uncut molasses grass grew in front of the shacks. Near the road the grass was brown and ragged, becoming green as it grew around the rundown shacks.

Most of the hovels looked empty, but as he passed the last one, Devlin saw three kids hanging around in front. A three-year-old boy wearing nothing but a filthy pair of underpants. His brother, six, wore shorts and a T-shirt with a hole over his belly. Their sister looked to be about ten. She wore a dirty, dismal one-piece dress. They all had that blank, listless look that goes with poverty and boredom.

Devlin caught a glimpse of the inside of their one-room shack lit by a single bare bulb hanging from the ceiling. A worn-out woman in a threadbare dress sat on a dilapidated couch. She held a baby to her breast and stared at a small black-and-white television.

This was the kind of misery that bred desperation and discontent. This was not the Hawaii for tourists and others who clung to the prosperous pieces of paradise on the coasts.

Devlin left the little slum area behind and entered the business part of town passing a 7-Eleven on one side of the road and a head shop, a medical clinic, and a pharmacy on the other side. A bit farther on stood a post office, a bank, and the locked-up police substation – a simple prefab structure that looked as if it had been dropped onto a patch of asphalt and left there.

He continued on into the old part of town and saw why one of the newspaper articles he'd read said Pahoa was reminiscent of an old Wild West town. The buildings were faded one or two-story wooden structures fronted by slightly elevated wooden sidewalks with handrails.

On one side of the street, Devlin saw a natural food store, a closed restaurant, a bar, a small grocery store, an alley, empty stores with darkened storefronts, a craft shop, an office of some kind, then Da Restaurant, the Thai food restaurant, and more empty storefronts. On the left, a long two-story building occupied almost a full block of Main Street. The building was painted dark green. The second floor showed a neat series of windows in white frames. The ground floor was empty except for a video store and something that looked like it might be a bookstore.

At the far end of Main Street, there were a few more buildings. All looked unused except for one that housed a bare-bones Laundromat lit by bare fluorescent lights. Devlin caught a glimpse of a young man and a girl sitting on top of a worktable. Long hair, scraggly beard, granny glasses, and tie-dyed shirts made Devlin think of late sixties Haight Ashbury.

Devlin continued driving for another hundred yards, then turned the car around in a school parking lot and drove back.

Even in the rosy twilight everything in the old town looked washed out. The colors of choice were faded blues, pinks, and cream. Maybe a tourist guidebook would call this place a quaint reminder of old Hawaii. This place wasn't quaint, thought Devlin. This place has no mana, no more spirit. This place is the end of the line. Certainly, for Billy Cranston.

The few people Devlin saw as he drove seemed to be walking around just to be out and about.

Devlin found the Village Inn. It turned out to be housed in the large green building that dominated Main Street. Next to the Inn was a dirt parking lot about sixty by a hundred and fifty feet, bordered by the street, the building and fields of tall molasses grass, ferns, and oleander shrubs that merged with a patchy forest of mostly ohia trees.

As Devlin drove into the lot, he saw a hulking local moke sitting on the running board of a rusty pickup truck talking to a tall, skinny teenage boy holding a skateboard. Devlin was sure that money and drugs would be exchanged any minute. The sullen man sat shirtless, staring at Devlin as he parked his brand-new rental car. Devlin stared right back at him, checking out his big, brown belly, crude tattoos, and unkempt black hair. Devlin kept staring at him until the man looked away.

A large banyan tree grew in the middle of the dirt lot rutted with grooves and holes filled with dirty rainwater. Three other cars were in the lot, none less than ten years old. There was also a beat-up commercial van with the words Sheet Metal badly hand-painted on the sides.

Devlin's rental car might as well have had a sign on it that said, 'Stranger in Town'. Devlin didn't care. He intended to make his presence known.

He parked, grabbed his bag out of the back seat, and found the entrance to the Inn. It faced the parking lot. Instead of a door, there was a tall, wooden gate that opened onto a stairwell that led up to the second floor.

The gate was unlocked. Devlin walked up the stairs and found himself standing in an old-fashioned South Seas-style interior veranda which overlooked a cluttered central courtyard on the ground floor. The Inn occupied two sides around the courtyard – the side running along Main Street, the short side facing the parking lot. The stairway brought Devlin to the corner of the two sides, where he stood looking at a huge parrot perched in a large wire cage.

A waist-high railing and wooden pillars bordered the veranda which was furnished with wicker tables and chairs. There were potted ferns, palms, and other plants artfully placed to give the area a lush feel. The floor, which was covered by a burlap rug, sloped badly, and as he walked across it, Devlin had to duck low under a ceiling beam, but overall the area was comfortable and quiet, a surprising haven from the rundown, mostly ugly town outside.

Suddenly the big parrot screeched so loudly that Devlin jerked away.

A stocky woman in shorts and a billowing Hawaiian shirt came out of the office to his left and smiled at him. She had long gray hair, strong features, and skin that had been weathered by the sun. She came over to him, smiled, and in a soft, cultured voice said, "Aloha."

It was the first Devlin had ever heard the word spoken so genuinely.

"I'm Rachel Steele. This is my place. You must be Mr. Devlin."

"I am. Nice to meet you," said Devlin

He looked down at Rachel. She was about five, five a sturdy woman with piercing blue eyes. She looked directly at him and seemed very comfortable in her bare feet and her surroundings. Devlin guessed she was near seventy, but she had a vigor and authority about her that made her age mostly irrelevant. Rachel Steele had aged gracefully into an elder.

She reached up and shook Devlin's hand. He wasn't surprised at the strength of her grip.

"How long are you going to be with us, Mr. Devlin?"

"I'd say a week or so."

"What brings you to our little town?"

"I'm investigating the death of Billy Cranston."

"Oh."

"Did you happen to know him?"

After a pause, Rachel said, "Perhaps we should discuss that some other time."

Devlin said, "I'm sorry if I was a little abrupt with that."

"No worries. Let me tell you about your choice of rooms."

"Sure."

Rachel waved at the long row of rooms that faced Main Street. "You don't want any of those. They're basically little sleeping rooms, and you have to use the common bathroom over there. That corner room isn't bad, but it's occupied. My two best rooms are the ones with their own bathrooms. Got the Don Ho room right there." She pointed behind Devlin. "And the Jack London room," she pointed off to her left, "over there."

Devlin calculated that the Don Ho room would have the better view of the parking lot.

"I'll take the Don Ho."

"Good. The door is open. Keys are on the dresser. We lock the gate downstairs at ten o'clock. Key for the gate is on the smaller one on the ring. If you need anything, let me know." She patted Devlin gently on the arm and said, "Welcome."

Rachel padded back to her office, which was the first set of rooms on the Main Street side of the building. Rachel hadn't closed the door, so Devlin looked in for a moment and saw that her workspace was filled with more potted plants, antiques, and general clutter. She put on a pair of half-glasses and continued with her paperwork under the light of a large table lamp made from a brass samovar.

Devlin stepped into the Don Ho room. It was small, but carefully furnished and decorated. There was a green bedspread on a bed that would be a bit short for Devlin, green ceiling, floral green wallpaper, and smooth wood floors finished in a mahogany stain and polished to a dull gleam.

A ceiling fan/light kept the air moving in the room. And yes, there was an original oil painting of Don Ho hung over a large antique floor radio.

He walked over to the double window facing the parking lot. He bent down and was able to see the front half of the parking area, the street, and the bar across the street.

Devlin stepped back and checked out the window coverings – horizontal mini-blinds and tied-back drapes.

There was a television in the room, but no phone, which Devlin knew would necessitate some improvising.

The bathroom was large, but held only a shower stall and sink, no tub.

He quickly unpacked, putting his clothes in the antique wardrobe that occupied the wall opposite his bed and the dresser near the door.

He unpacked three guns: The Browning Hi-Power, the Sig-Sauer P226, and the small 25-caliber Beretta. He carefully laid the Browning and the Beretta in the bottom drawer of the dresser, covering them with a nylon laundry bag, and shoved the Sig-Sauer in his waistband in front of his left hip.

Devlin checked the lock on his door. Surprisingly, it was a firm dead-bolt lock. He locked it and left the inn.

He walked out of the parking lot. The surly long-haired guy was in the same place, but now he had a new customer – a nervous, heavyset blonde woman in a black raincoat. Devlin made sure to once again stare at the drug dealer. He walked left to the edge of town, nodding and making eye contact with everyone he saw, thinking – that's right pal, take a good look. He crossed the street and walked to the other end of town, doing the same, walking into any store or restaurant that was open, stopping to carefully check out anything that interested him. He took particular notice of three pay phones in the 7-Eleven parking lot.

He doubled back and returned to his starting point in front of the Village Inn, crossed the street, and walked into the bar, a run-down place teetering on the edge of dive bar status. He stood just inside the doorway, looking around, looking back at the few people in the bar who wondered what a big, well-dressed, scowling haole was doing in their bar.

Devlin didn't speak to anybody or order a drink. He turned and walked out. He'd accomplished his purposes. Most of what was in Pahoa was now in Devlin's head. And he was the heads of most of the people in Pahoa.

CHAPTER 16

It had taken Eric Engle almost three hours to drive to Eddie Lihu's ranch up in Waimea on Oahu. Lihu made him wait thirty minutes before he called him into his office.

When Engle entered, the fat man barely looked up from the guest list for his daughter's wedding. The event was scheduled for a week from Sunday. Lihu's long-suffering wife had taken care of most of the arrangements. All the invitations had been sent out. Most of the invited guests had responded.

Lihu wasn't staring at the list because he was interested in his daughter. He didn't even like his daughter very much. She was a rather sullen girl who had inherited her father's propensity to be large and unattractive. It was clear to Lihu that her groom was marrying the family first and the daughter a distant second. Lihu's studied the list to pick out those who hadn't yet accepted the invitation. For Eddie Lihu, the main purpose of the wedding was to display his power. The more who attended of the 1,238 people who had been invited, the better the display. Lihu has spent the last three hours calling those who had not R.S.V.P.'d, eating, smoking Dunhill Monte Cristo cigars, and sweating. Even with the central air running, the room smelled terrible.

Lihu pointed to a chair. Engle sat in it. Charlie, the bodyguard, sat in a couch opposite Engle. They waited.

Lihu continued making notes next to various names on his list, deciding which of the guests really didn't want to attend, but had accepted the invitation so as not to insult him.

Lihu picked up his dead cigar and chewed on it for a bit. He knew there would be a handful who would never agree to attend. They were the ones who would eventually give him the most satisfaction, because they would become targets for his schemes and maneuvers to make their lives miserable. One way or another, sometime, somehow, Lihu would find a way to hurt them. The more powerful they were, the cleaner they were, the better it would feel to Eddie Lihu when he diminished them.

Finally, Lihu looked up at Engle and said, "So?"

"His name is Jack Devlin."

"I know what his fucking name is. What does he want? What did he say to Nishiki?"

Lihu tilted back his chair and folded his hands over his huge stomach.

"Nishiki contacted me yesterday. Said a woman from Pacific Rim had called to make an appointment regarding the Cranston case. When this Devlin character arrived, I sat in the cubicle next to Nishiki's and monitored their conversation."

Lihu had closed his eyes. Engle looked at Lihu to make sure he wasn't falling asleep. Just then Lihu opened his eyes and rumbled at Engle in a phlegm-filled voice, "What is it, you skinny cocksucker? I have to beat it out of you? I already asked you what I want to know. Don't make me fucking ask you again."

Engle related Devlin's conversation with Nishiki almost verbatim. Lihu occasionally grunted to indicate he was following Engle's words.

When Engle was finished, the fat man leaned forward and sat upright in his chair. He stayed motionless for about five seconds, then he pointed a sausage-like finger at Engle and said, "Okay, here's what you do. This Devlin is gonna show up in Pahoa next. Get over there and point Kee in the right direction. Let him know we don't want Devlin fucking up our situation. Just say that. Then stay out of it. Stick around to make sure Kee and his assholes take care of things, then get out of that town. Keep me informed."

"Yes, sir."

Lihu asked, "How much does Kee listen to you?"

"As much as he'll listen to anybody, and only because he knows it's coming from you. I can't guarantee anything with regard to Sam Kee."

Lihu grunted again. Lihu looked at Engle. Engle stared back at him. Lihu said, "Good-bye." Engle nodded, afraid he had appeared dull-witted just sitting there not realizing the meeting was over. He stood up quickly and walked out of the office.

As the door shut, Lihu leaned back in his chair, closed his eyes for a moment, then tipped forward to his desk. He grabbed the phone and dialed a number, one of dozens he had memorized. A beeper service answered, and Lihu punched in one letter on his phone pad: L. Then he hung up and tilted back in his chair, waiting. He looked at his watch and grunted. "Fucking Friday night." He stuck his giant cigar in his mouth and stood up. "C'mon Charlie, let's go eat."

#

The beeper that received Lihu's call started vibrating. It was clipped to a belt on a pair of pants hanging in the bathroom of a Hotel Street-district prostitute named Tay Williams. She was busy in the bedroom, squatting over the face of her client, George Walker. Tay was dressed in high-heel black boots, black leather crotchless panties, and a half-cup bra made of black leather and chains.

George Walker lay naked, his wrists and ankles handcuffed to Tay's brass bed. Tay had wrapped Walker's penis in a black ribbon from the base to just below the head, which was turning a purplish blue from the constricting pressure on his blood vessels. It kept his erection firm and painful. Occasionally, Tay would flick her leather riding crop at the exposed part of Walker's penis. She had been sitting on Walker's chest, rubbing her clitoris and squeezing her nipples. Now she squatted over Walker's face, tantalizing him, demanding he lick her but not getting close enough to let him. She kept taunting him to stick his tongue out farther. Stick it out until it hurt.

Walker was so excited he could hardly breathe. This would go on for at least an hour, becoming more cruel, more painful, more debasing. Tay William's was very good at her job. George Walker considered the thousand dollars he paid her in cash for every session worth every penny. Particularly since the money he was getting from Lihu made a thousand dollars seem almost like a small sum. Walker never stopped to think about the fact that Lihu was getting back forty percent of the thousand dollars.

Tay continued her taunts and teasing until Walker felt as if he were going to ejaculate, but Tay grabbed the head of his penis and squeezed it, quickly stopping the urge. How did she know when to cut him off at just the right moment? Did she know that he became aroused just remembering it was Friday night? Did she know that he became so excited his heart pounded, and he found it difficult to breathe getting into his car to drive to her apartment?

Eddie Lihu's beeper message was not going to be answered for quite some time.

CHAPTER 17

The next item on the Devlin's list was dinner.

Devlin figured the food at the natural restaurant would be too bland. He had considered the Thai restaurant but figured the menu might be too much of a mystery. That left Da Restaurant.

When he stepped under the low doorway, Devlin saw Walter Harrison sitting at his table near the kitchen.

With the dinner service almost over, Walter had returned to the activities he liked best, nursing a tall screwdriver and reading a thick hardcover book. He looked at his watch. Ten minutes to closing. The prospect of cooking another meal did not please him.

Walter casually indicated to Devlin he could sit anywhere. The only people in the restaurant were an obviously drunk mulatto man and his companion – a tired, thin brunette with a bad complexion who occasionally patted him on his forearm.

Devlin selected a small table next to a window so he could watch the street. The teenage hippie couple was still sitting in the dingy Laundromat across the way. The blonde woman in the black raincoat he'd seen earlier hurried past on the other side of the street. A pickup truck pulled into the parking lot. Friday night and the town seemed to be getting a second wind.

Devlin picked up the small menu on the table when his peripheral vision caught the waitress approaching. He looked up and immediately lost his appetite.

"Oh, Christ," he muttered and looked back down.

Leilani came to the table and said without hesitation, "I'm not taking any shit from you about this. You indicated quite clearly you don't want to have anything to do with me, so don't try to tell me what to do. What do you want to eat?"

Devlin fixed a smile at her and said, "What the hell are you doing here?"

"I'm not interested in anything you have to say."

"Did your father call you? I left word with him."

"I rarely answer his phone calls."

Devlin looked down, shaking his head.

Leilani said, "Do you want something to eat or not?"

Devlin looked up. "Why do you think I left you in that restaurant? You didn't notice the police outside?"

"What are you talking about?" she said.

Devlin took a deep, slow breath. He said, "We've been talking too long. Just write down an order and get me some food. Whatever you think is best. And a large glass of water, please."

"Are you going to explain what you just said?"

"Not here. Not now. I don't want anybody to think we know each other."

Leilani walked away quickly, and Devlin stared down at the table. He was just as much angry with himself as he was with Leilani. He had badly underestimated her. He should have made sure she knew not to get involved. He should have taken care of it himself. Gotten her number from Jasper Cranston and called her. Now he had a loose cannon on his hands. Now he was into damage control, and he hadn't even started this goddamn job.

Leilani returned with his glass of water. Devlin did not look up at her, and she did not linger.

But by the time Leilani brought him his food, Devlin had collected his thoughts enough to tell her, "All right, you have to know what's going on. Tonight. But I don't want anybody seeing us together."

"Do you know where the school is?"

"Yes."

"You have a car?"

"Yes."

"I'm finished here about ten-thirty. I'll walk to the school and wait for you in the parking lot. No one should see us there."

"No."

"Why not?"

"It's too isolated. Too many people could see you walking there. It'll look suspicious this time of night. How about you get me a cup of coffee, and I'll tell you what to do."

Devlin watched her walk over to the coffee station and fill a brown ceramic mug with Kona coffee. He found himself staring at her long legs and shapely ass. Her flimsy cotton top and sarong skirt covered her, but they certainly didn't conceal her body. He still looked at Leilani for the sheer enjoyment of it, even though he was furious with her.

What the hell did she intend to do? Did she have any idea of the kind of attention she could draw in this little backwater town?

When Leilani returned with his coffee, Devlin asked her, "Can you get to a phone where you'll be undisturbed?"

She hesitated for a moment and said, "Yes."

"Then write this number down and call it at ten-forty."

He recited a phone number. Leilani wrote it on her order pad.

"If that's busy, call this one."

He gave her another number he had memorized.

"We can't be seen together. Not even by accident. So let's use the phones."

"Okay."

"You'd better give me my check and walk away."

"I haven't added it up yet."

"I'll add it."

Leilani put the check on the table and walked.

#

At ten-forty Devlin stood in front of the pay phones outside the 7-Eleven. At ten-forty-five the first phone in the bank of three rang, and Devlin snatched it off the hook.

"Sorry," he heard. "I had to wait for someone to get off this phone."

"Is anyone around you?"

"No. I'm in a little cubbyhole here in the natural food restaurant. Where are you?"

"Outside the 7-Eleven." Devlin watched the street as he waved off mosquitos. "Why are you here?"

Leilani ignored the question and asked, "What happened with the police outside the restaurant? Why didn't you come back?"

"Two men attacked me in the small parking lot down the street."

"Did they hurt you?"

"No. I hurt them. Worse, they had a third guy driving a van they came in. The driver panicked and drove over one of the attackers trying to get away."

"He ran over him?"

"Yes."

"What happened to him?"

"I don't know. I don't think he killed him. I chased after the driver, but he got away. I tried to drive back into town to find you, but the cops had the main road blocked."

"You think it had anything to do with Billy?"

"Yes."

"How did they know to go after you?"

"I assume they've been watching your father's house. Did you tell anybody about our dinner?"

Leilani was emphatic. "No. Absolutely not."

"The only thing I can think of is that guy hanging around us on the beach heard our plans."

"What guy?"

"The one who decided to fish ten feet away from us."

There was a pause as Leilani tried to remember what Devlin told her.

"This is crazy."

"No. This is dangerous. Someone doesn't want your brother's case investigated. Now, listen to me. There's no place for amateurs in this. What are you doing here?"

"I'm going to set myself up in this town and see if I can find out anything."

"And then what?"

"I don't know. Tell the police. My father. You. This restaurant job is perfect. It's a small town. People like to hang out in a place like Da Restaurant and talk. They're still talking about what happened to Billy."

Devlin said nothing.

"What's the matter? You don't have anything to say. You don't think there's a possibility I might find out something that could help you? I'm going to make that dump the best restaurant in town. In a few days, I'll know everybody. If you'd stop and think about it for a moment, you'd realize I'm right and let me help you."

Devlin finally spoke.

"Leilani, you have to really hear what I'm going to say now. Whether your plan is good or bad is not the point. Maybe you'll find something out, maybe you won't. The point is, it's professionally, ethically, morally wrong for me to work with you."

"Why?"

"Because that will put you in danger. And I have no right to put you in danger."

"All right. I understand. But you're not the one putting me in danger. I'm the one deciding to do this. Not you."

"That's irrelevant. You don't have enough information to make a valid decision on this. You don't know what I'm going to do.

You don't know how dangerous this can or can't be. You can't judge how much danger you're putting yourself into. And me."

Devlin listened to her breathing. He pictured her face with the phone near her mouth, hoping he had persuaded her.

"All right," she said, "that may be true. But even so, I'm not going to leave."

"Christ," Devlin muttered.

"What?" she said angrily. "Why do you have to take it upon yourself to worry about me? I'm not worried about you."

"That's pretty goddamn obvious."

"What does that mean? Why should I?"

Just then a pickup truck roared into the 7-Eleven lot and pulled into the parking space behind Devlin. The noise of the engine drowned out any chance to talk. Devlin faintly heard the phone company recorded voice come on and ask for ten more cents to continue the conversation. He shouted at Leilani, "Do you have change?"

"No," she shouted back.

"Shit," Devlin muttered. "Get another goddamn quarter and call me back!"

"Go to hell!" Leilani shouted and hung up on him.

Devlin slammed his phone down so hard he almost broke the receiver. He shoved a quarter into his phone and dialed. Before the second ring finished, a questioning voice picked it up.

"Hello?" asked Leilani.

"Let me tell you something, I'm the wrong person to hang up on. If you don't start listening to me, Leilani, tomorrow morning everyone in this town will know who you are, and why you're here. I'll have your father on the first plane in here and make him go into that restaurant and drag your ass out of there. You try any shit with me for half a second, it'll be the last thing you do in this town. You got that?"

"You wouldn't dare."

"The hell I wouldn't."

"How did you know this number?"

"I memorized it. I walked the town tonight and looked for pay-phones and memorized all the numbers."

"Why?"

"Because it's the best way to talk to people without anybody knowing about it. I also make sure to have a bunch of change in my pocket. Do you?"

"I'm not a detective, or whatever you are."

"Exactly. You're not. What you are is somebody who could put me in jeopardy. As well as yourself."

"Look, I'm sorry I hung up on you. I have this thing about men telling me what to do."

"Well get over it, goddamn it. If I were a woman investigating what happened to your brother, I'd be telling you the exact same thing. And if you were a man, I'd be down there punching your head in and putting an end to this bullshit right now."

"What, you don't hit women?"

"No, but that's no guarantee I won't."

Devlin heard Leilani laugh softly at his answer. "Ah, Christ, I said I was sorry about hanging up. Come on, I'm too tired to fuck-ing argue with you."

"All right. Forget it."

"So what are we going to do here?" Leilani asked. "I take it you're threatening to blow my cover, as they say, but not yet if I listen to you."

"I didn't say that. I wanted you to listen to me, so you'd decide yourself to get the hell out of here."

"And that's not going to look suspicious? Right after you show up."

"That's irrelevant. By this time tomorrow, everybody is going to know why I'm here."

"Okay, so you think about it for a second. Do you think it might be an asset for everybody not to know why *I'm* here?"

The recorded voice came on asking for money. Devlin fed the phone another dime. Leilani continued. "I'm going to blend in with the people in this town. Listen to what they are saying. Ask a few questions. I won't sound like I'm anything more than curious. And then, if you allow me, pass on that information to you. If nobody knows I have anything to do with you, whatever you do shouldn't affect me."

Devlin stood in the 7-Eleven parking lot shaking his head, trying to figure out how to get through to Leilani.

"I just want to help. I already have information that might be useful."

"Like what?"

"I know that people in town are still talking about my brother. And from what I can tell nobody thinks he just walked out to the middle of nowhere and died. I know one person in this town that everybody is afraid of. Someone who looks like he's capable of killing someone."

"Who?"

"Sam Keamoku. They call him Sam Kee. The owner of the restaurant told me about him."

"And you saw him?"

"Yes. He came to the restaurant to check me out."

"Check you out? Why? Why would he want to check you out?"

"Same reason you would. Why do you think I'm prancing around in that place dressed like that? The damn food isn't going to attract anybody."

Devlin grunted in agreement, then asked, "What does Kee look like?"

"He's big. Muscled up. Has long black hair he wears pulled back. The left side of his face is pushed in. He's got a lot of Island tattoo work on his body. I asked Walter about him ... "

"Who's Walter?"

"The guy who owns the restaurant. He's a good source of

information, too. At first, he just told me to keep my distance from
Kee. Later on, he told me that Kee has a following of local toughs
that treat him like some sort of half-baked Messiah. Plays the native
rights, they stole our land card. I haven't got a lot of details yet, but
I'm getting the feeling that whatever crime is going on around here,
Kee is behind it."

"Like what?"

"I assume drugs. This town seems to be the center for it on this
side of the island. That parking lot next to your hotel is drug central."

"I know. I saw a couple of deals going down. Anything else?"

"He intimidates a lot of people. And apparently hates whites in
particular. A real haole hater."

"Did he know your brother?"

"I don't know, but I don't see how he couldn't. It's a small town."

Devlin brushed away another mosquito.

"When did you get here?"

"About noon. Had a job in Da Restaurant in time to work the
lunch hour."

"Okay, I'm impressed. You had a good idea setting yourself up
in that restaurant. And you worked fast."

"Thank you."

"But Leilani, don't lose sight of the fact that what you're doing
is dangerous. Somebody sent those thugs after me. Somebody who
has the resources to find out about me. And now, two strangers
have shown up in a small nowhere town on the same day. I made
a point of walking around tonight making my presence known.
Hopefully, that will take some of the attention off you, but don't
underestimate how dangerous your situation is."

"I won't. So are you saying I should continue?"

"Not yet. You've been here before, right? You said you know the
scene here."

"Yes, but I haven't been here in over a year. Even then I never
told anybody that I was here looking for my brother. And if someone

remembers I've been here before, so what? I don't need to deny it. In fact, it makes things more plausible. My story is I'm taking a break from my sculpting. Pahoa is a good place to do just that."

After a pause, Devlin said, "All right. Keep doing what you're doing, but please take my advice."

"Okay."

"You can tone down the, the ..."

"The what? Flimsy tops and tight sarong act?"

"Yes. You don't want to alienate the women in town."

"I agree. I'm counting on the women to be the best source of information."

"Good. Don't push things. Let information come to you. Mostly listen. Ask questions that sound natural. Go easy. Talk about me. That will bring up the topic of your brother."

"Sounds good," said Leilani.

"Never, ever write anything down. Ever."

"Okay."

"Do not confide in anybody. Ever."

"Okay."

"And follow your boss's advice. Tread very lightly around this Sam Kee fellow."

"I'm happy to leave him to you."

"Good. Are you open for breakfast in the morning?"

"No. Lunch and dinner. If you want breakfast, go to the natural food place at the other end of town, Paradise East. I hear they serve a good breakfast."

"Okay. I'll probably see you at dinner tomorrow. If you have anything to tell me, you can let me know, and we'll hook up over the phone again."

"Okay, anything else?"

"Yes. One last thing. Before we go forward with this, I need your word on one thing."

"What?"

"If I tell you to leave, you have to promise me that you will stop whatever you're doing, grab whatever you need to get on a plane, and disappear. Better yet, have your plane ticket, money, and ID on you at all times. You have to promise me that, or I won't go forward."

Leilani chafed against Devlin's demand but knew she really had no choice. She couldn't see herself obeying Delvin like he asked, but she tried to convince herself she would.

"Okay. I agree."

Devlin said, "That's it then. Good night," and hung up.

CHAPTER 18

Devlin walked slowly back to the Village Inn. It was almost eleven-thirty. He needed sleep. He still hadn't adjusted to the time zone.

As he walked through the dirt parking lot to the Inn's side gate, he saw cars in the lot and heard hear music playing in the bar across the street. Friday night in Pahoa.

Devlin took out the key to unlock the gate. As he walked up the stairs, he saw Rachel standing above him.

She asked, "You in for the night?"

"Yes," said Devlin. "I'm still pretty much on Mainland time."

"You'll be up early then."

"I suppose."

"I'm usually in bed by ten. Up to the bathroom at three. Up for the day at six. Old folks' hours." She laughed a hearty laugh that made Devlin smile. "However, this is the first Friday of the month. Paychecks and welfare checks came today. The bar across the street will be busy tonight. I hope the noise doesn't keep you up."

"I can usually sleep through most anything."

"All right, then." Rachel patted him on the arm again. "See you in the morning, dear."

Devlin smiled at the word, dear. Rachel padded off to her rooms, he unlocked his door, and stepped into the Don Ho room, automatically checking to make sure it was undisturbed. He went to his dresser and picked out a small waistband holster from the bottom drawer. He clipped the holster to the bottom of the bed frame, placed his Sig-Sauer in the holster, stripped, showered, and shaved.

Even when he was in the shower, Devlin could hear car doors slamming, voices, snatches of music from the bar.

It was too warm to close the windows, so Devlin tried to close his mind to the outside sounds. He lay in the bed with his feet hanging over the end. He let his mind wander and tried to concentrate on the soft swish drone of the overhead ceiling fan.

He fell asleep thinking of Leilani sitting next to him on the beach.

He managed to sleep the until shouts woke him up, and the unmistakable sound of fists against flesh got him out of his bed.

Devlin knew from experience that most street fights lasted seconds. He estimated that this one had gone on for a lot longer than that. It had taken at least a minute for him to wake up, decipher the sounds, and get out of bed. He kept the lights off in the room and pulled up the mini-blinds. The banyan tree blocked some of his view across the street, but he could see a knot of men shifting and moving in front of the bar. Suddenly a heavyset man broke free from the group and ran across the street into the parking lot. He was a haole dressed for his weekend night out. He wore a clean pair of jeans and a white long-sleeve Western-style shirt. The shirt was ripped at the shoulder. His face was already lumpy and swollen from the punches he had taken. His bleeding nose stained his white shirt with a spatter of crimson.

Four men ran after him like a pack of jackals. The first man to reach him shoved him onto the ground of the parking lot. He landed hard. The other four men surrounded him before he could even start to get up.

From across the street, a big man walked slowly toward the circle. Devlin knew from Leilani's description that this was Sam Kee.

The victim of the beating managed to get up on all fours. He struggled to rise, but he was too disoriented to stand. Kee walked leisurely toward the fallen victim as if he had all the time in the world. When he came within five feet, Kee suddenly took two quick strides and kicked the man in his ribs so hard that both Kee's feet left the ground. He kicked him like a field goal kicker. He kicked him so hard that he knocked the haole off his hands and knees onto his side. Kee stepped forward and stomped the man in the face and chest, yelling at him, "You haole piece of shit."

The man tried to block the kicks with his arms, but they were too powerful, too well placed. He grunted in agony and tried to roll away. He was crying now, screaming for them to stop, but as Kee stepped back, the other four men attacked him with vicious kicks and punches, fighting with one another to get to him. Devlin had the sense they were trying to prove to Kee that they could hurt the man as much as Kee had.

The man rolled up into a fetal position. Kee pushed his thugs away and stepped in. He jumped up and knee-dropped his entire weight on the man's side, grunting out a yell "Yeaaah!" He did it again, obviously trying to break the man's ribs. While he smashed his knee into him, one of his crew tried to kick the white man's hands away from the side of his head. Devlin kept waiting for it to stop, but it didn't.

Suddenly Kee yelled, "Hold it. Pick him up."

Devlin quickly stepped into his pants, pulled open the dresser drawer, took out the Beretta 21A and slipped it into his pants pocket. He looked out the window and saw that they had the man propped against a car now. The beaten man was bent over in pain. Kee motioned the others away from him and approached him with his hands up over his head as if to say, "See, I have no weapons." For a moment, Devlin thought he might be getting ready to talk to the man, to warn him or tell him something. Instead, Kee executed three flashing, full-strength sidekicks into the man's body, grunting his karate howls each time.

And now the others stepped in with full-strength punches.

Uppercuts, big roundhouse punches. One man threw a powerful left hook into the haole's head.

As he headed for the door, Devlin wondered where the hell the police were. He had no idea why it was happening, but he'd be damned if he was going to sit in the Don Ho room and watch a man being used as a human punching bag.

When he reached the landing, Rachel Steele was already at the bottom of the stairs pushing open the gate and walking into the parking lot yelling, "Stop it! Damn you, stop it!"

By the time Devlin was down the stairs, Kee and his men had turned away from the horribly beaten white man and were headed for Rachel. She stood about thirty feet from the gate, out in the lot. She was dressed in a long white nightgown and a red robe, her gray hair flowed past her shoulders and blowing in the night wind. She stomped her foot on the ground and yelled, "Leave that man alone and get out of here, Sam. I've already called the police."

Devlin walked out into the dirt parking lot and stood about five feet behind Rachel. He had his right hand in his pocket and his gun in his hand.

Kee swaggered over. His men followed behind him. Their victim folded down onto his hands and knees.

Kee stopped a few feet from Rachel and said, "Who the fuck you yellin' at, you old haole bitch?"

"I'm not afraid of you, Sam. You and your boys are drunk. Why don't you go home now and stop hurting people?"

Kee tilted his head and peered at Rachel with his good eye. Devlin could practically feel the hatred. "Who the hell do you think you're giving orders to, you stupid old cunt?"

Devlin could see Rachel shaking with fear, but she stood her ground. She yelled at Kee, "Go on. Go home. All of you."

Kee screamed, "This is my fucking home!" He looked as if he were going to backhand Rachel across the face, to smash her out of his sight. Devlin took two steps forward. Kee pointed to Devlin and said to Rachel, "What do we got here? You finally hire some kine a bodyguard. You keep trying to tell me what to do, you going to need one."

Rachel looked behind her, saw Devlin, and immediately turned sideways to keep the two men separate. She looked back and forth at Kee and Devlin. She could feel the anger arcing between them. Now, she was even more frightened.

Kee pointed to Devlin and yelled, "Who the fuck are you?"

Devlin answered quietly, "Someone who doesn't need four other assholes to help me beat up one guy. Why don't you do what this woman asked and get the hell out of here?"

Kee stood up to his full height, puffed out his chest, and smiled as he looked Devlin up and down for a few moments. He nodded his head a few times then announced, "Oh, we got a real tough guy here, huh? What you got in your pocket there, tough guy? Huh? You don't need any help, why you got that gun in your pocket?"

Kee patted his pants pockets and lifted his T-shirt. "I don't need any guns. You such a bad guy, put the fucking gun down and come throw me out of here yourself. Come on, haole tough guy. You want to give orders, let's see if you can back them up. Just you and me."

Devlin didn't move. His voice was steady and even. "Tell your friends to leave, and we'll see about that. Just you and me."

Rachel stepped closer to Devlin. She put her hand on his bare chest and gently trying to move him back, but it was like trying to move the banyan tree.

"Go on inside," she said gently, "it's all over."

Rachel's hand felt amazingly soft on Devlin's skin. Her quiet voice calmed him. Everything came into exquisite focus. Devlin could feel the cool night wind on his body. He saw the full moon gleaming as a strip of clouds blew by. For a moment, Devlin felt the Island mana move through Rachel's soft hand into his chest.

Then he looked at Kee's broken face and locked eyes with him.

He felt Kee's hate touch him, pushing out everything else. Devlin knew if he stepped back one inch, if he showed the slightest weakness, they'd be on him like a pack of wolves. Devlin shifted his gaze away from Kee for just a moment to check the others. He saw everything. The saliva flecks on one man's chin. The scraped knuckles on another one's hand. Three of them were large men. The fourth, half hiding behind one man, was the Filipino, Angel. The small man hid his right hand behind his back, and Devlin knew he held a gun or a knife. The Filipino was too far away for an easy shot with the Beretta, but Devlin knew he would fire at him first. That would scatter the others, but Kee would probably come for him. The rest of the seven bullets would be for Sam Kee.

Devlin gently moved Rachel behind him as he saw a second white man come out of the shadows on the edge of the lot. He helped the beaten man to his feet. Devlin was amazed that Kee's victim could still stand up. His friend must have hidden during the beating. At least he hadn't abandoned his companion completely. The two men stumbled back into the shadows and crossed the street toward the bar. If Kee and his men heard them, they didn't care now. They had Devlin.

Once more Rachel said, "It's over." But nobody was listening to her. Devlin and Kee stood facing each other, unmoving, and nobody else was going to move until the showdown between them ended one way or another.

Suddenly the whooping of police sirens shattered the moment. Seconds later, two four-wheel-drive vehicles skidded to a stop in the dirt parking lot. The cars bore no official insignia, but each had a single blue flashing dome light on its roof.

The standoff between Devlin and Kee ended. Kee broke off the staring match and turned to leave the parking lot.

Devlin kept his eye on Kee and all his men until they were completely turned away from him. He carefully watched the Filipino until he was sure the little man wasn't going to shoot him from the shadows.

Out of his peripheral vision, Devlin saw two uniformed cops approaching. Only now that the last of Kee's men were out of clear sight did Devlin look away from them and at the cops. They were both young local men. Both dressed in tight-fitting dark blue police uniforms, their shirts starched and pressed, their pants sharply creased. They swaggered onto the scene, hands on their holstered guns with knowing smiles on their faces. Devlin didn't think there was anything at all to smile about. He realized with disgust that the cops were going to take a 'boys will be boys' view of what was going on.

The two cops watched Kee walk away. The taller cop, the one closest to Kee, yelled, "What's going on, Sam?"

Kee turned to him but kept walking. "More haole shit raining down on my head, that's what. You ought to keep the trash out of my town, Kana. I'm tired of doing it myself."

The cops looked back at Rachel and Devlin. They didn't quite seem to know what to do.

Rachel turned to Devlin. "You'd better go inside," she said.

Devlin preferred avoiding any problems about the gun in his pocket, so he turned and walked toward the gate. Rachel immediately went toward the two young cops.

"What's the matter with you two? Can't we get any police presence out here on a first Friday of the month? I've told your people over and over again we need someone in this lot. You know there's going to be trouble. What good does it do anybody to come after it's over?"

"Hey, auntie, cool down," said the first cop, "we only got the damn call five minutes ago."

"One of these days Sam Kee and his gang are going to kill someone in that five minutes."

Devlin was walking up the stairs when he heard the second cop ask, "Who's that big guy who walked into your place?"

"He's my guest who got woke up because of those animals. And he's no concern of yours. You ought to go over to that stinking bar and see who else Kee and his boys hurt tonight."

Devlin heard the tall cop's voice. "Why don't you stop yelling at us, Rachel, and tell us what happened."

"Those boys practically beat a man to death a few minutes ago."

"Where is he?"

"I don't know. His friend took him away. He's probably on his way to the hospital."

"Well, what do you expect us to do if nobody is here except you?"

"Go arrest Kee for practically killing someone out here."

"Who? What someone?"

The taller cop waved off Rachel and told his partner, "Come on, forget this shit. Nobody aroun' to say nothin'. Let's go."

From the top of the stairs, Devlin heard Rachel mutter something unintelligible, then he heard her open the gate at the bottom of the stairs. He didn't wait for her. He walked back into his room and quietly closed his door. He didn't want to talk to her or to anybody about what had just happened.

He took the Beretta out of his pocket and placed it back in his dresser drawer. He took off his pants and laid back down on the bed. He consciously relaxed each group of muscles, starting with his legs, working his way on up to his face. It was going to be a while before his body absorbed all the adrenaline pumping through him. He didn't expect to fall asleep for the rest of the night.

#

When Kee and his men walked back into the Pahoa Lounge, Kee was still ready to raise hell, but there wasn't any opportunity. Most everybody other than his men had left. And then he saw Eric Engle quietly waiting for him. Engle motioned Kee over to his table.

"Where'd you come from, shyster, and what the hell do you want?"

"I have something to tell you from Mr. Lihu."

"Yeah, what?"

"What you're going to do about that guy across the street."

Kee sat back and tilted his head at Engle. "Lihu know somethin' about that haole?"

"He knows everything."

Kee leaned forward and dropped his elbows on the table. His face turned to stone. "Tell me."

CHAPTER 19

Devlin dozed off about an hour before dawn, but as the sun rose at six-thirty somebody banging a bag of ice against the bed of a pickup truck woke him. Devlin pushed the covers aside and got out of the bed. He felt stiff and out of sorts. He washed and dressed quickly, clipped the holstered Sig-Sauer to his waistband, covered it with his shirt, and left the Inn.

He headed east until he reached the 7-Eleven. He breathed in deep, almost tasting the fresh morning trade winds. He welcomed the chance to stretch and move.

He picked up the pay phone and dialed the Pacific Rim office and gave quick instructions.

Three minutes later his pay phone rang.

"Tuli?"

"Yeah, man. What up?"

"You got in okay. Found the house."

"It's all good."

Devlin gave Tuli instructions on when and where they would meet and hung up.

He walked back into town aching for food. The small dinner at Da Restaurant and the early morning encounter with Kee had built a fierce appetite in him. He found Paradise East and ordered pancakes with Portuguese sausages and coffee. The pancakes and sausage were delicious. He ordered a whole papaya with a toasted English muffin and more coffee.

By the time he finished, he had seen a good number of towns-people and checked out the three waitresses who ran the place. They were hardworking women, all Caucasian.

One of them was a short blond woman with scrunched-up features and a ready smile. Another was a tall brunette. Devlin decided she must live upstairs because when she started work, her hair was wet, as if she had just stepped out of the shower. The third waitress was the oldest of the trio, probably in her early forties. Her skin was weathered from the tropical sun, but she was a handsome woman with a firm, full figure. She had sun-bleached dark hair worn in a short easy-to-care-for cut, and a large tattoo of a rose on her right shoulder blade. Two of her children a boy about six years old and a pretty little blond girl played outside and ran in and out of the restaurant while she worked.

Leilani was right. A restaurant in such a small town was a good spot to see who lived in the area. The clientele that Saturday morning ran from the older wandering-hippie types who seemed to drift in and out, to men who looked like they worked construction, to mothers and kids.

Devlin paid his bill and walked outside. It wasn't lost on him that the people in the restaurant had looked at him as much as he had looked at them. Everybody knew when a stranger was in town.

When Devlin returned to the Inn, Rachel was sitting at a small work table on the veranda drinking her morning coffee. She asked him, "Did you have your breakfast?"

"Yes. Paradise East."

"I like their pancakes," said Rachel.

"So do I," said Devlin.

"I think we should talk if you have a minute."

Devlin sat on a wicker chair across from her and said, "Sure."

"You had a gun in your pocket last night, didn't you?"

"Yes," said Devlin. "I have a carry permit for the gun."

"Would you have used it?"

"If I'd had to."

"Yesterday you said you were investigating the death of someone named Billy Cranston."

"I am. I work for a private security company looking into the circumstances."

"Is he that poor man supposedly half eaten by feral pigs out in the forest reserve?"

"Yes. Did you know him?"

"I knew him by the name John Sunshine. Among others. He'd change his name every so often. For a while, it was John Q. Public. He also called himself, John America. Might have been other names. I don't remember him using the name Cranston."

"So people around here didn't even know his real name?"

"I don't think so. At least I didn't. Sometimes he'd do odd jobs for me. He'd work for a few days, then wander off."

"Anything else you know about him?"

"I thought he was a good man. When he worked for me, he worked very hard. He was quiet." Rachel paused and then decided she could confide in Devlin. "I think he was suffering inside, Mr. Devlin. I always felt that when he left town, he left so he wouldn't cause anybody any trouble. He was not comfortable being around people. When it became too much for him, he went off by himself."

Devlin nodded. "Did he have any friends?"

"I don't know about friends." Rachel nodded to herself as if she were remembering Billy. "He smoked a good deal of pakalolo, you know. Perhaps it made him a little aloof. In his own world. But, of course, I didn't travel in the same circles as he did. I don't know about who his friends were. I keep to myself up here more and more these days. The town seems to frighten me more and more. I just feel safer up here."

"You didn't act frightened last night."

"Well, I was. Not at first. At first, I was too angry to be frightened. But when I saw what I'd gotten myself into, I was terrified. When I got back up here, sir, believe me, I was shaking. I don't want to be crude, Mr. Devlin, but I barely had time to get to the bathroom. A woman my age can't stand much of that."

"Why did you go out there?"

"To stop what was going on."

"Why were you the only one?"

"Who else was going to? Most of the men in town do whatever Kee says."

"Why?"

Rachel paused. "I suppose a combination of things. He's a source of income for them, and he protects them."

"From what?"

"Mostly the police, I suppose."

"How?"

"Mr. Devlin, Sam Kee may look like a thug, and he may act like one, but he's also very clever. Nobody has caught him doing anything. He has a bunch of flunkies who do all the dirty work, and if anybody comes after him, he says their violating his civil rights. He has this creepy lawyer that threatens lawsuits. Kee makes a lot of noise, and the law enforcement people just say the hell with it."

"That's what those cops did last night."

"Exactly."

Devlin said, "If the police want to come to a crime scene with their sirens off, they don't usually turn them on just before they arrive. I heard their sirens maybe five seconds before they pulled into the parking lot. I'd bet you they were parked somewhere up Main Street and came barreling in when they figured the action was over."

"They said they were answering other calls."

"I didn't believe that. Neither did you."

Rachel nodded. "You're right. I didn't. But I wouldn't assume there's any real collusion there. I don't think the police around here like Sam Kee any more than we do. I just think they don't want to be bothered with him any more than they have to."

"It's their job to be bothered with him."

"As my father used to say, you're preaching to the choir, Mr. Devlin."

Devlin asked, "Do you know anything about the guy they beat up?"

"No. But this morning I heard he was one of the oil rig workers out at the geothermal plant."

"Oil rig?"

"They use the same type of rigs for tapping into the geothermal."

"I see."

"I'm sure it didn't take Kee and his thugs too long to pick a fight over that. They march around here making out like they're some kind of protectors of goddess Pele."

"You're kidding."

"Yes. It's nonsense of course, although I suppose some people believe Madame Pele is outraged by tapping into geothermal energy." Rachel laughed. "Can you believe it? People have been building for decades in the shadow of two of the most active volcanoes in the world. Two, mind you. One of which, Kilauea, is going off right now. It's been sending out lava flows for the last ten years. Still is. Flows that have wiped out entire communities. There is nothing to say that a year from now everything you see here won't be buried under ten feet of lava. And there isn't one damn thing anybody can do about it. That's why people end up praying to a mythical goddess. The whole idea of being on this island at all is rather foolish. I don't believe Kee and his simpletons are worried about a couple of holes in the ground. It's all just an excuse to act violently and scare people."

"Where does Kee get his money?"

"Mr. Devlin. I think people around here pretty much assume he's behind the drug trade in this area. Of course, if they ever caught him I'm sure Kee would claim it's his constitutional right to grow the sacred herb on the land his ancestors were tricked into giving away to the haole devils."

"Is he native Hawaiian?"

Rachel waved at the air. "Oh pooh! These days, every Polynesian who gets off the plane in Honolulu claims he's full-blooded Hawaiian. The sad fact is, there aren't any real Hawaiians left to speak of. Maybe one percent of the original Hawaiian bloodline has survived. And a good portion of that tiny percentage has intermarried along the way. Maybe Kee has some Hawaiian blood in him, but so what. I'm more native Hawaiian than he is. My father was born in these islands, and so was I. I doubt that man is even sure who his father is, much less his grandfather."

"So it's all a front."

"Of course. Mr. Devlin, Sam Kee is a brutal, nasty bully. The only thing he believes in is Sam Kee. He's just a little bit more clever than your average thug. He seems to have figured out how to get away with his crimes."

"Do you think he had anything to do with the death of John Sunshine?"

"I don't know, Mr. Devlin. The fact that you've come here to look into John Sunshine's death tells me that he was more important than the people around here realized. Who was he, Mr. Devlin?"

Devlin paused and thought about his answer for a moment. "It occurs to me, Rachel, that I'm going to be asked that question a few times before this is over."

"What's the answer?"

Devlin shrugged. "It depends. Billy Cranston was a lot of things."

"What was he to you, Mr. Devlin?"

Devlin looked at Rachel in a way that made her feel that the answer he was about to give wasn't going to be shared with anyone but her. His look made her listen carefully.

"Rachel," he said, "Billy Cranston was the closest thing to a true American hero that you and I will ever meet."

Rachel looked at Devlin with her piercing blue eyes and after a moment or two said to him, "Then I'm afraid we're part of a great, great tragedy, Mr. Devlin. And I'm sorry that I can't help you understand why it happened."

Devlin nodded. "I know you would if you could."

"You do?"

"I saw you last night, ma'am." Devlin leaned forward and put his big hand on top of Rachel's. The back of her hand felt as if the years had polished and softened the skin until it was almost translucent. He was instantly reminded of the moment in the parking lot when she had put that hand on his chest to hold him back. To try to protect him. He told her, "Rachel, the next few days I want you to settle in up here and stay out of harm's way."

"That's very kind of you, Mr. Devlin."

"What?"

"To give me such a gentle warning."

CHAPTER 20

After his talk with Rachel, Devlin spent the next two hours walking around town talking to people about Billy Cranston. It reminded him of the old days when he was a rookie beat cop in New York. He talked to a dozen different people but got similar answers from all of them.

"Yes, I knew him." "Kind of a lost soul." "Big guy. Used to drift in and out of town." "Never hurt anybody." "Such a tragedy." "Too bad." "Have no idea why it happened." "Nah, don't know anything about what happened."

Devlin hadn't figured he would find out anything useful, but he went through the motions, hoping to stir up a response, a reaction, hoping to shake loose the shroud of mystery surrounding Billy's death. He knew his next move might be just as frustrating, but it had to be done.

#

Sam Kee was having more success getting the answers he wanted. Five of his men walked around town watching every move Devlin made. Kee sat on the lanai behind his Main Street office and waited for them to come by and tell him what Devlin had just done.

Kee sipped a large mug of coffee and nodded at each bit of information. Angel and Loto sat with him. They served as his audience. Kee told them, "That dumb fucking haole don't realize he's in my town. Nobody gonna tell him anything, even if they knew something."

Angle and Loto made sure to give Kee the reactions he wanted: smirks and nods.

Kee said, "I know what that asshole's gonna do before he does it."

Loto asked, "What?"

"He ain't going to find out shit around here. So, logic says he's going to go look at where they found the body. Maybe find out something there."

Loto asked, "What we gonna do?"

"Make that fucking haole wish he never even heard of this island." Kee pointed a finger at his men. "Remember, anytime the haole come to your town, beware. He gonna take from you or fuck with you before you know what's happening. The damn haoles got it all, but it ain't never enough. Guy like this has to learn that bullshit don't work around here, boys."

#

Devlin's next move was as Kee had anticipated. He drove out of Pahoa, making sure nobody followed him. As he approached the intersection of 130 and Niaulani Street, he turned left, continued on for a few minutes, and at the first intersection he made another left. Near the end of that street, he saw the broad figure of Tuliima Mafa strolling on the country road carrying a large brown paper shopping bag. Devlin pulled up alongside Tuli.

Tuli bent over and said, "Hey, boss."

"Get in the back, big guy. Lay down."

"Dat's easy."

Again, Devlin made sure he was the only car around, then circled back to Niaulani and back onto Highway 130.

"How's the house?"

"Okay. Back off the road. It'll do good. We goin' out to where they found the body?"

"Yes."

ONE MAN'S LAW · 161

Tuli lifted a huge foot wearing the biggest hiking boot Devlin had ever seen. The rest of his hiking outfit consisted of a huge blue T-shirt with a Chicago Bulls logo on it and a baggy pair of black shorts.

"Holy shit, where'd you get those shoes, Tuli?"

"Got 'em in Samoa. In Apia, man. On Upolo. My home, brudda. Man, you got to have good shoes we go into that forest. They got everything in there, Jacky man. Big lava rocks. Jungle. Trees. Marsh. You got good shoes? Ola'a Forest Reserve. It's going to be tough in there, brudda."

"In the trunk. I checked the maps. We can come around from the south and make our way through an old subdivision north of Eleven. They cut some roads in there but never built anything. I think we can use those old roads to get within a mile or two of where they found the body."

"Mile or two through that mess gonna seem like ten."

"What's in the bag?"

"Food, brudda. And water. You gonna hike you gonna need fuel."

"Food, huh."

"Yeah, you gonna like it."

Devlin checked his rearview mirror again. The only vehicle in sight was a tanker truck about a half-mile behind. Devlin was sure nobody had followed him, but nobody had to. As Devlin made a right turn at the intersection of Highways 130 and 11, one of Sam Kee's men named Kimo Akai, parked in a small shopping center easily spotted Devlin's white Ford Taurus rental as it slowed down to make the turn onto 11.

Kimo dialed Kee's office in Pahoa. Kee picked up on the first ring.

"It's me, Kimo. Dat guy just went past here."

"You sure?"

"Same license plate."

"Good."

Kee broke the connection and dialed out quickly. When his call was answered, he yelled, "Okay, how many guys you got there now?

The voice said, "Eight."

"Good. Get 'em ready. I'm leaving town now."

Kee sprang out of his low-slung chair, moving fast. Loto and Angel scrambling after him.

#

Thirty minutes later, Devlin turned the Taurus onto an asphalt road that ran past hidden driveways, most of them gated, leading back to homes and small farms. The buildings were few and far between. Both sides of the road were bordered by scrub forest made impenetrable by a tangle of vines and undergrowth. Devlin saw electrical lines running into the houses, but rooftop rain catchment tanks told him that there were no water or sewage lines in the area.

After about three miles, the last of the buildings disappeared. Devlin continued on about half-mile until the asphalt turned into a rutted dirt road. Squinting at his topo map, he looked for a road on his right. He spotted an overgrown dirt path and decided that was it. He turned onto a trail so narrow that the sides of the Taurus were constantly scraped by the vegetation on each side.

A thousand yards later, the road became too rough and narrow to continue. They found themselves surrounded by the rainforest shrouded in a mist of intermittent rain.

Devlin turned to Tuli still lying on the backseat, his big arms folded across his chest. He held the map up and pointed to an X he'd drawn.

"We're here. More or less." He pointed to another X surrounded by green about two miles northwest. "They found the body there."

Tuli took the map and studied it. Checked the scale and announced, "A little over two miles. I bet guys used to grow a lot of pakalolo in there. Get a truck this far and haul the plants and fertilizer out into the reserve. What was your boy doin' in there? Maybe had a little patch. Maybe step on somebody's toes had a patch, too?"

"That's one theory. But they didn't find any plants near the body."

Tuli grunted. "What da hell does *near* mean?"

"I don't know."

"We'll see what we can find when we get in there, boss."

Devlin said, "That's the idea."

#

Further west and a bit south from where Devlin and Tuli had stopped, a sixty-five-acre chunk of fertile land had been carved out of an area known as the Ola'a Reservation Homestead. It had been turned into something that resembled a ranch. There were a few head of cattle, three acres of papaya, five acres of Kona coffee – just enough so that the owner, Samuel Keamoku, qualified for a variety of government subsidies.

Eight members of his crew sat in the main room of the ranch house waiting for him to arrive. They had been smoking fat buds of marijuana and drinking quarts of Mickey's Malt liquor from wide-neck bottles. When Kee walked in followed by Loto and Angel, their buzz disappeared. Kee began shouting orders before the swinging screen door shut behind him.

CHAPTER 21

Devlin opened up the trunk of the Ford and took out a pair of hiking boots along with a pair of new socks. He sat down on the lip of the trunk, tossed his lightweight Allen Edmonds slip-ons into the trunk, and pulled on the socks. He stepped into his hiking boots and told Tuli, "How bad can two miles be?"

Tuli laughed and said, "Ask me that when we get to the last half-mile, brah."

As Devlin laced up his boots, Tuli pulled a backpack out of his shopping bag and began transferring food and water into the pack.

Devlin walked around to the front of the car and looked into the forest. It was mostly ohia trees along with paperbark trees, kiawes, kukui, and quite a few Norfolk pines. The trees weren't very dense. About like a scrubby forest in the northeast of the Mainland. The ground, however, was thickly covered with ferns, molasses grass, mesquite bushes, and vines.

"Doesn't look too bad."

"From here." Tuli held a quart of water in each hand. He handed one to Devlin, reached into his back pocket and took out a bottle of mosquito repellant.

"Spray this. Drink that."

Devlin followed instructions and methodically drank half his bottle. Tuli did the same while Devlin covered himself in insect repellant. He slipped on his backpack and motioned for Devlin to lead the way.

Within ten minutes, Devlin had sweated through his shirt. He was doing more bending under tree limbs and vines, and more pushing aside ferns and bushes than walking. And it was more scrambling and stumbling up and down ruts and gorges than walking. His khaki slacks protected his legs, but his dark T-shirt didn't protect his arms and hands from scrapes and scratches.

Tuli seemed amused by it all. Instead of fighting the forest he seemed to use his bulk to lean into the greenery and push aside anything in his way with his big arms and hands.

Devlin cursed; Tuli smiled. After twenty minutes Devlin stopped to wipe the sweat from his face. They both finished off their first quarts. That left two quarts in the backpack.

"Is it all like this, you think?"

"Don't worry about it. Are you hungry?"

Devlin said, "We just started."

"So you want to wait?"

"What do you have in there, anyhow?"

Tuli slipped off the backpack and showed Devlin a pile of small Styrofoam lunch packs with compartments for a portion of meat, a chunk of cheese, crackers, a pickle, and pack of mustard. Plus, a tiny little napkin and a plastic spork.

Tuli laughed at his haul.

Devlin said, "Well, aren't you one big happy camper."

"It's good, brudda. All nice and neat."

"Let's keep going."

Twenty minutes later they had covered less than half a mile. Devlin had finished another half-quart of water.

The big Samoan laughed and said, "Hey, ranger, you hungry yet?"

"Not yet."

Devlin continued plodding ahead.

Tuli asked, "Hey, boss?"

"What?"

"This is thick as hell, man. How you gonna find the spot where that guy got killed?"

Devlin stopped, pulled out a compass on a long lanyard, and dangled it in front of Tuli. "Haole invention, brudda. Called compass. Don't have to navigate by the moon and stars like you Samoans. I kept track of the mileage on the car's odometer, so I know how far we traveled into the forest reserve. Made that the starting point. Plotted a line northwest from there. What do you figure our rate of travel is?"

"The way you stumbling through here? Maybe one mile an hour. At the most."

Devlin checked his watch. "Let's go another half hour."

Tuli grunted as they pushed their way forward. He said, "Yeah, boss, but I got one more kine question."

"What's that?"

"You really think anybody could drag a fuckin' body in through all this shit?"

"No way. I think Billy walked in and ran into somebody who didn't want him to be where he was."

"'Cuz he got into somebody else's pakalolo patch?"

"I don't know. Like you said, we'll have to check the area when we get there."

Both men slogged on in silence for another twenty minutes. Suddenly the forest gave way to a little clearing created by a mound of lava that bulged out of the floor of the forest. The only things growing on the mound were a few tufts of grass.

Devlin and Tuli shuffled into the clearing. Devlin sat down with a grunt of fatigue and tried to wipe the sweat off his face with the shoulder of his sweat-soaked shirt.

Tuli slipped off his backpack and dropped it on the ground. He looked around, looked up at the sky, and squatted next to Devlin. He pulled out another quart of water and six of the luncheon packs. He tossed three of the packs to Devlin, took three for himself, sat back, and crossed his legs.

Devlin opened his pack and scooped the whole section of lunch meat into his mouth, then the pickle, then two crackers. "How'd you know I was going to be so hungry?"

Tuli smiled, removed the spork, mustard, and napkin, folded his foam tray until everything fell into the middle, then tipped the entire contents into his mouth. He looked at Devlin with wide eyes and bulging cheeks as if they were sharing a private joke together. He chased the food with two large swigs of water and started on the second pack.

#

By the time Tuli and Devlin had stopped to eat, six of Kee's men had outflanked them and taken up positions north of their destination. Kee, Loto, Angel and two others had come up south of Devlin and Tuli angling east. All four of them were pulled along by a pair of whining, barking, howling mongrel dogs on leashes. The dogs were bred from different breeds of large dogs.

The dogs were raised in a filthy pack, fed rarely, and forced to fight for their food. They were always hungry. The dogs were barely controllable because of the constant fighting and near starvation. As long as the dogs were on leashes, they could be handled. Once off the leash, they would attack anything in front of them. They were called junk dogs because they were expendable.

Kee checked his watch. He would be in position soon.

He yelled to his men, "Get ready to welcome another haole piece of shit to our island."

#

Tuli and Devlin finished eating, drank their water down to a half-quart each, packed up what was left, and trekked back into the tropical forest following Devlin's compass line. After another ten minutes, Tuli patted Devlin on the shoulder and pointed to a muddy little trail to their left.

"Pig trail, boss. If it goes in our direction, we should stay on it. Move a lot faster."

"Pig trail?"

"Yah, a lot of dem wild pigs livin' in here, man. They root out some trails for themselves. They're not stupid like us. They don't wanna stumble around in here."

Devlin nodded and headed for the narrow trail. Just as they started on the trail, it began raining.

"Shit," muttered Devlin.

Tuli looked up into the downpour, rubbed his head and face and said, "No, feel good, man. Gets the sweat off you."

Devlin kept his head down and continued walking.

In ten minutes, the pig trail disappeared, but they didn't need it anymore. The forest had thinned considerably. It was almost all grass and ferns. Devlin told Tuli, "This might be the place."

"Uh-huh."

Tuli looked at his watch. "I'd say we did a little over two miles. You want to go a little farther. See if we find something else?"

Devlin looked around. "Yes. Let's go."

They walked through the clearing and were about five yards into the rainforest when Devlin felt Tuli's hand on his shoulder. He turned and saw the big man straining to hear something. Devlin thought he heard something, too.

"What is it?"

Tuli listened for another moment and then said, "Sound like dogs, man."

Devlin tried to pick out the sound and thought he heard a snatch of barking when suddenly the faint sounds of the dogs were overwhelmed by a thudding noise. As Devlin and Tuli turned back toward the clearing, they heard a deep growling grunt, the sound of forest undergrowth being crushed and pushed aside, and in the next second a beast from hell burst out of the forest into the clearing behind them.

For a moment, the crazed animal paused and looked around. Devlin had never seen anything like it. It was a massive wild boar, almost two-hundred pounds. The head was huge, the shoulders and back high and thick, tapering down to the hind legs. It had a long, ugly snout and two nasty curved tusks jutting out of its lower jaw, both stained red. Thick strands of bloody saliva hung from its mouth and grotesque snout. The beast shook its massive head, snorted, pawed the ground. A nasty flap of flesh hung from its neck.

Devlin heard Tuli mutter softly, "Holy fucking shit."

The sounds of the chasing dogs suddenly became clear, barking, wailing, almost akin to screaming. The boar spun away from the sound of the dogs and charged toward Devlin and Tuli. Their presence meant nothing. It was running for its life. They were in its way.

Devlin already had the Sig-Sauer out. He dropped to one knee, held the gun with a two-handed grip, propped his elbow on his knee, trying to get the beast's head in his sites. He gritted his teeth and steeled himself to wait until the charging wild boar came close enough to hit with a nine-millimeter handgun.

In seconds, Devlin could see a bloody foam spray from the beast's mouth with each enormous exhalation.

He squeezed off three quick shots. The boar shrieked, bellowed, shook its head, but none of the bullets seemed to penetrate the monster's skull. The animal hardly missed a step, charging at Devlin, who fired twice more and then dove to his right, but the side of the boar's head hit Devlin on his left side, the long bottom tusk just missed tearing out a hunk out of Devlin's leg.

The boar's momentum carried him past Devlin, one rear hoof slashing into his left shoulder, but thankfully missing his head and face.

Once past Devlin, the boar skidded to a stop, twisted back, and tried to gore Devlin's head with his tusks, but Devlin had rolled too far out of the way. The animal bellowed, grunted, and sucked in air. It shook blood and foamy saliva from its mouth and lowered its head to charge again when three-hundred pounds of fighting Samoan slammed into its back.

The impact flattened the beast for a moment. The beast twisted and writhed, trying to rear back and buck off or gore Tuli who grabbed a handful of bristle between the boar's massive shoulders with one hand as he plunged an eight-inch knife into the boar just behind its right shoulder, trying to pierce the boar's heart. The boar reacted by flailing harder. Tuli twisted the blade, shoving it in farther. The boar fell onto its side. Tuli rolled off as the desperate animal still tried to twist its head at him and get a tusk into the big Samoan.

Devlin was on his feet now, his gun pointed at the still flailing boar's head, helping Tuli to his feet with the other hand as the first of Kee's junk dogs, a bullmastiff, burst out of the forest in a full run, racing for the bloody boar. The sounds of more baying and screaming barking were near.

The mastiff threw himself onto the dying boar, snapping and biting its face, dodging the boar's tusks, trying to latch onto its neck or snout.

Devlin yelled, "C'mon."

Tuli took a last look at his knife jutting out of the boar and charged into the forest with Devlin as more of Kee's dogs poured into the clearing. The dogs went straight for the bloody boar. Amazingly, the beast was scrambling to get to its feet and fight back as more dogs slammed into it. A barking pit bull mongrel attached itself to the fighting monster's throat, bringing the boar down into the fighting, biting scrum and chaos of ten crazed dogs.

Tuli and Devlin ran and stumbled back into the rainforest just as the sky opened up and a downpour of rain fell on them. They continued putting distance between them and the fighting animals when suddenly automatic weapons fire crackled out from somewhere ahead of them. Vegetation shredded around and behind them. Both men dropped to the ground and flattened out.

Devlin peered through the pouring rain and forest ahead of him, trying to spot the rifle flashes, but the shots were coming from too deep in the forest.

"Shit!" he yelled. "That whole thing was to drive us into this ambush."

Tuli shouted to Devlin over the howling and barking behind them, "How many rounds you have left?"

Devlin held up the Sig and said, "Ten, plus a full clip in my back pocket."

"Another spray of bullets ripped through the forest over their heads."

Devlin asked, "You got a gun?"

Tuli had his backpack in his hand. "Yeah." He pulled out his own Sig. "Hold on, Jack. We might have to back out of here."

"What about those fucking dogs?"

"Hell with 'em. They busy with the damn pig."

Tuli disappeared into the foliage behind them.

Devlin looked out in front to see if he could spot any movement or muzzle flashes. Nothing moved. The downpour covered the sound Tuli made on his return until he crawled back next to Devlin.

"Bad news, boss."

"What?"

"Five more guys came out right at the edge of that clearing behind us."

"Armed."

"The two I saw were. Had M16s. We go back that way they'll cut us down fast."

"What the fuck is going on?"

"I know, man. Dis is Hawaii. Nobody supposed to have dat kine a weapon."

Suddenly, Devlin flashed back to the Vietnamese jungle with Billy Cranston and the approaching line of armed NVA regulars coming up the hill toward them.

"I know. This shit shouldn't be happening here. Hi-velocity rounds coming at us from fully automatic weapons." Devlin pointed to east. "Crawl over in that direction. I'm going to draw their fire. Try to spot the muzzle flash. Stay down. Watch. Then wait for me to come to you."

"Dis fucking rain ain't going to make it easy to see anything."

"That goes both ways. Go on."

Tuli scooted right and disappeared in the undergrowth. He kept going until he was behind a wide ohia tree.

Devlin took cover behind another tree, stuck his left arm out, and sprayed five steady shots in a wide arc right to left. The air around him exploded with gunfire. Devlin stayed low behind his tree as the foliage around him quivering and disintegrated under the barrage of bullets.

As soon as the shooting subsided, he crawled as fast as he could through the mud and the undergrowth in Tuli's direction. After about ten yards, he spotted Tuli's blue shirt visible about ten yards away and quickly joined him behind the cover of the ohia tree.

"See anything?"

"Five maybe six. About fifteen, twenty yards apart spread out in a line runnin' east to west. Closest to us is about ten yards to the left. Maybe twenty, thirty yards back in the forest."

"Okay. Take your shirt off. You're too easy to see. Let's stay low and move east as fast as we can. You go first. I'll stay here and watch if anybody follows or becomes visible."

"Okay. You see one of 'em, shoot the muddafuckers."

"Go."

Tuli scrambled east. Devlin crouched low, waiting to see if Tuli attracted fire. Without his shirt, in his black shorts and the pouring rain, Tuli blended in with the surroundings. Devlin watched and waited, saw nothing, then made his way after Tuli, who waved at Devlin to keep going.

Devlin continued on for fifteen or twenty yards, stopped, and waited for Tuli. Again, no gunfire, no movement, but the rain had tapered off taking away some of their cover.

When Tuli arrived, Devlin said, "Let's go. We have to get clear of this ambush. You think you can circle around and find that pig trial?"

"Yeah, follow me."

The continued east for another ten minutes, then turned south, hearing intermittent bursts of automatic weapons fire.

Tuli said, "They trying to flush us out."

"Drive us back into the ones behind us."

He and Tuli continued moving as fast as they could, pushing through the vines, bushes, and ferns. Devlin could hardly believe it when they ran into the pig trail. He hoped it was the same one they'd found before. Without a word, they turned left and began hustling through the forest. After ten minutes, Devlin stopped to check his compass.

"We're veering off to the east."

Tuli asked, "But still heading south?"

"Yeah."

"As long as we moving south, we'll hit the subdivision. We find one of those roads, we'll be able to get to the car fast."

"Okay."

"You know who the fuck those guys are?"

"No. But I know how I'm going to find out."

"Good, 'cuz I'm gonna kill them."

CHAPTER 22

Leilani looked for Devlin throughout the lunch service but didn't see him. There was a steady flow of people into the restaurant throughout the afternoon. Almost all of them had something to say about the stranger in town asking questions about the dead guy in the Ola'a Forest Reserve. The more Leilani heard them talk, and the longer she waited to see Devlin, the more tense and anxious she became. By dinnertime, she had a wretched headache. She kept thinking about the men who attacked Devlin outside Jameson's. She found herself surprised by how much she worried about him. All the comments about Billy from the townspeople tore at her.

Saturday had always been Walter's busiest night before she arrived, and now it was busier than ever. It was only because Walter agreed to let Leilani pitch in with the prep that they were able to keep up. All during the dinner service Walter's lack of speed in the kitchen gnawed at Leilani.

Every time someone entered the restaurant, she found herself hoping it was Devlin. By 10:15, the restaurant had been empty for almost an hour, and everything was just about cleaned up. She told Walter, who was already pouring his nightcap of cheap vodka and orange juice, "I'm done."

Walter said, "Sure. Go ahead."

She went up to her tiny room in the back of the second floor, took a shower to get the cooking smells off her body, and changed into jeans and a long-sleeve cotton shirt. She went back downstairs, walked through the kitchen, and slipped out the back door.

She made her way behind buildings until she was a few doors down from Da Restaurant, then cut back onto Main Street. She continued past the slum area of town, walked across the street to the 7-Eleven, and checked her watch. It was exactly ten-thirty-five. She drifted over to the pay phones and hoped she wouldn't attract too much attention waiting there. At ten-forty-three she had almost convinced herself she'd wasted her time. She was just about to leave at ten-forty-five when the first pay phone in the bank of three rang. She snatched up the receiver.

"Yes?" she asked.

"Very good," came back Devlin's voice. "I thought it was a long shot you'd be at that phone."

"Thanks for the vote of confidence."

"Sorry. That was a rather backhanded compliment."

"That's okay. I'll take it. I almost left. Last night you said to call at ten-forty."

"You're right, but you didn't call until ten-forty-five, so I decided to wait five minutes."

"We're over-thinking this."

"Better than not thinking at all."

"What happened? Why didn't you show up today?"

"I went out to the Ola'a Forest Preserve where they found Billy's body and walked into an ambush."

Leilani didn't respond for several seconds, and then her questions came tumbling out. "Who? When? What happened?"

"I'll tell you about it when I see you."

"Are you all right?"

"Not exactly, but I survived. Has anything happened at your end?"

"What's wrong? Are you hurt?"

"Just banged up. Do you have anything to tell me?"

"Who did it?"

"Leilani, take it easy. It's all right now. I'll tell you when I see you. I don't want you standing out there for a long time. Just tell me if you heard anything useful today."

"Everybody was talking about you walking around town asking about Billy. Also, about Sam Kee and the lady who owns the Village Inn. They said you had a run-in last night in the parking lot. Did Kee try to kill you?"

"Was he in town today?"

"I don't know. I didn't see him."

"What were people saying about last night?"

"Not too much. Just telling each other what happened or asking what happened. It seemed to me like nobody is very surprised by it. Almost like it's a regular thing around here. But they were surprised about you. Nobody in this town goes up against Kee like that."

"What else did they say?"

"Mostly what I said – everybody knows you're in town to look into Billy's murder."

"Anybody connecting Kee to that?"

"Not really. People around here just don't seem to be able to deal with it. They don't want to even think about who did it. Nobody's brought up Kee's name when they talked about Billy. It's not real clear why Kee would bother with Billy."

"Okay, Leilani. That's good. Very good. I don't want anything to happen to you, but I'm glad you're in such a good position to pick up information. I need your help. Can you hang in there?"

"Of course." Leilani found herself surprised at how good Devlin's praise made her feel. And at the same time, she felt annoyed that it meant so much to her.

"Any comments about Rachel Steele?"

"She's the lady who runs the Village Inn?"

"Yeah."

"People look up to her. Walter says Kee would love to drive her out of town. But beating up an old woman doesn't exactly fit his macho image, so he apparently just harasses and insults her whenever he can. I guess he figures she's going to die off soon anyhow."

"How are you doing?"

"Fine. Why are you being so nice to me now?"

"Am I?"

"Yes."

"Well, is that all right?"

After a moment, Leilani said, "Yes."

"Good. Anything else you can tell me about Kee?"

"He has a ranch somewhere north of here."

Devlin's interest sparked. "He does?"

"Yes."

"How do you know that?"

"Walter told me. He apparently got it through some bullshit application for Hawaiian homelands. Nobody quite knows how he pulled that one off, except they say his lawyer helped him."

"Do you know exactly where his ranch is located?"

"No. Some homestead area near the rainforest."

"Right. What the hell is that guy's real name?"

"Keamoku. Samuel Keamoku."

"Got it. If you can find out the location of his ranch without causing suspicion, do it."

"Okay."

"But be careful."

"I will. You know he rents one of those storefronts in town, too."

"Kee?"

"Yeah. The doors are usually closed, but there's almost always some of those scroungy guys that hang around Kee going in and out of there."

"What's he need an office for?"

"I don't know. A sign on the door says, Center for the Hawaiian Sovereignty Movement. When will I see you? Are you going to tell me what happened?"

"Yes. I'll try and be there tomorrow."

"Good. We only do brunch thing on Sunday. I think I found a young guy who can cook better than Walter, which isn't saying much. Main point, things will probably go faster. I should be free around two, two-thirty."

Leilani felt as if she were making a date. It was a strange feeling.

"Okay, I'll let you know Leilani, keep doing what you're doing. You'd better get off the phone. Keep your ears open and see if you can find out exactly where Kee's ranch is."

"Okay."

"And one more thing. If I don't show tomorrow, don't worry."

"Should I get to this phone same time if I don't see you?"

"No. If you're being watched, I don't want to set up a pattern."

"Do you think I am?"

"I was. I don't think you are but act as if you are. As long as no one connects you with me, you should be okay. Stick to your business. Don't be anywhere that doesn't look right."

"Okay. Bye."

Leilani hung up the phone quickly and walked into the 7-Eleven. She wanted to look as if she had had a reason to be there other than to answer the phone in the parking area.

#

Devlin hung up his phone. He was in a two-bedroom suite at the Hilo Hawaiian Hotel. By the time they'd humped back to the rental car, and the rain had stopped, they realized neither of them had avoided injury. Devlin had a deep gash on his left shoulder where the boar had stepped on him, and a blossoming, painful bruise on his back where the boar had run into him. Tuli had a deep wound on his right forearm where one of the boar's tusks had caught him.

Both of them had an assortment of scrapes and bruises from scrambling through the forest undergrowth.

Mrs. Banks had arranged for a doctor to stitch them up and check them for anything significant. It had taken the doctor two hours to clean and prep the wounds, stitch them, and bandage everything properly. Devlin considered them both very lucky to have avoided gunshot wounds, which would have been devastating from an M16.

The doctor gave Devlin phenylbutazone for his bruised rib cage.

Tuli was still sleeping in one of the bedrooms. Devlin walked into the suite's bathroom and stood in front of the mirror checking his injuries. He realized how lucky they were that the boar hadn't done more damage to them. But he couldn't accept that luck had saved them from getting shot. Tuli had counted at least five shooters. All of them had automatic weapons. There had been two sustained volleys of fire in their direction, but no bullets hit them. Devlin believed they had been firing over their heads. It was hard to tell because the rounds had flown way past them. Was there a large enough plot of marijuana growing in there to merit protection by seven or more men with M16s? If so, it had to be a massive field. And that seemed highly unlikely.

It seemed like whoever had fired on them were more intent on driving them off than killing them. Driving the boar into them with dogs might have been an attempt to run them off or injure them in a way that wouldn't necessarily involve the police.

All speculation, and none of it explained how Billy Cranston end up dead and half-eaten in that fucking rainforest. Was he alive when the animals began feeding on him? Did the people responsible for that also drive the feral pigs into him? And what did this guy Sam Kee have to do with it, if anything? Devlin knew his trek into the area had raised more questions than he had answers for, but he'd gotten a reaction. All he had to do now was do more of the same.

CHAPTER 23

Leilani walked on Main Street carrying a small bag containing a tube of toothpaste and a new toothbrush. She didn't need either one, but she wanted to look as if she'd had a reason to be at the 7-Eleven. When she came to Kee's storefront office, she stopped and pretended to check out the bulletin board nailed next to the front door, but she was actually surreptitiously looking in the front window. The lights were on inside, but there didn't seem to be anybody in the office. She listened but didn't hear anybody talking or moving around. Suddenly a phone rang inside. It spooked her, and she quickly moved off toward the restaurant.

In the back office, Eric Engle picked up the ringing phone, already knowing who was on the other end.

The phlegm-filled voice grunted, "So?"

Engle had prepared his response. "Nothing confirmed, yet. Both men have been out of town all day. Our friend apparently set up some sort of welcome for his guest. But I haven't heard how the party went."

"Ho'olohe! What the fuck is it with you, Engle?"

"I prefer to be discreet."

"Lolo. Did he run that asshole off or not?"

"I don't know."

Lihu hung up without another word. Engle didn't care. Just as long as the call was over.

#

Eddie Lihu hit the flash button on his phone and dialed another number from memory. A phone rang in a two-story bungalow situated in the officers' housing complex at Schofield Barracks on the island of Oahu. Lieutenant Colonel George Walker picked up his phone.

Walker had been enjoying a Saturday night alone, sipping generic Scotch purchased by the half gallon at the Army PX, watching CNN, and reading the latest edition of one of the many financial advisory newsletters he subscribed to. When he heard the voice on the other end, he knew his quiet evening at home was over.

"Did you get that information for me I asked you for?" the voice rumbled.

"Let me call you back on another phone."

"Fast. This is important."

Walker hung up. He hated it when Lihu called him at home. The Army's computerized phone system recorded every call that came in and out of the base. He never called Lihu from the base. And he disliked it very much when Lihu called him.

He put down his newsletter, left his cheap Scotch and droning TV, and went out to his car. He checked his watch. It was after eleven, so it would not be too unusual for him to drive off base to get something. The PX was closed. And although Schofield Barracks had more stores and facilities than most towns in Hawaii, they weren't open twenty-four hours.

Walker drove past the guard post and headed in the direction of Wahiawa. He pulled into a gas station, parked his car near the pay phones, and called Lihu.

Lihu didn't waste any time. "What's taking so long? I told you last night I need an inventory of everything that's gone off the Big Island and everything still there. Everything. How soon? And what about security?"

Walker could tell that Lihu's mouth was full of food. He pictured Lihu spitting it against the mouthpiece of his phone as he talked.

"I'll have a complete inventory by mid-day tomorrow. End of day, I'll have our usual security team cleared for duty at Pohakuloa. You can start day after tomorrow if you have your trucks and loaders lined up."

"First thing Monday. No excuses."

"None. How many days will you need security?"

"Schedule them for five days, but it'll be shorter than that."

"I take it you're shutting down operations."

"Never fucking mind what I'm doing. Have that inventory ready. And tell McWilliams to call me."

Walker frowned into the mouthpiece. He knew better than to press Eddie Lihu.

"Okay."

"Call me when you've got everything compiled and printed out. I'll come over there and pick it up."

Walker asked quietly, "Where should we meet?"

Lihu had a steamed crystal-shrimp dumpling poised to go into his mouth, but he paused for a smile as he answered Walker's question. "At your friend's place. How's that?"

Walker knew that meant he'd see Tay sooner than their usual Friday date. "That will be fine."

Lihu popped the dumpling in his mouth, hung up the phone, and said to himself goddamn right it will be, you sick fuck.

#

In his working hours, Lieutenant Colonel George Walker never took orders from anybody less than a brigadier general. But when Lihu spoke to him, he listened as if Lihu wore five stars. He went back to his car, pulled over to the self-service pump and stuck the hose nozzle in the tank of his Dodge Dart. While the gas pumped, he reviewed Lihu's requests, already sure he'd get everything done.

Lieutenant Colonel George Walker had not risen to the staff level by being incompetent. He was G4, the officer in charge of supply, transportation, and maintenance for the 25th Infantry Division stationed at Schofield Barracks, one of the largest Army installations in the Pacific.

Walker already had a general idea of the amount of material left to gather up. He assumed Lihu would ship it out of Hilo harbor. As usual, Lihu would be using his own trucks and men to do the job. Organizing, and printing the inventory information would take only three or four hours. No challenge at all.

Dealing with Captain Kensington McWilliams, however, was a different story. Walker compared it to handling explosives. McWilliams was volatile, unpredictable, and at least on some level, insane. If he weren't, he wouldn't have been doing what he was for Eddie Lihu. Even as he drove back to Schofield, Walker began figuring out the logistics and ways to manipulate McWilliams, both dangerous endeavors, but Walker had no choice. Eddie Lihu owned him. And the bitter irony was that Walker actually admired how deftly Eddie Lihu had done it.

Lihu had first contacted Walker when he held the rank of major. A major on the move, Lihu had said. And Lihu was right. During that first very discreet phone conversation, Lihu told Major George Walker that he was an important man. And Lihu wanted to do him a favor. Lihu said he wanted to make sure nothing happened to an Army officer while he was on Lihu's turf.

Lihu knew about Walker's interest in Hotel Street prostitutes. Lihu told Walker he was too important a person to be walking the streets looking for strange pussy. He offered to provide a woman who had her own apartment. A place where Walker would be well taken care of. It had started with Lihu asking Walker to allow him the opportunity to do him this favor. For everybody's sake.

Back then Walker had convinced himself he believed Lihu. Creating that belief had been the key. The rest was easy. The combination of blackmail, prostitutes, and money had been extremely effective. Lihu was a master at it. Within six months he had very tight control over the soon-to-be Lieutenant Colonel George Walker.

Within six months, Lihu had coerced Walker into using United States Army vehicles to transport marijuana crops off the island of Hawaii. Walker was in charge of moving thousands of tons of men, arms, and equipment. It was easy to hide four or five-hundred pounds of marijuana in a few two-ton Army personnel vehicles. Or a tank. Or sometimes even in one of the division's CH-47 Chinook helicopters.

And the movement of men and equipment onto and off the Big Island was almost constant. Although the 25th Infantry Division was stationed at Schofield Barracks in Oahu, almost all the training that required the firing of weapons was done 250 miles to the south on the Big Island of Hawaii at the Pohakuloa Army Training Center.

Everything worked without any major problems. And then Lihu and Walker got really lucky. The Federal Drug Enforcement Agency and the State of Hawaii decided to wipe out the marijuana trade that was ruining the good name of Hawaii. The DEA launched a ruthless interdiction campaign using military-style helicopter raids, crop spraying with herbicides, and property seizures. For Lihu and his partners, the drug raids couldn't have been better. They virtually wiped out the competition.

Lihu's network of informants kept him abreast of upcoming DEA helicopter searches. If his crops were in the flight pattern, Lihu simply harvested them, hid them, or gave them up. Even if he lost a few patches, there was always enough product left to reap good profits. The drug enforcement efforts forced the price of prime Hawaiian marijuana to almost triple what it had been before. The campaign not only helped Lihu build a near monopoly on production, it also guaranteed that every plant he cultivated would escalate in value.

And never once had the Army vehicles been searched. Never once had Lihu and Walker lost a shipment.

There were a couple of close calls. But McWilliams and his people had taken care of them. A timely accident here or there. A sudden death that appeared to be a knife fight between two drunken Army personnel. For Walker, the close calls were the exceptions that proved the obsessive bureaucrat's rule. Nothing was perfect. But risks could be reduced until they were negligible. Walker had restricted his core group so that on his side he had never used more than a total of twenty-one men. He had organized them in the classic Army three-unit structure. Three men to a team. Three teams used per shipment.

What made everything work so well was that Kee and his men packed the crops in containers used by the Army. Everything they handled ended up looking like Army property. Except for McWilliams, none of the Army personnel knew that they were transporting marijuana. They were loading containers that held Army supplies. All the containers were Army issue. Just a small fraction of them held marijuana.

But all that had been a prelude to their present operation. A once-in-a-lifetime opportunity had presented itself, and Lihu and Walker simply adapted the old system to a new product. One that was much more profitable than marijuana. Now for some reason, Lihu seemed to be rushing to either consolidate or wrap up the operation.

Walker had no idea why. But he didn't care. If Lihu wanted to phase out his scheme, or even take a hiatus, so much the better. George Walker believed in the investment adage: pigs go to market, hogs get slaughtered. Walker had already made more than enough to finance his retirement. Getting out from under Lihu's control would be worth it. And he'd still have enough for many afternoons with Tay.

As soon as he returned to his quarters, Walker wasted no time getting to his computer. While he listened to the beeps and whirs as the machine booted up, he opened a desk drawer and retrieved a small envelope. It contained clippings of Tay's pubic hair. Walker bent to the open envelope and sniffed delicately. He touched himself, gently squeezing his erection. There were still exquisitely tender spots on his penis where Tay's riding crop had disciplined him. He wished he could slip away right now. Walk out of his room in the two-story officers' barracks, get back into his car, and drive to her apartment.

Patience, he told himself. Soon he would be able to retire from the Army, build a little house somewhere on the Islands, and move Tay in. Keep her all to himself. The idea almost made him dizzy. He forced the image out of his mind and looked at the cursor blinking quietly on the blue computer screen. He exhaled slowly, replaced the envelope, and set his fingers to the keyboard. He punched in the password that would unlock the database files and translate the encrypted information: mistresstay.

CHAPTER 24

Devlin had sealed off his bedroom at the hotel in Hilo, cranked up the air conditioning, and hoped the painkillers would get him a night's sleep. They worked until dawn when he turned over on his damaged shoulder one time too many and woke to see the glow of morning light seeping in around the blackout curtains. He rubbed his face, moving his arms to see how it felt. Not bad. Then he sat up. Boom! There it was. Hard, sharp pain in where the boar hand banged into his side.

When he stood up, he felt stiff and sore all over from battling his way through an overgrown tropical forest, particularly his legs. But none of it was debilitating. He could move, walk, think. He could plan. He could do what he had to do.

After a hot shower, Devlin dressed in his ruined clothes, ordered room-service breakfast and phoned Mrs. Banks. She worked with him as if it were the middle of the week, even though it was seven o'clock Sunday morning. It took them almost thirty minutes to go over all of Devlin's requests. As Devlin hung up, Tuli opened his connecting door and padded into the room.

"How do you feel?" Devlin asked.

"Like shit. What about you?"

"Like shit warmed over."

Tuli stood there sullenly. Blood had seeped through the bandage on his forearm. He wore only his baggy shorts. He had washed them out the night before, but even though they were black the dirt and bloodstains were still visible.

"Who the fuck were those guys, man? And where do we find 'em?"

"I'm working on it."

"They must be da guys that fucked up your friend, hey, Jack?"

"Looks that way."

"What now?"

"Now we have a lot to do. Order your breakfast. We've got to get new clothes. Set up the safehouse. Get more transportation. I want to be out of here in an hour."

Tuli smiled and laughed. "Aaaiieee, Jacky, you sure fucked up da car. That's two. Car rental company gonna put a big X on your name."

"What do you expect? I had to back out of there almost a mile before I could turn around. It's okay. The car's just scratched up. I have to get wheels for you."

They checked out an hour later, drove to a shopping center near the airport to buy new clothes, and then headed for Pahoa-town.

Tuli directed Devlin to the safehouse. It was set back from the road. There was only a slight entrance cut out from a dense growth of bushes and ferns. The small A-frame house sat on a scrap of lawn overgrown with tropical ginger plants, orchids, and more ferns. A short set of stairs that led up to double sliding doors.

Tuli unlocked the doors with a key hidden under the stairs. Devlin stepped inside. The first floor consisted of a large open area and kitchen divided by a long counter. Farther back was a bathroom and bedroom. A steep flight of stairs led up to the second floor, which Devlin assumed was another sleeping area.

The place was clean, but it had been locked up for so long that a musty smell pervaded the rooms. Because it was surrounded by so much vegetation outside, very little light penetrated inside the house.

Tuli headed to the back bedroom and drop his bag of new clothes on the bed. Devlin checked the locks on the back door and walked upstairs to check those rooms. Once that was done, Devlin told Tuli, "Mrs. Bank has arranged for a pickup truck to be dropped off for you before three o'clock. You have to be at the airport to pick up our shipment by five."

"Got it."

"Pacific Rim will have a man at the airport to handle the paperwork. Meet him where freight comes in. When he has it cleared, load up and bring everything back here."

"How many containers?"

"Probably two. They'll put the ammunition in one and the weapons in the other."

"Good. We gonna need more than pistols to go up against whoever those ufa assholes are."

"That's what's coming. More. A lot more. Keep your eye out for anybody following you."

"I hoped somebody do follow me. Won't have to look for dem to buss 'em up."

"First get our stuff, Tuli man. I'll call you later."

#

Twenty minutes later, Devlin was in the Don Ho room at the Village Inn, shoving a new clip into his Sig. He pulled out the small Beretta 21A and slipped it into the pocket of the new pair of walking shorts he had bought at the shopping center. He changed from his Allen Edmunds slip-ons to a pair of cross-training shoes. He rinsed his hands and face and went looking for Rachel. She was nowhere to be found, so he stepped into her office and left four hundred-dollar bills in an envelope for her.

He left the Inn and headed for Da Restaurant. When he passed Kee's office, he considered pulling out the Sig and kicking the door in, but from outside it didn't appear as if anyone was in there.

He continued on to Da Restaurant.

Leilani was just coming out of the kitchen when he walked in. There were six other people eating. Devlin figured that was more than their usual Sunday business. Leilani even had Walter Harrison in a clean shirt and long pants bussing tables.

This time Devlin didn't sit near the window. He took a seat against the far wall, facing the entrance. The Sig-Sauer was holstered in the front of his waistband.

Leilani came right over and said, "Nice to see you again. Are you hungry?"

She was looking at Devlin as if she were trying to see if he had any obvious wounds. Devlin simply looked at her. She was wearing a peasant-style dress, but it was cut short above her knees and had a wide, scooped neckline. There was plenty of Leilani's flawless copper skin to look at. And as usual when she was working, she had her hair tied up on top of her head, so nothing obscured her face. Devlin decided she was so beautiful she was almost mesmerizing. He wasn't surprised Da Restaurant's business was growing.

"I am hungry. What do you recommend?"

"A fresh Ahi steak. And we have a new chef who won't overcook it."

"Sold."

"Steamed vegetables and rice?"

"Perfect."

Leilani tried to keep her voice matter-of-fact as she asked, "When can we talk?"

Devlin glanced quickly around the restaurant to see if anybody was watching them. All the customers were busy eating, so he asked Leilani, "Do you know if Kee is in town?"

"I don't think so. Why?"

Devlin dodged the question and asked, "What time do you think you'll be done?"

"Should be done by two o'clock. I was going to hike out to a black-sand beach I heard about yesterday. It's supposed to be very isolated. If you showed up there, no one would know."

"Okay."

"I'll draw you a map."

With that Leilani left Devlin's table and headed for the kitchen.

Devlin ate his lunch slowly. Leilani was right. The fish was nicely grilled on the outside and pink inside.

When Leilani returned with his check, there was another piece of paper under it. As she picked up his plates, Devlin looked at the map she had drawn and knew immediately he'd never find the beach. He asked her, "How far is this beach from town?"

"About five miles. Walter's letting me borrow his truck for the afternoon."

"I'll walk out of town for about a mile and wait for you to pick me up. We'll hike out together."

"I thought you didn't want us to be seen together."

"Once I'm out of town, I'll know who's around us. If it doesn't look right, I'll wave you off. The beach is isolated?"

"Yes. Very."

"We should be okay."

"Fine. I'll look for you on the road."

Leilani headed for the kitchen with Devlin's dishes. He dropped his money on the table and strode out of the restaurant. He stood on the raised wooden sidewalk for a moment, looking up and down Main Street. The town was quiet, but it seemed to Devlin that it was a nervous rather than a peaceful quiet.

The hot sun had burned away the morning rain.

Devlin turned to his left and walked about fifty feet along the wooden sidewalk until he was in front of Kee's office. He tried the door. Locked. Devlin took a step back, looked at the old wooden door, then pulled out the Sig-Sauer, and unleashed a perfectly placed front kick that shattered the doorjamb. The door flew open, and Devlin strode into the office as if he owned the place.

He looked quickly around the room taking in everything: Topographic maps of the Puna District on the wall. A small oil painting of a sugarcane worker in a field. Banners that proclaimed, "No to Geo" and "Hawaii for Hawaiians." Two desks, a few pieces of cheap wicker furniture, walls, and a sagging wooden floor painted a washed-out green.

Devlin held his gun pointed at the ceiling and walked toward the back. He passed a dimly lit storage area, a bathroom, and entered a large office. The office was well equipped. It contained a computer, a fax machine, a large worktable, and a file cabinet.

He walked out the back door onto a lanai. He saw an old couch, a coffee can filled with cigarette butts, a beat-up refrigerator. No snarling dogs. No island tough guys. No Sam Kee.

He holstered the Sig, walked back into the office, and exited past the broken front door. Several people had gathered across the street. Devlin stood in front of the door letting the people see him.

Just then, a four-wheel-drive Toyota Land Cruiser came barreling down Main Street and slid to a halt in front of the office. All four doors flew open. Angel, Loto, and a third man named Pali jumped out of the SUV.

Devlin grabbed the butt of the Sig and was ready to shoot at the first sign of guns. He expected automatic rifles, but none of them had guns. Devlin stood his ground.

The biggest of the three, Pali, grabbed the sidewalk handrail, vaulted over it, and landed lightly on his feet about two yards to Devlin's left. Loto and Angel ran up the steps on Devlin's right.

Pali shifted into a side stance, then without hesitation or warning, stepped toward Devlin and let loose a spinning kick aimed at Devlin's head. The kick was meant to intimidate and impress Devlin, and perhaps to drive him into Loto and Angel, but Pali had picked the wrong person for a demonstration. Devlin stood exactly where he was and simply leaned back away from the kick. Pali followed the kick with another spin in the same direction aiming a backhand fist at Devlin's head. That was the blow that was supposed to land, Devlin had seen the attack sequence many times. He turned into the spin, grabbed Pali's left wrist with his right hand and his throat with his left. He squeezed Pali's throat hard enough to half-crush his windpipe. Devlin kept turning and shoved him into Loto and Angel, who were closing in on Devlin's right.

The three bodies collided with a sickening thud and a crack as two head collided. Pali ended up on his hands and knees bleeding from his forehead. Devlin took one step forward and kicked Pali full force in the face. He didn't throw a kick. He didn't flash a kick at him. He drove his heel into and up through Pali's face and nose with enormous force. He broke three of his teeth and almost shoved the nose cartilage into the man's brain. Pali's head snapped back, blood sprayed up out of the broken nose in a long, graceful red arc.

Loto stumbled around Pali and rushed toward Devlin, head down, his muscular arms spread wide to grab him, but the last thing he should have done was get close to Jack Devlin. Before he had anything in his grasp, Devlin dropped low and timed a perfect uppercut, straightening his legs and bring up his elbow into Loto's jaw with so much force that Loto's jaw shattered. He broke through the wooden handrail bordering the sidewalk and dropped three feet down to the street. Loto landed so hard he cracked his collarbone, ending up flat on his back, unconscious. His chest heaved, and his cheeks puffed out with tortured exhalations.

The Filipino, Angel, had been clever enough to hang back behind the bigger men, but now he was desperate. He should have simply run for the SUV, but he pulled out his knife and slashed the point of the blade at Devlin's face. His fear gave him speed, and his frantic slash would have split Devlin's face open, except for Devlin's quick reaction. He leaned away from the blade, slapped Angel's forearm, pushing the blade away, then pivoted and punched Angel in the temple, sending him crashing into the broken front door. Angel's legs turned to water, and he crumbled to the floor. Devlin was on him in two strides. He stomped down on the Filipino's wrist and broke the bone. Devlin kicked the knife out the door. He bent over and picked up Angel by his belt and his long hair. He pushed the front door out of the way with the Filipino's head and threw the man over the sidewalk handrail and into the street. He landed on his chest and face.

Devlin paused only long enough to see that more people had gathered on the other side of the street.

He picked up the Filipino's knife. He turned and plunged the stiletto deep into Kee's front door, then snapped the blade and tossed the broken remains into the gutter. The jagged piece of steel stuck out of the door. Devlin had left his calling card.

From Kee's office, Devlin returned to the Village Inn. He ran into Rachel Steele holding the envelope he had left for her.

"Mr. Devlin," she said. "Do you have a check? I hate to keep large bills around here. I always think I could lose a hundred-dollar bill as easily as a dollar."

Devlin turned to her as he strode toward his room.

"No checks, Rachel."

"Oh?" She thought about that for a second "Well, why don't you pay me when you leave?"

Devlin stopped and faced her. He was still flushed from the fight, but he composed himself and told her quietly, "I'd rather you kept that money. That way I won't have to think about it."

Rachel took off her reading glasses and looked at Devlin. She had no idea he had just finished maiming three men he believed had ambushed him and Tuli with automatic weapons. But she could tell it was taking a great deal of polite effort on his part to deal with her. She became flustered and stepped back from him. "Oh," she said. "I'm sorry. Is everything all right?"

"Yes, Rachel, everything is all right. Keep the room for me, please, but as far as anybody else is concerned, I've moved out and you don't know where to."

"Oh dear. I'm not accustomed to such things."

"I know, Rachel. If anybody asks about me, just say you don't know."

"I understand."

"Thank you."

CHAPTER 25

Devlin went into his room. He checked the bandage on his shoulder to make sure his wound hadn't started bleeding. The stitches seemed to have held. He flexed his right arm and rubbed his elbow. There was going to be a bruise where he'd connected with that dumb son of a bitch's jaw.

He changed into a T-shirt and his hiking boots, pulled out a small daypack from his carry-on, and placed the Sig-Sauer into the pack along with a towel, a swimsuit, and a liter bottle of water. He switched the small Beretta into his waistband holster. He pulled his T-shirt over the gun and slung the pack over one shoulder. He left the Inn and made his way on the paths behind the buildings before he cut over to the main road, watching to make sure nobody followed him.

As Devlin walked, he tried to spot anybody eyeballing him in passing cars or from houses. He'd already decided that Sam Kee had been behind the ambush. If he had any doubt, it was gone after those three showed up. He had been careful to look for vehicles following him as he drove to the forest preserve. He doubted very much if Kee and his men knew how to set up a professional tail. For that, they would need at least three vehicles and drivers who were in radio contact and knew what they were doing. It had to have been done by stationing people along the route watching for him. The rental car was easy to spot in an area where most people drove pickups or junkers. There was only one road in and out of town.

Kee had enough men to keep watch. And it wouldn't have taken a huge amount of insight to figure he'd be going to investigate the place where Billy Cranston's body had been found.

He and Tuli had survived.

He'd flushed out the enemy. Now he had to keep one step ahead in a part of the Big Island that suddenly seemed like a backwoods Appalachian community with eyes and ears behind every rock, bush, and hollow. Devlin felt better on foot, out of the rental car. He could see what was around him. And even if someone chanced to see Leilani pick him up, it would look more like a stranger had offered him a ride than like a prearranged meeting.

He'd walked almost a mile loosening up his sore legs, letting the sun warm his back when he heard a pickup truck braking to a halt behind him. He had the Beretta in hand as he turned his head. When he saw Leilani behind the wheel, he relaxed, took a quick look up and down the highway, and climbed into the truck. Leilani pulled back out onto the road very quickly, without needing to be told.

Devlin holstered the Beretta and slumped down in his seat to be out of sight, just in case.

Leilani announced, "You are officially the number one topic of conversation in Pahoa."

"Is that so."

"Kee showed up about twenty minutes after you left. He went nuts. Screaming and yelling at everybody. Swearing he's going to find you and kill you."

"Good. He's welcome to try."

"The cops were there, too."

"What'd they do?"

"Nothing much. Watched while they loaded Kee's guys into the ambulance."

"They should be happy they weren't going to the morgue. Did you find out anything about the location of Kee's ranch?"

"Jeezus, you don't let up, do you?"

"I'm just getting started."

"What the hell is going on? What's gotten into you?"

"Kee set up an ambush. The object was to kill or maim me, not sure which."

"Where?"

"In that forest reserve where Billy's body was found."

"You okay? I mean, what did they do? Are you sure it was Kee?"

"Who else would it be? What did you find out about his ranch?"

Leilani looked at Devlin. "So you're not going to talk about what's going on?"

"I've pretty much told you what I know."

"Oh."

"What about Kee's ranch?"

"So far, all I've come up with is that it's in the Ola'a Homestead somewhere north of Highway 11, and west of Kurtistown."

"And where's that in relation to the forest reserve?"

"Just south of it. Near the western border."

"Well, that's a start. How are you getting your information?"

"Mostly Walter, and the girls' network."

"Interesting."

"Sisterhood is powerful, brah. There are a lot of women in that town. A lot of single mothers on welfare."

"How do they take to you?"

"What do you mean?"

"You're not exactly one of them."

"Why not?"

Devlin said, "Are you fishing for compliments?"

Leilani laughed. It was a natural, hearty laugh that made Devlin feel good when he heard it.

Leilani turned off the main road onto a gravel road that eventually gave out to hardpacked dirt.

"A few of them resent me. But most of them see me waitressing and busing tables in a shitty restaurant, and they figure I'm a working girl. Plus, they know I'm passing through so I'm not much of threat in terms of their boyfriends or whatever. The smart ones realize I got Walter to hire someone, so when I leave there might be a chance one of them can take that job."

"Interesting."

Leilani turned west onto a road that ran parallel to the ocean. Between the road and the ocean stood a vast field of hardened lava that had covered over every bit of ground, vegetation, and beach right down to the water. Devlin peered out at the solid black mass. It looked like Nature's way of turning everything into a massive, crudely-paved parking lot.

Leilani drove until she arrived at a wooden sawhorse that stopped vehicles before they ran into the lava that had flowed over the road.

"End of the line."

Devlin asked, "Where'd the flow start from?"

"Six miles northwest. Six miles long and almost two miles wide is now nothing but black lava. Took out a whole community on the way and a real nice beach near Kalapana. Actually, there is no Kalapana anymore."

Devlin stared out at the vast field of black.

Leilani said, "Let's go."

She jumped out of the truck wearing a pair of lightweight walking shorts, a plain red tank top, and a well-worn pair of jogging shoes. There wasn't anything extra on her long, lean body to inhibit her stride. She strapped on a fanny pack, spun it around so it rested on the small of her back, shoved a beach towel behind the pack, and strode off onto the lava field. Devlin could see it wasn't going to be easy keeping up with her long-legged strides.

He followed her out onto the hard, black surface that dipped and rolled like a gigantic field of pudding that had hardened into an uneven black mass. Some of it had splintered on the surface like a thin coat of burnt plastic. Other areas, called pahoehoe, looked like huge strands of rope laid side by side. There were also bubbled-up shells that had hardened with nothing under them but air, but most of the field was one thick, solid mass of dense black rock.

Every so often they would come upon narrow crevices that were five or six feet deep. As he strode over them, Devlin could feel the deep-down heat rise up against his legs. The lava was still cooling after more than three years.

Leilani had opened up about a fifty-yard lead on Devlin. They were halfway to their destination. She stopped to get her bearings and to pick out landmarks to orient them. When Devlin caught up with her, she shaded her eyes, pointed, and told him, "See that set of three palm trees sticking up out there?"

Devlin nodded. "Yeah."

"If you don't want to keep up with my pace, just keep heading for those."

Devlin peered off into the distance. "Are those trees growing on a beach?"

"Almost. Supposed to be a big kipuka. "

"What's that?" he asked.

"A spot where the lava flows around an area and leaves it untouched. Of course, once that happens, the area isn't much good because you can hardly get to it. There's a lot of folklore about how lava has flowed around ancient sacred places. Places of worship and sacrifice. Before the white man came in, there were dozens of those places all around the island. They marked ancient routes of travel along the coast. Even overland."

"Mostly gone now?"

"Oh yeah," said Leilani. "The holy places are dead and gone. Killed the island spirit. The white man did what the lava couldn't."

At that moment, in the burning sun out on the vast black nothingness, Leilani looked more Polynesian to Devlin than at any time he had been with her. Something was stirring in her that he would never feel. She turned quickly and hiked off, light-footed, agile, independent, completely sure of herself and of every step.

Devlin pushed and crunched over the undulating lava. Leilani seemed to glide. He had to ease carefully down a decline, then push his hands onto his knees to lever himself up the small but steep ascents. She gathered momentum going down and then used that momentum to carry her up and onward. Devlin settled into his own steady pace and watched Leilani go on ahead. She'd given him the palm trees to guide him.

CHAPTER 26

More and more of Kee's men came into town looking for someone to beat on. Eight of them had already gathered in Kee's office: two of Angel's brothers, Wilfredo and Ramon. Three of Kee's regular crew, Feto, Tommy, and Aka along with Aka's cousins Frank and Pana. And lastly, one of Kee's men who always showed up when there was trouble, a heavyset surly local named Kimo. More were coming.

Kee had riled up all of them with rants about the imagined and genuine injustices that plagued them and then left them muttering and goading each other toward violence as he retreated to his back office with Eric Engle.

Kee railed at Engle, "I'm gonna go across the street and choke the fuckin' truth out of that old cunt, Rachel. She knows where that guy is."

Engle said, "No. You're not going to attack an old lady who has nothing to do with this. You're going to get in your jeep and drive up to your place to meet Lihu. His plane lands in Hilo in ten minutes. You should leave now."

"Fuck Lihu. Who is this guy, Devlin, anyhow? He think he some kine guy can come in here and fucking pull this shit? Put down three of my men like that, and I'm gonna do nothing?"

"I told you who he is," said Engle patiently. "He works for a company called Pacific Rim. They're a private security company. He's been hired by Billy Cranston's father to look into his death. The idea here, Mr. Kee, was to convince Mr. Devlin to leave this island until we solve other problems. Not to make everything worse."

"You should have let me shoot him out there."

"No. That would have made things worse. Much worse. I thought you were going to cause him to run into wild animals or something."

"We did, but he got away."

"Apparently without injury."

"All right," said Kee. "Fuck this. I'll handle my way."

"No. You won't. Mr. Lihu is going to handle it."

"How?"

"I'm sure Mr. Lihu has it figured out."

Kee looked at the gawky, white-faced lawyer and fought back a nearly irresistible urge to punch him in the face.

"Let me tell you something you skinny fucking useless haole piece of shit. Lihu don't have this figured out, I'm going to find that guy and kill him and slice him up and feed him to my dogs."

Engle knew it was useless to argue with Sam Kee. He nodded and said, "I wouldn't keep Mr. Lihu waiting."

Kee ran his fingers through his hair, stared up at the ceiling, and yelled, "Fucking lolo hupo!"

Engle looked at his watch.

CHAPTER 27

Leilani reached the edge of the lava field, sat, and waited for Devlin to catch up. She looked in every direction. The only thing visible was Devlin.

When he came within a few yards, she motioned for him to follow her into a green oasis surrounded on three sides by the dead black rock. In the middle of the oasis were the three swaying palm trees they had used as guides. Up close now, they could see that the trees were over sixty feet tall.

Leilani skillfully walked along strips of the hardened lava that coursed through the thickening vegetation. Just as the lava gave way completely to the tropical growth, she spotted a small opening between a stand of bushes and the palm trees. They climbed up a six-foot cliff, and suddenly found themselves in a fragrant field of swaying, pungent molasses grass and sweet-smelling bamboo orchids – tiny purple and white flowers on tall grass-like stems. There were also flowering ginger plants, guava trees, gardenias, purple and crimson bougainvillea, and patches of small ti plants. Just a hint of a trail cut through the flower-filled area. Devlin followed Leilani as she glided along the trail, walking toward the sound of the ocean, pushing aside the grass, bushes, and orchids.

After a minute, they reached a line of tall ferns. They bent under two drooping fronds and stepped onto a perfect black sand beach about a hundred yards long and twenty yards deep. The north and south ends of the beach were bordered by twenty-foot-high cliffs of lava that ran right down to the ocean. The waves had pounded and shaped the cliffs, digging out sharp grooves in the rock. At the base of the cliffs were huge chunks of lava that lay in piles like natural seawalls.

Devlin and Leilani walked toward the ocean, crunching across the fine black sand. They had found a private patch of paradise.

"How did you hear about this place?" asked Devlin.

"One of the women in town told me about it. The last lava flow created it. Hardly anybody outside the area knows it's here."

"It's amazing."

"Yes, it is."

Leilani was a few feet in front Devlin, facing the ocean. She slipped out of her tank top and walking shorts. She wore nothing under the top. Without a word, she stripped off a small pair of white bikini panties and dropped them on top of her shorts. She turned and faced Devlin with nothing on except a thin gold ankle bracelet.

Devlin didn't even try to be discreet. He stared. She was flawless. Her skin. Her perfect teardrop breasts. Her sensuous, dark nipples. Even the trim, perfect patch of dark hair between her long legs. He wanted to see all of her, all at once, but he couldn't. He tried to see each part of her and all of her. Finally, he gave up and looked at her face.

She looked back with a knowing grin and said, "You've been looking through my clothes almost since the time we met. I'd never swim at a beach like this with anything on, so I figured this would be as good a time as any to get over the physical thing between us."

Devlin said, "The physical thing?"

"Oh, all these side glances and furtive looks. I just want to get through it, get over it. Whatever." Leilani came to him and lifted his T-shirt. "Come on, get your clothes off. I want to see you, too."

Devlin raised his arms and allowed Leilani to pull the T-shirt over his head. She stood and looked at him for a moment, but she didn't comment on the bandage covering his left shoulder or the other visible signs of old and new damage.

She folded his T-shirt and dropped it on the beach. Devlin reached out and put a hand on her shoulder so he could stand on one foot and unlace his hiking boot. Leilani opened his belt buckle and unbuttoned his walking shorts. She smiled as Devlin struggled with his socks. When he straightened up, she pulled down the zipper on his shorts and let them drop onto the black sand. Then she gently pulled the elastic waistband of his briefs over his fierce erection and slid his underwear down until it dropped to the sand. She reached out, took his erect his penis in her hand, and gently squeezed it once.

"Very nice," she said, letting go so Devlin could step out of his walking shorts and briefs.

She picked up his shorts and underwear, folded them and placed them on top of his T-shirt. Then she stepped into Devlin, put her arm around his neck and pressed into him. Devlin embraced her, feeling her body next to his. Her copper-colored skin felt cool and sleek.

"Is this what you mean by `getting over the physical thing'?"

"I suppose."

Devlin felt her soft, firm breasts against his chest, the flat of her cool abdomen against his upright cock. Leilani went up on her toes, he bent to her, and they kissed gently. Her lips were soft and full. Their tongues searched tentatively, then Leilani leaned back to look at him. Devlin caressed her silky-smooth back. Leilani felt his shoulder muscles and massaged the back of his neck.

"You're almost not real," he said.

"Is that good or bad?"

"Bad, very bad."

"Why?"

"We shouldn't be doing this."

"Bullshit."

Leilani continued to caress Devlin, and he did the same to her. Suddenly she stopped and said, "You're not married, are you?"

"No."

"Promised to anybody?"

"No."

She resumed stroking him. "So is telling me we shouldn't do this is some sort of reverse psychology move?"

Devlin said, "If it is, I wasn't clever enough to think of it. But even a dimwit would know this is probably a bad idea."

"Probably?"

"Certainly."

"Why?"

"How can you possibly think I'd come up with an answer to that with you standing here holding onto me naked."

Leilani stepped back. "All right. We can leave it at this. Plus, I hate making love on a beach. The sand gets everywhere."

"Yeah, I know, that's so annoying."

Leilani laughed. "Okay, I just wanted to see you. To feel you. The rest can happen, or not."

Leilani turned and headed for the tropical blue water. Devlin watched her step carefully into the ocean, deftly dive over an incoming wave, and disappear into the liquid blue.

Devlin joined her, and they swam naked in the warm waters. Devlin started out slowly, careful with his left shoulder, stretching out, testing the pain along his left side where the wild boar had slammed into him. The salt water burned his scrapes and bruises, but eventually, that gave way, his muscles loosened up, and he swam out into the deep water and back, all the while with Leilani at his side effortlessly swimming at whatever pace he set.

Devlin came out of the ocean first, managing to make his way out without too much bashing from the waves. He stood on the beach letting the sun dry his shoulders and back, burning a little more color into his haole skin.

A few minutes later, he watched Leilani as she calmly strode out of the water. The stones and coarse sand didn't seem to bother her at all. The water fell from her limbs as if her shining bronze skin were oiled. She wiped the salt water from her face with her graceful fingers and was next to Devlin in a few strides.

They walked to where Leilani had set her towel, took turns drying off, slipped on their clothes over their salty skin, and sat side by side, facing the ocean.

Neither one spoke for a while. Finally, Leilani asked, "Now what?"

Devlin didn't say anything.

"Why the silence?"

"I'm thinking."

"About me wanting to get over the 'physical thing'?"

"I don't think that's actually a way to get over that."

"Oh?"

"Maybe if we went back to my room in that shitbag hotel, took a long shower together, and spent the afternoon in bed we'd get over it. For a day, maybe. Better yet, we could fly over to the Kona coast, check into one of those super lavish destination hotels, have a few drinks, a sunset dinner, a cold bottle of bone-dry Sauvignon Blanc, and spend the night getting over the physical thing."

"Sounds lovely."

"Yeah. But instead, I'm going to ask you to come back with me, throw whatever you have in a bag, and get off this island. Today. On the first plane back."

"What?!"

Devlin held up his hand. "Not as a way to deal with our attraction for each other. Hear me out."

"You're really something, you know."

"Leilani, hear me out. In the truck, I didn't tell you everything about what happened in the forest reserve. But now is the time to explain it."

"You might have decided to explain it before I got naked in front of you."

"Uh, I didn't see that coming."

"Whatever, go on, explain."

"This thing with your brother's murder has gone to a whole new level. Kee's men, and even if it wasn't Kee's men it doesn't matter, whoever they were, opened fire on me with M16s. There were at least eight, nine of them. Nine guys with automatic weapons is so far off the charts as to be crazy. That many military-style weapons in the hands of civilians is unheard of on the Islands. It's unheard of anywhere in the United States."

Leilani said, "There are a lot of guns and rifles on the islands. A lot of semi-auto stuff."

"Leilani, best case scenario these were military-style assault weapons that were retrofit to full auto. Even that's off the charts. But that's not what it was. Trust me, I know the sound of military M16s on full auto. Those were M16s.

"Maybe one of two of those weapons find their way into civilian hands. But when that happens, a whole base can be shut down until the Army finds out who's behind it. I know the drill. I was an MP. The Army comes down full force on that stuff. We're talking about close to a dozen M16s in civilian hands. If your brother's death is connected in any way to that, we're looking at something way beyond murdering a homeless vet who stumbled into somebody marijuana patch. I told you from the very beginning, this could get dangerous. Now it has. I can't let you stay. Please, listen to me."

For a few moments, Leilani didn't speak. She stared down at the sand between her feet, looked out at the ocean. Devlin waited. Finally, she asked, "What are you going to do?"

"Find out what's going on here. Then shut it down."

"How?"

For the first time, Devlin turned away from the ocean and faced Leilani.

"We're not talking about me, Leilani. We're talking about you."

"*We're* not talking about me. *You're* talking. Giving me orders. And I'm just supposed to sit here listen, nod, and do what you tell me."

"I'm not telling you, Leilani, I'm asking you."

"And what if I refuse?"

"Please don't."

"Then answer my question. What are you going to do? Unless you have a hell of a lot more information than I think you do, I can't see you finding out what's going on and shutting it down. You don't even know where Kee's ranch is. Or how many guys he controls. Or what he's up to. You don't even know if he's the one who ambushed you, or if he's the one who killed Billy."

Devlin said nothing.

Leilani turned to him. "Listen, I heard what you said. Yes, it's frightening. It's crazy. Sam Kee is clearly crazy. He might have twenty or thirty of those ignorant losers following him around lapping up his native rights bullshit. I've been in this town less than three days, and I already know the women in this town hate him. Everybody is afraid of him."

"All the more reason you should get out."

"But tell me, how are you going to solve this? Your method seems to consist of stomping around that town attracting attention and kicking everybody's ass. Okay, you flushed out the bad guys, now what?"

"I can't do what I need to do if I'm worrying about you."

"Then don't. Listen, you're the one who's the focus of attention around here. Nobody is looking at me. Why don't you let me keep doing what I'm doing for at least a couple of days? If I don't come up with anything, or you figure this all out by yourself, I'll go home. If you've already figured this out to the point you don't need me, tell me. Go on. Tell me. What do you know?"

"I know that somehow, Sam Kee has control of that town.

I know all that Hawaii for Hawaiians crap he's spouting is self-serving nonsense, but apparently, it's worked. He has a cult-like following that will risk their lives if he tells them to. I watched him, and his crew, nearly beat a man to death. I doubt very much that Sam Kee is the only one involved in whatever is going on. Somebody has been tracking me, probably since I arrived in Honolulu. For sure since I met with your father."

"Because of what happened at Jameson's?"

"Yes."

"Don't get pissed, Jack, but it doesn't sound like you have nearly enough information to solve whatever is going on here. Don't you think I might be able to find out information that will help?"

"Not if it gets you killed."

"Isn't that my decision?"

Devlin shook his head. It was becoming clear he wasn't going to win this argument. He could blow Leilani's cover and cause her to leave, but that would put her in immediate danger. He could call her father and tell him to come get her, but that, too, would blow her cover, and there was no guarantee she would listen to him either.

Devlin turned to Leilani and said, "Tell me one thing."

"What?"

"I want to know why you're here. Why you're really here? What you want out of this?"

Leilani had been ready for Devlin to give her more reasons to leave, but this question cut to the heart of it.

She looked away from him, took a long slow breath.

"That's a little hard," she said.

"Why?"

"It's embarrassing. And painful."

"I'm sorry, but I think it's a fair question. You being here doesn't just put you in danger. It's going to be more dangerous for me, too."

Leilani didn't respond.

Devlin waited and watched her.

She sat on his right, staring straight ahead. He could only see the left side of her face. Suddenly, he saw her wipe at the cheek facing away from him. At first, he thought she might be brushing away an insect. And then, he saw a tear running down her left cheek.

And then she told him.

CHAPTER 28

The Chevy Blazer pulled up in front of Kee's ranch house five minutes after Kee arrived with Eric Engle. Eddie Lihu drove. Next to him in the front passenger street sat Captain Kensington McWilliams. Behind them, jammed onto the Blazer's rear bench seat sat McWilliams's three-man team of Rangers. Their equipment filled the luggage area behind them.

Lihu climbed out of the driver's seat and lumbered into the ranch house. McWilliams, dressed in spotless Army fatigues followed close behind. Inside the house, Engle and Kee sat at a large wooden table in the middle of the large main room. Engle tried to hide the anxiety caused by Kee barely arriving before Lihu. Kee sat with his arms crossed looking defiant.

Lihu sat across the table from Kee, ignoring the general disarray around the room and the condition of the beat-up couches and chairs. Mc Williams stood in the doorway, doing nothing to hide his distaste for Kee, the surroundings, and the situation.

Lihu started by pointing a finger at Kee and saying, "So, dis guy Devlin, he's still around."

Kee said, "Yeah. And thinking he got the right to put three of my men in the hospital."

Lihu made a guttural sound and nodded. He turned to look at McWilliams, and then back at Kee.

Kee said, "What?"

Lihu stared at Kee, his face without expression, but there was something in the silent, baleful look that silenced Kee.

Finally, Lihu spoke.

"Lot of fucking up going on. Don't wanna waste time talking about it." He held up a fat finger and pointed to Kee. "First, you and your people are gonna get everything you got stashed in the lava tubes and on this ranch, pack it up, truck it over to Hilo in the next two days. I don't give a fuck you have to work non-stop. You get it done. I got three half-tons comin' in here this afternoon.

"Pack everything up. I don't want one fucking bit of it left anywhere on this island. Don't fuck up. That's all you got to do."

Kee said, "What about dis asshole, Devlin?"

Lihu stared at Kee. "Don't goddamn ask me any questions, Sam. Time to listen. Devlin dies tonight. It's set." Lihu pointed over his shoulder. McWilliams is going to handle it now. You listen to what he says. Don't make me tell you a third time."

Lihu stared at Kee, daring him to speak.

Engle looked at the stare down. He glanced over at McWilliams, the poster boy for a trained military killer. Buzz cut hair, dead eyes, no expression on his face, his hand on his sidearm in a canvas holster at his waist. Engle knew that Lihu needed Kee, but he also knew that Eddie Lihu would not hesitate to have McWilliams shoot him if he gave him any trouble. Lihu's patience with Sam Keamoku had just about run out.

Fortunately, Kee had enough sense to keep his mouth shut.

Lihu nodded once, got up, and walked out, motioning for McWilliams to follow him. Just before Lihu got back into the Chevy, he turned to McWilliams standing near the driver's side window and said, "Two seconds after everything is loaded, and you're sure this place is clean, kill him. Burn this goddamn place down and put his fucking body someplace nobody will find it.

CHAPTER 29

Leilani continued to stare out at the ocean as she spoke.

"Billy was two years older than me. He was the big brother every girl wants. Handsome. Strong. Protective. But it wasn't easy for either of us in that house, or in that community. People think Hawaii is a big melting pot, but it isn't really. There's a lot of racism here. Kids are the worst. The Island kids give the haoles shit and vice versa. I was in between. I got it from both sides, but it would've been a lot worse without Billy around. He always stood up for me. There were a lot of fights. He never backed down. He just got tougher and stronger. And I loved him more and more. I worshiped him."

Leilani paused and dug her toes deeper into the black sand. "When I was fifteen, I looked like I was eighteen or twenty. I attracted a lot of attention." Leilani lifted an eyebrow and gave Devlin a side-long glance. "Can you believe it?"

"I don't know, that's a real stretch."

"Yeah," said Leilani. "I wish. Sometimes I liked it. The attention. The power it gave me. Just as often I hated it. Sometimes I wished I could just disappear. It was all about power, after all. Age, race, male/female, this high school clique versus that clique.

"Billy and I were half-siblings. As you know, he was haole. All haole. I came out looking mostly Island. By the time I was sixteen, he was nineteen. Around that time, we started drifting apart. I tried to convince myself it was the big brother, little sister thing. And then for a while, I convinced myself it was the racial difference that made us drift apart."

"But it wasn't that?"

"No. It was something else."

"What?"

"Just let me tell it my way. Billy didn't just grow distant. He *kept* his distance. It hurt me. My mother kept saying Billy just didn't want his little freshman sister tagging after him. She didn't want to admit what was going on either. What made it worse – as much as Billy rejected me, his friends were all over me."

Leilani stopped. Shrugged. "The only thing I liked about the attention from Billy's friends was that it gave me a way to get Billy's attention. I knew he didn't like it, so I kept letting it happen. Looking back, I can't believe I was capable of that."

Devlin sat motionless, saying nothing, watching the tears sliding down Leilani's cheek. She wiped them away as if annoyed by them.

"Then, out of nowhere, came the day."

"What day?"

"The day Billy left. No warning. Nothing."

"Left?"

"For the Army, Jack. You see, he'd tried every way he could. I was too young, or too stupid, or maybe deep down I knew the truth, but I didn't give a damn."

Leilani turned to Devlin, "The day he left, he knew it was finally safe for him to feel the things he felt for me. He knew there was nothing I could do about it. He knew the minute he got on that bus, I was safe. And the second he let his feelings come out, I felt it, too."

Leilani spoke slowly. "I swear to you, when we embraced to say goodbye it was like we'd been married for all our lives. The passion that passed between us actually took my breath away. I couldn't breathe. The lust, the pure desire – it was beautiful and sensual and horrible.

"Billy didn't have to enlist like that. He could have gotten student deferments. Christ, he could have gone to West Point. But he knew he had to go right then and there. To go where we would be completely separated from each other. If I had just let him hurt me a little and stayed away from him, he wouldn't have had to run off to that pathetic, stupid, useless war.

"I did that to my brother. I did. I killed him, Jack. But before I ensured his death, I made it so he would lead a horrible, pitiful life devolving down to a terrible, terrible, lonely end. I did that. And I'm telling you right now, you're going to have to kill me to stop me from doing whatever I can to avenge his death. Because if I don't do that, if I don't at least try, I don't want to go on living."

Devlin didn't respond. He looked down at the black sand. After a few moments, he said, "I think I understand."

Leilani shrugged.

After a few moments, Devlin said, "All right. I won't try to talk you out of staying, but I'm still going to ask you to let me tell you what I think is the best way for you to help me. Assuming you agree that helping me is your best shot at doing something about Billy's death."

"I agree. You're the professional. You tell me what you think I should do, and I'll do it. Your way."

Suddenly, Leilani stood up. She had no desire for more talk. She slipped on her shoes and her fanny pack, and said to Devlin, "We should go back."

They walked across the lava side by side, Leilani going slower now, taking long easy strides, letting Devlin keep pace with her. They were closer now. Devlin could still feel the sensation of her naked body against him, but at the same time, the barrier between them was palpable. It was a self-imposed distance. But that seemed to make the separation more intolerable. Despite their attraction to each other, they knew if they crossed the barrier any chance they had of avenging Billy's death might be destroyed.

CHAPTER 30

Devlin gave Leilani directions to the safehouse. When she pulled over Walter's truck, Devlin pointed to the mailbox and said, "You can't see the house from the road, so remember that mailbox. The house is in past those bushes. If for any reason you need to get out of town, lay low, whatever, you come here. Even if you have to walk."

"Okay."

Devlin made sure Leilani had memorized the numbers for the phone in the safehouse and for Pacific Rim.

He said, "The phone here will record a message if nobody is here. Pacific Rim will have a person answering calls twenty/four seven. You can leave detailed messages for me anytime."

Devlin nodded once, then asked, "You okay?"

"Sure. I think I know an angle for finding out more about Kee's men."

"What's that?"

"There's a women's group that meets tonight in that crafts store across the street from the restaurant. Kind of a consciousness-raising thing. I'm sure I can bring up the topic of Sam Kee. Find out more. Maybe even where the ranch is."

"Sounds good. Make sure you don't attract too much attention."

Leilani said, "Only yours, honey." And then she laughed out loud. "You should have seen the look on your face just then."

"What was it?"

"You tell me."

Devlin said, "I don't know. A combination of lust and dread?"

"Don't worry about it."

"I don't have time to worry. You should get going. We don't want to be parked out here for too long."

Leilani shifted into drive and said, "Okay. Bye."

Devlin jumped out, and she pulled away.

Devlin entered the house. Tuli sat at the kitchen table, grinning, surrounded by two large metal containers, each one bearing a stenciled label that said they were the property of the University of Hawaii Anthropology Department. Although there was no anthropology department in the world that would use what was in the containers.

Tuli had carefully laid out the contents on the long countertop that separated the kitchen from the living room. There were three military-spec, pump-action Mossberg 590 12-gauge shotguns fitted with laser sites. A fourth rested in Tuli's lap. Three dozen boxes of shotgun shells in various gauges and two dozen boxes of 12-gauge slugs were also on the counter, along with two full-body Kevlar bulletproof vests and two lightweight vests. Also, two Heckler & Koch submachine guns, two night-sight goggle systems, a bolt-action Mauser rifle, plus clothes, rain gear, packs, and other equipment Devlin had ordered.

"When did the truck arrive."

"Just before three, like you said. Nice little Tacoma."

"Any trouble at the airport?"

"Nah, dat guy knows his business. Don't know how he got this stuff on the plane, but it just came out with all the regular suitcases and freight. Just scoop 'em up off the carousel." Remembering it made Tuli laugh. The weapons had also made him very happy. "Man, we could make kaukau out of dem fucking ilos, hey. Kill every fucking one of dem quick."

"Not yet, Tuli."

"When?"

"We'll see."

Devlin checked his watch. It was almost seven o'clock. "I'm going to wash up. Did you buy any food?"

"Oh yeah. Got some beer. Spam. Papaya. Coffee. Milk. Cereal."

"Anything green?"

Tuli thought for a moment. "I bought some toilet paper I think is green."

Devlin looked in the refrigerator. One shelf was filled with containers of Spam. Hawaiians ate more Spam than anybody else in America. Devlin didn't even want to imagine that mysterious chunk of meat sliding out of the container. He quickly closed the refrigerator door.

He found the bathroom upstairs, stripped, showered off the sea salt, dried, and dressed in clean clothes. He switched the Beretta in his backpack for the Sig and went back downstairs.

He poured himself a bowl of cereal, sliced up a papaya, and dumped the pieces into the cereal. No Spam.

Tuli had finished stacking all the equipment against the living room wall and was eating his dinner: Spam, bread, and beer. A loaded Mossberg 590 was on the table next to him.

Their dinner was interrupted with the insistent ringing of the phone on the kitchen counter. Devlin answered it. The night duty officer at Pacific Rim confirmed it was Devlin and then read him a message: "A man named Nishiki called. Said he has important information for you. Wants to meet tonight. The McDonald's in downtown Hilo. Pukihae Street. Ten o'clock."

The duty officer recited a phone number to confirm the meeting with Nishiki.

Devlin hung up the phone and looked at his watch. He had plenty of time to drive the thirty miles up to Hilo but wondered what was so important that he'd have to. He dialed the phone number Nishiki had left. An answering machine came on. Devlin thought for a second, then decided he'd do what Nishiki asked.

Better to cooperate with the local police honcho than to piss him off.

"This is Devlin. I'll be there at ten."

He hung up and turned to Tuli. "You want some dessert?"

"Sure."

"How about McDonald's?"

"Yeah, I could go for a couple of Big Macs."

Devlin picked up the shotgun next to Tuli. He pumped a shell out, checked it, put it back in. Tuli had loaded up with double-aught shot. He shouldered the shotgun, checked the laser sight, flipped the safety off, then back on, and handed the weapon to Tuli. It was a combat weapon. Pump action. Eight-shell capacity. Made for U.S. Marine quick-strike anti-terrorist FIST teams.

"Bring the Mossy. We'll go separately. You take the pickup truck. I'm supposed to meet that police sergeant I spoke to in Hilo. He's the cop in charge of Billy's case. Says he has information for me."

Tuli shoved the last forkful of food into his mouth, nodded, and followed Devlin out the door. Devlin walked Tuli to the truck. Tuli climbed in and sat waiting for Devlin to tell him more.

Devlin leaned into the window and said, "Listen, I don't have much idea what this is all about. This cop acted like an asshole last time I talked to him. I don't know why he'd want to be giving me information now, so let's play this carefully. I'll give you a few minutes head start. Shut down someplace where you have a view of the parking lot and the restaurant, but where you won't be easily seen. Stay out of it unless it looks like I need you. I'm only taking my registered gun. I don't want any trouble about other weapons."

"'At's okay, Boss. I'll have you covered."

"Good. Go ahead, then."

Devlin knocked the side of Tuli's truck and watched him drive off. He was alone now. Standing under a full moon glowing in the Hawaiian sky, the trade winds sending a string of clouds scudding overhead.

Devlin looked up for a moment and then down. He let himself

think about Leilani. It seemed as if whenever any natural elements of the Islands touched him – wind, ocean, moon, sun – he thought of her. He saw her face. Heard her voice. Remembered the feel of her silky copper skin. Then he pushed away all feelings about her, knowing that he was probably going to have to do that quite a bit before he finished what he had come to do.

He walked over to his scratched-up Ford Taurus, drove to Highway 130, and headed for Hilo.

He turned on the radio. Nothing happened for a second, then Bruce Springsteen's "Kitty's Back in Town" blared over the speakers. Devlin cranked the volume up and listened to the guitar and saxophone twang and bang, picking out the vocals behind the instruments. He remembered the picture on the back of the album cover – a young, skinny, relaxed Springsteen standing with his musician buddies in front of a Jersey Shore storefront. A worn-out storefront. Faded. Like the ones in Pahoa.

He tried to remember other songs on the album, then just listened.

\#

As soon as he pulled into the McDonald's parking lot, Devlin felt uneasy. He was in an old section of town. Fronting McDonald's was a street that had a regular flow of traffic, but behind the fast-food restaurant, it was quite desolate. There was an unlit back street bordering about fifty yards of empty space, then a set of old warehouses that looked long-abandoned.

Devlin spotted Tuli's Tacoma parked across the street outside the glowing circle of light created by the last set of high-intensity lamps in the parking lot. The greenish color of the truck blended in with the shadows. He couldn't see inside the truck, but he knew Tuli and the Mossberg were there.

Despite his unease, the prospect that Nishiki might have something useful to tell him made Devlin feel energized.

He steered the Ford into a handicapped parking spot right near the entrance of the McDonald's and felt a ripple of anticipation run through him. In the next second, he had an image of himself in some godawful Hawaiian hospital bed, intubated and stitched and wired together, waiting for wounds to heal, knowing he would never be quite the same. He pushed the image out of his mind and shut off the car. What the hell was that about? Some sort of flashback to the rainforest? Parking in a handicapped spot?

He felt the Sig-Sauer press into his stomach as he bent over to step out of the car. He scanned the parking area. Two cars were parked close together in the middle of the lot. A third car occupied a space in the row bordering the east edge of the lot. Three cars seemed about right for late on a Sunday night.

Devlin turned away from his car and walked toward the entrance of the restaurant. He pushed open the first set of double doors, then the second, and stepped into the clean, brightly lit fast-food outlet that had become a cookie-cutter piece of America, duplicated over and over again in cities all over the world. It felt familiar and strange to him at the same time. He scanned the seating area and saw Nishiki sitting alone in the center of the restaurant. Nearer to the serving area was an elderly man sipping coffee, and a few tables to his right sat a local family: mother, father, and two young daughters eating frozen yogurt sundaes with hot fudge topping.

Devlin figured the cars parked in the lot belonged to the family, the old guy drinking coffee, and Nishiki who Devlin ignored as he walked up to the counter.

There was only one person at the registers, a stout Hawaiian girl who smiled and asked what she could get him. She wore maroon pants, a maroon striped shirt, a maroon baseball hat. The papaya and cereal he had eaten weren't nearly enough, but he just said, "Coffee."

The girl poured the cup and loaded little containers of half-and-half, packets of sugar, and a plastic stirrer on his tray. Devlin handed her back everything but one container of half-and-half, paid, and carried his tray over to Nishiki's table.

The policeman looked the way Devlin expected he would be. Tired. Distracted. And dressed exactly like the last time he'd seen him in his white shirt and dark pants, his tie loosened.

"What's so important?" asked Devlin.

Nishiki looked at him as if it were the first time he had ever seen Devlin. As if he had no idea why Devlin was there; as if he were trying to decide what to say.

Devlin flipped the top off his cup and poured his little container of half-and-half into the coffee. He stirred it, took a sip, looked back up at Nishiki.

Devlin said, "So?"

Nishiki started to talk. "Look," he said, "we got some information about your guy. Seems like maybe some of the local boys are involved."

"Local boys? What local boys?"

"I can't tell you that, but I can tell you that we're going to be making arrests. Soon, hey? Point being, we're asking you to stand aside. Stay out of it until our investigation is over."

"Sounds like your investigation is over if you're going to arrest somebody."

"You know what I mean."

"No. I don't know what you mean. Who's 'we' that's asking me to stand aside?"

Nishiki looked surprised at the question. "We?"

"Yeah," Devlin said, "who's we?"

"What the fuck you talking about? Us. We. The police. Word came down from the brass you should stay the hell out of this."

"Brass? What brass? Your boss? Who's your boss, Nishiki?"

"Major Olohana. Crawford Olohana."

"You guys use military ranks on the force?"

The question confused Nishiki. "Uh, yeah. Why?"

Devlin said, "So you're telling me Major Crawford Olohana told you to come here, ten o'clock on a Sunday night, to tell me to step aside."

"Yeah," said Nishiki.

Devlin said, "Uh-huh." He took another sip of the coffee. It was still too hot to drink. "I don't suppose this meeting has anything to do with the fact that your local boys didn't kill me yesterday out in the rainforest, does it?"

"What?"

"Or because a few of them landed in the hospital today."

"What are you talking about?"

"You know something, Nishiki, I didn't like you when I first met you. Your tough-guy act. The bullshit you tossed at me. And here you are, bullshitting me again. What the hell is going on?"

"What do you mean?"

"Don't fuck around with me, Nishiki. On Friday, you didn't know shit. No leads, no information, nothing. Two days later, the case is solved, and you're ready to arrest the bad guys. You expect me to believe you?"

"I give a shit what you believe. Just stay out of our business."

"Or what? Why don't you tell me who's telling you what to say and do, and you and I can skip this part. I'll go talk directly to them."

Nishiki looked down, shaking his head. "It don't work that way."

"Well, this isn't working."

"Devlin, you got no kine idea what's going on here. Your friend knew. Your friend knew what they were doing, that's why they killed him."

Devlin said, "Who? Who killed him? What did he know?"

"I don't know. But I do know you're in over your head. The people behind this will crush you. You ain't gonna do shit about anything. You want to..."

Nishiki mouth moved, but Devlin didn't hear it over the sounds of a shotgun blasting outside, and the front window of the McDonald's collapsing, as a 5.56 x 45 mm bullet hit his back. The force of the impact was like a giant fist that sent Devlin slamming into the table in front of him.

At that moment, a series of thoughts flashed through Devlin's mind: He hoped the bullet wasn't going to penetrate the metal plate in the Kevlar vest he was wearing. The old man didn't drive to the restaurant. One of the cars belonged to the shooter. He hoped Tuli had blasted him with the Mossberg. His back was going to hurt like hell.

Devlin managed to get one hand on Nishiki's throat, dragging him down as he fell over to his left.

He heard another blast from Tuli's shotgun and the sound of tires squealing.

Nishiki managed to break free of Devlin's grip and crawled behind the serving counter to take cover.

Devlin rolled over onto his back, gasping for air, pulling the Sig-Sauer from his waistband holster. The three other customers were all on the floor. The little girl screaming non-stop. Glass from the shattered front window covered the tables, chairs, and floor in the seating area.

Devlin struggled into a half-sitting position, trying to see outside without making himself a target, but the restaurant's bright fluorescent lights prevented him from seeing into the dark. He rolled over, keeping low, crawled past the counters into the kitchen, hoping whoever had shot him wasn't going to come into the restaurant to finish the job. And that they hadn't taken out Tuli.

In the kitchen, Devlin made it to his feet, moving faster now, still bent over. There was no sign of Nishiki, but he saw three workers huddled in a corner. He shuffled past them to the back door, pushed the release bar, and leaned out to take a look. He saw a black topless Jeep Wrangler parked in the unlit alley, two men in the front seats. The passenger held a rifle. Devlin jerked back and pulled the door shut as three-round bursts of bullets banged and cracked into the heavy door.

The firing stopped. Devlin kicked open the door, stuck his gun out, and fired five shots at the Jeep. Whoever was in it, returned fire. But now, Devlin heard the roar of an engine and the sound of brakes squealing, followed by booming shotgun blasts from a Mossberg 590. Tuli was still in the fight.

Devlin dropped low and peered out the door and saw the big Samoan walking calmly toward the jeep laying blast after blast at the vehicle. Staying low, Devlin ducked out of the McDonald's and aimed a volley of slow, steady shots at the Jeep as it roared off down the alley with the passenger spraying return fire aimlessly behind them.

Devlin stood up, shouted out, "Tuli!" and ran as best as he could toward the pickup truck.

The Samoan turned and ran for the truck. Devlin heard the first sounds of police sirens in the distance. Flushed with the fire of battle, Tuli made it to the truck before Devlin. He could barely wait for him to climb in before he floored the accelerator and raced after the Jeep.

Devlin yelled, "Gimme the Mossberg. Careful, one of those guys has an M16."

"Grab the Mossy behind your seat. We got to get these mudderfuckers."

Tuli reached the end of the alley and slid to a halt in the middle of the intersection. He looked left. Devlin looked right. Tuli yelled, "There," and turned left heading for the dark warehouse area about fifty yards away.

Devlin saw two figures getting out of the Jeep on the right side of the street. They ran toward a dark-colored van parked near a warehouse at the next intersection. Whoever they were, they had planned this well enough to have a backup vehicle.

Devlin could see the back of the Jeep had been hit by the 12-gauge shot. Both rear tires were flat. Devlin saw that the larger of the two men, wearing shorts and a white T-shirt, carried the M16. When he saw the headlights of Tuli's pickup, he turned and fired bursts of bullets back and forth across the road. It was Sam Kee doing the shooting. Most of the shots started low, ricocheting and skipping off the asphalt, but the last spray ripped across Tuli's pickup, knocking out a headlight, cracking the corner of the windshield.

Tuli veered left out of the line of fired and ran his truck along the side of a brick building sending sparks flying and making a horrible tearing screech.

Devlin leaned out the passenger side window with his Mossberg and fired blast after blast at Kee as Tuli awkwardly wrestled the truck back onto the street.

Kee backpedaled toward the van. His partner was already in the driver's seat. Kee fired a last blast as he climbed into the van, yelling a curse.

Devlin let off two more blasts as the van disappeared past the intersection heading right.

Devlin wanted to end this right now. He'd match two Mossberg 590's able to unleash nine rounds as fast as a man could pump and pull against an M16. They could fill the air around one man shooting an automatic rifle who clearly couldn't aim the damn thing, but Tuli's truck wasn't going in the direction Tuli steered. Nor was it able to get up speed.

Tuli cursed and stopped the truck.

Devlin didn't want to be caught by the police with a bullet-riddled truck filled with guns and ammo.

They both ran around to the front of the pickup. Banging into the wall had pushed in the front fender far enough so that the left, front wheel couldn't turn all the way. Nor could it roll without scraping the fender.

Tuli, still mumbling and cursing lumbered over to the damaged fender, grabbed the section above the wheel, and pulled the sheet metal away from the tire, yelling, "Mudder-fucking-piece-of-shit-fuck," until he had the wheel free.

Tuli kicked the tire and said, "Let's go. We might find 'em."

"No. They're gone. We have to get out of here. The cops get us now, it's over. C'mon."

Still grumbling, Tuli got behind the wheel and shoved his shotgun behind his seat. Devlin did the same on the passenger side. Tuli pulled out slowly, and when he reached the street near the warehouses, he turned left and made the first right putting distance between them and the flashing red and blue lights filling the sky around the McDonald's.

"You know who dat fuckin' guy was, boss?"

"Yes. Sam Kee."

"That's twice now, boss."

"Three times if you include the bullet that hit me in the restaurant."

Tuli said, "No. That bullet wasn't from those two guys."

Devlin turned to look at Tuli.

"What?"

Tuli shook his head. "Different guys. They were dressed in dark clothing and ball caps. In dat car on the far side of the parking lot. One driver. One shooter. One rifle. One shot. I didn't see nuthin' till after the one shot. And they was already rolling onto the sidewalk and straight out onto the street.

"I just let off a blast so you'd know I was out there covering the front, but the shooter was moving out. I figured you'd go out the back, so I came around to get you."

"Son of a bitch. Kee was just covering that exit in case they missed."

"Somebody else involved now, boss."

"No. Not now, Tuli. They've been involved since this started.

CHAPTER 31

Across the street from the McDonald's, on the empty second floor of a derelict wood-frame building that had once housed a massage parlor and Tarot card reader on the ground floor, Captain Kensington McWilliams scanned the scene in front of him with high-powered field glasses. Three police cars, two ambulances, an Emergency Services vehicle, and several unmarked cars with single flashing blue lights attached to their roofs had all converged in the parking lot.

McWilliams put his field glasses down and stepped away from his window. One of his men having returned from his post at street level stood near the doorway awaiting orders from McWilliams. Both wore civilian clothes.

McWilliams turned to his soldier.

"Status report."

"Positioned myself as spotter, as ordered, ready to provide support if needed to the shooting team."

"Go on."

"One shot took down intended target. Our team made its way out of the area without resistance."

McWilliams said, "A third party did, however, step out of a green pickup truck and fired one shotgun blast into the air."

"Yes, sir."

"Your analysis?"

"My first priority was to confirm the kill."

"And?"

"Negative. I proceeded into the McDonald's. Four civilians. Mother, father, child, older man. Police personnel Nishiki. No sign of our target."

"Conclusion?"

"Target must have been wearing body armor protection."

"Mistake number one, soldier. Describe it."

"Insufficient intelligence. If we knew the target was wearing body armor, we would have taken a headshot."

"Why didn't we take the headshot from the beginning?"

"Too much chance of killing police sergeant Nishiki."

"Correct. Subsonic round with the right load should have remained in the body of our target but not the head. Anything else?"

"I proceeded to check the kitchen area and exit area behind the McDonald's."

"And?"

"Signs of a gun battle. Multiple rounds in the back door of the restaurant. No sign of target, driver of the green truck, or team in place to cover that exit."

"Mistake number two. Relying on ignorant, ill-trained, illiterate Island scum. I assure you, soldier, that will not happen to our team again. Police the immediate area, be ready to leave in three minutes."

"Yes, sir."

Kensington McWilliams turned away from his soldier. Debriefings were fine, but it amounted to one thing. He and his men had failed. Kensington McWilliams did not countenance failure. Worse, this failure happened because he had allowed his operation to be exposed to ignorance and incompetence. The list of people he had to eliminate from the world of the living was growing longer.

CHAPTER 32

Leilani walked across the street from Da Restaurant and entered the crafts store where the women's meeting was scheduled to take place. She found herself in a combination crafts store/bookstore/ coffeehouse. An eclectic jumble of furniture was scattered around the front of the store, mostly comfortable chairs with lots of cushions, bolsters, and pillows. There was also a square wooden table by the entrance with four straight-back chairs. On the table were napkins, milk, and sugar. A display counter for handmade jewelry, small wooden boxes, rings, and bracelets, separated the front of the store from the next section.

Farther back was a coffee bar with an espresso and coffee machine, and a six-gallon dispenser for mineral water. The back section contained a magazine rack and shelves filled with books on New Age topics: health, cooking, holistic medicine, feminism, religions, meditation, and more. Sweet incense burned somewhere. A tape of tinkling bells and soft percussion was playing.

As soon as she entered, Leilani felt relaxed and welcome. Three women sat around a well-worn coffee table near the front of the store, all sipping tea. Leilani recognized two of the waitresses who worked at the Paradise.

The older of the pair smiled and said, "Hi, my name's Janet." She was the brunette with the flower tattoo on her shoulder. It was her kids who played around the restaurant while she worked.

Janet pointed to a small blonde and said, "This is Wendy." She waved and smiled at Leilani.

The third woman, a dark-haired, heavyset lady in a peasant blouse and long black skirt, said, "I'm Louise. This is my place."

Leilani shook hands all around and said, "My name's Leilani. I'm new in town. I just started working at Da Restaurant across the street."

"We know," said Janet. "Most of the men in town are talking about you."

Leilani said, "Oooo, good. What are they saying?"

Whatever distance there might have been between Leilani and the others disappeared with that response. Janet laughed. Wendy smiled.

Two more women walked in. "What's so funny?" one asked. Janet turned and said, "Oh, we're just about to tell Leilani what the local boys are saying about her."

"We're supposed to be talking about the health center tonight."

Janet waved her hand. "In a minute." She turned to Leilani and said, "Okay, honey, first thing you have to know about Pahoa-town – eighty percent of the men around here are pigs."

"Ninety," said Wendy.

"Ninety-five," said one of the new arrivals.

Over the next two hours of gossip, serious discussion about the town's needs, and exchanging of histories, Leilani learned much more about what was going on in the town and the Puna district. She was proud that she had found out so much information for Devlin. And she was happy because she felt she had made a friend in Janet.

Janet was tough, smart, and confident. She had lived in Pahoa for ten years, had gone through two men and ended up with three kids she was raising on her own.

As the meeting broke up and the women rinsed out their mugs, Janet took the initiative and asked Leilani, "How about a nightcap?"

Leilani was anxious to call Devlin but agreed to a quick one.

They walked into the Pahoa Lounge and headed straight to the bar. A tall, sullen guy in his early twenties stood behind the bar with his arms crossed. He wore paint-stained canvas pants and a T-shirt with a cartoon on it of two dogs humping and a caption that said, "Bury the Bone."

Janet put ten dollars on the bar and asked for two beers. The bartender placed two longneck Budweisers on the bar, took the ten, and placed the change down all without saying a word. Leilani ignored his rudeness and drank down about a third of the beer before she set it back on the bar. The beer was so cold it left a dull ache in her temple, but it tasted great.

Janet took a swig said, "Good, huh?"

"Better than tea." Leilani downed another long swig and sat down on a bar stool.

Leilani had heard that the town bar was not exactly a safe place, but it was Sunday, it was quiet in the bar, and she was with a regular, so she felt relaxed. She looked around. The place was larger than she had expected. A small dance floor and a stage filled the back of the space. The stage was empty except for a set of drums that looked as if it hadn't been used in a long time.

In front of the stage, there was enough room for five tables with chairs. The bar where they were sitting was long enough to accommodate ten stools. The back bar area was cluttered with liquor shoved together in no particular order, photographs, signs, a clock that didn't work, and a large color television tuned to a cable music station. The picture on the TV was clear, but the sound was turned off. In the back of the room stood a well-used coin-operated pool table.

The only other people in the bar were three women sitting at one of the tables, quietly sipping beers and talking. Leilani thought one of the women was somewhat overdressed for the Pahoa Lounge. Janet noticed Leilani looking at her and leaned over to tell her, "That's the owner. Name's May. She's a very nice lady. She's got breast cancer."

"Oh shit, no."

Janet nodded.

Wendy walked in, waved at Janet and Leilani, and sat down to talk to May. Sunday night seemed to be ladies' night in Pahoa-town.

Leilani had seen many of the women before, but now she was learning their names and backgrounds. It made her feel almost as if she belonged in Pahoa.

She had turned back to take another drink from her bottle when two men walked in and headed for the bar. One was a short, mostly Chinese man with eyes so squinty they looked perpetually shut. He wore cutoff jeans, a red striped T-shirt, and an incongruous red tam-o'-shanter with a white tassel. His partner wore a threadbare black-and-white checked cowboy shirt and dirty jeans. He looked like an Australian aborigine. They stared at Leilani as they passed.

Janet stared back at them and said, "Evening, boys."

The Chinese man laughed and said, "Oh, hi, Janet. Hi, hi. Didn't hardly see you there."

"Yeah, what happened, you get nearsighted all of a sudden? Or maybe I should just knock you in the back of your head so's your eyes go back in?"

The Chinese hit himself in the back of the head, blinked a few times, and said, "There you go. Who's your friend?"

Leilani spoke up and extended a hand. "Leilani. What's your name?"

"My name's Wing, Nestor Wing. This is Phillip. What you drinkin'?"

The aborigine said, "Seven and seven." Nestor slapped his knuckles into his buddy's shoulder and said, "Not you. Ladies?"

"Just beer," said Janet. "One more and I'm going home."

"One more will do it for me, too," said Leilani.

Nestor slid a twenty toward the bartender and nodded. "Another round for the ladies. I'll take a vodka. Give Phillip a seven and seven."

Phillip said, "Make it a double."

Nestor said, "Put some damn money on the bar you want a double."

The bartender went to work without a word. Nestor and Phillip sat on the stools next to Leilani.

"What brings a pretty woman like you to Pahoa-town?"

"Kind of taking a break from my regular work. Change of scenery."

"How do you like it?"

"Okay so far. Some things around here make me a little nervous, but it's okay."

"Like what?"

"Oh, that fight in here the other night."

"You in here for that?"

"No. But I heard about it the next day. Were you here?"

"Nah. Not the first Friday of the month. Not me. Yeah, Sam Kee and his boys up to their usual shit."

"He came in the restaurant where I work. He gives me the creeps."

"I'll tell him you said so. No, just kidding. You might want to keep that to yourself."

The aborigine laughed, and Nestor elbowed him in the ribs. "Mind your manners, Phillip."

"Oh yeah," said the aborigine.

"It's a pretty good town if you watch yourself, right, Janet?"

"I guess so."

"Don't think anybody's really been hurt since I've been around."

"How long is that?" asked Leilani.

"Five years."

"What about dat guy they found in the rainforest?" said Phillip.

"He was plenty fucked up."

"Who, that Sunshine guy?"

"Yeah," said the aborigine.

"Fuck knows what happened to him," said Nestor.

Leilani frowned at hearing Billy spoken of that way. Without thinking, she blurted out, "Did you know him?"

Nestor said, "Who? That guy they found all et up?"

"Everybody knew him," answered Janet. "He was around here a long time."

"Were people upset about what happened to him? Did he have many friends?" asked Leilani.

Nestor shrugged. Janet fell silent. Phillip took a sip out of his drink and said, "Lyman was his friend."

"Lyman?"

"Yeah, another nutbag. They used to hang together."

Nestor said, "How do you know?"

"I just fuckin' know. Lyman lives down near Opihikau. Somewhere in there."

Leilani wanted to ask more. Luckily, Nestor asked for her. "Who's Lyman?"

"That haole guy. You know. From the Mainland."

"Lyman?"

"Yeah, come on, you know dat guy. Works at the health food store sometimes. Skinny fuckin' dude. Or at the garage outside of town. Near the high school. He works at both places now and then."

"Oh yeah, I know who you mean. He's lolo, man."

"Yeah, yeah." Phillip nodded. "He's into the herb pretty heavy. Same as that Sunshine dude."

"Seems like most everybody smokes around here," said Leilani.

"Do you?" asked Nestor.

"Occasionally. Can't really afford it."

"Yeah. Me neither. Not like it used to be around here. People didn't mind sharing a little."

"What kind of work do you guys do?"

Nestor giggled and waved, "Cane, honey. We work sugarcane."

"Right," said Janet. "Which conveniently means they don't work, since the sugarcane industry has been going to shit ever since I been here. The last field up north is ready to close down."

"Can't help that," said Nestor.

Leilani settled in and followed Devlin's advice. Listen ninety-nine percent, ask one percent. So far it had worked.

The four of them talked about the town until she and Janet finished their second beers, then Leilani announced that she wanted to turn in. Janet said she did, too. Nestor and Phillip urged them to stay. Leilani was about to politely refuse when a blond woman walked in. She sat down on the other side of Nestor and Phillip and said, "Come on, Philly, buy me a drink!"

Phillip laughed and said, "Okay, Amanda, just one."

Her slurred voice and rheumy eyes told Leilani that the woman was already drunk, but nobody seemed to mind.

She didn't wait for Phillip to order for her. She yelled to the bartender, "Joey! Rum and ginger."

The only response she got from the bartender was a frown, but he grabbed a glass and made her drink.

Janet and Leilani walked out as the boys struck up a conversation with Amanda.

Leilani heard her ask in a raspy, drunken voice, "Who's the fuckin' Polynesian princess with Janet? She end up here by mistake or somethin'?"

Back to the real Pahoa-town, thought Leilani.

CHAPTER 33

Devlin and Tuli brought the shotguns and ammunition into the safehouse and laid everything on the table for cleaning, including Devlin's Sig-Sauer. Then he picked up the phone and dialed Pacific Rim. As soon as the night-duty officer came on, he started talking. He gave instructions to pick up and replace Tuli's damaged truck and his Ford in the McDonald's parking lot.

There was one message on the safehouse phone answering machine left twenty minutes ago telling Devlin to call Leilani at the restaurant.

Devlin dialed the number from memory. A woman answered.

"Leilani?"

"Yes."

"Can you talk?"

"Not too long. It's a little late. I'll make it fast. Learned a lot tonight from the Pahoa ladies. I found out where some of Kee's followers live. Some at his ranch. A few near town. The Filipino guy, the skinny one you got in that fight with, lives nearest town."

"Do you know his name?"

"Angel. He lives south of town. You have to go around on the old Red Road and take it to Kamailli Road, then turn back north about a mile. They said the front yard is filled with rusted-out cars, but it's apparently a decent-looking house. There's supposedly a small avocado orchard out back."

"How'd you get such an accurate description?"

"I told them I couldn't believe such a scummy guy could live on a nice piece of property. They gave me a lot of details. Christ, everybody in this town knows everything about each other. Apparently, his mother owns the property."

"He lives with his mother?"

"And other family members. Brothers, aunts, cousins. You know how it is around here."

"Is he home from the hospital?"

"Oh yeah. The whole clan is supposedly after you for what you did to him."

"Good."

"What are you going to do?"

"Bring him a get-well card."

"Jeezus, Devlin, you'd better be careful."

Devlin didn't respond.

"I also got a line on Kee's ranch, too. Not the exact location, but I can show you the approximate location on a map."

"All right, look, you're doing great, but I want you to relax now and lay low."

"What happened?"

"I'll tell you when I see you."

"When will that be?"

"What time do you finish lunch tomorrow?"

"About two-thirty."

"Can you get wheels?"

"Yes."

"Pick me up a hundred yards west of the safehouse at three. Just stop on the side of the road. I'll climb in if there's nobody in sight."

"Are you all right?" Leilani asked.

"Yes. You better go."

"See you tomorrow."

"Tomorrow. Thanks."

Tuli had re-filled the magazine for Devlin's Sig-Sauer and reloaded both of the shotguns.

Devlin carefully removed his polo shirt and Kevlar vest. He tried to look over his shoulder where the bullet had hit him.

Tuli said, "Don't look. Gonna be even more big and ugly tomorrow. Did it break any ribs?"

Devlin raised his left arm, rolled his shoulder. "No. I don't think so."

"Be just a bad bruise."

Devlin pulled open the Velcro closure on the back of the vest and pulled out a metal plate. The fibers of the vest had mushroomed the bullet, setting it up to be stopped by the plate. None of that reduced the impact to Devlin's body.

Tuli said, "Good stuff, huh."

"Yeah. This vest is something new. Made in the Netherlands. You should try it."

"Got one big enough?"

"We'll have to work on that. Listen, clean up, eat, grab some sleep if you can. We're heading back out soon."

"What for?"

"It's time to go on offense. Whoever these guys are, they've been ahead of us every step. Every time we make a move, we get shot at."

"These lolos weren't that far ahead of you, Jacky boy. Dat's why you wore the damn vest."

"And why I brought you along."

"Think we'll have the vehicles by then?"

"If not, your truck will good enough for now."

Tuli smiled. "This time we be the ones who shoot first, aye, boss."

CHAPTER 34

Sam Kee didn't speak as he drove from Hilo to the high school parking lot outside Pahoa. He thought about getting out of his truck, walking up to that asshole McWilliams, and shooting him, but he knew he'd have to swallow more haole shit from the maniac before this was over.

He hammered his fist on his knee. "Fuck."

His driver looked at him but said nothing.

"One fucking guy. All set up. They couldn't take him out. Supposed to be some kine of super-soldiers. Didn't do shit."

"What'd you think happened?"

"I don't know. They must've missed. Don't ask me how. Fuck!"

McWilliams stood waiting in the dark behind the high school when Kee arrived. His men were nowhere to be seen, but Kee knew they were somewhere with eyes on their boss.

Before Kee got within three feet of McWilliams, the soldier said, "I presume you weren't successful preventing the target's escape."

Kee yelled back. "He was supposed to be dead."

"Lack of intelligence, my friend. He was shot center mass. Bullet didn't penetrate. He was wearing body armor. That, plus following bad orders to avoid a head shot so as not to kill the policeman ruined the kill."

"He fucking had a back-up, too. Did you know that? Fucking giant with a goddamn shotgun."

"Please don't raise your voice, Mr. Kee. Every battle isn't a win.

Let's refocus and move on. Devlin will be taken care of."

"How?"

"Leave that to me. For now..."

Kee yelled, "You fuck up one more time, I'm going to kill that fucking guy with my own fucking hands."

McWilliams spoke calmly. "Yes, I understand. But for now, you're going to lead us to where the fucking shipment is stored. I want it fucking loaded and on its fucking way before fucking daylight. Am I making myself fucking clear, Mr. Kee?"

"Yeah, yeah."

"Give me coordinates for the trucks."

Kee handed McWilliams a piece of paper with numerical values for latitude and longitude.

"Just the one location?"

"Yeah, plus what's at the ranch."

"How many men have you lined up?"

"Ten. They're waiting for us now."

"Excellent, Mr. Kee."

Standing in the field behind the school, the moonlight revealed the deadpan expression that seemed to be McWilliam's only look. Kee hated that look, but he feared the eyes. They were the eyes of a someone who enjoyed killing humans.

McWilliams interrupted Kee's thoughts. He shined a penlight on a topo map of the southeast quadrant of the Big Island. Kee pointed to an area southwest of Opihikau. "See this section here. The old '85 flow?"

"Yes," said McWilliams.

"There's a lava tube right about here. It's a big tube, but it's hidden by a pali."

"The coordinates are accurate?"

"Yeah. The half-tons can get within about a mile or so. My guys have two ATVs you can use to bring the stuff to the trucks."

"Understood."

McWilliams raised his arm, and a Humvee appeared in the school parking lot. The only person in the car was the driver. There was no sign of McWilliams's other two men.

McWilliams led Kee to the Humvee's passenger seat, as he radioed in the coordinates and an explanation of where the trucks should meet them.

McWilliams climbed into the backseat where he could keep an eye on Kee. As they pulled out of the high school parking lot, Kee folded his big tattooed arms and sat back. He was tired. And he knew he was going to be more tired very soon. But not too tired to kill crazy fucking McWilliams. And that goddamn haole bastard, Devlin.

CHAPTER 35

Pacific Rim delivered the replacement vehicles just before Devlin was about to leave. This time a blue Toyota Tacoma for Tuli. A white Toyota Camry for Devlin. By 2:06 A.M. they were slowly driving the blue truck past Angel's house south of Pahoa.

There were no lights on in the house. No streetlights. Tuli had turned off his headlights. The black asphalt road was barely visible under the cloudy sky.

Devlin told Tuli to continue past the house and turn around at a bend in the road about three hundred yards ahead of them.

When Tuli finished turning the truck, Devlin said to him, "Okay, here's the drill. Keep the lights off. Drive back slowly. Park near the house. Leave the keys in the ignition and the doors closed but not shut. We walk into the front yard together. There's probably some mongrel dogs living around the place, probably in those junk cars, so when we set foot on that property, they're going to raise hell."

Tuli held up his weapons. In his left hand, he held a Mossberg 590, fully-loaded. He'd added a tactical flashlight under the barrel and a sling. In his right hand, he had a lead-filled, twenty-six-inch, hardwood fighting stick.

"I'll smack or blast 'em. Don't worry."

"Just do it fast and keep moving."

"Fast or slow, whoever is in there is gonna wake up quick quick, boss."

"Just don't let anything stop you from getting around to the back of the house. I'll go in the front door. If I flush him out the back, take him."

"What's he look like?"

"Little guy. Long hair, goatee, and a broken wrist."

"Shit. That's all we're after?"

"That's all. But we have no idea who else is in that damn house. Put down anybody who comes out of there fast. And if it's this Angel guy, don't give him a fucking inch. He's a sneak. He'll have a bullet or a knife in you before you know it. Take him down quick and get him in the truck. But don't hurt him so bad he can't talk. I need answers tonight."

"Okay, boss."

Tuli drove the Tacoma up the road and parked it. The house still looked quiet. Devlin realized that all the windows in front were covered.

Devlin said, "I think we might be lucky on the dogs. Nothing's barking yet."

"Probably all in the back."

"Careful."

"You, too, Jacky, man. Dat fuckin' house is creepy."

They both stepped out together, both with shotguns. Devlin reached behind him and checked the Sig in his waistband holster. Devlin looked at the house, then up and down the road. All was quiet.

Devlin tipped his head toward the house, and they slowly walked to the driveway on the left. Devlin held his hand up again and went down on one knee. He looked closely at the house in front of him. It was so quiet that he thought the house might be empty, but the place fit Leilani's description exactly. There were two rusted-out cars in front, and the area was overgrown with a tangle of grass and bushes. Vegetation around one of the rusted-out junkers had grown almost to the roof of the car. There was a four-foot-high crumbling rock wall running along the road, ending at the driveway. Parallel to the house on the right side, a two-track road led out to the fields. The house was one story, which gave Devlin some consolation. He hated the idea of going into a strange, dark house, not knowing who or what was inside, but at least there wouldn't be anybody coming down on him from above.

His only advantage was surprise. He wanted to get in, find Angel, and get out before anybody was fully awake.

Again, Devlin checked his waistband holster to make sure the Sig was secure. He pointed to the left side of the house and made a circular motion. Tuli nodded.

Devlin whispered, "Ready?"

Tuli nodded. Each pumped his shotgun to chamber a round and stood up. The sound of the guns was all it took to make the first dog start barking. Both men ran full speed toward the house.

Tuli charged forward, the Mossberg slung across his chest, the fighting stick in his right hand.

Devlin took off quicker than the big Samoan, but Tuli was moving amazingly fast for a man his size. He peeled off left and headed for the back of the house just as a pack of three dogs came skidding around the corner into the front yard. A fourth dog, a huge mastiff who had been sleeping under the front porch, burst out heading straight for Devlin.

Tuli stopped, dropped the stick, pulled the Mossberg into position, pumped two shots into the snarling, barking pack. He picked up his stick and ran. The two blasts of double-aught shot, fired from less than ten yards away, blew the two lead dogs into pieces and knocked down the third. Tuli leapt over the carcasses, smacked the dog still alive in the head and kept right on moving.

The dog after Devlin was closer and faster than the others. Devlin slowed down so he could steady the Mossberg with two hands and fire. Most of the snarling dog's head disappeared in the explosion. The mastiff let out one shriek when it was hit, the torso twisted backward, and the remains landed in a bloody heap as Devlin ran for the front porch.

Somebody must have been sleeping in the front room, because just as Devlin leapt onto the porch, the front door of the farmhouse opened, and a man stepped out with a rifle. As the occupant tried to shoulder the rifle, Devlin levered the butt of the shotgun up into the underside of his jaw. The shooter's head snapped back, he fell into the doorway, the rifle banged into the door frame and fell onto the porch. Devlin smashed the butt of the Mossberg into the shooter's chest, knocking him back into the house and onto the floor.

The front door opened onto one large room, cluttered with furniture. The man fell in an awkward heap, his head cocked at a sharp angle. Devlin kicked a lever-action Winchester .22 out onto the front yard, dropped into a crouch, and swept the dark room with his Mossberg's tactical flashlight.

If other people had been sleeping in the front room, they were gone. Devlin heard noises from the back of the house. It sounded like someone banging into a door. A woman was yelling something over and over again in Tagalog, and Devlin thought he heard a dog whining and yelping in the backyard.

Devlin stood up from his crouch and ran into the front room toward a dark hallway three yards ahead of him. Just before he reached the hallway entrance, a dog came running out of the darkness as if someone had just released it. The dog hardly made a sound except for its feet scrabbling on the hardwood floor. The flashlight showed a dark shape coming at him so fast that Devlin was barely able to duck as the dog lunged for his throat. The belly of the dog slammed into Devlin's head, knocking him on his back. The dog landed behind Devlin, slid, and spun around trying to sink his teeth into Devlin's head. Devlin was flat on his back with the shotgun pointing behind him. He pulled the trigger blindly, rolled over, and jumped to his feet looking for the dog. He saw an inert shape and turned back into the hallway, stumbling forward, off-balance, intent on getting to the back of the house as fast as possible. He could see now that there was a light on back there. He kept the Mossberg pointed straight ahead and had gone forward only four or five steps when a large body burst out of a room to his left and crashed into him, driving him through a door and into a bathroom.

Devlin was driven into a sink, painfully smashing his right hip. Somebody had him in a crushing bear hug. He turned his head and saw that the man was Chinese. He had to be one of the biggest Chinese men Devlin had ever seen. Devlin's arms were pinned to his sides. He had managed to hold onto the shotgun in his right hand, but he couldn't point it or pull the trigger. The shotgun was useless and holding onto it meant Devlin couldn't do anything to break the crushing grip that was preventing him from breathing and caused incredible pain to his already bruised back.

He managed to engage the safety on the Mossberg and then drop it. Both of Devlin's hands were empty now, but the Chinese man lifted him and smashed him against the bathroom wall on the left. Devlin grunted in pain. He could just barely inhale. And just then another man appeared in the doorway holding a club of some sort. He was angling to smash Devlin's head with it, but the first attacker was in between, and he couldn't get a clear shot.

Devlin tried to pull his arms apart to break the giant's grip, but the Chinaman increased his pressure and twisted Devlin around so that his partner could hit him. Devlin saw now that the second attacker, a Filipino, was holding a cut-down pool cue. He heard a man and a woman yelling in Tagalog. The one with the pool-cue butt reared back and swung again. Devlin was just able to twist away from the downward blow, but the cue butt caught his right shoulder.

The next attempt was sure to connect. Devlin snarled. No way he was going to let some bastard crack his skull in a stinking bathroom on a back road in Hawaii.

He threw himself backward, using all his strength to crook his arms at the elbow, trying to gain leverage to raise the Chinese attacker's grip higher. He managed to lift the giant's vice-like grip, but the attacker responded by increasing the pressure. Devlin felt as if his chest and spine were being crushed.

The second attacker near the doorway had the pool cue upraised and was aiming for a third try. Devlin braced his feet and just managed to turn and get the Chinaman in between them. Then he reared back again, this time with all the snap he could muster and smashed his forehead into the Chinaman's nose. The bone cracked, he howled in pain, and Devlin felt the strength in the big man's grip waver. Devlin reared back and butted him again, and the grip weakened further. He exerted a huge, sudden effort, lifting his arms, and finally broke free from the giant, just in time to duck another swing from the pool cue. He pulled the Chinese in front of him, blocking any more swings, grabbed him by the head, and pulled his bleeding face down hard into his right knee.

The giant collapsed onto the bathroom floor.

Devlin then threw himself at the man with the pool cue, driving him into the wall outside the bathroom. He held him by the throat against the wall with his left hand and snapped a brutal right hook into his temple. The man's eyes rolled back, and he collapsed. When he hit the floor, Devlin drove a foot down into his head.

Devlin picked up the pool-cue butt and threw it out into the front room. He turned back and went into the bathroom. The first attacker was on his knees, struggling to stand, but he was too disoriented. Devlin looked for the Mossberg and found that it had been kicked over next to the bathtub. He shoved past the Chinese man to get the shotgun, but the big man grabbed for Devlin, caught the back of his pants, and dragged him back. He wrapped his arms around Devlin's waist. Devlin curse. The giant didn't know how to fight, but he sure as hell knew how to grab and smash. Suddenly Devlin heard shotgun blasts from outside the back of the house. A man shouted in pain; women screamed. Devlin quickly twisted two elbow shots into the big man's face, breaking teeth and sending blood spattering against the bathroom mirror. The giant fell back against the sink, and his huge weight tore it out of the wall. The pipes behind it broke, and water sprayed all over the bathroom.

Devlin turned to look for the shotgun as a man came rushing past the bathroom. He turned back into the hallway to see if it was Angel, but whoever it was had already made it out of sight into the kitchen and probably out the back door.

He turned once more to retrieve the Mossberg and could hardly believe it. The big Chinaman was staggering toward him.

Devlin yelled, "Are you fucking crazy?"

The attacker responded by trying to grab Devlin again. Devlin straight-armed him and punching hard right-hand shots into the man's already broken nose and teeth. The giant gurgled in pain, grabbed for Devlin's head, and toppled backward like a felled tree. Devlin kept punching his face until he hit the floor.

The man was finally unconscious. Devlin straightened up and grabbed the Mossberg lying in a pool of bloody water. He wiped it on the shower curtain and turned back toward the hallway.

When he stepped into the hallway, he caught sight of a man in the kitchen with a gun. He just managed to duck back into the bathroom before the gunshot exploded.

There was enough light in the kitchen for Devlin to see that it was Angel. He was shooting with his left hand. His right arm was in a cast. Probably why he had missed.

A woman in the kitchen started screaming when Angel let off another round.

From inside the bathroom, Devlin aimed the Mossberg toward the hallway ceiling and fired, blowing apart plaster and lathe. He stepped out of the bathroom turned, pumped, and fired the Mossberg at the kitchen ceiling, and kept firing as he advanced step by step toward Angel, who was covering his head and trying to shield himself from the falling debris.

The explosions from the Mossberg disoriented Angel. The Filipino blindly held his gun out and steadied himself to fire, but it was too late. Devlin smacked the gun aside with the barrel of the Mossberg and shoved the hot muzzle of the gun into Angel's face. Angel almost fell down as Devlin yelled, "Drop it! Drop the fucking gun."

Angel threw the gun down. Tuli had been standing right outside the back door. When he saw that Devlin had Angel, he came into the kitchen holding his Mossberg, ready to shoot anyone who tried to intervene.

"What the fuck took you so long, boss?"

"Next time you go in the front door. Here!" Devlin shoved Angel toward Tuli. The Samoan punched him in the back of the head, grabbed him around the waist, and lifted him to his shoulder like a child. He turned and strode out the door.

Devlin turned and told the still screaming Filipino woman, "Shut up and get out!" He grabbed her by the arm and pushed her out the door. He had no idea who she was.

Tuli stood in the yard, waiting for Devlin.

"Did you shoot anyone?"

"No."

Devlin pushed the woman down onto the ground. There was a teenage boy, a middle-aged woman, an older man, and a dead dog.

"All of you stay down there for ten minutes. You move, I'll shoot you. You call the cops, I'll come back and kill you."

Tuli turned and trotted back toward the car with the unconscious Angel bouncing on his shoulder. Devlin followed silently, making sure nobody moved and watching for anyone who might be hiding. He kept the Mossberg pointed and ready to fire. He looked to make sure the crazy Chinaman wasn't coming out of the house, then turned and ran to catch up with Tuli.

Tuli deposited Angel in the bed of the pickup, immobilizing him with duct tape. He and Devlin jumped in the truck and drove off.

CHAPTER 36

Tuli parked the Tacoma out of sight behind the safehouse. He carried Angel into the inside. Devlin followed with the weapons.

"How hard did you hit him back there?"

"Not enough to break his head."

"I want him to be able to talk."

"He'll talk. Tuli gonna play the Mu for this guy. He'll be talking so much you gonna have to yell at him to stop, boss."

"What's the Mu?" asked Devlin.

Tuli said, "You'll see."

When they entered the house, Tuli deposited the semi-conscious Angel in a sturdy wooden chair set at the end of the dining room table. Devlin headed for the bathroom. His hands, face, and clothes were spattered with blood and spit and dirt.

He came out of the bathroom as cleaned up as he could get without taking a shower. He didn't look forward to this. He wished he could make it fast and easy, and avoid the disgusting, demeaning parts that he knew were coming, but he had no choice.

Devlin was going to play the good guy. He knew Tuli had no trouble playing the bad guy. Tuli considered Angel as no more entitled to mercy than the mongrel dogs they had shot an hour ago. Even less so since Tuli knew that unlike a dog, Angel had a choice. He chose to be the kind who would shoot you or stab you the second you turned your back. There wasn't any doubt in Devlin's mind that if necessary Tuli would snap Angel's neck in a second.

Devlin sat at the corner of the dining table with a glass of water. He said nothing to Angel and didn't offer him anything to drink. Tuli had disappeared into the kitchen which gave Angel back some of his bravado.

Devlin said, "Who was that fucking big Chinaman trying to kill me?"

"My cousin, asshole. An' you are a dead man whether you know it or not."

Devlin didn't react to Angel's threat. He drank most of the water as Angel watched him. He stood up, walked over to his backpack, and extracted a manila folder. He laid the folder down on the table in front of Angel. Tuli appeared with a coiled rope. Angel turned when he saw Tuli and tried to stand, but Tuli shoved him back in the chair and looped the rope over his head and shoulders, pulling Angel's left arm free before he wound the line tightly around the small man's body, securing him to the chair.

Angel said, "What the fuck you doing?"

Nobody responded. Tuli motioned for Angel to raise his left hand. Angel didn't. Tuli slapped him hard across the face and grabbed Angel's arm. He tied the rope tightly around Angel's left wrist and dropped his arm on the dining table. Tuli walked out of the room and came back carrying a two-by-four length of wood about a foot long, a hammer, and a handful of three-inch nails. He went to the other end of the dining table and nailed the two-by-four to the end of the table.

During Tuli's preparation Devlin sat and looked through the file that Chow had given him at the Mandarin Hotel in San Francisco.

Next, Tuli grabbed the rope attached to Angels left wrist and looped the rope around the upright two-by-four one time, then slowly pulled the slack out of the rope until Angel's arm was extended across the table. When Tuli was finished, Angel's chest was tight against the dining table, his arm out in front of him.

Devlin looked up. "Okay," he said, "here's the deal." He laid out the pictures of Billy Cranston's ravaged body in front of Angel. "You and your friends did this. You either did it yourselves. Or you caused it to happen. Or you know who did."

Angel would not look at the pictures. Now Devlin's nice-guy act disappeared. He grabbed Angel's long hair and forced his face down until his eyes were inches from the photographs.

"Look at them."

Angel screamed, "You can't do this. You can't do this."

Devlin pulled Angel's head up. "Why? Because this is against the law?"

"Yes," yelled Angel.

Devlin said quietly and slowly, "Look at the fucking pictures. Your rights died with him. You have no rights here. There is no law here except my law."

Tuli pulled the rope just a bit, then looped it once around the two-by-four to keep the pressure on. Pain stabbed at every joint in Angel's arm.

"Do you know what the law was on this island before scum like you came here? Before the haole like me came here?" Devlin pointed to Tuli. "Men like him were the law. If someone like you broke the kapu, broke the trust of civilized people – they'd rip you to pieces and let you die."

Devlin pointed to Tuli holding the rope, staring at Angel, no expression on his broad face. "He would have killed you already. I'm giving you a chance to live."

"What do you want?"

"The truth. Everything you know. And if I don't think it's the truth," Devlin looked at Tuli. The Samoan pulled the rope tighter. Angel screamed. "He'll snap every joint in your arm. And the next arm. And then he'll kill you, and we'll leave you in the forest for the pigs like you left my friend."

Angel gasped for breath and said, "Okay, okay."

Tuli eased off on the rope a bit so Angel could breathe. And then he started talking, just like Tuli said he would. He talked so much Devlin couldn't shut him up.

Devlin had very little information to verify what Angel was saying, so he had to make him repeat each part of his garbled story so he could sort out the truth from the half-truths and lies. The fact that English was not the Filipino's first language didn't make it any easier.

Twice Tuli had to pull the rope, the last time nearly tearing apart Angel's shoulder joint before Angel's story became somewhat coherent and consistent.

It took almost an hour, with Angel screaming and sobbing at the end of it. It disgusted Devlin to see the mean little man with his long hair and stylish goatee who had been posturing and threatening him turn into a pathetic, sniveling coward.

Devlin raised a hand to Tuli, and he released the rope.

Devlin pushed Angel back in the chair and said, "We go through it once more. You have one chance to tell me the truth. You do, we're done. If not, I'll have to walk out. I don't want to see what he'll do to you."

Devlin tried patiently for another half-hour. So did Angel. Devlin motioned for Tuli to step outside. They left the Filipino slumped at the table.

Devlin said, "He's done."

He rubbed his face and looked at his watch. It was nearly five. The sun would be up soon. His clothes stank from the fight at Angel's house and the stress of the interrogation.

Tuli nodded. "Ought to throw the little piece of shit into a hole and cover 'im up. He worthless, man. What do you think about what he said?"

"To get everything out of him and make sense of it would take days. Right now, it's a jumbled mess. He keeps blaming Kee for everything. Swears he wasn't out there in the forest preserve when whatever happened to Billy took place."

"You believe that?"

"Yes."

"Me too."

"He's also saying something about Kee working for the big man, but I don't believe he knows who that is. Then there's all that shit about nobody messes with the big man. And all that babbling about moving stuff. Smuggling stuff along the old routes they used for pakalolo, which they're still running. He says the new stuff is military arms, but he says Kee doesn't let him around that so he doesn't know what they're smuggling."

Tuli said, "That don't surprise me. He's a worthless little shit."

"Then there's the bullshit about Sam Kee going to take over the island. Return everything to the natives. I've already heard that nonsense."

Tuli said, "Yeah, but a bunch of lolo assholes with automatic weapons still can be a lotta trouble."

"I know. Clearly, Kee and his men have military assault rifles. They were crazy enough to try to use them on us in that goddamn jungle and on a public street in Hilo." Devlin tapped Tuli's shoulder. "Fuck it. Tie him up, lock him in the basement. Let's clean up and get some sleep."

"Then what?"

"We keep at it."

CHAPTER 37

After meeting with Kee, Engle, and McWilliams at Kee's ranch to plan the ambush of Devlin, Eddie Lihu had driven to an area just outside Hilo called Wainaku. He owned a small house there and used it as his headquarters when he had dealings on the Big Island. The house was completely nondescript. It was a fifteen-minute drive to the harbor and the airport, two very important locations for Lihu's business dealings.

A woman named Alina White lived in the house. She functioned as Lihu's housekeeper/mistress. Alina had worked for eight years as a Madame at one of Lihu's whorehouses in Honolulu, ruling with the iron fist of a privileged kahuna. She was a big woman, a very big woman, but Lihu found her size appealing. On the rare occasion when he had sex with her, it was mostly perfunctory pushing and grunting between two extremely overweight people, but Lihu was able to satisfy himself quickly and, most importantly, without embarrassment. In Alina's company, he didn't feel obese or ugly. And she treated him like a king. She prepared his food for him in the ancient Hawaiian custom of always using utensils, so she never touched any of the food with her own hands. She kept a special set of sheets, pillowcases, and towels for him. If Alina were menstruating, she wouldn't even be in the same room with him unless he insisted. She never raised her voice around him and kept her eyes down in his presence. It was a ridiculous old act based on outmoded Hawaiian kapus (laws), but Alina was very good at it, and Lihu liked it. And since he only used the house once or twice a month, Alina had no trouble playing her role as an outcast slave to the Big Alii.

But on this morning, nothing she did satisfied him. Lihu had slept through the night and awakened at eight o'clock. He sat in her kitchen reading the morning papers blazing with the news about the shooting at McDonald's. A huge amount of publicity and risk that accomplished nothing. Because no one had been killed, much of the story had to do with an extraordinary number of bullets fired in the area behind the McDonald's. Lihu pictured what had happened. McWilliams most likely assigned Kee to guard that area, figuring he'd take care of Delvin, and Kee would have nothing to do. Somehow, Devlin had tried to escape out the back giving Kee an excuse to fire twenty rounds into the McDonald's backdoor, and dozens more in the alley.

The paper speculated about military-style assault rifles. Luckily, they didn't speculate that the weapons were actual military rifles. But this was getting way too close to Lihu's operation. Worse, Devlin was out there able to cause trouble. What should have been one bullet in the back was now a complete fucking mess.

Lihu sat at Alina's kitchen table, not even touching his breakfast, his gross features set in deep thought. "Fucking shit," Lihu muttered to himself. All he had needed was four more days. Two to transport his material to Hilo harbor, one or two to get it all on a ship. And then this guy shows up. If anything more happened, the island would be shut down tight. It might not even be possible to get himself off the island.

Lihu calmly calculated his options and decided had no choice. He had to keep doing what he was doing, faster than he'd ever done it before. He had to transport the rest of his stolen goods off the island, shut down the operation, and eliminate all traces. Cover his trail. Sell everything, whatever the price.

Yes, eventually it might all lead back to the Army, but he could cover his tracks there, too. No good thing lasted forever. Time to end it.

He picked up the phone on Alina's kitchen table and dialed. This time he didn't use the beeper number. He dialed Walker's office at Schofield directly. He gave the code name he and Walker had agreed on. When Walker came on the line, Lihu didn't waste time. "Get up from your desk, get the inventory information, and leave the base now. Now. Don't talk. Don't do anything but leave. Stay out of sight and meet me at the bitch's apartment, noon, not twelve-thirty, not two minutes after twelve, noon."

Lihu didn't wait for an answer. He hung up and dialed again, and this time Engle picked up the receiver in Kee's office.

"It's me," said Lihu.

"Yes."

"Where's Kee?"

"I assume with McWilliams and his people loading up the last shipments."

"You haven't seen him since last night?"

"No."

"Call me when you hear from McWilliams that they're done loading. As soon as that's confirmed, get the fuck out of that town and get back to Oahu."

"Understood."

Lihu hung up the phone and yelled, "Charlie."

The big bodyguard walked into the kitchen. Lihu checked his watch. He told Charlie, "Get the fucking car. We're going to the airport. I got something to do in Honolulu."

CHAPTER 38

The official police report went through channels very quickly. On Sunday morning at exactly 9:48 A.M. a report that provided more details than the newspaper stories was placed on the desk of Major General James Hawthorne, CO of the Army 25th Infantry Division, Schofield Barracks

General Hawthorne was a 1990s version of a 1950s Army officer. Thin, intense, and Army-issue right down to his plain black-frame glasses. Hawthorne had served in both Korea and Vietnam, but at heart he was more bureaucrat than warrior.

By 10:22 A.M. he had finished reading the report. Twice. The first reading told him something serious was going on. The second reading helped him assess the most important part – how much this bad news going to affect his career?

Hawthorne went about his analysis systematically. He hadn't risen to the rank of major general without being systematic. He prided himself on being an objective analyst.

First, although the newspapers only speculated, the official police report stipulated that the rounds fired behind McDonald's were almost definitely from an Army-issue M16. Luckily, they could not assess if there was more than one rifle. But even one missing M16 would cause great concern. Hawthorne's instincts told him if there was one M16 missing from his base, there could be more. One rifle, maybe even two, Hawthorne could probably contain the publicity. Particularly, if they quickly found those responsible.

But more, and his career would be in serious jeopardy. Hawthorne could not let that happen.

The General called in his aide-de-camp, a West Point lieutenant who would never be any good at combat, but who was hell on wheels when it came to administration. Hawthorne began talking the minute the lieutenant entered.

"Issue the following orders: All division personnel will report to their immediate commanding officer. All personnel will be restricted to base immediately. I want a roll call report of every man assigned to the division on this desk by twelve-hundred hours, and the exact location of any man not on base. I want the entire command staff assembled in my conference room at fourteen-hundred hours."

"Yes, sir. Is that all, sir?"

"No. Get Crimmins from Military Police, and the PM Weisman, in here ASAP."

"Yes, sir."

"Get it done."

CHAPTER 39

Waking up was easy. Getting out of the bed wasn't. Devlin's arm's, chest, and shoulders hurt from the Chinaman's bear hug. His hip ached where he banged into the sink. The impact from the bullet hitting his back made it difficult to breathe. The knuckles on both hands were scabbed and swollen from hitting the guy with the pool cue and the Chinaman. He had a painful bruise on his forehead from the head butts.

The only things that didn't hurt were his feet.

He spent two hours icing his swollen hands and bruises. Then he ate. Then he sorted and arranged their cache of weapons. All the while thinking about the jumble of information Angel had spewed out.

He called Mrs. Banks. He made several requests and then left the safehouse leaving Tuli sleeping peacefully in the downstairs bedroom.

He walked down the road. It was a quiet afternoon. Overcast. The sky was hidden by a thick bank of rain-filled gray clouds. Devlin hoped Leilani arrived before the rain started.

He was wearing a short-sleeve denim shirt, hiking shorts, and cross trainers. The Sig was in his waistband holster. He carried his backpack. Inside were the small Beretta, a towel, and his swimsuit. But he really had no intention of hiking or swimming. He heard Leilani's truck. He checked his watch. Three o'clock exactly. She pulled up, and Devlin slowly climbed into the cab.

Leilani looked at him and said, "My God, you look terrible."

"I feel terrible."

"What happened?"

"Where are we going?"

"Not far."

"You're not planning another hike, are you?"

"Not really."

"Okay, I'll tell you what happened while you drive. Then you can tell me the latest.

Leilani drove west, and Devlin talked.

She took the first turnoff toward the ocean. Within ten minutes, she slowed down and drove off the highway onto an overgrown two-track road. About a hundred meters in, the road ended at a mound of rocks and dirt. She parked Walter's truck. Devlin had finished giving her a summary of the previous night's events. By the time he was finished, Leilani had lapsed into silence.

She knew Devlin was skimming over the details, but she couldn't help filling them in for herself. He had been sent to a meeting where he was supposed to be killed. At least two men were involved in trying to shoot him. Maybe more. Kee was involved, too. Devlin had used her information to break into a house in the middle of the night and abduct someone in order to get information.

"What's the matter?" asked Devlin.

Leilani frowned. "I'm not used to this sort of thing."

Devlin said, "Of course not. Why should you be?"

"With all that, I'm surprised you're not telling me I should leave."

"We've covered that. It's up to you."

Leilani nodded and said, "I have a lot to tell you. But you need to see this place first."

Leilani handed him a bottle of water from her backpack.

"Drink. I heard about something that will help you feel better."

Devlin took several swallows.

"Drink more."

"Why?"

"Because you're going to be sweating soon. Come on, I'll show you."

They left the truck, and she led Devlin down an overgrown, rocky trail for about two-hundred meters. They continued past a pile of lava rocks covered in ferns. Even in the overcast, misty air Devlin could see trails of steam rising through the dark rocks. It reminded him of the mysterious wisps of steam that often rose out of sewer covers in Manhattan. As they walked, Leilani explained.

"One of the women in town told me about a natural steam bath around here. Very healing. Very special."

"A natural steam bath?"

"Yes, deep underneath this area, all around, there's heat from active lava flowing under the surface, from lava that's still cooling. Some of it rises up as thermal heat. All that heat makes the sub-surface very hot. Rainwater percolates down and hits hot rock and turns into steam. Sometimes it finds a way out."

They continued on, following the trail around a bend until they came upon the base of what looked to Devlin like a miniature mountain about thirty feet high. The trail ended at the base. Leilani walked around to the other side. Devlin followed. On the far side, what had looked like a little mountain now looked like a miniature volcano. Wisps of steam rose from an open crater at the top.

Leilani climbed up the side to the rim. Devlin followed and at the rim saw clouds of steam rising from inside. As soon as the steam rose above the rim, the brisk winds dissipated it.

They climbed over the rim and stood on a small ledge that ran around the inside of the narrow crater. At the bottom was a flat surface about ten feet in diameter. A makeshift wooden ladder that led down to the bottom. At the far side, there was an oval opening in the rock wall. Billows of steam flowed gently out of the opening, exuding a soft, inviting mineral smell.

Leilani stepped onto the ladder and climbed down.

"Come on."

Devlin followed her down and across to the opening in the wall. He felt the hot steam as it flowed around his bare legs.

Leilani took off her backpack and propped it on a natural shelf in the wall. Then she leaned back against the side of the wall and pulled off her hiking boots. She carefully placed them next to her pack and continued undressing much as she had done on the beach. T-shirt, shorts, panties, all folded neatly on top of her boots.

Devlin slowly took off his T-shirt while he watched her. He decided Leilani didn't need clothes. Her body was perfect without them. Now that she was naked again, Devlin knew this was the way he wanted to always picture her. Open, free, natural. With her perfect breasts. Her long arms and legs. Her sleek, silky, copper skin. A gust of cool misty air blew down through the opening above. Devlin watched Leilani's aureoles crinkle and pucker as her dark nipples became erect.

Leilani stood before him naked, waiting with a mischievous turned-down half smile, letting him stare at her while she watched him undress.

"Come on," she said. "Strip."

Devlin asked, "You want a strip, or should I just take the rest off?"

"Are you moving that slowly because you're hurt, or because you just want to make me wait?"

"Wait for what?"

Leilani smiled, this time to herself, and said, "Come on Devlin, you need to sweat."

She turned to her backpack and took out two towels, quickly crouched down and ducked into the narrow opening in the wall. Devlin went after her, bending to half his height so he could walk through. He emerged in a circular inner chamber about six feet wide filled with steam that made the walls slick and wet with condensation. Tiny lichens and other mossy growths thrived on the constantly moist surface. Hot steam engulfed him, but occasionally a cooler drop of water would fall on him from above.

For a moment Devlin felt it was too hot to breathe, but his lungs adjusted to the heat, and he slowly breathed in the naturally steamy air.

Inside of the steam-filled cave, just about big enough for two people their size, Leilani had made a pad out of her towel and sat against one wall. Devlin was able to fit into the space if he sat against the wall facing her. She handed him a folded towel, and he placed it down and sat awkwardly, barely able to move in the compact space without making some part of his body hurt.

The wall behind him was flat, wet, and warm. The stone curved nicely so that it supported his back. He settled back against the wall opposite Leilani, then opened his long legs and place a foot on either side of her. She sat opposite him with her legs inside his, her feet inches away from his genitals.

Devlin stared at her in the dim light of the cave, trying to see through the wafting steam that flowed past them toward the entrance. Leilani looked like an ethereal manifestation of a Polynesian goddess. Her dark, wet hair, her perfect South Seas features, the long, perfect nose and erotic down-turned mouth all looked so entrancing as to verge on the unreal. The exquisite folds of her vagina echoed the entrance to a place that suddenly seemed removed from the earth. Devlin felt dizzy and closed his eyes for a moment, letting the naturally moist healing heat of the steam surround him. He could feel his sore muscles loosening, his joints creaking free of the tension, the pain easing away.

He rolled his head to loosen his neck muscles. He felt the moist heat of the steam going in and out of his nose as he breathed in the sulfurous smell, feeling as if it would heal him from the inside while the steam soothed him from the outside. It seemed as if a long time had passed in no time at all.

And then he felt Leilani's lift and bend his knee and begin to slowly massage his right foot with her long fingers. At first, she was gentle, but soon her strong fingers began to probe and knead each part of the bottom of his foot. She squeezed and worked his heel and Achilles tendon. She took each toe and massaged it, worked it, and then quickly pulled it, cracking the joint, releasing more tension.

Devlin looked at Leilani through the mists of steam intently focused on what she was doing. Her muscles rippled under her slick golden skin. Her beautiful face was a vision of concentration. Devlin hoped she would never stop. He relaxed even more, surrendering himself to her.

Now she was working on the left foot. Then the right calf. Then the left. Then the long, tender muscles that ran along Devlin's shins. Devlin was afraid to say anything to break the moment. He sat back and watched her work. Drinking her in. She was dripping with sweat. A drop ran down her long, slender nose and fell off the tip, landing on his knee. The cool drop made an instant electrical connection between them. He watched the muscles in her shoulders and arms and forearms flex and glisten and felt a twitch in his own shoulders.

Now she was working on his knees, using Devlin's sweat as a natural lubricant for her work. Wherever she touched him, the muscles seemed to come alive. It felt almost too good to bear. She leaned forward and effortlessly shifted from her sitting position, flattening the towel in front of her so she could sit up, her legs folded under her to get more reach.

Devlin watched her perfect breasts sway slightly as she gently massaged his left thigh with long, slow, intense two-handed strokes. He felt his cock harden and ached for her to touch him there as her fingers worked up his thigh toward his crotch. He opened his legs farther, silently inviting her, but Leilani slid her magic hands over his hip and across his hard-muscled belly, up his chest.

"You have a beautiful body, Devlin."

Devlin could only make a small guttural noise in response.

She slid her hands over his stomach and chest and started to massage his shoulders now, gently, lightly stroking the bruise where he'd been hit by the butt of the pool cue.

"You have too many battle scars, honey. You've been hurt too many times."

Devlin responded with a quiet "Hhhmmm."

Her face was inches away from his now as she worked on his right shoulder and biceps. Devlin was entranced by the perfect bone structure of her exquisite face. He was suddenly fascinated by the long line of her flawless nose. Her hair had fallen across one eye, but Devlin looked deeply into the other one, seeing past the deep, dark brown, picking out what looked like flecks of gold set deep in the iris.

Devlin tried to breathe in her scent. She smelled like sweet salt and soap. He realized that her face had never been this close to his for so long. He wanted to kiss her, to kiss any part of her face, but he didn't want to do anything that would make her pull away or stop massaging him. Without planning to, Devlin found himself reaching around behind her so he could massage her shoulders and back. She inched forward between his legs, to reach around behind his neck, and her knees nestled into his crotch. He spread his legs farther apart to accommodate her. His breathing quickened, as did Leilani's. His from sexual tension. Hers from exertion.

He slid his hands over her shoulders and down the sides of her rib cage. Her glistening skin was slick and smooth and wet. It felt oiled. He reached up and slowly, slowly cupped her breasts, giving himself time to feel everything about them – the silky skin, the weight, the shape, the soft yet firm give of them. He let his thumbs find her hard nipples and gently massaged them. She bent her head back and let out a small sigh. But she kept massaging the back of his neck, his hard, trapezoid muscles, and the base of his skull.

Devlin let his head fall forward, resting his forehead on her collarbone so he could enjoy each penetrating pull on his neck muscles. He had started to become lost in that one feeling when he felt Leilani straddle his left leg and drop down on his thigh. He felt the slight bristle of her pubic hair and the wetness of her vaginal lips on his skin. He brought his legs together so she could open hers and straddle his lap. She was wide open now, backed up slightly so that her clitoris just touched the bottom side of his erect penis. Gently she moved her hands up from the base of his head and pulled his mouth to her hardened nipple. He licked and tasted her as she slowly pressed her clitoris into the base of his cock.

Devlin took the muscular cheeks of her buttocks in his hands and pulled her toward him. Leilani raised herself up, and Devlin watched the long muscles in her thighs flex as she reached down and took hold of his erection. She held him in position as she slowly put the head of his penis inside her. Devlin groaned quietly as he fought the urge to pull her down on him and penetrate her deeply.

Somehow, she controlled him, made him wait as she slowly, millimeter by millimeter, lowered herself onto him. Devlin felt each exquisite bit of her inside silk as he finally arched up and entered her all the way.

When she had him completely inside, she squeezed his cock with the muscles of her vaginal wall, and then quickly released him. She slid up and down several times as if to test the reality of their being locked together.

Now that they were finally, irrevocably joined, she ground down onto him as if to confirm it once and for all. And then she allowed some other force to take over, and she slowly lifted and lowered herself. Devlin held her rear end tightly, amazed at the firm flexing of her buttocks, helping her up and letting her down. She had both hands on his shoulders and rode him. Now they were each trying to move into the other. And now the urge to climax took over. Devlin released his grip on Leilani's bottom and tried to touch her everywhere before he exploded. She pounded down on him two, three, four times, and Devlin ejaculated. She felt his release inside, and she squeezed him hard, writhing, coaxing, heightening every last bit of his orgasm as she reached her own undulating orgasm.

After a few moments, she slowly leaned down to him, resting her head on his shoulder. They sat and held each other for what seemed a long time, their sweat sealing their skin together. They didn't say a word until finally, Leilani spoke. "We'd better get out of here before we melt."

Devlin croaked out an answer. "Yeah."

They slowly separated from each other, stood up halfway, and ducked back through the opening. They stepped out into a clean, warm, torrential tropical rain pouring down through the opening above them.

Devlin was amazed at how he felt. He had left so much of his pain behind in the steam that he felt as if Leilani had worked some sort of Island magic on him.

Leilani smiled her gleaming white smile and turned her face up into the downpour. The soft rainwater was coming down in sheets.

"Perfect," she yelled.

She stepped over to her pack, pulled out a small bar of soap, and began lathering herself all over. Devlin enjoyed watching her handle herself with such vigor and pleasure. She washed everywhere. She even washed her thick black hair. She handed the bar to Devlin, and he began lathering off the sweat and mineral residue of the steam bath and the scent of their lovemaking.

He scrubbed himself until the small bar of soap disappeared into a sliver. His body felt renewed. The plateau they stood on was covered in foamy, soapy rainwater. Devlin rinsed and rubbed all the soap off as the rain continued to pound down on them. They both rushed, knowing that if the rain stopped suddenly, they'd never get all the slick soap off them. But the rain kept on until they felt new and fresh and clean.

Leilani stayed on her side of the plateau, working the soap out of her hair, edging the soapy water off her body with the palms of her hands. When she finished her rainwater shower, she grabbed her shoes, pack, and clothes in one pile and glided up the wooden ladder. The rain was easing off, but still coming down hard enough to keep them wet.

Leilani slipped into her boots and kept her clothes in a bundle, held close to her to shield them from the rain. She deftly made her way back down the side of the crater and took off at a fast trot toward the ocean, yelling for Devlin to follow her.

Devlin pulled his cross trainers over his wet feet and jogged after her. They found shelter under a large palm tree. Leilani saw goose bumps covering Devlin, and she vigorously rubbed him down with her towel, carefully blotting the wet bandage on his shoulder. She was completely unaffected by the wet. Her dark skin glowed, and she was moving more energetically than Devlin had ever seen her.

By the time she finished rubbing him down, and he had pulled on his T-shirt and shorts, the rain had turned into a fine mist that couldn't penetrate the palm fronds over their heads. The sun was beginning to break through the clouds out over the ocean. Devlin could just see the first glimmer of a huge rainbow forming in the overcast sky.

He dried Leilani off with his towel. When he started on her derriere and long legs, Leilani wisely took the towel from him and finished the job herself.

She dressed as quickly as she had undressed. Devlin enjoyed watching that almost as much as he had enjoyed seeing the reverse.

They sat at the base of the palm trees, dry under the large fronds. Leilani pulled out her bottle of water, and they finished it quickly. There was an awkward moment of silence. Devlin felt like he ought to say something about what had happened, but the feeling faded. It seemed superfluous. Instead, Devlin asked, "You said you had a lot to tell me?"

"Yes. First, I have the location of Kee's ranch." She pulled a map out of her pack and pointed to an area southwest of the Ola'a forest reserve. She pointed to a spot on the map, saying, "It's here. North of Mountain View, west of Kurtistown, off Highway Eleven. I've marked it."

Devlin said, "Great. That's great. You said that some of his men live on the ranch. Do you know how many?"

"No. But the women in town say he has a loose group of about twenty or thirty guys who are part of his gang, or whatever you call it. It's common knowledge that Kee raises whatever big crops of pakalolo are grown around here. It's not anywhere near the volume it used to be, but if it's drugs, Kee controls it."

"And he has thirty men in his crew?"

"At the most. They come and go. All these local guys have cousins and brothers and family. I don't know how many in his group are hardcore."

Devlin nodded. "Anything else?" he asked.

"A couple of things."

"Yes?"

"I finally heard about one person who seemed to be something of a friend to Billy. His name is Lyman. I don't know if that's his first name or last name. He lives not far from here."

She pointed out another spot on the map where Lyman's house was located.

"You find out anything else about him other than he was a friend of Billy's?"

"Well, the description I got was he's kind of a burned-out stoner. But he definitely knew Billy."

"I'll have to talk to him. What else?"

"Well, I'm not sure it's relevant. Kind of like telling you a murderer is a terrible person. But just in case you might want to know, Sam Kee is also a rapist."

"How do you know?" Devlin asked quickly.

"I told you about my women's group meeting last night at the crafts store. Two of the women started talking about how Kee had raped them. He'd come on to them, asked them out, then rape them."

"Did they describe how?"

"Took them to a house, pushed them into bed, and fucked them until he was satisfied. He's probably done it to a lot more than just those two. One said he came to her house and did it again."

"And nobody pressed charges?"

"One of them did."

"What happened?"

"The police said she didn't have enough evidence."

For a few moments, they lapsed into silence. Devlin watched the ocean. Leilani watched him. He seemed to be analyzing what she had told him. Then he turned to her and said, "Okay." He paused. "Listen... "

Leilani cut him off. "Don't start. Don't say it."

"All I want to say is, you've really helped me. Beyond expectations."

"Oh, okay. Thanks."

"But..."

"Oh, here it comes."

"Wait. Listen. All I'm saying is, you should back off now. Lay low. I think I've got everything I need to bust this wide open. And when that happens, you don't want to be here. If you don't want to go now, that's up to you. Just be ready. By that I mean, from now on, you have whatever you need in your pockets to get on a plane and leave in ten seconds. Money, ID, ticket, credit card, whatever. I want you to be able to walk out of that damn town, call a car service, hitchhike, whatever is fastest, go to the airport, and fly out of here."

Leilani made a conscious effort to relax. Despite what Devlin said, she didn't feel close to resolving what happened to her brother, much less punishing whoever was responsible.

She calmly asked, "Do you know who killed Billy?"

"Not yet. But I will. And it goes way beyond Kee. He was involved, I'm sure. But it's more than Kee and marijuana crops and that crap."

"What? What is it?"

Devlin paused. "Trafficking in military arms. I don't know how far it's gone. I do know it involves at least M16s. And if it's more than that…"

"What?"

"Like I said, you won't want to be here."

"What about you? What are you going to do now?"

"Keep going until I find out exactly what happened to Billy and why."

Leilani stood up and looked out at the ocean. She knew now that it had gone beyond her. That there wasn't much more she could do.

"Why do I feel so useless?"

"I don't know. You're the one who's given me what I need to figure this out."

Leilani turned to him. "I guess that's the whole point. It seems to all depend on you. What you think. What you're going to do. I'm the one who has to sit quietly and wait for you to solve this."

Devlin didn't say anything for a while. They both watched the clouds clearing out over the ocean. The hot Hawaiian sun appeared over the water.

Finally, Leilani said, "How much longer until you figure it all out?"

"I'd say a day, two at the most."

She turned to him. "Well, I guess that's it, then." Leilani nodded once. Quickly. As if to confirm the decision with herself. "Walter's been too nice to me to just walk out on him. Let me finish dinner tonight, and set him up for lunch tomorrow, then I'll go."

"Okay. Fine. Here's what I want to do. I'll leave a car for you in the parking lot next to the Village Inn. A white Toyota. The keys will be on top of the back tire. Passenger side."

"Outside the car?"

"Yes. People don't look for keys outside."

"What if they fall on the ground or something?"

"They won't. I'll stick them in the tire tread."

"Okay."

"And there'll be a gun locked in the trunk. Just in case."

"A gun?"

"Just in case. Do you know how to use a gun? It'll be a semi-automatic. Small caliber. Nothing you can't handle."

"Yes. My father taught me. You don't really think I'll need it, do you?"

"No. I don't expect you will. When you're finished with the restaurant, just get in the car and drive to the airport. Leave the car in the lot, the gun in the trunk. Take the first plane home."

"Then what?"

"Stay in Oahu until I get there."

"And then what?"

"Then it will be over. I'll sit with you and your father, and you'll hear my report. If you're satisfied, I'll file it with Pacific Rim."

"And if we're not satisfied?"

"We'll talk about it then."

Leilani burned to ask more, talk more. But she didn't know what to say. And she could tell that Devlin was already planning his next move. Working it out. He was done with her.

She felt deeply unsettled. A combination of anger, sadness, loss, and frustration. She had come to Pahoa to finally, once and for all, do right by Billy. She had done her best, but now she knew that she had been shunted off to the side. She had ended up doing what women always seemed to. She had attached herself to a strong man. Helped him. Comforted him. Enabled him. And now, he had moved on from her. Yes, with honesty and decency, but it still felt the same. Step aside and let the man take over.

But it was more than that. She wanted to do something that

Devlin couldn't do. With her own drive, her own vision. For Billy. For herself. She wanted to move his spirit. To touch the damaged soul of her brother who had died in a world of agony.

Leilani knew she had grown away from the old South Seas myths and religious beliefs that her mother had imbued in her. Even so, the folklore of Polynesia still influenced her enough that she believed joining one's ancestors in the afterworld life of Po was a great gift. Relatives who were not accepted by the deceased were doomed to wander in a netherworld of torture as ghosts or lapu. Leilani knew she had not saved Billy from his ghostly wanderings while he was alive, and she had not saved him from being condemned to ghostly wanderings now that he was dead.

Whatever she had done, it was mostly something that would help Jack Devlin. Devlin was strong, implacable. He'd had a genuine bond with her brother. But could he do anything to affect Billy now?

Leilani didn't know. Nor did she know what she could do. All she knew was that accepting her place made her feel empty and without power.

The silence lasted as they began walking back to Walter's pickup. Devlin stayed next to her, silently willing her to follow a track that would lead her to safety. Leilani just walked.

They drove back to the safehouse. Still not speaking. When they arrived at the mailbox, Leilani leaned over from the driver's side, put her arm around Devlin, and kissed his cheek.

Devlin said, "You get home tomorrow, Leilani. Everything is going to be all right. Billy will rest easy soon. I promise you."

Devlin's comment touched Leilani. She knew then that she was going to cry, and she didn't want Devlin to see that. She touched him once on the cheek and said, "Good. You come back to me, will you?"

"Yes, I will."

"Promise?"

"Yeah," said Devlin. "I promise."

She quickly looked straight ahead. Devlin got out of the pickup, and she drove off. She didn't even look in the rearview mirror. And she didn't bother to wipe away the tears.

CHAPTER 40

Colonel George Walker had been reading the morning papers when Lihu called. The newsprint story of the "McDonald's Shooting" had just about paralyzed him. But Lihu's terse orders over the phone fired the synapses in his brain that responded to a direct command, and Walker began to move.

He checked his watch. A few minutes after ten. He hung up the phone. His military training came into action. He moved swiftly and mechanically. Not even bothering to put on his uniform jacket, he walked quickly out the back door of the admin building, got into his car, and drove to the officers' housing area. He walked into his bungalow and went through the moves that he had rehearsed in his mind. He opened his bottom dresser drawer and took out a canvas bag. In it were his mutual fund statements, transaction codes, bank account statements, passport, safe-deposit-box key, five-thousand dollars in cash, a change of clothes, and a shaving kit. He went back to his living room, stuffed the computer printouts of Lihu's inventory into the bag, and walked out to his car.

Going through the movements he had mentally rehearsed so many times brought Walker a sense of calm. He began to calculate what was going to happen. He knew it was all going to unravel soon. He was sure McWilliams and his team had been behind the shooting at McDonald's. He was sure the fact that no one had been killed signaled that McWilliams had failed. And nobody had to tell Walker that the firepower unleashed in the area would indicate military assault rifles had been used.

Conclusion: it was all going to unravel. But it would take time. Walker knew the Army tech-teams would descend on his files. But he had constructed them in ascending layers of completeness and then added cross-references that made everything more complex. The tech specialists would have to drill down through successively redundant files before they could begin to analyze the data.

Walker estimated it would take at least a few days to find out the discrepancies. More time to realize the full extent of the missing equipment. More time to match the data on replacement equipment with the material cycled out.

By then, Walker estimated, he and Tay would be safely settled in another part of the world. There was time. Walker had decided on London where the sun didn't shine so mercilessly so often. It would be perfect. European sensibilities would suit them both better, he decided. By the time Walker arrived at the exit gate, he was beaming. His current world was about to collapse, but his twisted logic told him it would actually mean liberation. Not to mention that Lihu would be closing down the operation and paying him off. That final payment would help secure the future for a good long time. It was all going to work out. Walker felt invulnerable.

As up pulled up to the exit, the MP at the gate stepped into his booth to answer the phone call that would tell him to shut down Schofield. Walker hardly even slowed down. He breezed past with a waving salute that the MP barely acknowledged as he picked up his phone. By the time the soldier had logged the latest order in the day book, the next car pulling up was a beat-up Ford Pinto driven by a heavyset black woman. She had a large bag from the Popeye's fast-food outlet near the PX and six bags of groceries in the backseat. The soldier recognized her. She was the wife of a staff sergeant who lived off base. He let her go and dropped the gate. She'd be home tonight, but not her husband.

In less than an hour, Walker was driving through the downtown commercial district of Honolulu. He parked his car in an underground garage on Bishop Street. He stripped off his uniform shirt, pulled out the envelope with Lihu's inventory, hid his canvas bag in the trunk, and walked out of the garage. He looked a bit strange in his white undershirt and uniform pants, but Walker decided the important thing was that no one remember seeing an Army colonel walking around downtown Honolulu.

He thought about taking a roundabout route to Tay's apartment but found himself walking directly there. He checked his watch. 11:40 A.M. So what if he got there a little early. He'd have some time to flirt with Tay.

He stopped in front of a large glass window and bent over to tie his shoe while looking into the reflection to see if anyone was following him. He had learned the technique in an Army intelligence course he had once attended many years ago. It was a ridiculous move. He couldn't really distinguish any of what he saw reflected in the glass, but it somehow reassured him. He finished tying his shoe and quickened his pace.

He allowed himself to play with the idea that Tay would be there waiting for him in her leather outfit. Ready to accommodate him with a quick dose of play before Lihu showed up. By the time he turned onto Tay's block, he had an erection. He half ran up the narrow flight of stairs that led to her second-floor apartment. He put his key in the door, thinking of her and at the same time realizing how far gone he was to be fantasizing about what might happen with Tay when his entire working life for the last eighteen years was cratering.

When he opened the door, he turned to see if she was in the living room. But as he turned, he smelled the unpleasant aroma that announced the presence of Eddie Lihu. And yet there was Tay, lounging on her couch as she often did. But this was a different Tay. This Tay wore no makeup, no black corset or boots or undergarments. This Tay looked painfully plain and washed out. She was dressed in faded jeans and a sweatshirt with a Nebraska Cornhusker logo. She barely looked up when he entered the room. She looked so bland and ordinary that Walker's eagerness to be there evaporated along with his withering erection.

When Lihu walked out of the bathroom zipping his fly, Walker's only desire was to be someplace else. He hadn't seen Lihu in months and had forgotten just how big a man he was. A big man gone to fat. At least three hundred pounds, thought Walker.

Lihu seemed to be sweating even more than usual. His usual excessive dose of cologne only made his body odor more pungent and nauseating. Walker suddenly felt sick to his stomach.

Lihu pointed his fat thumb over his shoulder and rumbled at Tay, "Go in the bedroom."

He spoke to her, but he looked at Walker.

He pointed to the small dining table and told Walker, "Sit."

Walker stepped to the dining table and took a seat. It gave him an opportunity to watch Tay go into her bedroom. He stared in her direction, even after she closed the door.

Lihu pulled a chair a good distance away from the table, but he still barely had room for his enormous belly.

Lihu said, "So, everything got fucked up."

"What happened?"

"You tell me."

"Not at my end. I got clearances for McWilliams and his team, arranged transportation, put in place requests at Pohakaloa. Everything you ordered. I assume what I read in the papers today wasn't good news, but how did my end get fucked up?"

"You hear from McWilliams yet?"

"No. I did leave the base rather abruptly, but I wouldn't normally hear from him unless he needed something."

Lihu grunted. "You bring the information I asked you for?"

"Of course."

Walker pulled the computer printouts from his back pocket, unfolded the pages, and laid them on the table, proud that he had hit the mark on everything Lihu asked him for.

Lihu grunted and picked up the pages. He scanned them.

"This accurate?"

"Absolutely. Down to the last cartridge. Of course, I don't have much of an idea what you've already shipped off the Islands. I only know what went in from my end."

"All of it?"

"All of it. And now I think you owe me something, Mr. Lihu."

Lihu made a noise that sounded like a rumbling "Yeah."

He reached around to get something from his back pocket. It was quite an effort to get his arm around his girth. Walker pursed his lips impatiently. When Lihu brought his hand around, it held a hammerless Taurus .38 revolver. A small gun designed for easy concealment. Lihu shot Walker between the eyes before he even had time to reflexively raise his hands.

The crack of the gun startled Tay, even though she was behind her closed bedroom door. Charlie, Lihu's bodyguard, turned in her direction and raised his eyebrows conspiratorially. She looked back at Charlie and didn't move from where she sat at the corner of the bed. She sat very still. Something in her was hoping that if she remained in that position, didn't react, didn't say one word, Charlie would get up and leave her alone, and Charlie and Lihu would walk out of the apartment. She waited without moving, but it didn't work. She heard Lihu's rumbling voice. His fat voice calling her name.

Charlie nodded toward the living room, and Tay obediently got up and went out.

Lihu was standing over the body, staring down, examining the startled look on Walker's face.

"What an asshole," he said to himself. "Fucking prick thinks he's actually something special. Supposed to be a fucking soldier, and he walks in here like some kine a damn accountant."

Lihu turned to Tay and said, "Come over here."

When she was within arm's reach, he gently pulled her next to him.

"Look at that. Pathetic, huh?"

Tay looked down at Walker but didn't say anything. She watched the blood seeping out the back of his head, puddling and soaking into her carpet, staining it. At that precise moment, when she watched the blood spreading, she knew it was hopeless to think this would all go away so she could just clean up the mess and go on with her life.

She felt Lihu's hand on the back of her neck. His sweat smell reeked. She tried to breathe through her mouth. He pointed her head down so she had to look at Walker's dead body. Then she felt him slipping the butt of the.38 into her hand.

"Sick fucking pervert. Used to come up here and let you beat him. Piss on him. You ever shit in his face?"

"I don't know."

"Yes, you do. You know. You shit on him, didn't you?"

"I guess so."

"You guess so? You shit on a guy's face, and you guess so?"

"Not on his face."

"Oh, not on his face. I see. You piss on his face?"

"Yeah."

"Tell him he was a piece of shit?"

"Yeah."

"Sure you did. He was a piece of shit."

Slowly Tay felt her hand rise. Then she felt Lihu's big hand engulf hers. Her hand was inside Lihu's, but it was her hand that held the gun, the butt of the weapon firmly inside her palm.

Now the gun was pointing at Walker. And suddenly it jumped and banged and flashed. It jerked her arm, and the sudden noise made her flinch.

"Go ahead, shoot that piece of shit. He's already dead, but you can put a couple in for yourself. Shoot him!" yelled Lihu.

His bark made her squeeze the trigger, and another bullet went into the body.

Now she couldn't stop looking at Walker. She tried to see where the bullets had entered, but she couldn't find the spots. She was sure she had seen the body twitch when the trigger was pulled, but she didn't see any big holes or more blood.

And then Lihu was slowly pushing her onto a chair. Now she could smell the sweaty tang of the fat man's body odor mixed with the acrid smell of the gun smoke, and she felt as if she would vomit. And now his huge hand was gripping the top of her head. Pulling her head back so that it was firmly wedged against his fleshy belly. It hurt. She tried to move, and the pressure immediately increased. Her head was trapped against his big, soft, fleshy belly. And now the gun in her hand was being firmly pressed into her temple. The hot muzzle burning the soft, tender temple. It hurt more than the grip on her head. More than anything, until a terrible noise exploded mixed with a terrible split second of brilliant light and more pain than she had ever felt in her entire lifetime.

Lihu stepped back quickly as he fired the bullet into her head. He checked to see if any of the blood had sprayed on him. The right side of his shirt was wet. Didn't matter. He'd burn all the clothes he wore. Shoes, too.

He came around in front of the chair and looked carefully at the scene. The gun was still in Tay's right hand. She had fallen off the chair, collapsed on the floor onto her side. Lihu pictured the angles of bullet entries into the bodies, the positions of the corpses, the residue on Tay's hand. All of it would fit with a murder/suicide scenario. Lihu knew exactly how the scene should appear. After all, he had been the district attorney of the Big Island. That's why he had taken care of George Walker and Tay himself.

Lihu stood carefully examining the crime scene, going over it piece by piece. Lihu pursed his lips and sneered at the bloody mess he had created. Charlie walked out from the bedroom and stood next to him, watching Lihu evaluate his work.

Finally, Lihu said, "Too bad I had to lose a good whore."

Charlie nodded.

"Well," said Lihu, "that should end the trail here."

"You don't need this guy Walker anymore?"

"Nah. I gotta shut down everything over there. It's over. And I got all the information out of him I need. Stupid for such a clever guy. He actually liked it when I talked that pidgin Hawaiian shit to him. Hey, brah?"

Lihu mopped his face and neck with a large handkerchief.

"You touch anything?"

"Nope."

Lihu thought through all his moves once again. He walked into the bathroom and looked around. He wiped down the toilet handle one more time, left the bathroom, and motioned for Charlie to follow him. They took the stairs down to the ground floor and left the building by the back entrance. As he walked across the alley and ducked into the parking garage, Eddie Lihu wondered how long it would be before the smell led the cops to the apartment.

CHAPTER 41

Devlin watched Leilani drive off, then he walked back into the safe-house. Tuli was awake, dressed, and eating. Devlin suddenly was so hungry that he fixed himself a Spam sandwich.

He told Tuli, "We're going to make a visit to someone."

Tuli asked, "Who this time?"

"A friendly. But take the Mossberg just in case."

The sun was low in the sky as Devlin and Tuli pulled up to the ramshackle plywood houses belonging to Lyman, the man Leilani had told Devlin about. Devlin drove this time. He pulled the Camry up to the house very slowly. A bearded man with long dreadlocked hair and a wild-eyed expression sat on the front porch with his bare feet up on a rickety handrail. Sections of the house behind him looked like they were on the verge of collapsing.

An overweight Rottweiler bitch lying a few feet away from the man eyed Devlin and Tuli as they stepped out of the car. Devlin was in no mood for dog trouble, and neither was Tuli. The Samoan stood behind the open front door of the car holding his Mossberg out of sight, keeping an eye on the dog.

Devlin walked toward the porch, stopped about five feet away, and smiled at the man staring at him.

"I'm Jack Devlin. I'm a friend of John Sunshine. I knew him as Billy Cranston. Are you Lyman?"

"Yes."

"Can I come on up?"

"Okay."

"How's the dog?"

"Just don't make any sudden moves or noises."

Devlin walked toward the porch. Tuli stayed by the Camry.

The dog stood up slowly as Devlin approached. Devlin squatted in front of the dog and extended his hand.

"Good girl," said Lyman.

The dog didn't bother to smell Devlin's hand, but she did allow him to pet her big head. Devlin stood up. The bitch ambled to the other side of Lyman and settled back down near his chair.

Lyman had on a pair of faded, worn denim overalls. No shirt, no shoes. The gaps in the overall's side buttons showed he wore no underwear either.

Devlin judged Lyman to be about forty-five, but he looked older. He had the wasted sunken-cheeked look of someone who was physically and mentally ill. His hair and his beard had grown to the point where they stopped getting any longer because the ends just wore off.

But even though his body seemed to be wasting away, Lyman's eyes had fire. They were as wide open and blazing as a possessed Old Testament prophet.

Devlin brought over an old wooden stool from the other end of the porch and set it down next to Lyman. He said nothing for a few moments, hoping the fearful look in Lyman's eyes would subside a bit before he started asking questions.

"You okay?" Devlin asked.

"I get a little nervous. Shook up, you know."

"Well, you don't have to be nervous about me. I'm not here to cause you any trouble."

Lyman took a deep breath and tried to breathe out slowly. "I'm not nervous about you. I just am. Nerves are shot. I know about you. Billy said you'd be coming."

"He did?"

"Yes. He said you would be coming. You fit the picture I had in my head."

"Well, here I am."

"And Billy said there'd be more coming after you. Lots more. He said that to me. I heard it."

"I believe you."

"Yes, sir. Billy knew why he was on this earth. He had a mission."

"What was that?"

"Don't know exactly." Lyman took another deep breath and exhaled the air with a quivering sound.

"Well, I just wanted to ask you a few questions."

"About Billy?"

"Yeah."

"He had a vision. He said I should tell you when you came here."

"A vision?"

"From the herb. Like one of God's chosen gets. All God's chosen used the herb. It's in the Bible. Christ smoked herb. Krishna, too. All the mystics and bodhisattvas. Johnny knew the bad times were coming."

"How so?"

"The Spirit is gone. The garden is polluted."

"By what?"

"Hate. Greed. Weapons of destruction."

"Is that what Billy said?"

Devlin noticed a slight tremor in Lyman's hands as he nodded quickly. "Yep."

"What did he mean by the weapons of destruction?"

"You never seen a war?"

"Yes, I've seen war."

"Me, too. I seen war. I been to war. That's how I got this way. Can't eat right. Can't sleep. Half the time can't shit right. Only thing that helps is the blessing of the herb, and they'll lock you up for using it. If they catch you."

Devlin nodded.

"Lock you up. Send the engines of war to spy on you. Swoop down. Tear up the herb. Take you out of the garden and off to hell."

"You mean the police?"

"Police. Army. DEA. All of 'em. Swoop right down on you."

"In helicopters."

"Just like in 'Nam."

"Have you seen any helicopters lately?"

"Not them kind. But I heard trucks. They're gonna gather the weapons of destruction."

"Gather?"

"Yes, sir."

"Gather from where? How many weapons do they have?"

Suddenly Lyman stood up, and Devlin could see more clearly how skinny he was. He thought for a second that Lyman might have some kind of cancer.

"'Scuse me. Gotta piss."

Devlin nodded and remained on his stool. He took a quick look at Tuli, still standing in the same place, watching, Mossberg out of sight.

Devlin listened to the bathroom sounds, and then he caught the unmistakable pungent aroma of burning marijuana. Lyman came back out onto the porch carrying a fat joint. He stuck the joint between the little finger and ring finger of his left hand, cupped the joint with both hands and toked it four or five times, each time inhaling deeply, sending up thick puffs of smoke that surrounded his head. He'd smoked down a good part of the big joint in just a few seconds. His eyes didn't lose their wild look, but he seemed calmer, and his hands stopped trembling.

"So, Lyman, about these weapons. You have any idea how many they have?"

"Lots. Billy knew. He saw them."

"Where?"

Lyman waved at the air. "Out there. In the isolated areas around here. We walked in all them fields. In the rainforest. Up near the volcano. Lava fields. All over."

"Is that what Billy was doing the day he was killed? Looking for the weapons?"

"I don't know what he was doing that day. Whatever it was, it wasn't no random thing. Billy knew exactly what he was doing. He decided he should stop it. Said he was going to bring the judgment down on them. I think he was setting out to maybe start killing them, but I guess they killed him instead."

"Who killed him?"

"The masters of war. But they didn't count on Billy's plan. He was a righteous warrior, you know. He feared no man."

"I know."

"How do you know?"

"I fought with him."

"Then maybe you're a righteous warrior, too."

Devlin didn't respond.

Lyman stared at Devlin for a moment. Nodded. "You're one of the warriors Billy called down on them. Huh?"

"Maybe. Are you saying getting killed was all part of Billy's plan?"

"Billy's plan was Billy's plan. He was peaceful, but he was still a warrior. You read about Christ in the temple, didn't you? Didn't you ever think about how one man like that goes and kicks ass? Moneylenders. Powerful people. Billy was righteous. He didn't fear them at all. I'm too afraid now. I'm useless for that. Don't have the strength no more."

"Did he tell you how many places they hid the weapons?"

"He said all throughout the garden. But it doesn't matter now."

"Why not?"

"I told you. The weapons have been gathered."

"How? Who gathered them?"

Something in Lyman closed up. "I don't know."

"You said you heard trucks."

Lyman looked away from Devlin. Nodded again, but this time to himself. Devlin asked, "When?"

"Yesterday."

"Do you know where?"

"No."

Lyman took another series of tokes from the marijuana. It looked for a moment like he was done with Devlin. Suddenly, he opened his eyes wide, almost as if he'd come back to himself.

"Where Kalapana used to be. Billy said that."

"Do you know who killed Billy?"

Lyman stared at Devlin.

Devlin asked again, "Do you know?"

"Do you?" asked Lyman.

"Sam Kee?"

Lyman nodded. "Maybe. Sam Kee's strong. But I don't think he could kill Billy. Unless Billy wanted him to."

"Why would he want him to?"

Lyman answered, "I just told you why. Part of his plan."

"If not Kee, then who?"

Lyman finished the joint. Devlin waited. Everything around him seemed to move in slow motion. Lyman. The dog. Even how the vegetation around the ramshackle house moved in the gentle wind.

Lyman said, "The masters of war, that's who." Then he stared blankly out into the scraggly field in front of his house. He looked as if he was watching something far off in the distance. A stillness came over Lyman. Devlin knew the conversation was over. The meaning, of course, was still obscure, but Devlin was completely sure that Lyman believed everything he had said.

Devlin left the porch and climbed behind the wheel of his car. Tuli took one last look at Lyman and the dog and settle in the passenger seat. Devlin drove in silence back to the safehouse.

Tuli watched Devlin trying to decipher the conversation. As they pulled into the hidden driveway, Tuli asked, "What do you think, boss?"

Devlin shut down the engine and turned to his partner.

"I think Billy Cranston knew when he decided to walk into the rainforest that day it would lead to his death."

"Why'd he want to die?"

"After what he went through in Vietnam, Billy Cranston had plenty of reasons to die. But he didn't. He kept hanging onto a miserable, painful life. Until he found a reason to die."

Tuli said, "To bust up whatever is going on around here?"

"I think so. He knew his father wouldn't rest until he found out how and why Billy ended up dead. His sister, too. I'm sure he knew about his father's connection to William Chow and Pacific Rim. And Billy was certainly smart enough to find out that I was part of Pacific Rim."

"So what we lookin' at, boss? M16s in the hands of the local bad guys?"

"That's only part of it. Lyman was talking about a lot more than a handful of military rifles, Tuli."

"I guess we gotta find out, huh, boss?"

"Yeah. See if you can get some sleep, partner. We'll head out about midnight."

"Where to?"

"Sam Kee's ranch. The answers are at Sam Kee's ranch."

CHAPTER 42

Eddie Lihu and his bodyguard Charlie arrived back from Honolulu at 5:16 P.M. Charlie drove Lihu's Chevy Blazer out of the Hilo airport short-term parking lot and arrived at the edge of the Kahaualea Reserve with about an hour before sunset. Charlie drove through a sparsely populated housing development called Fern Forest until the asphalt ended at a two-track road that disappeared into the rainforest leading toward the nearly thirty-five square mile lava field that extended all the way down to Kalapana.

Charlie pulled over and left the engine on, the air-conditioning running. He'd grown accustomed to the strange body odor of Eddie Lihu, but now there was the added odor of gun smoke still on his clothes from the execution of George Walker and Tay Williams. He discreetly aimed the air vents in his direction to get the maximum amount of fresh air flowing toward him. Lihu sat in the back seat, carefully studying the pages of the inventory compiled by Walker.

Fifteen minutes later, they heard the rumble of GMC A C5500 flatbed truck coming toward them out of the rainforest. Captain Kensington McWilliams rode the running board on the passenger side, holding onto the side view mirror support. He wore full-camo utilities that nearly matched the canvas cover hooped over the truck bed. The truck paused just long enough for McWilliams to jump off, then roared past Lihu's parked Chevy.

McWilliams strode toward the vehicle and climbed into the back seat next to Lihu.

Lihu checked his watch and asked, "Where are we at?"

McWilliams looked a little more wired than usual but spoke matter-of-factly.

"We've been at it non-stop." He pointed out to the two-track road ahead of them. "That's only good for about eight clicks. After that, we can't turn the trucks around for the trip out. The lava tube is about two miles farther. We use the ATVs in between. We got four ATVs and three trucks. Men loading at both points. I'd say we got another five, six hours until we're done here. Then we hit the Kee's ranch. He swears there's not more than one truckload of munitions there. We'll see. Should be done before dawn tomorrow, or soon thereafter. Assuming this riff-raff keeps working at this pace. Can't guarantee that."

Lihu asked, "How long does it take for the trucks to cycle between here and the harbor? You need more?"

"No. There's always a truck waiting for the next load."

"All right. Make sure the drivers never leave the trucks. Don't let any of 'em see what's going down."

"We're following protocol."

"Good. Finish the clean up here. Then do Kee's ranch. Then the rest."

McWilliams lifted an eyebrow and glanced at Lihu. "Don't worry about the *rest*. I assure you, there won't be anybody around to identify me or any of my men. Or you."

"What's your exit plan?"

"We'll go back to Pohakuloa like we're coming in from training maneuvers. That's what Walker's orders say. We'll fly back to Schofield out of Bradshaw. I'm sure Hawthorne is calling everybody back to base. Hopefully, we won't be the last ones in. How bad is the fallout from Kee spraying M16 rounds behind McDonald's?"

Lihu grunted. "It doesn't matter. In forty-eight hours they can look all they want and find nothing. A week, a month from now, they'll know what they lost, but not where it went. If they ever find their shit, it'll never link to us. I'll be in touch after you're back at Schofield."

McWilliams nodded, climbed out of the Chevy, and walked into the forest along the two-track trail to wait for the next truck.

Lihu told Charlie, "Head over to the harbor."

As they drove off, Lihu was already thinking about how to get rid of the last person who could link him to one of the largest thefts of Army weapons ever perpetrated: Captain Kensington McWilliams.

CHAPTER 43

Devlin managed to fall into a tortured sleep minutes after he laid down in the upstairs bedroom. The images were horrible: Billy's gaping dead mouth morphing into the black hole where his stomach and heart had been; the blood of Devlin's own wounds mixing with Billy's; Kee's snarling lopsided face spewing heat and spit at him. Devlin saw Lyman's trembling hands and wild eyes; volleys of bullets shredding the Hawaiian rain forest and turning it bloody. It all pinballed in Devlin's nightmare until he finally put a stop to it and struggled back to consciousness. He checked his watch. It was a few minutes past eleven. He had slept three hours.

He swung his feet off the bed and onto the wood floor, moving mechanically: wash, dress, this time in dark clothes, long pants, and sturdy hiking boots, head downstairs.

Devlin opened the back door of the house. It was overcast with light rain falling. The weather was going to make this more difficult, but safer. A tradeoff Devlin would take.

Tuli came into the main room, and they sat down for a late-night dinner. Eggs, bread, and Spam for Tuli. Fruit, bread, and fried Spam with coffee and water for Devlin, who wasn't too happy that Spam might be part of his last meal on earth.

While they ate, Devlin told Tuli "Okay, here's the plan. We hike into that goddamn rainforest one more time. Find Kee's ranch. Nail down what the hell is going on. Clearly, Kee and his men have access to military weapons. If Lyman is right, and they're using trucks to get it out of Puna, it has to be more than M16s. We go in, find out the extent of it, document it with photos, and get the hell out."

"We go back in there, boss, we gotta go in heavy."

"Goddamn right."

"So we see what they got, then what?"

"We make sure we finish what Billy started. I report back to Pacific Rim. William Chow will unleash the U.S. Army and every other law enforcement agency who wants a piece of this. We'll get the hell out of the way. The Army will come down hard and fast. They'll find out who's behind this. They'll shut down this whole island if they have to. Call in the Coast Guard, close the airports, whatever they have to do."

"Then what?"

"See how it plays out. Hopefully, whoever was involved in Billy's death will be taken down with the trafficking arrests."

"And if they ain't?"

Devlin stared at Tuli saying nothing for a moment, and then said, "We'll see."

Tuli nodded back. He knew Devlin wasn't going to say more.

It was just after before midnight when they drove away from the safehouse. Devlin drove the Toyota Camry for Leilani. Tuli followed in the pickup truck which had been carefully packed with everything they needed.

Pahoa was quiet when they pulled into town. Devlin drove slowly, looking once again at the run-down buildings, the faded storefronts. He passed Da Restaurant and thought about Leilani sleeping on the second floor. As soon as he thought about her lying alone in bed, he wanted to stop the car, run up the stairs, and wake her. Put her in the Camry and watch her drive out of town. Instead, he drove past the restaurant, forcing himself to stop thinking about her.

He pulled into the parking lot next to the Village Inn and

parked the Toyota near the back. He stepped out, placed his Beretta 21A in the trunk near the spare tire, and locked the trunk.

Upstairs Rachel Steele stood at her bathroom window. She had been on one of her usual late-night visits to the toilet. The sound of Devlin's car in the lot attracted her attention. She stood silently at her window, watching as Devlin placed car keys on top of the Camry's rear wheel, then walked out of the lot disappearing in the early morning rain.

#

Using Leilani's map, Devlin and Tuli had taken a road that bordered the southwest edge of the Ola'a Forest Reserve, heading north up toward the Waiakea Reserve, skirting east of Mauna Loa.

Devlin had been carefully tracking their progress on his topo map. He told Tuli, "Find a place you can pull over. Try to get cover under some of those hanging ferns so the truck isn't too visible."

Tuli did as Devlin asked.

"How far away from da place are we?"

Devlin pointed straight ahead. "I'd say about a five-minute walk on this road. I'm assuming the ranch is set back a ways. Once we spot it, I want to see if we can hike around it, get up somewhere we can hunker down, and observe. If it looks quiet, we'll decide if we want to get closer and look around."

Devlin's estimate was correct. After a five-minute fast walk, they came upon the ranch. They could see plenty of light through the trees and foliage and hear the sounds of men and equipment.

"Pretty hard to miss this shit, huh?" said Tuli. "What do you think is goin' on?"

Devlin pointed to their right. "Let's swing around over that way. See if we can find out."

It was still raining lightly. The clouds overhead obscured the moonlight. Both men were nearly invisible in the dark. But it also made walking through the forest more difficult. Even with the bit of light spilling from the ranch area, they had to step carefully. Loaded down with weaponry didn't make it any easier.

Devlin had a .308 bolt-action Mauser rifle Model 86 fitted with a precision night scope strapped across his back. In his right hand, he carried one of the Mossberg 590 Intimidator shotguns loaded with eight 12-gauge shells, plus one in the chamber. The shotgun had a forearm-activated laser sight. He also had his 9mm Sig-Sauer P226 with a 15-shot magazine and SIGLITE night sights. Devlin also carried a small backpack with extra ammunition for all the weapons. It amounted to almost thirty pounds of destructive firepower.

Tuli was armed with the same shotgun and handgun, but instead of the bolt-action Mauser he carried a 9mm Heckler & Koch MP5N submachine gun with a Beta night sight. It was loaded with a 30-shot magazine, and Tuli was skilled enough to fire the entire magazine into a six-inch circle out to almost a hundred feet. He, too, carried a backpack with extra ammo, plus water and food.

Both men wore bulletproof vests. Tuli was too big for the vest to close around his torso, so Devlin had used duct tape to secure it to him.

Back in the Tacoma were a second HK MP5N machine gun and another Mossberg, duplicating the weapons they were carrying.

The rainforest here was similar to the area where Billy's body had been found, except there were more trees and less ground cover. The elevation was higher making it cool enough so that the moisture in the air turned into thick billows of fog that filled in every gulch and rut. Visibility inside the rainforest was minimal, which was fine with Devlin.

After about twenty minutes, they found a suitable vantage point – a ridge that bordered the east side of Kee's ranch. Behind them was the dense, fog-filled rainforest. In front of them lay a steep drop-off that went down for about forty feet, leveling out into a circular work area occupying about four acres.

Devlin crouched down behind a small outcropping of rock and set about packing a mound of muddy red earth on which he could rest the Mauser. Tuli set up his firing position about twenty meters north of Devlin.

Once he was set up, Devlin surveyed the area below him. His position on the ridge was at three o'clock. To his left at six o'clock stood Kee's ranch house, a simple wood frame house, two-floors, with a red asphalt shingle roof. Devlin figured it held a living room, kitchen, eating area on the ground floor. Bedrooms and bathrooms on the second floor. Two pickup trucks, an SUV, and three beat-up cars were parked in front of the house.

At the nine o'clock position, directly across from Devlin, there were two rusting metal Quonset sitting next to each other. Each one was fifty feet long and twenty feet wide. There were large double doors on the front, and three windows punched into the sides of the huts.

A fairly new GMC C5500 truck was parked in front of the Quonset huts, midway between them both. From his angle, Devlin could see men coming out of both huts loading the flatbed. Some men used hand trucks. Others worked in pairs pushing rolling carts loaded with boxes and containers of varying sizes.

Devlin peered through the scope on the Mauser. The truck faced him, so he couldn't see what was being loaded in back, but he could catch glimpses of what was being hauled out of the Quonset huts: 50 caliber M2A1 Ammo cans, wooden cases of rifles, green aluminum cases for arms or weapons systems, more than enough to convince Devlin this was a massive theft of U.S. Army weaponry.

At the top of the circle, opposite the ranch house, stood a large rainwater catchment tank. Next to the tank was a large dog pen about thirty feet long and fifteen feet deep surrounded by a cyclone fence. Despite the lights and noise from the loading, most of the dogs were quiet.

There were no other structures in view. Beyond the water tank,

Devlin could make out a cyclone-fence gate that closed off a two-track road that led to a pasture holding a small avocado grove that faded into ohia forest. Dozens of avocadoes lay rotting on the ground.

Suddenly, Devlin heard the doors of the Quonset hut on his left creaking and slamming shut. He peered above the Mauser's scope and saw a small group of men coming from behind the truck heading toward the ranch house. It seemed as if they had finished their loading, but there was still a line of men bringing out and loading equipment from the other Quonset hut.

Devlin muttered a curse and pulled a Fuji portable camera from his breast pocket. He had to get whatever evidence he could, fast. Rushing to catch images before it was too late, he brought the camera to his eye, shielded it from the rain with his left hand, and looked through the viewfinder to aim for a shot of the men loading. The image was blurry, dark, and obscured by the rain.

"Shit."

He'd have to settle for what he could get.

Devlin depressed the shutter button half-way to focus. Before he knew it, the camera clicked off and produced a flash.

Devlin cursed. For a second, he tried to convince himself his left hand had shielded the flash. In the next second, any notion of that was literally blasted apart as down in the work yard Kensington McWilliams, burst out of the Quonset hut where the men were still working, raised an M16A2, and sprayed automatic fire in a deadly line toward Devlin's position.

Tuli unloaded a stream of return fire from his position, as McWilliams ducked back into the hut. Devlin turned off the flash and kept taking pictures, grabbing as many images as he could.

The remaining men loading the truck either ran toward the ranch house or back into the Quonset huts. Sam Kee appeared out of the house brandishing an M16, yelling at his men to get inside, looking to shoot somebody, anybody.

Inside the Quonset hut, McWilliams was yelling at Kee's men to grab weapons.

Outside, one of Kee's security team who had been positioned in the work yard ran up the far end of the ridge to get into a flanking position.

Another member of McWilliams's team suddenly appeared out of a second-floor bedroom window of the ranch house and began firing steady, methodical single shots at Tuli's position.

The dogs were screaming, barking, leaping against the fence trying to get out of the pen.

Devlin shoved the camera in his breast pocket, pivoted, swinging the Mauser a quarter circle to his left, bringing the image framed in the window into the crosshairs of his scope. It was a U.S. soldier dressed in combat camo. Tuli had crawled back just under the protection of the ridge which was being methodically chewed apart by the heavy caliber fire from the house. Devlin sited in his target and squeezed a shot into the center mass of the shooter. The figure disappeared from the window. Dead if he hadn't been wearing body armor. Knocked down and out if he had.

Devlin yelled to Tuli above the shouts of the men below and the baying, screaming barking junk dogs.

"Fall back, this way."

Devlin didn't stop to watch Tuli make his break. He worked the bolt action Mauser and fired shot after shot from one side of the work yard to the other, picking targets one after another: the cargo truck, Quonset huts, dog pound, back to the ranch house.

As Tuli lumbered past him, Devlin yelled, "Go straight back into the forest. We won't have any cover on the road."

Devlin kept firing until he heard Tuli open up with suppressing fire from the HK MP5. He rolled away from his position, leaving the bolt action Mauser behind, and ran hunched toward Tuli who kept firing to give him cover. When he reached the big Samoan, he grabbed his arm and pulled him into the forest as return fire exploded behind them.

Devlin yelled, "This way! We have to use the forest for cover, get clear, and angle over to the road and get the truck.

Devlin knew they would be coming for them from behind. Could they outrun them? How many were there? How heavily armed? Devlin didn't know. But he knew whoever they were, they were the ones who had killed Billy Cranston. And he knew he was going to kill as many of them as he could before he died, too.

CHAPTER 44

Major General James Hawthorne and his command staff had been working a little over eighteen hours since the initial report of M16s being fired in Hilo. Various personnel had been cycling in and out presenting information to Hawthorne who made it clear to everyone they would be working around the clock in the coming days.

Just before two in the morning, Hawthorne's second in command, Colonel Mitchell Wyse, stood behind an overhead projector with a small stack of transparencies on the table next to the projector.

Wyse cleared his throat and placed the first transparency on the projector.

"This is a summary page for what we've managed to document regarding all M16 rifles issued to the division for the past six months."

Hawthorne interrupted Wyse immediately.

"Goddammit, Mitchell, I can't see those fucking numbers. Do you have printouts?"

"Yes, sir."

There were twenty-three officers of varying rank in the conference room. Wyse had one set of printed pages. The set he was going to talk from. He handed it to the closest officer who passed it up the table to Hawthorne.

Wyse went back to his presentation, reciting and pointing out numbers. Hawthorne ignored him and quickly read through the first five pages of his report.

He interrupted again. "All right, all right. So, the only thing we've tracked in the last eighteen hours are M16s. Correct?"

"The only thing accounted for top to bottom, sir."

"What else is there?"

"A few more categories of squad-size weapons."

"Which ones?"

"We're starting with the premise that anything missing is most likely connected to the weapons upgrade that commenced twenty-five January of this year. The majority of that ordinance consisted of M16s, SAWs, grenade launchers..."

Hawthorne interrupted, "But you've only gathered full information on the M16s?"

"Yes, sir."

"Why?"

Wyse said, "We're working at a disadvantage."

"Which is?"

"We're missing the officer in charge of the operation."

"George Walker?"

"Yes, sir."

Hawthorne muttered a curse. That one piece of information told him they had a major problem. He asked, "Where's Weisman?"

A tall, thin man with close-cropped dark hair stood. Hawthorne pointed to his provost marshal, Lieutenant Colonel Sam Weisman, and said, "Sam, you get me George Walker. You find that bastard. I don't care where he is in this world, you fucking find him, and you get him back on this base."

Weisman said, "Yes, sir."

"And if he's dead, I want the body."

"Yes, sir."

Hawthorne turned back to Wyse, "Give me the big picture. The logistics. Timeframe. Personnel involved."

Wyse forgot about his transparencies and spoke from notes on a legal pad.

"The operation rolled out over a period of six months. It's scheduled to end in two months, end of October. During that time, pla-
toons in varying numbers have been shipped over to Pohakuloa for
weapons upgrade and training. In terms of rifles, older M16s were
exchanged for M16A2s. The first shipment of decommissioned
M16s were crated, sealed, and shipped from Pohakuloa to Hilo on
ten February. The sealed crates transferred to Merchant Marine
Ship William Case for transfer to the army weapons depot in Red
Bank, New Jersey, arriving eighteen March, three days late due to
inclement weather at sea."

Hawthorne asked, "And every crate was accounted for at Red
Bank?"

Wyse answered, "Yes. All numbered. All intact. All signed for.
Crate numbers matching at Red Bank with crates shipped. The
objective of the upgrade was to increase squad efficiency since
we're reducing the division's overall troop levels. Upgrading our
weapons was deemed the most cost-efficient method in lieu of personnel cuts."

"What percentage of our arms have been upgraded?"

"Eighty-five percent."

Hawthorne told Wyse, "Issue orders that the program stops
immediately."

"Yes, sir."

The staff watched a grim-faced Hawthorne sit silently in front
of them. After a few moments, Hawthorne started speaking again.
Slowly at first. Then the pace quickened, and his voice rose with
each sentence.

"Eighty-five percent of a twelve-thousand-man infantry division." He paused to let that sink in. "Gentleman, I want an exact
number ASAP, but I don't need it to know we're talking about one
holy hell of a lot of weapons. Right now, you're tracking crates, gentlemen. Sealed crates that might not be opened for months until the
Army decides what to do with these weapons. Nobody in this room

goddamn knows what's actually in those crates. We know what's supposed to be in them. But we won't know until we locate them and goddamn open them.

"We're talking about sealed crates that had to travel halfway across the Big Island on the Saddle Road to get to either Hilo on the east side or Kawaihae on the west before they were shipped off the island. How many miles is that? Thirty, forty miles in either direction. Forty goddamn isolated miles. Half of it in constant rain and fog. How many shipments went out over eight months? Hundreds? How many crates? Thousands?"

Nobody volunteered an answer.

Hawthorne leaned forward, "That's not a final question, gentlemen. The only question that matters is how many crates did they get, gentlemen? Two percent? Ten percent? A dozen? A hundred? Two goddamn hundred crates of my weapons! Does anybody fucking know?"

Hawthorne sat back, organizing his thoughts.

"Sit down, Wyse. All right, here's what we're going to do. Broad strokes first. Itemize every category of weapon upgraded: Older M16s, grenade launchers, Dragons, LAWs, SMAWs. SAWs, whatever.

"Track down every shipment to Red Bank. Contact Red Bank. Inspect and inventory the contents of every crate. Do the same with any ordinance on Merchant Marine ships en route.

"I want a complete list of all personnel under George Walker's command. Assemble every single one of those troops, from officers to noncoms to privates. Everyone in Supply and Transportation who had a hand on those weapons. And anybody else who was on any kind of work assignment out of Walker's office."

"Yes, sir."

"Confine them to their barracks. Start interviewing them one by one. I don't want to hear any shit about legalities. Someone has declared war on this division, and I want to know who. I want to know everything every one of those troops did starting back in February. If there's any soldier who worked out of Schofield back then and isn't here now, find him and get him back here."

"Yes, sir."

"I don't care where they are, get them back here."

"Yes, sir."

Hawthorne stood up. "Gentlemen, we are going to find out what happened to our weapons. We are going to find out how it happened. And we are going to get our weapons back, even if it means closing down the entire goddamn island of Hawaii and going through every structure on that island."

CHAPTER 45

Captain Kensington McWilliams stood beneath the cover of the ridge with the two surviving members of his security team. They were both armed with M16A2 rifles that had M203 40mm grenade-launchers attached. McWilliams gave them fast, precise orders while pointing southeast and northeast.

The soldiers split apart and ran full speed over the ridge and into the forest, one veering north, the other south.

McWilliams walked over to Sam Kee and his five men standing at the base of the ridge. All were armed with stolen M16s. McWilliams told them, "We'll come in behind them while my guys flank them and drive keep in front of us. Spread out in a line. You see anything moving, kill it."

Kee yelled, "You heard him, let's go."

The men ran up the ridge, over, and into the forest. McWilliams and Kee fell in behind them. McWilliams told Kee, "You take the right side of the line, I'll take the left. Keep them moving straight. My guys will keep them in front of us. We'll catch them, cut them to shreds, and get the hell out of here."

McWilliams ran left. Kee headed right as his men disappeared over the ridge.

#

Devlin and Tuli had made it five hundred yards into the forest, fighting the darkness, the rain, and the uneven ground when they heard the first whump of an exploding grenade off to their left and behind them.

They flinched. Tuli cursed. They both kept moving through the dark morass as fast as possible.

Even though McWilliams's soldiers were behind Devlin and Tuli, their grenade launchers had a range of 400 meters, so the first grenades fired landed almost parallel to where Devlin and Tuli stumbled through the forest. The chances of a direct hit were still slim, but McWilliams didn't care. He knew the intruders had fled east. Unless they wanted to stumble through the rainforest for days, the only way out lay to the south where a little-used road would take them over to the Pu'u O'o Volcano Trail, which would get them back to Highway 11. McWilliams had instructed his soldier taking the south flank to veer over to the road that led to the Volcano Trail and keep pace with the intruders. If they made it to the road, his job was to blast whoever emerged from the forest with grenades and bullets.

Of course, McWilliams didn't tell his soldiers the rest of his plan.

#

Devlin stopped in a dense section of the tropical forest to take a quick reading on his compass, trying to figure how far they had come, and the best angle to take them out on the road near the hidden Tacoma pickup. Tuli leaned against a large tree, peering out into the rain and darkness, trying to see anybody coming their way.

Another grenade landed. This time a hundred feet behind them and somewhere off to their left.

Tuli said, "What's the play, boss?"

Devlin quickly calculated the possibilities. He pointed to his right.

"We have to get out of here before they pin us down. Hopefully, we're far enough ahead of them." He pointed to his right. "We have to make it to the road before they surround us. Let's see if we can find out how close they are."

Devlin pointed to a thick tree ten yards ahead of them.

"You set up there. I'll lay down fire from here and then take cover. If they see my muzzle flashes and shoot back, use their flashes to get a bead on them. Fire off about five seconds of your HK. Draw their fire, then cut right and head straight for the road. If we're lucky, we'll get a sense of how many are following. If we're really lucky, we might take out a couple of them."

Tuli nodded, they turned, and ran to take up their positions, as another grenade fell, much closer this time. Devlin turned, drop to a knee, and pumped five fast blasts from the Mossberg over a thirty-degree angle.

The return fire came quickly. Devlin couldn't see Tuli because he was flat on the ground behind a Koa tree. As the return fire began to fade, he heard Tuli open up with the HK. It seemed like it went on for ten seconds or more, sending over a hundred rounds of 9mm bullets into the forest behind them.

Neither Devlin or Tuli saw Kee's man, Feto, hit by the bullets from Tuli's HK. They were running toward where they hoped the road would soon appear.

Behind them, the two men near Sam Kee dropped and took cover. Kee was the only one who fired back, but he had no idea where to shoot. Kee stopped firing and yelled at his men to get up and move.

Kensington McWilliams watched the exchange of gunfire in the dark forest hidden behind the north end of Kee's line of men. He had been drifting quietly in the dark and the rain, trailing behind the advancing line of men. Perfect, he thought.

Unlike every other man in the forest, McWilliams was not loaded down with a rifle and ammunition. His only weapon was a Beretta M9 pistol. In the dark and the rain, wearing camos that let him blend in with the foliage, he was close to invisible. He was light on his feet, nimble, and focused on taking full advantage of the opportunity at hand. Let the intruders kill as many of Kee's men on the right flank as they could. He'd pick off Kee's men one by one on the left end.

McWilliams spotted his first target, stumbling forward, looking around for his compatriots, struggling to keep pace and hold his weapon. McWilliams smiled. He was already close enough to take him out, but there wasn't much fun in that. He moved closer. Still no reaction from Kee's man. He got within six feet, hoping the idiot would turn and try to take a shot at him. When McWilliams came to within three feet, Kee's man, Tommy, still had no idea he was being stalked.

McWilliams disgustedly shot him in the back of his head.

#

Kee had seen his man, Feto, go down. He stopped firing his M16 and looked to the next man on the left, Loto, the short, wild-haired muscular half-Chinese he had been with when he first came into Da Restaurant. Loto was still standing. Kee yelled at him, "Loto, Loto, get down, man. Down!"

Loto dropped to one knee, peering out into the dark, rain-filled forest in front of him.

Kee yelled, "Loto, you see Frank or Aka, Or Tommy?"

Loto turned his gaze. "No."

Just then, both men heard the crack of McWilliams's Beretta 9mm pierce the sound of the rain.

Kee froze. That single sound seared into him like a hot knife into his gut. He couldn't admit it, yet he knew it was true. He cursed. He knew that sound was his death knell. He should have seen this coming. He wondered if all this had been a set up right from the beginning. This guy Devlin, all of it. He could see Lihu putting it all together. Keeping him alive until he had the last of the stolen weapons loaded and delivered to Hilo harbor. Then get him out in the fucking forest all set up to be killed off by McWilliams and his men. They weren't after the intruders. They were after him.

Kee stayed low and made his way to Loto. He put his hand on Loto's muscular shoulder. In the rain and dark he moved close enough so that his mouth was near Loto's ear.

"Hey, brah, we got fucked, man. This is some kine trap. They're trying to kill us. Take us out one by one."

This confused Loto. He whispered back, "Who?"

"McWilliams and his men. Lihu must have ordered it."

"What you going to do?"

"What the fuck you think, brah. Kill dem first. Come on. Stay low, move fast. We got to get back to the ranch. Get some heavier firepower."

#

Devlin had stumbled and fallen three times in his run to the road. Every time, Tuli had helped him to his feet. It seemed they had been pushing through the forest for much too long. Where the hell was the road?

Devlin stopped. "Hold it, Tuli."

He dropped down to one knee again, catching his breath, pulling out the compass one more time. He had to make sure they were heading due east. He oriented himself in the direction they had been moving. The compass told him that they had veered too far south. Devlin turned directly east.

"Okay, we go straight for it. That way."

"You think we're past the truck?"

"Maybe. Probably. Hard to figure the distance we traveled quick-walking on a road for five minutes and stumbling through this shit for half an hour. Let's just get the fuck out of here."

"Remember, boss, as soon as we get out on that road, we're visible."

Just then, another grenade exploded almost directly behind them. Both men felt the shock wave.

Devlin yelled over the ringing in his ear's. "I'd rather get blown up where they can find my body parts."

#

McWilliams had taken out two more of Kee's men, Frank and Aka, both with headshots. That would leave Kee and two more assuming the intruders hadn't taken out any of Kee's men.

He moved quickly to get behind the survivors, just in time to see Sam Kee and Loto moving fast heading back in the direction of the ranch.

McWilliams leaned out of sight and smiled. He was glad that Kee had made this more interesting. He let Kee and Loto get out ahead of him and then moved silently in behind them. It looked like only two left. Easy. Well, not *that* easy. Both men were armed with automatic rifles. The trick would be to stay out of sight. They couldn't shoot what they couldn't see. But then again, McWilliams wanted to see Kee's face when he shot him. First, a gut shot thought McWilliams. Then get up nice and close and tell him what a moron he was before he shot him in between his eyes.

Then jump in the truck. Pick up his two guys on the road. Hopefully, after they blew the shit out of whoever had been spying on them. Then off to Hilo. From there, McWilliams realized his Army days would be over. Get the final payoff from Lihu and disappear. He might have had a chance to get back to Schofield via Bradshaw, but not with one of his men dead. Nope, that had fucked this plan.

No problem. Just set up another plan. Take care of the two buffoons stumbling around up ahead, pickup up his two surviving soldiers, deliver the last load, and disappear.

McWilliams felt a sense of relief mixed with the disappointing realization that he wouldn't be doing much killing for quite some time.

CHAPTER 46

Leilani Cranston woke with a start. Her entire body convulsed as if she had stepped out over a cliff. She blinked. It took a few moments to recover from the shock before she realized she was in bed, above Da Restaurant, on the Big Island. She had no idea why she had jerked awake like that. She hadn't been dreaming. Or at least she had no memory of a dream.

She rolled over and looked the small digital travel clock on the night table. 2:27 A.M.

She had to pee. She walked barefoot down the back steps. She wore only briefs and a tank top. The early morning air felt chilly. Rain was falling outside.

She used the restaurant bathroom, and then walked through the restaurant to the front window and peered outside. A single overhead floodlight illuminated most of the parking lot next to the Village Inn. She saw a car parked near the back. Just as Devlin had promised her. A white Toyota Camry. She knew the keys would be on top of the back tire on the driver's side. Just as Devlin had promised.

It would be so easy.

Go upstairs, dress, shove everything into her backpack, drive to the airport. She could leave Walter a note. Make up any bullshit excuse. But then what? The first flight out was probably around six-thirty or so. She'd get to Hilo around three, three-fifteen. Nothing would be open. Flights might be delayed of the rain. Why not just get back into bed? Get some sleep. Help Walter through breakfast. Tell him she had a family thing back on Oahu. Leave with her head up. Not sneaking out like she had something to hide or be ashamed of.

CHAPTER 47

The forest started to thin out a bit. Devlin and Tuli were moving faster. There was no gunfire behind them, and the grenades behind them were falling with less frequency. Maybe the attackers were running out.

Suddenly, an empty space loomed in front of them. The road. It seemed to be raining harder now. Or maybe it just looked that way out as they came out from under cover of the dense overhead foliage.

As they approached the muddy road, Devlin stopped and grabbed Tuli's arm.

"They've been driving us in this direction. They must have men set up out there somewhere."

"Yeah, but where?"

"If it was me, I'd be out there looking for the vehicle that brought us in."

Tuli laughed quietly. "Dat means we all gonna be lookin' for that damn truck. Where the fuck you think it is? Right or left?"

"I'm betting right. Back north. I think we overshot it."

"Okay."

"Let's stay back in the forest and track north parallel to the road."

"Okay."

Within two minutes, Devlin felt Tuli's big hand on his shoulder. He turned around. Tuli was smiling and pointing ahead. Devlin stared until he spotted the back of the blue Toyota pickup fifteen yards out in front of them.

Tuli said, "You see anybody?"

"No. But that doesn't mean they aren't there."

"How we gonna flush 'em out?"

"We go for the goddamn truck. I'm sick of this rain, this bullshit, these fucking grenades. You stay back in the forest and walk to the far side of the truck. Keep going for a hundred count. I'll start counting, too. When you get to a hundred, step out onto the edge of the road, and come back this way. I'll step out at a hundred and come toward you. Anybody shoots at you, I take them out. Anybody shoots at me, you do the same."

"Got it."

"My bet, they'll be hiding in the foliage on the other side of the road."

"Maybe."

"Let's try not to shoot each other while we're at it."

"Good idea."

Tuli headed off. Devlin hunkered down, counting. At one hundred, he stepped out onto the road. He stood still for a moment looking up ahead to spot Tuli. He couldn't see anything in the rain and the dark. He started walking.

Devlin figured the odds of getting ambushed were at least fifty/ fifty. But by how many? Where would the lie in wait?

Ten steps, nothing. Twenty, nothing.

Devlin figured he'd be damned if he was going to let them wait for him to walk into it.

He shouldered the Mossberg, aimed into the forest opposite the car and fired off a round. He continued walking, pumping in another shell, firing. Nothing. Devlin had guessed wrong.

McWilliams's soldier had been hunkered down in front of the Tacoma betting the approach would be from the north. He was half right. He kept out of sight, waiting for whoever was shooting to come into view.

As soon as Tuli heard Devlin's first shot, he broke into a run. He clocked Devlin's location by the muzzle flash from the Mossberg, but he couldn't figure out what Devlin had been firing at. He kept running, seeing the truck now, looking for Devlin, looking for someone to shoot.

Devlin slowed down so he could reload the Mossberg. He slid more shells into the Mossberg trying to spot any enemies lying in wait down the road, but he didn't see McWilliams's soldier lean out from behind the front of the Tacoma, staying low, raising his M16 to his shoulder, setting it on full auto. He was a second away from squeezing off a stream of bullets at Devlin, when he heard the pounding and huffing sound of a large Samoan coming up behind him.

He turned.

The M16 and the IIK erupted at almost the same time.

Devlin broke into a run, looking for a target.

The gunfire stopped almost as soon as it had started.

Ahead, Devlin saw Tuli standing over a heap, pulling the rifle out of the dead soldier's hands. Tuli heaved the M16 into the rainforest and climbed into the passenger seat of the truck without a word.

Devlin stepped under the palm frond covering the truck and got into the driver's seat. He made U-turn and headed south.

"Just the one, huh?" said Devlin.

Tuli staring out the windshield muttered, "No."

Devlin looked ahead and saw McWilliams's second soldier stepping out of the forest about 100 yards ahead of them. Tuli was powering down the passenger side window to get a shot with the HK, but not before the soldier got his shot off first – another grenade.

Devlin cursed and floored the accelerator.

The grenade fell wide and behind the racing Tacoma, but close enough to lift the truck off its back wheels and blow out the back window.

Tuli held the HK in one hand out his window and sent a stream of return fire at the soldier.

Devlin cursed and aimed the car at the soldier. They both knew now the only shot the soldier could take would be right at the car.

The Tacoma shuddered and bounced over the rutted road. Tuli's stream of bullets flew everywhere but at the soldier. It did distract him. Between looking at the oncoming truck and ducking away from the automatic weapon's fire, McWilliams's soldier fumbled the grenade. He got it into the launcher tube but pulled the chamber back too soon. The grenade wasn't all the way in. He slid the chamber open, angled the rifle down to get the grenade in the launcher, closed it, but too late.

Tuli's HK was empty, but Devlin had his weapon, a pickup truck, aimed right at the soldier. Devlin aimed the truck at the soldier who threw himself to his left. Too late. The truck hit the soldier's legs at 52 mph, shattering both and spinning him around so fast that he banged against the side of the truck as they roared past.

It sounded like they had hit a tree. Devlin fought to keep the Tacoma from sliding off the muddy road. He braked, muscled the car back on the road, and kept going.

Devlin turned to Tuli. "Done."

That's when he saw the blood on Tuli's face and shoulder.

CHAPTER 48

Back in the rainforest, McWilliams ran full speed, abandoning any effort to conceal himself. He had to take them out before they reached the ranch.

Kee and Loto were out in front of him, both firing blindly behind them. They made it out of the forest. Another fifty feet and they'd be up and over the ridge.

McWilliams spotted a fat ohia tree, he slid toward it like a runner sliding into home plate, turned over on his stomach taking cover behind the tree. He held the Beretta in a two-handed grip and fired at Loto just as he made it to the top of the ridge.

The impact of the bullet sent the Loto over the ridge as if someone had shoved him from behind. Kee jumped over the ridge and disappeared.

McWilliams was on his feet, moving fast out of the forest, smiling to himself thinking, okay, asshole, just you and me now."

Kee dropped his M16 and ran full speed toward his ranch house. He never looked back.

McWilliams made it to the top of the ridge, just in time to see Kee disappear into the house. He stopped and took cover behind the ridge. No point running into the open before he saw what his enemy had in mind. He took the time to shove a full clip into the Beretta, realizing that a shot from sixty yards with a handgun didn't give him very good odds.

He peered over the ridge and saw Kee's last man lying dead,

face down, on the incline. McWilliams didn't hesitate. He threw himself over the ridge and slid down to get the M16 under Loto's dead body.

He made it down to Loto and got a hand on the barrel of the M16 just as Kee came out of the ranch house carrying a SMAW (Shoulder Launch Multi-Purpose Assault Weapon).

McWilliams cursed. He knew the SMAW could shoot a variety of deadly rockets. Anyone of them could blast him off the ridge as soon as Kee spotted him. McWilliams flattened himself behind Loto's body.

From down in the ranch yard Kee yelled, "Come on out you fucking haole piece of shit. Fucking traitor. You think you're going to kill me, come on, take your shot."

Kee shouldered the SMAW and walked toward the ridge.

McWilliams smiled and kept his position, hidden behind Loto's thick body. Fine. Let the asshole come closer.

But Kee didn't come straight toward the ridge. He veered off away from where McWilliams lay behind Loto and then slowly climbed up the ridge.

McWilliams cursed. "Shit." Not as dumb as you look. He wasn't going to shoot the rocket until he could see what was behind the ridge. Another twenty paces and Kee would be high enough on the slope to spot him. Could he get a shot off first?

McWilliams slowly brought the M16 into position. Kee kept advancing up the slope coming into McWilliams sites.

McWilliams tried to merge with the dirt and stone and mud underneath him. The first light of dawn had come up. The rain had tapered off into a slight mist. He saw Kee coming closer, his wet shoulder-length hair blowing in the wind.

McWilliams curled his finger around the trigger. He would wait until Kee came a bit closer. Two steps.

Kee dug his foot in for the next step. One more. McWilliams had him in his sites, ready to squeeze off a burst of bullets. Kee took another step. McWilliams fired just as Kee's slipped in the mud and went down on one knee. McWilliams shots flew over Kee's head and revealed his position. Kee turned and pulled the trigger on the SMAW. McWilliams knew the rocket wasn't going to be very close. Kee had been falling sideways and back when he fired. But McWilliams knew it didn't matter. Kee hadn't loaded the SMAW with a rocket. He'd loaded it with a fuel-air warhead.

McWilliams buried his head in the dirt.

The rocket roared out of the short barrel spewing a deadly mist of fuel over an area exceeding two hundred square meters. And then the rocket exploded, instantaneously igniting the nearly vaporized fuel. The ensuing explosion shook the entire area, igniting into a massive ball of fire that vaporized every particle of oxygen and immolated everything around it. The vacuum pulled the air out of Kensington McWilliams's lungs and incinerated the back of his body from head to toe.

Kee fell backward onto the ridge. In seconds, the fireball dissipated. Suddenly it was over. There was no more fire. No more shooting. Almost no sound at all.

ONE MAN'S LAW · 339

CHAPTER 49

There wasn't much left of the Toyota Tacoma's suspension by the time Devlin bounced it onto Highway 11. The left front headlight was gone, the bumper cracked, and the fender crumpled. There was a huge dent on the driver's side, but the pickup's engine was intact. Devlin kept his foot on the accelerator until the speedometer needle twitched at 87 mph.

Now that they had finally turned off the jarring, rutted road, Tuli calmly improvised a field dressing for the bullet wound that had torn out a piece of his right trapezius muscle.

Devlin fought to keep the car on the road. Within five minutes, he was approaching Kurtistown, and he screeched to a halt in front of the first pay phone he saw. He got out quickly, pulled off his Kevlar vest, and rushed to the phone. Tuli slowly stepped out and stood next to the car with the HK submachine gun at his side.

Devlin punched in Pacific Rim's number. He was put through to Mrs. Banks immediately.

"Mrs. Banks, please turn on the tape. I'm going to dictate a message. You have to get it to the commanding officer at Schofield. Do you know who that is?"

"Yes, Major General James Hawthorne."

"Do we have any relationship with him?"

"My husband and I have met him socially. More important, Mr. Chow knows him."

"Good. As soon as I'm done, tell Mr. Chow to listen to my message and assure the General he can rely on the accuracy of what I'm about to tell you."

"Yes, Jack, go ahead. The tape is running."

Devlin quickly described his assessment of the amount and scope of arms that he had seen being loaded onto the truck at Sam Kee's ranch. He emphasized the high probability that what he had seen was only a portion of a much larger quantity of stolen arms. He stipulated he had photographic images taken with a disposable camera, although he couldn't guarantee the quality. He detailed the presence of Army personnel at the scene. He identified Samuel Keamoku, AKA Sam Kee, as involved in the theft, describing him as an unstable, dangerous person with a group of fanatical followers. Finally, he described the location of Kee's ranch. He said nothing about the running gun battle that had occurred.

When he was finished, he told Mrs. Banks, "Include the Army liaison in Honolulu, but go straight to the top with this."

"Understood."

"Then I guess you'll have to pass on the information to local law enforcement."

"Okay."

"Thanks."

Devlin hung up and dialed the phone number he'd memorized for Da Restaurant. It was time to get Leilani out. Now.

The phone rang seven times with no answer. He checked his watch: 6:27 A.M.

Maybe too early.

He cursed, slammed down the phone, and jumped back into the Tacoma.

He knew now that the chain of events Billy had started with his death was going to be unstoppable. The U.S. Army was now involved, and there wasn't a force in the entire world that could confront and defeat them.

Devlin had to hand it to Billy. He'd unleashed the dogs of war. The only option now was to get out of the way, then sort out exactly who killed Billy Cranston later. Whoever they were, Devlin was going to make sure they weren't alive much longer.

CHAPTER **50**

Walter Harrison sat at his usual spot at the table outside Da Restaurant's kitchen drinking coffee and his usual morning eye-opener – a shot of warm vodka, along with chunks of cantaloupe. The phone in the kitchen rang. Walter checked his watch. A little early for a phone call. He didn't bother to answer it. More likely than not, it was for Leilani. She'd taken over talking to most of his suppliers.

Walter felt himself descending into a funk and decided that was fine with him.

He finished his vodka, chased it with coffee and another piece of cantaloupe. The phone stopped ringing. They'd call back, whoever it was.

Forty-five minutes later, Walter was into his first tall glass of vodka and orange juice when Leilani came down.

"Morning, Walter."

Walter answered with a silent forced smile. It seemed to Leilani as if Walter knew what she was about to tell him. She had a pang of guilt about using him and his restaurant for her own reasons. Maybe she would work until the end of the day, get everything set up for Walter, and leave tomorrow.

She sat down. Before she could say anything, Walter said, "What's that look for?"

"What look?"

"You look like you're about to tell me something I don't think I want to hear."

"Oh. Well, yes, something has come up at home. Family issues. I should go over to Oahu."

"When?"

Walter's petulance dispelled her guilt about leaving. It seemed like he wanted to be rid of her so he could sit and wallow in his cheap vodka and orange juice. So be it.

"I should leave today. I'll work through lunch and catch an afternoon flight."

"Why not leave now?"

Leilani looked at Walter for a moment, trying to figure out what might have set him off.

"What's the matter?"

"Nothing's the matter. We both knew this was temporary. You've improved things a lot, which is nice. But why kid ourselves? Your improvements will disappear soon after you do."

"You know, Walter, you could keep going with some of them."

"Yes, dear. I could."

Leilani was about to fall into Walter's trap and get into an argument with him. She decided not to.

"Okay, Walter. Thank you very everything. I'll go upstairs and get my things together and clear out. I think you'll be more comfortable with that."

It didn't take long for Leilani to pack up everything and clean her room. She carried her small carry-all bag and backpack downstairs. She stood next to Walter's table and extended her hand.

Walter frowned and tried to look put out as he pushed his chair back and rose to his feet. He shook Leilani's hand with a crooked smile.

"Thanks for everything, Walter."

"You're welcome."

"I'm sorry if I upset things around here."

Walter waved a hand. "Oh stop. Don't worry about any of it. I'm just being pissy. It's fine. That's what old washed-up drunks do."

"You're not old and you're not washed up. You're just doing what you want to do. You're entitled."

"Well, that's the nicest thing anybody has ever said to me."

"You're welcome."

"Thank you. How are you getting to the airport?"

"A friend lent me his car."

"Oh. And here I was thinking we'd have to take an awkward drive together."

"Nope."

Walter nodded and said, "Well, you better get a move on."

And then gunfire erupted on Main Street.

CHAPTER 51

Kee walked back into his ranch house carrying the SMAW. The heat and stench of the burning fuel oil mixed with the incinerated forest and human bodies filled the air around him. McWilliams and Loto for sure. Maybe one or two of his men if they had been close enough. Too bad the SMAW didn't get whoever had spied on them. Most likely that Devlin asshole and somebody helping him. Unless McWilliams soldiers got them, they most likely got away. Fuck it. It didn't matter. It was over now, or soon would be.

Kee picked up his phone and began making calls. He spoke to three of his men, telling them to get on the phone tree and spread the word. He told them, "This is it. Every damn thing I been predicting is coming true. The government's coming to take our land, our freedom, everything. Tell every son of a bitch to get into Pahoa-town, now. Everybody. The war starts, today!"

Kee ran to the loaded cargo truck still parked in front of the Quonset hut. There were bullet holes in from Devlin's Mauser, but nothing hit the engine or the tires. He tossed the SMAW in with the other munitions and weapons, slammed shut the tailgate, and headed for Pahoa-town, leaving whatever was in the Quonset huts or on the ground where it was.

By the time he skidded to a halt in front of his office on Main Street, there were already eighteen of his men milling around, including: Angel's Filipino cousins Efren and Tommy, Omar

Kahele, a notoriously mean drunk, Hani Isua, a heavyset balding man, and Tim Carpenter, a thin, bearded man of mixed Caucasian and Polynesian heritage who was always looking for a fight.

Kee jumped up on the hood of his truck holding an M16. His bare chest and cutoff shorts covered in dried blood and dirt, his hair a wild mane, yelling, "They're coming for you now, boys. You got one chance. Fight or die like homeless dogs."

The men surged toward Kee.

He yelled out, "Unload this truck. Grab whatever weapons you want; the rest goes into the office."

"Efren, Omar, take some men and vehicles, block off every access road into and out of town. Nobody gets out. Nobody gets in."

Kee lifted his rifle and fired into the air screaming a war cry. It seemed to release years of pent-up frustration and anger. More rifles fired. More yelling and screaming. The men around Kee were turning into a mob.

Kee yelled out. "They took our jobs. They took our money. They took our property. Today, we take it all back. Today, we take back Pahoa-town."

Kee organized a group to load the remaining weapons into his storefront and assigned four men to guard everything.

"The rest of you, get a rifle, divide up, go door to door and take everybody in this goddamn town and put 'em in the community center. Anybody gives you shit, shoot 'em and leave the damn body where it falls."

CHAPTER 52

The first thing Devlin did when he walked into the safe house was to call Da Restaurant. Again, no answer.

Next, Devlin looked at Tuli's bullet wound. He was going to need a doctor to properly deal with the injury, but for now, they cleaned and dressed the gash in Tuli's thick Trapezius muscle as quickly and effectively as they could.

Devlin said, "Clean up, dress, and then start packing all our weapons into the cases they came in. Throw your dirty clothes in with everything."

Fifteen minutes later, they were carrying the weapons and ammunition down into the basement.

Once everything was locked away, Devlin told Tuli, "Let's get the Filipino out of here."

Devlin checked the house one last time and locked up as Tuli led Angel out of the basement. He'd taped his arms behind his back and put a pillowcase over his head. Outside, he dropped Angel into the bed of the pickup. Devlin got in the pickup and drove off. A mile later, he pulled over.

Devlin and Tuli climbed out of the truck. Tuli lifted Angel out of the truck bed, the pillowcase still on his head. Tuli held him up by the back of his neck. Devlin cut off the duct tape and pulled off the pillowcase. The Filipino stood hunched over, blinking at the bright sunlight.

Devlin stepped up next to Angel. "Go home. Pray I never see you again, because if I do, I'll kill you."

Tuli shoved him down a slight embankment. By the time Angel got to his feet, the truck was no longer in sight.

Tuli asked Devlin, "Now what?"

"I have to make sure Leilani Cranston is out of that town. She may already be gone. Nobody's picking up the phone at the restaurant. We'll see if the car I left for her is still there."

"Then what? We gonna get out of here, too."

"You are. I've gotta get you to a doctor. Pacific Rim should be able to get one lined up for you in Hilo. Get that wound attended to, and then fly back to Honolulu."

"What are you gonna do?"

"Not sure. I'll check in with Chow. Once the Army gets in here, it'll be chaos for a while. I'll wait until things are sorted out. I know why Billy Cranston died, but I still don't know who actually killed him."

"Think you'll ever know?"

"I'd like to, but the way this is going down it might not matter all that much. Anybody connected to this mess will be either dead or locked up for a long time."

Tuli was about to argue that he wanted to stay on the Big Island as long as Devlin did, but police sirens and flashing lights interrupted him. Devlin looked in his rearview mirror.

"Shit."

Devlin pulled over to let three police cars stream past him. As he drove back onto the highway, he heard the first muffled explosion coming from the direction of Pahoa.

Tuli and Devlin exchanged looks. Neither of them said anything.

CHAPTER 53

Back in Oahu, Lieutenant Colonel Sam Weisman hadn't needed to look for Major George Walker. The Honolulu police notified his office they'd found his body.

The HASP officer, an Army sergeant whose job it was to act as a liaison between military and local police, was waiting on the street for Weisman outside Tay Williams's apartment when he arrived. The sergeant saluted the provost marshal and opened the downstairs door, reminding Weisman how much dead bodies and rotting blood could stink.

The soldier muttered, "It's a mess. The cops are waiting for you before they release the bodies."

Weisman thanked the tired soldier and walked slowly up the stairs. A uniformed Honolulu cop guarded the doorway. Inside, Weisman saw the usual scrum of detectives, uniformed cops, morgue and medical examiner people milling about the death scene.

Weisman looked at the bodies. Surprisingly there wasn't as much blood as he had expected. The cops had opened all the windows, but the dead bodies had been in an airless apartment in the tropics for almost twenty-four hours. One detective smoked a cheap cigar to counter the smell, but Weisman thought that just made the nauseating stench even worse. The odors of death and body waste had soaked into everything.

Weisman found the homicide detective in charge, Lieutenant Edward Kaolani. He introduced himself and asked the detective, "What do you know?"

Kaolani was dressed in the standard dark pants and white short-sleeve shirt with a dark tie. He was a heavy man. His neck was too big for him to button his collar. His eyes blurry from lack of sleep. Kaolani looked as if he would have left the scene long ago except that he had to wait for the Army official.

He pointed to the dead bodies and spoke in the familiar Hawaiian lilt that tended to turn every sentence into a question. "The blonde? She's a Hotel Street hooker. Drug addict. Heroin. Her sheet goes back three years. Arrests for prostitution, soliciting, and two drug possession charges. The man is your guy, George Walker. We talked to some of the neighbors. Looks like he was a regular customer. We're checking bullet holes and angles and all that, but we figure she shot him and then did herself."

Weisman stood for almost a minute looking at the scene. Kaolani waited patiently. The minute seemed like a long time.

Finally, Weisman asked, "Why?"

"Why what?"

"Why'd she shoot him?"

Kaolani shrugged. "You tell me."

"I can't. I mean, why shoot a regular customer? Customers are not the ones you shoot."

"Maybe he stiffed her."

"Then why shoot herself?"

"What are you saying, Colonel?"

"I'm saying the murder/suicide scenario doesn't make any sense without some kind of motive."

"It's early in the investigation. We'll find out the motive. You got a better scenario?"

"I know Walker left the base yesterday morning for no reason. Got up, left his office, didn't tell anyone anything. No explanation.

Nothing. Like he's running off to an emergency. What kind of emergency could there be in his whore's apartment?"

Kaolani scratched his left eyebrow and then rubbed his eyes with his thumb and forefinger. "The kine gets you shot I guess."

Kaolani wasn't interested in developing theories with Weisman. "You want to look at anything else?"

Weisman turned toward the body and squatted down. Weisman lifted Walker's hip, rolled the body onto its side, and lifted his T-shirt so he could see Walker's back. The skin of the dead man's back was clouded with blood turned purple.

Weisman stood up and looked at his watch. Almost 10:15 A.M.

"Looks like he got shot pretty soon after he left his office." He looked at his watch. "About twenty-four hours?"

"That's what the M.E. guy said."

"No other bruises or wounds?"

"Nothing obvious. We looked pretty careful."

"And the girl right after him?"

"Looks like it."

Weisman said, "No signs of struggle? Nothing broken?"

"Nope."

"Notes, letters, money lying around?"

"No. Couple of glassine bags of heroin and her works in the bedroom."

Weisman nodded.

"Okay. Let's get out of here before our clothes stink forever."

"I can release the bodies?"

"Yes. I'll check with my superiors about getting the body from you."

"Yeah. You gotta file and all do all the paperwork for the body."

"I'll tell my sergeant downstairs to go with your people and give the morgue whatever information they need."

"Fine."

Weisman and Kaolani walked out of the apartment. As soon as

they hit the street, they both bummed cigarettes from a uniformed cop and lit them.

Kaolani rubbed his eyes and spoke first. "So you think it's a setup?"

"I do. There's no reason I see in there for that to happen. If anything, it should be the other way around."

"Why's that?"

"Walker had problems."

"Other than sneaking off to fuck whores?"

"Yes. And by the way, she didn't look dressed for sex."

"True." Kaholani waited for a beat then asked, "You gonna tell me Walker's problem?"

"Yes. But not just yet."

"Makes it harder for me to explain why I can't close a case looks cut and dried."

Weisman inhaled deeply on his cigarette and said, "Okay. Between us, Walker was into something that had to involve civilians with criminal backgrounds."

"What thing?"

"Don't know enough about the extent of it to say right now. Let's just say it was bad enough someone would want to kill him. Let's assume for a second the hooker is the connection between Walker and the bad guys. Got any idea who was running her?"

"Sure. I'd have to confirm it, but most of the whores down here are run by Eddie Lihu. I mean, not directly. He doesn't pimp them, but he runs the scene. Not that you could prove it."

"Lihu?"

"Yeah."

Weisman made a non-committal sound.

"What?"

"I can see how Eddie Lihu would have more reason to kill George Walker than his whore did."

"A reason you ain't gonna tell me."

"Not at the moment," said Weisman.

"Which leaves us where?"

"Needing a little more time."

"For what? More time ain't gonna get you any connection to Eddie Lihu. That ended in that apartment."

Weisman frowned making another non-committal sound.

Kaolani said, "So what do you want me to do?"

"Just sit on this a few days. Can you investigate for about a week before you close it out?"

"A week?"

"Yes."

"I can fuck around for a week, but I'm not putting in time on something I can close right now."

"Good enough. If I don't come through for you, file it whatever way you see it."

Kaolani threw his cigarette butt into the street. "I will. I got a shitload of other work to do before this anyhow."

"Just one other thing?"

"What?"

"If you confirm that this was one of Lihu's whores, would you let me know that?"

"I'll ask around." Kaolani handed Weisman his card. "If I don't call you, you call me."

Weisman nodded, shook hands with the police detective and walked back to his car trying to think it through.

Assume George Walker had been involved in stealing military equipment. Assume it was a significant amount. For sure, Eddie Lihu was one of the few people on the Islands who could traffic a large amount of stolen military weapons. But how could they prove it? Just tracking and itemizing what had been stolen was going to take weeks. Maybe months. How cold would the trail be? And how could they discover the buyers? And then connect them to Eddie Lihu through a dead whore?

As far as Weisman knew, Eddie Lihu had never even been indicted for a crime.

He folded in long frame into his car and rolled down the windows. The smell of death was in his clothes, his short-cropped hair, his nostrils. Eventually, the smell would go away. But not this case. Not for a long, long time.

CHAPTER 54

After he left Kee's ranch, Eddie Lihu dozed in the back seat of the Chevy Blazer while his bodyguard Charlie made the drive to Hilo. It took almost an hour to skirt around the western edge of the airport and make his way up to the port.

Charlie kept driving until he reached the main harbor area. He stopped in front of the security guard's booth and presented a wallet with identification. The guard recognized the card which had been issued by his own security company and waved the Chevy into the harbor area.

Charlie drove slowly, passing shipping containers, trucks, wooden pallets, and ten-foot-high triangular stacks of six-foot-wide steel pipe. He continued past a five-block-long terminal building that ran parallel to the waterfront docking area on his left.

A seagoing passenger ship was tied up in front of the shipping terminal. In front of the passenger ship was a Japanese fishing trawler, and in front of that a large ferryboat with a stern big enough to accommodate about a dozen cars.

The area on the east side of the terminal building was mostly in shadows. Charlie drove through another lot past rows of tractor trailers parked in groups. At the far end of the lot, he pulled the Chevy in between two empty Matson trailers, hiding the Chevy Blazer in the dark shadows.

When Charlie turned off the headlights, the surrounding area fell into darkness. The only discernible sound was the ping of the car's engine cooling in the night air.

In front of them was the southern edge of Hilo Harbor. About a quarter of a mile out in the ocean, a natural coral reef protected the harbor. Man-made breakers calmed the ocean further so that by the time the water reached the shoreline, it was quite still. Instead of the rustle and crash of waves along a shoreline, there was only the slight wallop of sluggish green swells against a cement breakwater.

Lihu and Charlie walked out of the parking lot, toward a small, rundown shack at the far edge of the harbor area, mostly hidden by surrounding palm trees and vegetation. The shack was dark inside, but a single floodlight nailed to its roof illuminated the area in front of the shack. They walked through the circle of artificial light and down a narrow walkway that led to a secluded park and dock area.

The dock was just big enough for three or four small boats. The out-of-the-way anchorage was so unused that an old wooden sailing ship had remained tied up there until it rotted and sank in the shallow water.

Lihu and Charlie veered to the right, away from the water, and crossed a grassy area. At the edge of the grass, four local men sat around a picnic table finishing off a case of beer. Somebody had stretched the ubiquitous blue plastic tarpaulin between several of the palm trees. An old rusty pickup truck was parked nearby. It was a typical local poor man's enclave, set up near another piece of Hawaiian shoreline.

Lihu's three men were mixed-blood Islanders. All three had that burnt-skin local moke look. And all three were sullen and mean enough to get up and pound heavy fists into anybody that bothered them.

They had set up a tent on a little strip of sand between the palm trees and the breakwater. Their location gave them a good view of any boats entering the small docking area, as well as a view back to Hilo Harbor.

Lihu dropped into a plantation squat in front of their tent. Charlie disappeared in the shadows beyond the faint glow of a two-burner Coleman camp stove set up in front of the tent. A dirty fry pan was on one burner and a pot of coffee on the other. The burner under the coffee pot set at a low flame gave off a dim orange light that barely illuminated the men.

All three men waited for Lihu to speak.

"When's the boat get back?"

The man next to Lihu answered, "Should be 'bout an hour. Turnaround takes two."

Lihu asked. "Where do you load?"

The man opposite Lihu pointed to the corner of the little harbor. "Boat comes in on the other side of that wreck." He pointed behind Lihu. "Truck comes in past those storage tanks onto the access road. We load the boat from right over there. How many more loads you got comin'?"

Lihu said, "One more truckload. You should be able to get everything out to the ship in three loads. As soon as the truck gets here, you unload everything and send him out. Tell the transfer boat to haul ass back and forth. No breaks. Keep going until you're done."

"We still got about four loads stacked up from the other trucks."

"Just keep loading. I want you guys done here today. Don't stop when the sun comes up. Nobody can see what you're doing down here."

The men stirred, looked down. Lihu knew what they were thinking. "Don't stop. Don't give me any bullshit about the hours. Most of that time is waiting."

The men didn't say anything, but they each knew that loading during the day was going to increase their risk.

Lihu looked around the circle. "Any problems with that?"

Nobody spoke.

"You finish today, you get paid today, plus a bonus. The sooner you get done, the bigger the bonus. After the last load, get the fuck out of here."

All three men nodded. Lihu looked around the group, waiting for any questions or complaints. There were none.

Lihu stood and walked away from the glow of the Coleman stove. Charlie slipped out of the shadows and fell in behind him. Lihu looked at his watch. He had about four hours to kill before the first flight back to Oahu.

CHAPTER 55

As soon as the last police car raced passed them, Devlin pulled back onto the highway and followed. Even from a mile away, they could see the black smoke rising into the sky. As they came around the bend leading into town, they saw the more police cars, an ambulance, and a fire truck jammed together about two hundred yards south of a burning gasoline tanker truck blocking the road into town. The truck's 10,000-gallon tank had been blasted apart, spreading burning gasoline all around the surrounding area.

That alone was enough to blockade the town, but there were also four of Kee's men standing on the roof of a gas station about fifteen yards back from the truck. They fired random burst of gunfire into the flaming wreckage.

Devlin pulled the battered Tacoma over to the shoulder as two of the cops yelled and waved at their fellow officers and the ambulance driver to fall back.

Devlin cursed, pulled out, made a U-turn, raced back to the first intersection, and made a right turn.

Tuli asked, "Is there another way in?"

"Maybe. This leads to a bypass road that meets Main Street on the other side of town."

"What chance you think they haven't blocked that?"

"Zero," said Devlin. "But at least we won't have to breathe in that black smoke."

The scene at the west end of town was even more chaotic. Large sections of road and the surrounding area had been cratered by grenades. A telephone utility truck had been blasted into pieces and left blocking the road. There were four other abandoned vehicles including one police car riddled with bullet holes. The front of the police car sat in a crater with the driver's side wheel blown off the axle.

Devlin and Tuli pulled the Tacoma over, jumped out, and headed toward a cop standing in the middle of the road holding people and traffic back.

Devlin said, "Stay with the truck, Tuli."

Devlin walked toward the cop. He was one of the two cops who had arrived at the scene in the Village Inn parking lot when Kee and his men beat up the oil rig worker. He didn't look so confident now.

Devlin yelled, "Officer, you have to get these people back at least five-hundred yards."

"Who are you?"

"I'm ex-military. This mess was made with grenade launchers that have a range of over 400 meters. "

The cop decided not to argue. He waved and yelled for people to get back.

Devlin walked alongside him as he herded the bystanders to a safer distance. Devlin asked the cop, "What do you know?"

"Word is Sam Kee took over the town. Somehow, they got ahold of military weapons. Army's coming in heavy. Supposed to be coptering in at least a battalion. Helicopters are landing out at the high school now. Nobody's goin' in or out of that town. You'd better move out of here."

Devlin made his way past a man complaining about his truck being shot up, catching snatches of people talking about crazy Sam Kee, predicting he was going to go down shooting and killing people until every last person in that town was dead.

When he reached the truck, Devlin stopped and looked around.

Tuli asked, "Now what?"

Devlin stared past the wreckage toward the town.

"Kee made it back. With that truckload of munitions and weapons."

"Shit. He hole up in dat town with all that, he gonna be able to make a damn big lot of trouble, brudda."

"I have to get in there."

"Why?"

"I got to find out if someone is still in there."

"Who?"

"Billy Cranston's sister."

"What the hell she doin' in there?"

"Helping me. Us."

"Keeping secrets from Tuli, huh?"

"And from her."

"I get it. Safer that way." Tuli shook his head. "Meantime, you go in there you gonna be dead pretty damn quick, boss. Army gonna be here soon. They the only ones can stop that guy now."

Devlin looked at his watch. 11:32 A.M.

Tuli was right. Devlin had no idea what he might be facing if he snuck into town. Or if Leilani was in there, where she might be, or how many of Kee's men might be guarding her.

"Shit." Devlin climbed behind the wheel. "How's your wound?"

"It's nothing. Don't worry about it."

"Let's see what's happening with the big guns."

CHAPTER 56

As Sam Kee and Willi Pohano walked toward the community center. Willi, a thickset man with unruly hair that grew low down his forehead and a scraggly beard, slipped a bandanna over his face. Most of the men had taken to covering their faces. But not Sam Kee. He strode toward the community center checking out the town, a 9mm Beretta holstered on his right hip. Men stood on the roofs of the old wooden buildings that ran along Main Street. Several were outside Kee's office. Others were in the town bar drinking. The rest were guarding the community center. At last count, Kee had thirty-two men in town with him.

The community center was set back about two-hundred feet off Main Street on an undeveloped plot of land. A narrow dirt path led to the squat, flat-roof building made of concrete blocks painted a bilious green that was supposed to blend with the tropical greenery in the area.

Kee and Willi walked past two men guarding the center's front door and into the main meeting room, which was forty feet wide by sixty feet deep. There were two rows of Formica-topped tables set up end to end running parallel to the walls on the long sides of the room. In between the tables were six rows of metal chairs, ten chairs to a row. At the front of the room stood a lectern. The back wall was dominated by a set of wide double doors.

There were twenty-eight men, women, and children in the meeting room, guarded by five of Kee's men, all of them armed with

366 · JOHN CLARKSON

military issue M16s and Army issue 9mm Berettas. Whoever had been in town when Kee and his men had arrived were now hostages.

The captured townspeople sat in the chairs set up in the center section of the meeting room, between the rows of tables. There were three of Kee's men in the back of the room and two in front. The five guards turned their attention to Kee when he entered.

Kee had changed into a black T-shirt and loose black cotton drawstring pants. His hair was once again bound tightly in back. On his feet were black Kung Fu-style slippers.

Indoors, Kee appeared larger than usual. He walked directly to the front of the room, stood next to the lectern, pulled out his Beretta, and announced, "Everybody stand. Women over on the right side. Line up in front of the tables. Men to the left. Line up in front of the tables on your side. Men face the wall. Women face the center."

People slowly stood up and started to shuffle around one another and quietly sort themselves out. Of the twenty-eight captives, seventeen were women, and three were children, Janet's kids. Eight hostages were men.

The women moved to their side of the room. All the men stood up and shuffled over to their side except for a surly, rugged man named Moon, who could usually be found sitting in the parking lot next to the Village Inn nursing a wide-necked bottle of Mickey's Malt Liquor. He was accustomed to people giving him a wide berth. He sat sullenly on his chair with his thick arms folded. When Kee saw he wasn't moving, he told him, "Moon, go."

Moon scowled at Kee. "What the fuck are you doing, Sam? What is all this bullshit?"

Kee looked at Moon without any expression, raised his Beretta, and shot him twice in the center of the chest. The gunfire was so loud in the enclosed space that everyone flinched or ducked, even Kee's guards. The bullets knocked Moon back with such force his chair crashed into the chairs behind him. The orderly shuffle of the crowd turned into a pushing panic as the hostages tried to get away from the bleeding corpse in the middle of the room where Kee still pointed the Beretta.

Kee stood glaring at the hostages, a cloud of gun smoke swirling around him. Kee yelled at them. "My name is not, Sam. The next person that shows me any disrespect or defies me will be executed. You are hostages. You belong to us. No one can help you. We will kill you if you disobey us. If you obey, you might live to enjoy life without the haole's foot on the back of your necks in a free Hawaii."

Kee aimed his weapon around the room. "Does anyone want to die?" he yelled.

Each time he pointed the Beretta at someone, he or she cowered. Not one person in the room doubted he would shoot anyone who gave him cause.

Kee shoved the hot Beretta into his hip holster and walked toward the women, who were huddled together near the back of the room where they had moved to get away from the dead man. Kee grabbed the nearest woman by the arm. He pulled and shoved her toward the front of the room with such force that she almost fell. He did the same with the next two women, and the next, until they all moved forward.

Kee yelled, "Spread apart. Move. Line up along the tables. Face the middle. Move!"

He shoved and slapped the women, giving them instructions until he had them lined up in the order he wanted – divided from left to right according to race, and within race according to age.

"Put your shit on the table behind you."

The women did as they were told. On the far left was the oldest white woman Rachel Steele. Seven more haole women were lined up. The blond waitress from the Paradise Cafe, Wendy, was the youngest white. Next in line were ten mixed-race women. The non-Caucasian lineup started with the elderly Chinese woman who ran the convenience store and ended with a sixteen-year-old local girl.

She was pretty, but she had the stocky build of many Polynesian/ Hawaiian teenagers. She stood at the far left of the line, head down, trying to hide the fact that she was crying.

Kee told Janet's three children, two boys and one girl, to sit in the last row of chairs by themselves. The men were lined up opposite the women facing the wall.

Kee turned to the women. He walked down the line looking at each woman, poking and prodding their bodies, grabbing a few breasts, making some of them turn around so he could grope their rear ends.

Leilani stood almost exactly midway among the darker skinned women. She wore only her white walking shorts and a tank-top T-shirt. Kee stopped in front of here. He pulled out his handgun, cocked the hammer, and pointed it at Leilani. "You got anything to say to me, you half-breed bitch?"

Leilani said, "No."

Kee smiled. He eased the hammer back on the Beretta. He nodded, then he swept his arm across the scene and told his men, "The spoils of war, boys. You can take 'em when I say, all except for this one." He pointed to Leilani. "She's mine. Gonna make her last hours on earth real special for her."

Kee surveyed the women one more time. They stood awkwardly. Afraid. Embarrassed. And then Kee looked at the end of the line where the sixteen-year-old Hawaiian girl stood.

He looked back and nodded at Leilani, then walked over to the girl. His steps in his rubber-soled slippers were very quiet. He stopped in front of the girl. He held his Beretta in one hand, aimed at the ceiling. He gripped her chin with the other hand and forced her head up so that she had to look at him.

"Why you got your head down?"

The girl muttered, "I don't know."

"You think your ancestors walked with their heads down?"

"No."

"You think you're too fat?"

"I don't know."

She began to cry, at first quietly, then more openly.

Kee punched the muzzle of the Beretta into the side of her head, softly at first, then with more force.

"Stop it."

She tried, again lowering her head.

Kee yelled, "Look up!"

She looked up, too startled for a moment to cry.

"You need to be with men, not all these stupid, fucked up bitches."

Kee grabbed her shoulder, turned her toward the doors, and pushed the Beretta into her back.

"Walk."

As he marched the young women toward the rear doors, Kee told his guards, "Take the rest of the bitches to the craft store across from the office. Keep 'em handy. Leave the men here."

Kee pushed the girl out the back door.

Most of the women looked straight ahead. Two didn't. Rachel Steele and Leilani Kilau Cranston.

CHAPTER 57

There was only one cop standing by his police car guarding the entrance to the high school parking lot. Devlin held up his driver's license and lied without hesitation.

"General Hawthorne has requested my associate and I meet with him immediately."

The cop looked at Devlin and Tuli, then at the group of four fully-armed soldiers dressed in combat gear standing in front of a sawhorse barricade blocking the entrance to the high school. He pointed his thumb at the soldiers and told Devlin, "Go talk to them."

As Devlin drove through the parking lot, he saw troops jumping out of a Bell Iroquois Huey transport helicopter sitting at one end of the school's football field, while a second Huey took off from the other end. Past the football field, a massive CH-47 Chinook sat unloading men and equipment.

Devlin kept showing his driver's license and repeating his line of bullshit until he and Tuli were escorted into the high school gymnasium. Major General James Hawthorne, commander of the Army's 25ᵗʰ Infantry Division, sat at the far end of the gym behind a line of six long tables brought up from the school cafeteria. There were five staff officers seated with him. Two rows of long tables had been placed at either end of the six tables forming a U. Dozens of soldiers were setting up computers, printers, communication equipment, and power lines.

Hawthorne sat yelling into a cell phone, "Listen, a goddamn Stinger cruising around up there at Mach 2 will find any passenger jet that comes near this island. Shut down everything. No incoming commercial aircraft coming in or out until further notice. None. Shut it down, now."

Devlin and Tuli stood in the middle of the U waiting for the general. Hawthorne turned off the phone and looked up to see two big men staring at him.

"Who are you?"

"Jack Devlin. I reported seeing a truckload of your weapons."

"Who's the man with you?"

"My associate, Mr. Tuulima Mafa."

"He with you when you saw my weapons?"

"Yes, sir."

"How'd you get in here?"

"Kept telling people you need to talk to me."

"You're right. Both of you, follow me."

Hawthorne motioned for his aide, Colonel Mitchell Wyse, to come with him as he led Devlin and Tuli out of the gym into the boy's locker room. Hawthorne sat on a bench in front of a row of lockers, pointed to a bench opposite him, and said, "Take a seat." He turned to Wyse. "Mitch, close that door. Make sure nobody walks in." He turned back to Devlin, "First of all, anything you tell me doesn't leave this room. Agreed."

Devlin said, "Fine by me. Did you get the report I dictated to Pacific Rim for you?"

"Listened to it flying over. What else can you tell me?"

Devlin asked, "Have you had any contact with the town yet?"

"No. But in the next hour, every phone line out of there will be directly connected to this location. What am I looking at, Mr. Devlin?"

"Bottom line, a fanatic named Sam Kee who's been running drugs and pushing around people in that town for years looks like he's taken over that town with a truckload of your weapons. He seems to have accumulated a following by spouting a bunch of native-rights rhetoric. The usual they stole our islands act. Maybe he actually believes some of it. Or, maybe it's a total con. His followers haven't got much else going for them, so I'd say they swallow most of it."

"What else do you know about this guy?"

"He's a thug, a rapist, a bully, and I believe he's responsible for the death of a highly decorated Vietnam vet named William Edward Cranston. I also believe that William Cranston was killed because he tried to expose the trafficking in stolen Army weapons and the people involved. From what I've found out, the people involved included Sam Kee and some of his followers, as well as whatever Army personnel were behind this."

"What Army personnel?"

Devlin hesitated. Then said, "I can't identify them. I saw at least four soldiers loading stolen weapons at Sam Kee's ranch. Early this morning."

"What weapons?"

"Everything was in crates. My guess, squad-size weapons of all types. M16s, grenade launchers, SMAWs, ammunition. You probably have a pretty good idea based on what they're firing off in that town."

"And you know William Cranston how?"

"Served with him briefly in Vietnam."

"And you're investigating his death?"

"Hired by his father, Jasper Cranston. Also ex-Army. Retired as a brigadier general."

Hawthorne took a moment to absorb Devlin's information, then asked, "What does this maniac Sam Kee want?"

"I can only speculate."

"Go ahead."

"He knows we saw what was on his ranch, so he knows it's only a matter of time before he's caught or killed. My guess, he wants to go out in a blaze of glory and take as many with him as possible."

"How many men do you think he has in there?"

"Fifteen, twenty, maybe more. They're petty criminals as far as I can tell. Amateurs. Angry, out-of-work, disenfranchised people. Pretty good fodder for an armed riot. I doubt if they have a clue about what they've gotten themselves into, but I think most of them will follow Kee wherever he leads them. They haven't got much else."

"Do you have any idea how many people are in that town?"

"I'd say somewhere between twenty and thirty. Maybe more. Most of them women. Most likely a few children."

"Do you have an idea of how much ordinance they have?"

"The cargo truck I saw on Kee's ranch was a fairly new GMC. A flatbed about twenty-foot long. Had wood-slat sides and a canvas cover about six feet above the truck bed. Big knobby tires to get over the rough terrain. I'd say it could carry six, seven thousand pounds easy. I couldn't see how full it was, but if it was only half-full that's a hell of a lot of ordinance."

Hawthorne grimaced.

Devlin asked, "How much more did they steal, General?"

"A hell of a lot more than one truckload," said Hawthorne. "I can't go into details. We're still investigating."

Devlin thought for a moment. "Well, obviously it was stolen here on the Big Island. That means Pohakuloa Training Center..."

Hawthorne interrupted Devlin.

"All right, listen Mr. Devlin, I read your file on the way over here. You're Army. You served honorably in a lousy war. I'm assuming you don't want to do anything to harm the service. I'll tell you one thing, and then we drop the subject. The Division was upgrading squad-size arms. A significant portion of the old weapons was diverted."

"You made the switch and trained your men on the new weapons at Pohakuloa?"

"Yes."

"How'd you ship the old stuff out? Through Bradshaw?"

"No. Too expensive to fly it out. Everything was trucked over to Hilo. Shipped out of there to the Mainland. New Jersey."

"Which means you hauled everything over the Saddle Road. Lot of opportunities there. That route is covered in rain and fog off and on for miles. By the way, my sense of it is that Kee and his men hid weapons all over this island. There may still be..."

"Rest assured, we are going to find every goddamn crate, rifle, weapon, and every last bit of ammunition."

"Kee isn't doing this on his own. There's got to be Army personnel involved. There's got to be someone he's selling this stuff to. Do you know who's behind this?"

"I will." Hawthorne turned toward Tuli. "Mr. Mafa, I'm relying on you to keep this information private."

"I wasn't listening."

"Good. All right gentlemen, let's deal with the immediate problem. What else can you tell me about that town?"

Devlin said, "One road in and out. The main part of town is about ten blocks long. There's a bypass road that swings around east. Only a couple of roads hook up the bypass with Main Street. All the other streets leading from Main Street dead end a couple of blocks east or west. You can close the whole thing off fairly easily."

"Anything else?"

"Yes. You should know that Billy Cranston's sister, Leilani Cranston is one of the hostages in there. I intend to get her out."

"Shit."

"She's been helping me with my investigation. I have to get her out."

"Nobody is going into that town except my men, when and how I say."

"When is that going to be?"

"When I say so."

"I suggest it's before they start killing hostages. Assuming they haven't started already."

CHAPTER 58

After Kee left the community center with the young Hawaiian girl, two of his men dragged out Moon's body. They told the women to clean up the trail of blood they smeared across the linoleum floor. The women were taken to the crafts store where they settled into small groups around the room. They took turns using the bathroom. They improvised a sleeping area. When they asked about food and drink, the guards allowed two women to walk to the grocery store and bring back whatever they could carry. There was no way to cook anything, so the women settled for fruit, bread, and cold canned food.

Three times, Kee's men came into the store and dragged a woman out at gunpoint. Their intention was clear.

For two hours, Leilani sat by herself and fumed. She should have left last night. What had she accomplished by staying? Nothing. And now this – sitting, sweating, in a stinking, fucking backwater crafts store waiting to be raped by that maniac, Sam Kee.

She looked around the room at the wan, helpless women. They seemed so resigned. Whispering to each other. Clinging to each other. She was worn out from feeling tired and afraid and helpless.

Devlin. Devlin. "Christ," she muttered to herself. How did he always know what to do? Devlin never seemed trapped or worried or outsmarted. No matter what happened, he always seemed to know the next move. But damn it, Leilani thought, he didn't know any more than me. I was the one who gave him most of his information.

Even he said that. So how the hell did he always know what to do? Why was he always so sure of himself? Was he just faking it? How did he do it?

She sat alone in the corner of the hot, stuffy room and thought about it. Her brain seemed frozen. Stuck. Her head ached. She felt like crying. Like screaming. She thought about praying. She tried to crystallize a thought, a silent appeal to her ancestors, to feel their spirit, but her attempt at prayer just made her feel stupid and more weak.

And then, in a final moment of loathing, she rejected everything and everybody: Devlin, her ancestors, these women, everybody. Everything. And in the next moment, she understood. It hit with such sudden impact that she grimaced. Fucking men, she said to herself. Devlin didn't know any more than she did, except for one thing. The moment he knew who his enemy was, he went for them. He didn't question himself or second guess. He went straight at them.

That was the difference

She was surrounded by frightened, sweating women and whining children. Trapped. But suddenly none of that mattered. Despite the heat and the thirst and the confusion, one thing was clear. Sam Kee was the enemy. And Kee was going to come for her. Eventually, she would face him.

Leilani stood and walked to the nearest guard. She kept her face expressionless, her head slightly bowed. She asked permission to go to the bathroom. He nodded and motioned her ahead with the barrel of his rifle.

She quickly walked to the ladies' room. The bathroom was occupied, and two other women were waiting. The lack of movement, the waiting, the not knowing had been driving her crazy before. But now all that disappeared. Now she stood in the bathroom line and spent her time thinking, planning, picturing it. The waiting time meant nothing.

When Leilani finally entered the small bathroom, she immediately went to the dispensing machine bolted to the wall and bought a tampon. She went into a stall, slid off her shorts and panties, sat down, and unwrapped the tampon and carefully slid it of its cardboard holder, being careful to leave the bottom third in the holder. She had a small nick on her index finger from cutting potatoes. She put her finger between her teeth and chewed at the cut.

When she thought about why she was doing this, a ripple of fear passed through her, like an electric current hitting her in the abdomen. She remained sitting on the toilet and emptied her bladder. Suddenly a rifle butt banged against the bathroom door, and her stomach knotted. Leilani cursed quietly to herself then yelled, "Be right out!"

When Leilani walked back into the store, she saw that Rachel Steele was sitting in the spot she had occupied. The older woman was staring right at her, making eye contact, motioning ever so slightly, angling her head to indicate that Leilani should sit next to her.

Leilani did not want to deal with the old woman now. She had more to do. More to think about. But there was something so insistent in the lady's fierce blue eyes that she could not ignore her.

Leilani strode casually across the room and sat down next to Rachel. The room was fairly quiet. Many were sleeping. Those who were awake talked quietly.

Only two guards were watching over the seventeen women and three children. Leilani wanted to be by herself. Think about how to deal with Kee. How to go right at him and hurt or kill him before he hurt or killed her, but first she'd have to deal with this old lady.

Rachel spoke quietly to Leilani without looking at her. She said, "You're next."

"What do you mean?"

"I think you're going to be the next one they take out of here."

"Why do you think that?"

"I'm surprised Kee hasn't taken you out already. He must be busy."

"If he does, he'll wish he hadn't."

"Good," said Rachel. "I was certain if anyone had any spirit in here it would be you."

Leilani turned to Rachel but didn't say anything.

"And I have the feeling you're working with Mr. Devlin."

A fresh pulse of fear hit Leilani, and she said, "What? Where did you get that idea?"

"Don't worry. I don't think anyone else knows."

"Why did you say that?"

"Oh, a bit of logic. Two strangers in town about the same time." Rachel paused to look at Leilani. "You and Mr. Devlin both have the same quality. The same look about you."

"What look is that?"

"I don't know. Anger. A fierceness. I don't know. Maybe it's just that you and Mr. Devlin don't seem as afraid of things as other people." Leilani didn't say anything. Rachel continued. "Be that as it may, my dear, I thought I should tell you that I have a gun. And I have absolutely no idea what to do with it."

This time Leilani made sure not to look at Rachel. She spoke quietly. "Did you say you have a gun?"

"Yes. But I don't know how to use it. Do you?"

"Where did you get it?"

"It belongs to Mr. Devlin. I was up in the middle of the night to pee. I looked out my bathroom window and saw him leave it in the trunk of his car, and then put the keys to the car on the back wheel. When I heard the gunfire and commotion up the street near Kee's office, I went down into the parking lot and got the gun out of the trunk. I put the car keys back on the rear tire where I saw Mr. Devlin put them."

Leilani didn't say anything for a moment then asked, "Where is it?"

"It's in the middle of my waistband, in front. One of the advantages of age is that it makes you less appealing to men like these." Rachel paused. "I wasn't going to let them touch me anyhow."

Leilani looked over at Rachel. She had on baggy cotton pants and a pullover top that was loose enough and large enough so that Leilani couldn't discern the shape of the gun.

Both women sat in silence for a minute. Rachel spoke again. "Do you know how it works?"

"Is it a revolver or an automatic?"

"I don't know."

"Does it have a barrel that spins?"

"No. No, it's all one piece. Kind of rectangular."

"Yes. I know how it works."

"Then I'm going to give it to you. I'm going to lie down under that table. You get in front of me, so they can't see me. Face toward them so you can keep an eye on them. I'll take the gun out and tuck it under your butt. You reach around and take it when nobody's looking."

Rachel moved stiffly and awkwardly as she slowly lowered herself down to the floor. She inched her way back until she was lying out of view under the table.

Once Rachel was in place, Leilani slid in front of her, blocking the view. Rachel reached under her clothing and eased out the small Beretta 21A. She held the small gun tightly in one hand, covering it with the other. Just as she was about to slide the gun toward Leilani, she heard the double doors bang open at the other end of the room. She quickly put the gun back under her top and shoved it into her waistband.

Leilani slid away from Rachel, cursing softly, "Shit, shit, shit."

CHAPTER 59

Major General James Hawthorne was seconds away from ordering Jack Devlin to remain in the high school so he wouldn't try to enter the town when there was an insistent knock on the locker room door.

Colonel Mitchell Wyse opened the door part way. The officer standing there said, "We have a situation. General Hawthorne needs to know ASAP."

Hawthorne heard his officer talking to Wyse. He told Devlin and Tuli, "Don't leave this building."

He went out into the hallway.

"What's the problem?"

#

Fifteen minutes earlier, Hawthorne's soldiers manning the barricade set up at the east end of Pahoa-town spotted Janet's oldest boy approaching from two hundred meters. He was six-years-old. Blond. Thin. Wearing a torn Batman T-shirt, a pair of shorts that were too big for him, and worn-out rubber thongs. There was a 9 x 13-inch manila envelope taped around his neck. He walked normally except for the fact that he was crying and holding his right hand away from his body. Something too big for the boy to hold on his own had been secured inside his right fist with silver duct tape.

The sentry focused his field glasses on the boy's hand. He looked carefully at the magnified image, then immediately picked up his field radio and called into his commanding officer.

"Sir, a young boy is walking out of town toward us. It appears his right hand is duct-taped around a grenade."

The officer, a Lieutenant, had the sense to act immediately rather than wait for instructions.

By the time the boy was within fifty feet of where the road had been cratered by Kee's men, a female Army nurse had made her way past the ruined cars and broken asphalt. She motioned for the little boy to keep walking toward her. She was close enough to see that the child was so terrified he had wet his pants.

"It's all right," the nurse told him. "Come on, honey. We know what to do. Come to me."

The Army nurse knelt on one knee and held her arms out to the boy.

"That's right, come to me. What's your name, dear?"

Through his tears, the boy said, "Eric."

"Come on, Eric. Everything is going to be all right."

He walked within reach of the nurse, but she didn't move, letting Eric come to her. She hugged him close with one arm while carefully enclosing his small fist with her free hand.

She held his face against her chest so the boy couldn't see the Army technician wearing his bulky bomb suit that protected everything but his hands.

Eric asked, "Where's my mom?"

"Don't worry. We'll find out for you. Why don't you just sit down right here?"

The boy started crying again. "I'm wet."

"I know. That's okay. Just sit down, honey."

The nurse sat down on the asphalt and gently settled the boy in her lap. She stroked the back of his head and kept him close to her chest in a reassuring hug as the bomb squad specialist cut away enough duct tape so that he could slide a pin into the M67 fragmentation grenade.

#

Hawthorne stood in the corridor outside the locker room reading the contents of the envelope that had been taped around the six-year-old Eric's neck.

In the locker room, Tuli asked Devlin, "Now what?"

"I don't know."

Hawthorne returned.

"Would you gentlemen please come with me?"

Devlin and Tuli exchanged looks. Something had changed. There was no command in Hawthorne's voice.

They followed the General and Mitchell Wyse back to the gymnasium. There were more people in the big space now. Devlin spotted a Marine colonel and a Coast Guard officer at one of the tables. Opposite them, sat Crawford Olohana, the Hawaii chief of police. There were a few civilians at the table Devlin figured were FBI agents.

Devlin, Tuli, Wyse, and Hawthorne had entered at the far end of the gym. All eyes were on them as Hawthorne continued walking across the basketball court and out a door on the other side. Wyse stayed in the gym. Hawthorne led Devlin and Tuli into an empty classroom.

Hawthorne sat at a teacher's desk. Devlin and Tuli pulled chairs out from behind student desks and sat in front of the General.

Hawthorne said, "Give me a minute. Wyse is making copies of something for you."

Devlin said nothing. Tuli folded his massive arms across the chest and looked around the classroom thinking about how much he disliked high school.

Five long minutes later, Wyse entered with three soldiers of varying ranks and a handful of printed pages. The soldiers sat behind Devlin and Tuli as Wyse handed out the pages.

Hawthorne said, "We have information from the people who took over Pahoa. Right now, most of it concerns you, Mr. Devlin."

If Hawthorne expected a reaction from Devlin, he didn't get it.

"We have a bit of a situation here, Mr. Devlin. And apparently, you're part of it." Hawthorne continued, "As you can see, the top sheet lists the names of all the hostages. They've provided us with a piece of identification from most of them. Driver's licenses and so on. They sent a child out with an M67 grenade taped to his hand carrying this information. The pin was pulled on the grenade. There're twenty-six hostages left and twenty-six demands. The next pages list them. You can read them carefully when we're finished here, but I'll direct you to paragraph number three."

Devlin read the paragraph carefully.

His Royal Majesty Samuel King Keamoku demands that the haole oppressor, Devlin, appear before me this day. He must be unarmed, without clothing, in front of my headquarters at exactly 4 P.M. to face the justice of the New Kingdom of Hawaii.

Devlin tossed the pages on the table in front of him. "He thinks he's the King of Hawaii, and he wants me naked on Main Street in forty-five minutes."

"Yes."

"He's crazy."

"We know that, Mr. Devlin."

"And if not, what?"

Hawthorne answered. "It's on the last page. Says he'll start killing one hostage every five minutes until you show up. Starting with the Caucasians."

"You've got to take him out first. Kill him, and the rest will fold."

"It's not going to be quite that simple." Hawthorne lifted the pages and continued. "Kee states here that he has the hostages divided into several buildings. Each building is ringed by Claymore mines that have been daisy-wired together. Each set of Claymores has a detonator that will ignite them. It says there are men holding ignitors round the clock. We can't just go in there and wipe them out. We have to know where the hostages are. We have to know where the men are who are holding the ignitors. There could be multiple men. We have to assume they have enough wire to hide them far from the hostages.

Devlin asked, "What was your battle plan before you had this information?"

Hawthorne looked at one of his officers.

"This is Major Jim Hawkins. He's been working on that. Where are we at Major?"

Devlin looked at a compact man, intense, salt and pepper hair.

"Our plan was to use snipers and elite three-man squads to go in after dark when our night vision equipment gives us an advantage. We haven't discussed this yet, but I'd say that's still the basic plan. Snipers take out any bad guys visible. Troop on the ground take out the rest. Only difference now is to figure out how to disarm the ordinance around the hostages before we attack."

Devlin nodded.

"So you want me to go in there and do what?"

Hawthorne leaned forward. "Keep Kee busy until nightfall. Try to negotiate with him. Try to get us information on the hostages. Do whatever you can to disrupt his plans until we attack."

Tuli said, "How the hell he gonna do that? They put a bullet in his head soon as he show up."

Hawthorne said, "That's not necessarily a given."

Devlin said, "What about the rest of this nonsense? Broadcasting a call to the Hawaiian people to rise up and take back their lands? Telling all the people who believe in Hawaiian sovereignty to gather in Pahoa?"

"We can tell him we're working on it, but it's not going to happen."

Colonel Wyse said, "We already have a couple hundred people showing up to see what's going on. Maybe that will give this guy Kee the idea that something is happening."

Hawthorne said, "I don't give a damn if everyone on this island shows up. They're not getting into that town. I intend for this to be all be over an hour after nightfall."

Devlin said, "Even if those hostages have to die?"

"We're their only chance for survival, Mr. Devlin. Nobody else is going to intervene here. This is a military issue. It's not a political issue. Nobody is going to stop us from doing what we have to do."

Devlin said, "Nobody's stopped the Military doing what they wanted for the last hundred years. Why should it be different now?"

Hawthorne didn't take the bait. "My sentiments exactly."

Devlin picked up the pages and read off the words "Amnesty, land, reparations' what about all this?"

Hawthorne says, "I'll agree to whatever he wants to hear."

"You think Kee will believe you?"

"I don't know, Mr. Devlin. What do you think?"

"Me? I think we stole Hawaii in 1893 and we're not giving it back, and Kee knows it. I think the U.S. military just about owns these goddamn islands, and he knows that, too. I think if most people in the U.S. knew the kind of arms and ammunition and troops you have spread out over these islands, there might not be another tourist within a thousand miles of these islands."

Devlin shoved the set of papers aside. "Kee is crazy, but he's not stupid. He knows he got caught stealing from the Army. Which means he's going to a military prison for the rest of his life, and he'd rather go down in a blaze of glory and take as many of you people and as many of those hostages with him as he can. He can't win, so he's turning over the game board, General. That's what I think."

Hawthorne was clearly not accustomed to anyone speaking to him as Devlin did. He fought for control. "There'll be no blaze of glory for that bastard."

Devlin was about to say something, but Hawkins interrupted. "Please, Mr. Devlin. This isn't the time for a political debate. We need your help. We have to have somebody inside that town who can get us the intelligence we need to mount an attack that will save those people. Do you think you can do that? Twenty-six men, women, and children in that town deserve a chance to live. Go in there and keep Kee and his men occupied whatever way you can. Give us until nightfall, and we'll obliterate them. We have night-vision equipment. We'll have a laser target on the forehead of every one of his men. If you locate the hostages for us, I don't care how many ignitors there are or how many men holding them. We'll cut the firing wire on those Claymores, and we're done."

"Assuming I survive the first contact with Kee, you're asking me to help you slaughter those poor fools following Kee."

Hawthorne broke in. "They don't have to die with him. Go in there and tell them to put down their guns. Any man who walks out of that town unarmed will be treated fairly."

Devlin looked at the other men in the room. "I think General Hawthorne and I need to talk for a few minutes."

Hawthorne and his colleagues exchanged looks. Then Hawthorne looked at his watch and said to Devlin, "Ten minutes." Hawthorne told the others. "Give us the room, gentleman."

As the room emptied, Devlin moved his chair in front of Hawthorne's desk.

"Tell me everything you know."

Hawthorne opened a folder.

"We've been taking high altitude surveillance photos for the last two hours. We've spotted eighteen men in various locations. Some of them are on roofs."

Hawthorne pulled out an overhead shot of the town. Four buildings were circled in red.

"These are the buildings with the most traffic in and out."

Devlin leaned forward and pointed to each building. "This one is Kee's office. This is the community center, that's the town bar, and that one is a crafts store/bookstore."

Hawthorne said, "We believe the hostages are probably divided up among all four locations. But that's all we know. That's why we need you in there. Kee hasn't said that he'll kill you. We don't know what this justice is he's ranting about. Maybe he wants to make you some kind of prisoner."

Devlin didn't respond.

Hawthorne continued. "Mr. Devlin. You've served your country well and honorably. We recognize that. And we sympathize with the work you're presently engaged in for Pacific Rim. Unfortunately, that work has opened you up to quite a bit of scrutiny. There's going to be an extensive investigation into all this, starting with what happened on Kee's ranch. Preliminary reports say there are at least two dead military personnel in the area. You may be completely innocent of any crime, but you could be involved in criminal proceedings for years before it all gets sorted out. That's not good for people in your line of work."

Devlin looked at Hawthorne. "That's the stick. What's the carrot?"

"People who help us are our friends. We're not going to let someone serving his country be harmed. It's that simple."

Devlin asked, "How far does that go?"

Hawthorne paused, then said, "In this situation, quite far."

Devlin nodded. "And that has to include Tuulima Mafa. Whatever his involvement, it was on my orders. He did nothing on his own initiative."

"Agreed. So do I have your cooperation?"

"Not yet."

"Why? Half-hour ago, you were demanding I let you into that town to save Cranston's daughter."

Devlin leaned forward. "A half-hour ago you weren't asking me to walk into that town unarmed, locate the hostages, somehow get that information to you, and keep a maniac and thirty trigger-happy armed idiots busy for two hours."

Hawthorne nodded. "All right. What do you want?"

"If I don't make it out of that town alive, I want your word that you will pursue this case until you find out who ordered Billy Cranston murdered. I figure Sam Kee and some of your soldiers actually committed the murder. I figure they helped steal your weapons and transport them. But I don't see them able to sell military weapons on the open market. I need to know you'll go after the guy at the top. The guy who directed this."

"Of course, we will."

"And if I die in that backwater town, you'll share your findings with Jasper Cranston, his daughter, Leilani Cranston, and William Chow."

Hawthorne hesitated.

Devlin said, "They need to know."

"All right, but only if I believe they will keep the information absolutely confidential and do nothing to impede the Army's investigation."

"Fair enough."

"And if you survive, Mr. Devlin?"

"We'll talk about it then."

"Done." Hawthorne extended his hand. Devlin shook it.

Devlin asked, "What's next."

Hawthorne said, "I want you in there as close to nightfall as possible."

"I don't think we can wait that long."

"We've already told Kee you fled to Oahu. I told him you're flying back now and you'll meet with him as soon as possible."

"He bought that?"

"Not completely. He said at five o'clock he starts shooting."

"And if he starts before then?"

"We go in full force. Look, this is a standoff. We know he can kill every hostage before we can stop them. He knows if they kill the hostages, we'll wipe them out. That's why we need you in there. Do you want to meet with one of my specialists to conceal a weapon on you? Maybe wire you up with a small transmitter?"

"No. No weapons. No radios. You said all the phones in town will connect to you here. That'll have to do. Anything else will get me killed before I could use either."

"All right then. I'll leave you alone." Hawthorne handed Devlin a two-way radio. "Keep this and stay close. We'll call you if anything changes. Otherwise, report back here at four-forty-five."

CHAPTER 60

Leilani walked out of the crafts store, a guard on each side of her. Both men had bandannas covering their faces. They headed for Kee's office. She looked up and down Main Street. The town was empty except for Kee's men and their collection of beat-up cars and trucks.

The sun was low in the sky. A sudden wind blew past her, unsettling the empty street.

She continued walking, thinking about what she'd do if she'd gotten that gun from Rachel. Pull it out. Shoot these two. Run between the buildings into the backstreets and out into one of the empty fields surrounding town? How many men would be shooting at her by then? Too many. Any scenario she pictured ended up with her dead.

And then she was being led up on the sidewalk that ran in front of Kee's office. The guard on her right grabbed her upper arm in a tight grip. So tight it hurt.

The guard on her left opened the door to the office, and they pushed her inside. Bright bare fluorescent overhead lights illuminated the office. Kee sat at a desk reading three typewritten sheets of paper. He had a pen in his hand and had marked the papers with thick arrows and lines. The lawyer, Engle, stood with one hand on the desk, leaning over to look at the parts Kee had marked. Engle's face was ghostly pale. He seemed haggard. On the verge of exhaustion, driven there by worry and tension. Kee handed him the pages and said, "Fix it. We have to send this out immediately."

Engle nodded, pursed his lips seriously, and said, "Right." He took the papers from Kee without comment or argument. He didn't even look at the scrawled markings. He simply took them and walked to the back office.

Kee rose from his seat and looked at Leilani. He pointed to a wicker couch at the far side of the room and said, "Sit down over there."

Before she could comply, one of the guards pushed her toward the couch. Leilani stumbled over to it. When she turned around and sat down, she saw Willi Pohano sitting on the other end of the couch. She didn't remember knowing his name, but she remembered his flat, mean face. He held a rifle in his right hand, the barrel pointed toward the ceiling. He leered at her.

Kee walked over to Leilani. He said, "Take off your clothes."

The guards who had brought her to Kee's office moved a few steps closer.

Leilani sat up straight. She stared at Kee. She kept her arms folded over her chest. Kee stood three feet in front of her. He looked huge. She wondered if she could kick him between the legs when he moved close enough. And then Willi placed the barrel of his M16 against her left temple.

He said, "Do what he says."

Leilani kept looking at Kee. There was no expression on his face. After being in one space with seventeen women constantly shifting and talking, the office was unusually quiet and calm. It was clear that everyone in the office wanted to see this.

Willi pushed the muzzle of the rifle into the side of Leilani's head.

Kee smiled at her and said, "You and I are a pair. The best on this whole fucking island. Think of our children. Fucking princes and princesses."

Leilani said, "I'd rather mate with a dog."

The blow came so hard and fast Leilani never even saw it. Pain exploded on the side of her head. Everything went black for a split-second, followed by a flash of light. Her head banged into the wall behind her. She couldn't remember anything hurting as much as Kee's slap.

Kee loomed over her. Without even thinking, she kicked at him, aiming between his legs. The blow missed its target, but Kee felt it.

She knew Kee was going to hit her again. This time with a fist. She had both hands up and her arms crossed when the punch came at her. She blocked part of it, but Kee's jab hit her in the center of the forehead, knocking her back into the wicker couch. It surprised her that the blow hadn't hurt as much as the slap. And then Kee stepped forward and punched his fist down onto the top of her thigh. Full force. Like a karate instructor trying to punch down and break boards. The pain exploded, and she screamed an agonizing grunt. It felt as if he had broken her femur.

Kee stepped back and smiled. "You like to kick people, let me see you pick up that leg now."

Leilani couldn't move it.

"You like to hit people?" Kee punched her once, hard, in each bicep. She had never been hit by a man, much less a man as strong as Kee. Her arms were paralyzed. She had never felt such pain in her life.

Kee dropped down, his lopsided, leering face in front of her. "Come on. Hit me now."

Leilani screamed through tears of rage and pain. She tried to lift her arms. She couldn't.

"Oh God," she muttered.

This time Kee slammed the side of his fist onto her other leg. Not quite as hard as the first punch, but hard enough to make Leilani scream again.

Kee knelt in front of her and undid the button of her shorts. He pulled at the zipper, then lost his patience and ripped the shorts down her legs, breaking the zipper, muttering, "Fucking stuck-up whore." He pulled down her panties and kicked her immobilized legs apart. Leilani's right arm was twitching with the effort to move it. She tried more than she had ever tried to do anything in her life to get her arm to move. She couldn't.

Kee had his penis out, stroking himself, and then he stopped. "Aw fuck." He looked between Leilani's legs and said, "What the fuck is this, you bitch. Stinky time, huh?"

Leilani felt the tampon she had doctored with blood from her finger being wrenched from inside her.

She saw him throw the stained tampon toward his front door. "You gonna have to do me this time with your mouth. Open up!"

Leilani spat at him and yelled, "Fuck you."

Kee didn't bother to wipe off the spit of his leg. He smiled at her and shoved himself back in his pants. "Oh yeah. One tough wahine. But not for long, cunt. You'll open your mouth nice and wide after a few more beatings. Guarantee it."

The last blow was so hard that it broke Leilani's nose. It felt as if her face and head had exploded. She gagged once and passed out.

CHAPTER 61

Devlin stepped out of the high school main entrance into the light of a late Hawaiian afternoon. He shaded his eyes and squinted up at the sun for a moment, then put his head down and walked toward the Tacoma. Tuli fell in behind him, sensing that it wasn't the time to say anything.

They both got into the truck, Devlin behind the wheel heading south. After a mile or two of silence, Tuli finally asked, "Where we goin', brudda?"

"A beach I know."

"How come?"

"I'd like to see it one more time."

"What's going on, boss?"

"I'm going into that town."

Tuli shifted his big body in the passenger seat. He furrowed his brow. He wanted to say something, but he didn't know how to say it.

Devlin drove, trying to remember the route Leilani had taken that first day when they hiked over the lava field to the hidden beach. He managed to find his way and parked the truck off the old Red Road near the wooden barricade. He looked out over the black expanse.

"You want to see a nice beach, Tuli?"

"Sure."

Tuli walked next to Devlin across the hardened lava. Devlin kept up a good pace. Neither man spoke.

For the first five minutes of the walk, Devlin tried to concentrate on nothing but walking up and down the rolling surface of the lava field. He felt the warmth flowing up from far beneath the deep cracks in the black stone field, as well as the hot rays of the sun. He tried to let his body feel everything and his mind hold nothing.

After about ten minutes, he began to carefully consider what lay ahead of him. He visualized walking into the town, up Main Street, past the bar, past the Village Inn, toward Kee's office. He tried to visualize it. He could see the buildings. Feel the asphalt street. He imagined several scenarios. Considered each of them until he could no longer reasonably foresee what might happen. Once he had considered the possibilities, he stopped thinking about it. There was nothing more to plan.

He put his mind on automatic pilot and continued the hike. By the time Devlin walked past the three swaying palm trees onto the exquisite isolated black-sand beach, he was calm. He slipped off his shirt, dropped to his knees, then sat down in the warm black sand with his legs folded under him, spine straight, totally focused.

The air was fresh. The sky mostly clear, except for a few fast-moving puffs of white clouds. There was no rain in the air. The sparkling water was calmer than the last time he had visited the beach. With Leilani.

He closed his eyes and carefully, precisely, attentively watched and observed each thought as it bubbled into his consciousness. Ever so gently he forced his breathing into a clean, steady pattern. For a while, his thoughts rose and fell with each breath. He thought about how secure he felt knowing that Tuli was somewhere behind him, watching over him. He allowed a surge of emotion to well up in him. For a moment, his feelings for the big man almost overwhelmed him. He savored his sense of gratitude toward Tuli. Feeling it. Holding it. A wave crashed on the beach, and he was back in the moment.

Devlin rode the waves of his mind; listened to the ocean;

breathed in and out. Eventually, an image of Leilani took hold of him. It was that first luxurious view of her walking languidly on the beach in front of her father's house. Her long legs, her shoulders, her face. That exquisite nose. The rich silkiness of her skin. The exotic lines of her tattoo. In the next instant, he saw her face close in front of him, surrounded by the steam. Devlin let images of her take hold of him for as long as they had power. But gradually thoughts of Pahoa-town, and Sam Kee, and the desperate, foolish ragtag men he had surrounded himself with intruded.

He tried to visualize each of the men he had seen with Kee. Picture their faces. Their eyes. See into their souls. How many enemies were in that town? What was their state of mind? How many were drunk or stoned? How much fear did they hold? How much anger? And how would they respond when blood and pain and violence and sudden death hit them?

From back among the palm trees, Tuli carefully watched over Devlin. He quietly sang the chant of an ancient Polynesian prayer, calling on his ancestors, on his South Pacific gods. Tuli wished Chief Aseososo were with him to give him prayer and advice. He prayed for the Matai, the clan. For himself. For Devlin. He felt very alone at that moment until he heard a faint noise in the tropical forest behind him. Maybe no man in the world could have moved so quickly and had the gun in hand so fast.

But when Tuli looked, he saw nothing. The wind stirred the vegetation behind them. The moment passed. Tuli slowly replaced the gun in his waistband, turned to watch Devlin, and sat back down on his piece of black beach.

On the walk back to the Red Road, Devlin seemed unusually relaxed. He smiled at Tuli and clapped him on the back.

"Don't worry, brother. It'll be all right."

"You sure you want to walk in there, boss?"

"I have to. There's a woman in that town I can't leave alone in there. And I sure as hell won't run away from Sam Kee. He's hurt too many people. He's tried to kill us twice. He's one of those who killed my friend. And if I don't go in there, he's going to kill more."

Tuli listened and nodded but didn't say anything.

"And it's the only way to flush the big rat out of his hole."

Tuli said, "The one that little Filipino bastard called the big guy."

"Yes."

Finally, Tuli nodded and said, "So what about me, boss? What does Tuli do?"

The walk across the lava field gave Devlin more than enough time to tell Tuli what he wanted him to do.

CHAPTER 62

General James Hawthorne had worked non-stop while Devlin was gone, operating at a pace beyond anything he'd ever experienced, even during his time in Vietnam. He wasn't prepared for the calm and reserve that emanated from Jack Devlin when he walked into the high school gymnasium with less than fifteen minutes until their five o'clock deadline. Hawthorne resisted the urge to raise his voice at Devlin. He made sure to give his last order calmly.

"We don't have much time, Mr. Devlin. We got Kee to agree to seventeen-hundred hours. Sunset is around six. Figure around six-thirty before our night vision equipment will give us the advantage we need. We'll cut all power to the town around then unless we hear something different from you. Try to survive in there until then and get us any information that will be useful. Pick up any telephone in that town, and you'll be connected to us. Good luck."

#

Devlin drove the pickup truck up to the burnt-out husk of the fuel tanker, then slowly maneuvered around it. He stopped in front of a barricade of cars set up by Kee's men. Three of them came out to meet him, all of them armed with M16s. One of them motioned with his M16 for Devlin to drive to the side of the road.

Devlin parked the Tacoma and got out. All three men pointed their rifles at him. Devlin raised his hands above his head. One of Kee's men reached inside the truck and took out the keys.

The man nearest Devlin poked him with his rifle barrel and said, "Walk."

Devlin lowered his hands, turned away from the men and their weapons, and headed for town. He tried to check himself, to gauge the adrenaline rush, the beating of his heart, the tension in his muscles. The walk seemed very much as he'd imagined it would be. Only more so. With each step toward the possibility of his death, Devlin felt himself moving into another reality. He noted that he could see individual pieces of grass. When he looked at the sides of the old wooden buildings, he saw deep into the grain of the wood. The road under his feet felt more real. The colors around him – the foliage, the faded paint on the buildings, the shades of blue in the sky – all seemed more intense.

By the time he walked past the town bar, he'd spotted the first of Kee's men on the roof of the laundromat. He continued walking and saw two more on top of the Village Inn and one more on a roof across the street.

When he was fifty feet from Kee's office, he saw two more men standing outside the two-story building. And by the time he arrived at the office, several more had come out onto the wooden sidewalks that ran along Main Street.

With their civilian clothes, dark faces covered in handkerchiefs, and automatic rifles, Kee's men looked like a third-world group of armed revolutionaries. Hawthorne's estimate had been eighteen men. Including the three men at the east barricade, Devlin's count had reached eleven.

All the men that Devlin spotted were looking at him. He was the focus of attention. The next item on Kee's insane list of events.

By the time he was in front of Kee's office, a group of four guards had formed a circle around Devlin.

Devlin stopped and turned toward the elevated wooden sidewalk, topped by the handrail. Devlin took off his white T-shirt and dropped it on the ground. Then his white linen pants and his underwear. For a second, he was taken by a realization of how one could live in Hawaii and spend very little money on clothing. And in the next second, he was struck by how absurd it was to be thinking that at such a time.

He stood in front of Kee's office, naked except for his shoes. They were lightweight boat shoes. The kind with tan leather tops and white rubber non-slip soles. He left the shoes on his feet because the sun had made the asphalt too hot to stand on barefoot.

First, Willi came out of the office, leaning toward him, scowling. Then, Sam Kee stepped out onto the wooden sidewalk. The big man. Grinning. Dressed in a sleeveless black top and black pants, his long hair unbound, flowing past his shoulders. He strode to the handrail and looked down at Devlin. Devlin looked up at Kee, at the classic Polynesian face, marred by the deformed left side. He took in the intricate South Sea tattoos, the big arms and bright white teeth. Except for the disfigured face, Devlin decided Kee did look rather regal in a primitive sort of way.

Kee told him, "Take off the shoes, too."

Devlin slipped the shoes off but stood on top of them to prevent the asphalt from burning the soles of his feet.

Kee told the man closest to Devlin, "Search his clothes."

The guard on Devlin's right shifted his M16 into his left hand, holding it by the top handle. Devlin watched him carefully, convinced that the man was not accustomed to handling the rifle. He picked up Devlin's shirt. There were no pockets to search, so he just shook it out, feeling it with one hand. He threw the shirt back on the ground and picked up Devlin's pants. He shoved the rifle under his armpit and felt the pockets with both hands. Empty. He dropped the pants on the ground.

Devlin thought about making a move for the rifle stuck awkwardly under the man's armpit, but he didn't. He wanted to talk to Kee.

The guard checked Devlin's underwear by moving it around

with his foot and stepping on it several times. He pushed Devlin off his shoes, picked them up, and looked inside them. Everyone watched while Devlin stepped onto his shirt to protect his feet from the hot asphalt.

When the guard was finished, Devlin reached down and picked up his underwear and pants, but the guard yelled, "Hey!" and jabbed the butt of his rifle at Devlin's head. Devlin leaned to his right, just avoiding the rifle butt, but the edge of it clipped him painfully on the tip of his shoulder.

Devlin hissed at the sharp pain. The guard took a step closer and tried again. Again, Devlin ducked the blow and then stepped back out of range. He still held his underwear and pants.

The guard turned the rifle into a firing position and yelled at him, "Asshole, put 'em down."

Devlin stood his ground and stared into the man's eyes as he dropped his pants and stood on them to get off the hot asphalt. He didn't drop the underwear. The man raised his rifle. Kee yelled, "Not yet."

Kee pointed at two of the larger men surrounding Devlin. "Grab his arms."

Devlin just managed to pick up his shirt and slip it on before they took hold of his arms. Willi, who was standing next to Kee up on the sidewalk, stepped down into the street. He carried a fat roll of duct tape.

Willi said, "Raise your arms."

He checked Devlin's armpits.

"Squat."

Devlin dropped down, and Willi kicked Devlin in the stomach. He doubled over and landed on his knees.

Willi turned to Kee and said, "Nothing on him."

He kicked the side of Devlin's leg and yelled, "Stand up. Put your fucking pants on."

As soon as Devlin was dressed, Willi wrapped duct tape around

Devlin's wrists and arms until they were tightly bound in front of him.

When he was finished, Willie punched Devlin in the kidneys. Devlin grunted. The guards turned Devlin so that he faced Kee, one man on either side of him holding his arms.

Willi walked back to his spot next to Kee up on the sidewalk.

Kee slowly took the Beretta M9 out of his holster, chambered a round, and laid the pistol on the handrail, cocked and ready. He pointed to Devlin and said, "Jack Devlin, I'm charging you with treason, murder of citizens of the new Kingdom of Hawaii, trespass, and attempted assassination of a member of the royal family."

"Which member of the royal family would that be?" Devlin yelled up to Kee.

"Me. Are you ready for sentencing?"

Devlin said nothing.

Kee said, "Sounds like yes to me. I sentence you to death. You'll be decapitated and your head sent to the occupying forces."

Devlin turned away from Kee and yelled out, "Just because he's crazy doesn't mean you all have to die. There's three thousand Army troops outside this town ready to take it back from you. They're going to shoot every single one of you if you don't surrender. They don't give a shit about the hostages. They don't give a shit about you. They're going to kill all of you and take back their weapons."

Kee pointed the Beretta at Devlin and yelled, "Shut up, or I'll put a bullet in you now and then cut off your fucking head."

Devlin turned to Kee.

"You don't really think you can get away with this, do you? You don't really believe you're going to have people rally to your Kingdom of Hawaii, do you?"

Kee smiled. "Why not? What else they got to do?"

Devlin said, "Let me loose, and maybe I can help you live."

Kee sneered down at Devlin. "How 'bout I help you be the first one to die."

"The first one to die was Billy Cranston. John Sunshine. Who killed him? Was it you?"

Kee lowered the Beretta, smiled, and nodded at Devlin.

"You're right. He was the first one, wasn't he? Walked right up and practically asked to be killed, just like you."

"How'd it happen? Who killed him?"

Kee stared off into the distance as if picturing it. "Man, it was fucking weird, hey? Walks up to the ranch. Early one morning. When we was first bringing the stuff in there. Like he knew we'd be there. Just shows up and yells at us. Telling us to stop what we was doing. Yelling all kine shit at us. He didn't have no gun, no knife. Nothing, hey? Sent a couple of boys out to take care of him. He kicked their ass, man. Crazy old haole bum was a tough son of a bitch. Forcing it. A bunch of us went out after him, but that nasty Army motherfucker McWilliams just punched the knife into him. You know? Wham! Fast. Didn't kill 'em, though. He just knifed him in the gut."

"Then what?"

"We strapped him onto one of the ATV's and drove him the hell out into the middle of the rainforest. I sliced 'im open and left him for the fucking pigs. You saw how we done it. Told the boys to run the dogs out in that direction. Drive whatever pigs, rats, mongoose, insects and shit out there into the body. Thought that'd be an easy way to get rid of the fucker. Pigs'll eat anything, you know. But somebody found him, I guess. What was left of him. Should have just buried the crazy piece of haole shit, hey?"

"You should have."

"Strange motherfucker. You know what he said to me when we loaded him onto the ATV?"

"What?"

"Said he was sorry it had to come to this. Sorry I was going to have to die."

"Billy Cranston was a better man than me, Kee. I'm not sorry you're going to die. Not sorry at all."

"Yeah, well, like I said, you first." Kee yelled to the men around Devlin, "Put him on his knees."

Devlin told the men, "This is your last chance."

Kee yelled to all the men nearby, "Beat his ass down while I get my blade. Now!"

Kee turned and walked back into his storefront office as five men moved in on Devlin, but Devlin moved first. Even though he was off balance with his hands bound in front of him, he managed to deliver a fast, powerful front kick right between the legs of the man closest to him.

In almost the same motion, Devlin stomped on a second man's knee. He ducked a fist aimed at his face, charged into a man with his shoulder and knocked him down.

Something rammed into his back sending him forward. Devlin managed to headbutt a face in front of him before he went down onto the asphalt. He tried to stand up, but somebody knocked him down again. More men appeared. An avalanche of fists and feet came down on Devlin. He managed to curl into a fetal position and get his hands up over his head trying to protect his skull and face.

He felt most of the blows land on his back, arms, legs, and hands. Devlin knew if the beating went on too long, they would eventually break his ribs, and if someone kicked a broken rip hard enough, it could puncture a lung. But he had already detached himself from the brutality and violence, analyzing it dispassion- ately. Most of the attackers weren't wearing heavy footwear. Also, there were too many men vying to hurt him. They were getting in each other's way. And dropping down to hit him with fists would put an attacker in danger of getting themselves kicked.

Devlin took the blows, the pain, the possibility of death until a foot caught the side of his head and everything went black.

Kee had come out with a machete during the beating. When he saw Devlin go slack, he yelled, "Stop. I want the fucker awake when I slice his throat."

The men backed off. A few giving Devlin final kicks.

Kee turned to Willi and said, "Drag his ass into the crafts store. Leave him with the cunts in there until he comes around. Make sure you tape up his legs, too."

Devlin didn't feel them lifting him off the ground, but he came spinning into consciousness as two of Kee's men dragged him across the street. He stayed limp, his eyes closed, waiting for the ringing in his ears and nausea to subside. They had him under the armpits, dragging him with his head down. He felt his feet dragged over the door saddle as they hauled him into the store.

They dropped Devlin by the table near the front of the crafts store. Willi squatted next to Devlin and quickly wrapped two turns of duct tape around his ankles. Two guards who had been watching the women came over to look at Devlin.

Willi told them, "When he comes around keep your eye on him. Don't touch him. Don't let any of these bitches near him."

The two guards, an on-again, off-again heroin addict named Honi and an alcoholic named Po, looked at Devlin saying nothing.

Willi asked them, "You got your eye on all these women?"

Po answered, "Yeah, but there's always one of 'em in the shitter doing something."

Willi headed out the front door, the guards walking him out.

Devlin curled into a fetal position, bringing his bound hands near his mouth.

Willi paused at the front door to tell Honi and Po, "When he comes around, one of you let us know."

Devlin slid his index finger between his back teeth and right cheek to carefully move a single-edge razor down into his mouth. From there, he maneuvered the blade between his front teeth.

Nobody in the room noticed what Devlin was doing, not even Rachel Steele who had been looking at Devlin, worried about the dirt and blood on his clothes, hoping they hadn't beaten him to death. And then she saw Devlin's head and hands moving near his mouth.

Honi came in and walked to the back door to keep watch. Po stayed near the front door. Rachel thought she heard Devlin cutting the duct tape. She stood up and took a few paces toward Po, making sure she blocked his view of Devlin.

"Bathroom, please," she said.

Po turned to her, and said, "Somebody's in there. As usual."

Rachel said, "I'll wait."

Rachel turned to head for the bathroom. Po reached out and grabbed Rachel's hair and pulled her back.

"Sit down, bitch. You go when I tell you."

He shoved Rachel onto the floor. Too far away from Devlin to give him the Beretta.

Devlin continued slowly working at the tape around his wrists.

Rachel heard the sound of the tape separating. The guard at the front door would hear it any second. She called out to him, "I really have to go. I'm sorry."

"Shut up."

"Please."

Po cursed, pulled Rachel to her feet and held her arm as he walked toward the bathroom located near the middle of the store. He held her arm as he tested the door. Seeing it locked, he pounded on the door.

"Get the fuck out! The old lady has to go. Open up before I pull you out of there."

Devlin's hands were free. He now had the single-edged razor blade between his thumb and forefinger. He reached down and quickly sliced the tape holding his ankles together. He shifted slightly, still curled up on the floor, and waited for the guard to come back toward the front of the store.

CHAPTER **63**

Kee stormed back into his office. Leilani sat on the couch trying to recover from his brutal punches. Trying not to cry. Trying to picture some way she could survive this. She'd had a partial view of what Kee's men had done to Devlin through the open front door. With each punch and kick, her hopes for survival faded.

Kee walked past her, headed for his desk, yelling orders to nobody in particular.

"Anybody find Engle? Find that piece of shit. The first execution takes place in fifteen minutes. I need a volunteer to present the head to the occupiers. I want a count of all hostages before then."

Kee was interrupted when a man came hustling into the office. Leilani saw that he was carrying her travel bag and backpack. Everything she needed to get off the island was in her backpack: Hawaiian Air ticket to Honolulu, money, and her driver's license.

The flunky walked over to Kee's desk and held up the items.

Kee glanced at him and asked, "What's that?"

The man nodded toward Leilani. "Her stuff. You told me to bring it over from Da Restaurant."

"Right." Kee pointed to his desk. "Put it over there."

Another man came out of the back office with printed pages listing all Kee's demands. Kee grabbed them from his hand. He glanced at the list, then picked up the phone on his desk. Without waiting, he said, "You have fifteen minutes to provide your response to our justifiable demands. Fifteen minutes."

He slammed the phone down without waiting for an answer, sat down, and picked up Leilani's backpack.

CHAPTER 64

Devlin watched Po shove Rachel Steele into the bathroom and slam the door. He wore a dirty T-shirt with a Cheerios logo, ragged jeans, and unlike most of Kee's men, work boots instead of flip-flops or sandals.

Devlin moved as imperceptibly as possible, turning his neck, tensing and relaxing the muscles in his arms and legs. He was going to have to take out this guard without having moved much since the beating. He had no idea what kind of pain he would experience, or if anything would lock up or give out. He knew he'd have one chance. He knew he'd have to get it done before the guard at the other end of the store could react. It didn't matter. He had no choice.

Po was taller than most of Kee's men. Wiry. Long hair. He had an older M16A1 hanging by the strap on his left shoulder, the handle facing back, the pistol butt and magazine facing front. He held the rifle by the strap with his left hand. He also had a long knife in a sheath strapped to the leather belt on his pants.

The duct tape was still on Devlin's hands and feet. He spread them slightly apart, making sure they were free but keeping them close together so it appeared as if he were still bound.

The guard headed toward the front of the store but gave Devlin a wide berth, keeping his distance. Devlin grimaced. He couldn't close the distance without the guard seeing it. He had to let him pass. Take him from behind. Even more difficult.

The guard passed Devlin. Devlin rose from the floor. His entire body felt stiff and immobile. Bent over, he moved in behind the guard. He brought his right hand up to grab the guard's throat from behind, but the guard was walking with his head down. Devlin grabbed the hair on the top of his head with his left hand, wrenched the guard's head back and grabbed the guard's throat with a crushing grip. The guard made a guttural sound. Devlin kneed him in the small of the back, pulled him down to the floor, rolled on top of him still holding his throat, squeezing the larynx.

The guard hit the floor with a soft thud, a gurgling choking sound coming out of his mouth. Devlin covered his mouth with his left hand, crushing his windpipe with his right as Po bucked and kicked under Devlin's weight.

Devlin rolled off, stripped him of the M16, pushed the safety switch to single shot, turned and rose to one knee as Honi turned toward the choking sound of the dying Po struggling for to breathe.

In a normal tone of voice, pointing the M16, Devlin told the guard, "Drop the rifle. Hands up or I'll shoot you. Now."

For a moment, Devlin and Honi eyed each other. The guard held his M16 by the top handle. He hadn't dropped the weapon or lifted his hands. Devlin didn't want to alert any of Kee's men in the area by shooting the guard. He rose to his feet and walked toward the guard, ready to shoot if he had to. He repeated, "Gun down. Hands up. Now."

When he was almost close enough to punch Honi with the muzzle of his rifle, the man lowered the rifle to the floor and slowly raised hands.

Devlin pointed to a chair near the coffee bar.

"Sit."

The guard had given up. Women began to gather in the back of the store. Devlin told the women nearest him, "Tie him up. Put something in his mouth so he can't call out."

Rachel Steele appeared next to Devlin.

"You came back."

"Yes. You okay, Rachel?"

"Yes."

"Gather up everybody near the back door. Have them ready to leave here when I tell them. You all have to move fast and stay quiet. Are there any other women being held?"

"Leilani in Kee's office. And a few others I think are in the bar."

"Okay. Is there a phone in here?"

"Behind the coffee counter."

Devlin picked up the second M16, strapped it across his back, and walked behind the counter. He picked up the phone. He heard a tinny ring sound and a click. He didn't wait for an answer.

"This is Devlin. Tell the General I'm sending women hostages out the back door of the crafts store on Main Street. They're going straight into the field heading for the tree line. Get men to meet them."

A voice said, "Done."

Devlin came back to the women. He motioned them to come closer and spoke quietly to them.

"I'm going outside to cover you. When I signal, everybody come out fast and quiet. Head straight for the field and run for the tree line. Keep coming until I say stop."

Devlin made his way to the back door and slipped outside holding one of the M16s. Daylight was seeping out of the sky. Last light was about forty minutes away. Devlin walked backward toward a rusted, derelict Chevy Impala sitting on bare rims, keeping watch on the rooftop of the crafts store. He saw nobody and immediately waved for the women to come out. He glanced at them but mostly watched the roofline. They weren't coming out nearly as fast as he wanted, nor as quietly. He waived furiously, urging them forward.

The first few women streamed past him. He couldn't believe how noisy they were, whimpering, talking to each other, making noise at the effort to run. One woman fell and cried out in pain. He

gave up motioning or saying anything, took cover behind the derelict Chevy, and kept his eyes on the roof.

He saw Rachel waiting at the back door for the last woman to
leave. She was the mother with a young boy and girl. He looked
back at the roof just in time to see a guard appear. Devlin got him
in his sights and squeezed off one shot that hit him almost center in
the face before he could raise the alarm. It didn't matter. The crack
of the M16 was unmistakable.

The women started to scurry and run faster, abandoning any
effort to keep quiet. A second and third guards appeared on the
roof. Devlin managed to shoot only one before the second guard
yelled at the women to stop and opened fire on them. Devlin flipped
his M16 to full auto and fired off three bursts of three shots, taking
out the guard as Rachel hurried past him, urging the mother and
children to move faster.

Before more guards could appear, Devlin began firing short
bursts back and forth across the roofline. A wave of nausea hit him,
a result of the beating he'd taken. He dropped down on one knee
behind the front rim of the Chevy. From a crouching position, he
leaned out and kept firing, driving one of Kee's men who came into
sight back from the edge of the roof. He kept firing until he was out
of ammunition.

He moved back behind the car, took the second M16 strapped
onto his back, leaned out, and pulled the trigger. Nothing. Devlin
knew the old M16s were notorious for jamming if not properly
cleaned. There was no telling when the battered rifle had last been
maintained. He swallowed hard, prepared himself to run for cover
behind the next building in the direction of the community center
when he felt a tug at his shirt.

He looked behind him to see Rachel Steele holding out his
small .25 caliber Beretta.

She said, "I hope it's all right. I took it from your car. But I don't
know what to do with it."

Devlin wanted to kiss the beautiful elderly woman, but he simply smiled at her. She had helped distract the guard in the crafts store. She had helped get the women out safe. She had risked staying to give him the gun.

He took her hand in his and slipped the gun from her grip.

Bullets were pinging into the rusted car and plowing into the ground nearby.

Devlin knew the chance hitting anybody with the small Beretta were slim, but it would be better than nothing. He looked Rachel in the eyes and said, "Thank you. Now, when I start shooting, stay low, run as fast as you can, and get out of sight. Ready?"

CHAPTER 65

Kee grabbed Leilani's backpack and opened it, turned it over, and spilled the contents on his desk. He pushed around two paperback books, a raincoat, hat, makeup bag, and other items. He pulled the water bottle out of a side pocket. He unzipped an interior pocket and found a slim wallet and a plane ticket. It didn't take him long to find her driver's license. It took less time for Kee to match Leilani's last name to John Sunshine/Billy Cranston. And from there to that bastard Jack Devlin.

"I fuckin' knew it."

Furious, he stormed into the front room, yelling at Leilani. "You fucking traitorous bitch." He threw her driver's license at her face. "You come into my town and work with that haole bastard to take me down? I'm gonna fuckin' cut off your head with him."

Leilani yelled back, "I don't know what you're talking about. I came here on my own to find out what happened to my brother. Fuck you!"

Kee reached for her just as the first shot from Devlin's M16 sounded across the street. He turned and ran toward the door, grabbing and pushing men out to the street as he went. More gunfire sounded. Then a pause. Then a series of three-shot bursts.

Kee ran across the street into the crafts store. He saw one guard on the floor dead, the other tied to a chair in the back. More gunfire sounded outside back of the store followed by shots from the roof.

There were four men with Kee. Someone yelled, "He's shooting from out back."

Kee grimaced. His women hostages were gone. He began screaming orders.

"Get those men off the roof. You and you, move the Claymores to the back, facing out. Run the lines out to the street. Then everyone get the fuck out of here."

Kee heard two shots that sounded like small arms fire. He heard the pounding of feet overhead as his men ran off the roof. He watched until the Claymores were in place, then backpedaled out of the store carrying the firing device and reeling out the 200 feet of firing wire. The four Claymores had been daisy-wired so all four could be set off with one electric impulse from the firing device.

Kee made it half-way across the street before he reached the limit of the wire. He waited until the second guard and the two men who had untied him made it out of the store.

Kee yelled, "Fire in the hole" and repeatedly depressed the ignitor. All four mines, each containing one-and-a-half pounds of C4, exploded, each of them driving seven hundred steel balls through the back wall and door of the crafts store.

The wall was obliterated, turned into flying shreds of wood, plaster, and lathe. The lethal range was 50 meters, but the steel balls could do major damage to a human body as far out as 250 meters. The wall obstructed the steel balls, cutting their range to about 100 meters. Most of the women had made it past that distance, and some had made it into the trees. None of them sustained injuries. Devlin was not so lucky.

He'd made it just past the far edge of the 60-degree kill zone of the nearest Claymore. Two steel balls missed his head by inches. Unfortunately, the explosion of the four mines not only blew out the back wall of the crafts store, it also blew off a section of the roof. The blast concussion knocked Devlin unconscious, and he fell in the area where flaming debris from the roof rained down around him. A burning hunk of wood hit his right calf, the pain jerking him conscious.

He scrambled away from the burning debris, looking for his Beretta and found it a few feet away. He grabbed the gun and limped south toward the community center, his ears ringing, every part of his body hurting, his eyes tearing and burning from the explosions.

#

As soon as the explosion subsided, Kee and his men walked through the wreckage of the store and out the back looking for bodies, particularly Devlin's. Kee became more and more agitated. Clearly, Devlin and the women hostages had gotten away.

He turned to four of his men and told them, "Get over to the community center. Reinforce the guards. Make sure the Claymores are still in place. If that haole bastard shows up there, shoot him. Keep shooting 'til he's dead."

Kee stormed back through the crafts store to his office. If his men didn't kill Devlin, he knew how to flush him out.

#

Devlin made it past the back of the Village Inn, through the parking lot, to a spot where he could see the back of the community center. There was no sign of any guards in the back, or of men with ignitors, unless they had been clever enough to hide out of sight.

He retraced his steps back toward the Village Inn through the connecting parking lot, using parked cars to conceal his movements. The Inn's gate was open. He made it upstairs and ducked into his room. The door had been smashed open. All his weapons were gone as well as the ammunition. From his window, he could see across the parking lots to the front of the community center. He saw four men out front. Two held firing mechanisms attached to two sets of firing wires leading into the center. The other two men held M16s.

They had two separate possibilities to ignite the Claymores but had reduced their advantage by having both men so close together. Obviously, the Claymores inside the center had to be facing the back. Otherwise, the men in front would be injured. There was a possibility of more men on the other side of the community center with ignitors for Claymores facing in Devlin's direction, but that could also injure men out front.

Devlin stepped back from the window and rinsed his head and face in the bathroom sink. He swished water in his mouth to get the grit out and tried to blow some of the soot and dirt out of his nostrils. He felt more steady and focused. He went into Rachel Steele's office, picked up her phone, and waited for the tinny ring to be answered.

"Command center."

"This is Devlin. Listen carefully. You should have most of the women hostages. There are a few more in the town bar. There is one more in Kee's storefront office. All the men are in the community center. I can't get in there. There are Claymores wired to explode inside the center. Four hostiles are in the parking lot in front of the center. Two holding ignitors, two men with M16s protecting them. Take out those four first. I've eliminated at least five hostiles. Be ready to move soon."

Before Devlin got a response, he heard Sam Kee screaming his name. He looked out Rachel's window facing Main Street and saw Kee standing with a pistol to Leilani's head. Her wrists were tied with rope. Kee held both the rope and a handful of her hair with his left hand.

"Jack Devlin, you have ten seconds to come out, or I shoot this bitch."

Kee began a countdown.

CHAPTER 66

Leilani stood next to Kee, grimacing from pain. With Kee grabbing her hair and holding her roped together hands up, she had to keep her arms raised to lessen the pull on her hair. He pressed the muzzle of his Beretta against her head to add more pain.

She had to breathe through her mouth because her nose was so badly broken. She found herself panting out of fear and the strain holding up her arms. Her legs and arms throbbed where Kee had punched her.

She heard Kee tell the men around him.

"Don't shoot that fucker when he comes out. I'm going to shoot that haole piece of shit, cut off his head, and throw it at the cameras."

Kee continued his countdown. He was at five.

Devlin stood just out of sight on the west wall of the Village Inn. He looked at the horizon. The sun had dropped below the horizon ten minutes ago. Another beautiful Hawaiian sunset filled the sky. The trade winds were pushing in the nighttime complement of gray clouds. But even with the clouds, Devlin estimated it would be another twenty minutes before it was dark. He didn't have twenty minutes. He didn't have twenty seconds. And he had no idea if any of Hawthorne's soldiers were within shooting range.

Out on Main Street, Devlin heard Kee ending his count.

"Three, two...one more second and I shoot the bitch, Devlin."

Devlin stepped out on Main Street, his hands up, the compact Beretta shoved in the waistband of his pants at the small of his back.

Kee pulled Leilani along next to him as he walked toward Devlin in the darkening street, flanked by five of his men.

Devlin felt a wave of fury come on him at the sight of Leilani's swollen, battered face.

Kee's lopsided face snarled into a grin of victory.

Leilani tried to walk forward, but Devlin could see there was something wrong with her legs. She staggered instead of walked. Kee kept a tight grip on the rope around her hands and her hair, pulling her along next to him, his gun still pointed at her head.

Kee's men followed. They all pointed their rifles at him. Five men, plus whoever Devlin couldn't see. He might get close enough to shoot Kee before Kee shot Leilani, but not all the others. It was impossible. There was no way. He didn't even have enough bullets left in his Beretta. The magazine held eight. The barrel one. He'd taken five shots to cover Rachel's escape. Only four left for six men.

Kee stopped about ten feet away from Devlin. He snarled at Devlin and punched his gun into Leilani's head. "I know who this bitch is. Her name's Cranston. We killed her brother. I'm going to kill her. And I'm going to kill you."

Suddenly, Leilani let out a snarling, screaming roar. She wasn't going to let this happen to her. Not without a fight. She knew who her enemy was.

She turned, lifted her arms higher, and brought her fists down with every bit of strength she had onto Kee's forearm.

She almost broke his grip, but he held onto her hair. Bent over, she reared up again lifting her arms to hit him. Devlin had already dropped to one knee, going for the Beretta.

Kee's gun fired, shooting Leilani.

Devlin fired almost simultaneously putting two bullets into the center of Kee's broken face.

Leilani went down. Kee went down. Devlin shot the guard closest to Leilani, and the next guard over. He shifted, pulled the trigger on the third guard just to be sure and heard the Beretta click empty. Two of the guards were too startled and confused, but the one Devlin had pointed at raised his rifle. Devlin threw himself to his right, knowing he was dead, but just then the top half of the shooter's head disappeared in a burst of blood, bones, and brains.

And then Pahoa-town exploded in the sounds of automatic weapons fire, stun grenades, the roar of a helicopter suddenly appearing.

Devlin rolled away from the bullets that were smacking into the street. He felt a sting tear across the back of his thigh as he crawled across the asphalt, desperately trying to reach Leilani. He thought he saw her move and was terrified that it might be from the impact of a bullet.

He didn't care if somebody shot him. He didn't care about anything now except getting to Leilani. He reached her arm, her shoulder, and pulled her to him, frantic to cover her body with his. He lifted and half carried, half dragged her out of the street to the sidewalk getting her under a corrugated metal awning. He had her now, but there was no letup in the shooting.

Devlin dropped back against the wall of the building and pulled Leilani into his lap. He gently held Leilani's chin and turned her head, trying to see where Kee had shot her. Her blood soaked into his chest and lap. In the dim light, he could see that the right side of Leilani's head and face was covered in blood. He gently wiped the blood away with his hand and saw an ugly tear in her scalp on the left side of her head. He felt for a neck artery, searching for a pulse, and felt a strong beat.

He put one hand under her back and the other under her legs and lifted her as he struggled to stand up. His right leg felt like it had no strength. He made it upright with one leg but fell back against the building. He grunted. He screamed. You have to do this, he told himself. If they were caught on the street, one of Kee's men could still shoot them, or maybe even the Army soldiers.

Leilani was not a small woman. Devlin wasn't sure if he could make it with one leg buckling. He staggered toward the Village Inn parking lot. The Toyota Camry was still parked there. He had to get her out of this war zone.

He tried to cradle her head against his chest as he walked. At the far end of town, he saw Bradley fighting vehicles slowly rolling into sight on Main Street. Regular troops walked on foot behind the armored vehicles.

When he reached the corner, his leg was just about to give way. He dropped down on one knee and gently propped Leilani against the wall. He didn't want to risk carrying her across the open lot. He cursed himself for parking the Toyota so far away. He stood up and hobbled toward the car. It seemed a mile away. He grabbed his right leg behind the thigh and lifted it forward with each step. He was moving, but the car didn't seem to get any closer. He heard shouting and more gunfire, but he ignored it, eyes on the car. He heard the crackling sound of an M16 and saw the black ground in front of him erupt. He fell, but he didn't stop. He crawled toward the back wheel of the car, looking for the keys on top of the tire. With a final effort, Devlin made it to the back bumper of the Toyota. He pulled himself up, found the keys on the back tire, and grabbed them. He rolled, crawled to the front door, opened it, and reached over the front seat to pull himself into the car, frantic knowing Leilani was a helpless target sitting where he'd left her.

Using the steering wheel, he pulled himself onto the seat, but he had to pull his damn right leg into the car. He turned to put the keys in the ignition, fumbled, and dropped them.

Devlin screamed and pounded the steering wheel. Just as he reached down for the keys, a Humvee with flashing lights skidded to a halt in front of him. Devlin saw a huge white cross painted on the side. The driver's door opened, and the biggest soldier Devlin had ever seen stepped out. Devlin wiped sweat and blood from his eyes. He felt an arm wrap around his chest and pull him out of the car.

"Come on, brudda, we gotta get you out of here. They killing everything in this town."

"Tuli!" Devlin grabbed his meaty arm and pointed toward Leilani. "Leave me here. Get Leilani."

Tuli didn't argue. He placed Devlin down against the Camry and jumped back into the ambulance. Devlin watched the Humvee screeched to halt by Leilani. He saw Tuli lifting her into the ambulance. And with that done, Devlin's last bit of strength left him. He barely felt the hands pulling him into the ambulance and laying him onto the stretcher built into the wall of the Humvee.

He heard the doors slam, the sirens wail, felt the Humvee lurch forward. And then nothing but deep, dark, black exhaustion.

CHAPTER 67

The Army doctor Tuli had commandeered when he drove the Humvee ambulance into Pahoa knew his job and didn't question why he was treating civilians instead of soldiers. He worked quickly and expertly. By the time they had loaded Leilani into the ambulance, her blood pressure had dropped dangerously, and she was deep in shock, conditions the Army doctor hadn't treated many times before. By the time they reached the private hospital in Hilo, her head wound was bandaged, she was stable.

Devlin's vital signs were more normal, so the doctor mostly attended to his wounds and started IV fluids.

At the hospital emergency room entrance, doors flew open, hospital personnel rushed out with rolling stretchers, and Devlin and Leilani were swept up in the rush of the emergency medical care.

As they wheeled him into an examining room, Devlin made Tuli swear he would watch over Leilani. In addition to his general trauma, a concussion, bruises, burns, and cuts, they discovered three bullets wounds, the most serious being the wound across the back of his thigh. Devlin hadn't even been aware of the other two. A bullet had taken out a small piece of his left ear on top. And a ricochet had nicked him on his right side.

Five hours later, Devlin sat quietly in Leilani's hospital room. He was on one side of the bed. Tuli on the other side with a fresh bandage on his bullet wound from the raid on Kee's ranch.

The only illumination came from the glow of medical machinery and a small night-light. Leilani's doctors had reassured Devlin that Leilani's injuries were not life-threatening. The hematomas on her legs and arms, and her broken nose were painful, but minor. The bullet wound to her scalp turned out to be superficial. The most serious injury was the likely loss of hearing in her left ear.

Despite the doctors' reassurances that there was no skull fracture, Devlin insisted on staying with Leilani. Before Hawaii, he'd seen his brother fall into a coma and have a stroke from a head injury.

Two days later on Wednesday morning, Leilani had recovered enough to leave the hospital. Devlin and Tuli accompanied her on the flight back to Honolulu. Jasper Cranston had insisted that Devlin bring his daughter to his home to recuperate, but Leilani had refused. She wanted to be in her own house. And she wanted Devlin to be there with her.

Devlin agreed. Tuli made it clear he would come, too. Nonnegotiable. Tuli considered Devlin to still be under his protection. Devlin knew it there was no point in arguing about it.

The three of them settled into Leilani's small house on the beach about a mile from her father's house. Devlin and Leilani shared her bedroom. Tuli slept on the pullout couch in the living room, a good portion of his arms and legs hanging off the bed.

They had arrived late afternoon on Wednesday. Leilani fell asleep immediately and didn't wake until mid-day Thursday. That gave Devlin a chance to meet with General James Hawthorne at Schofield Barracks. Hawthorne kept his part of the bargain, sharing all the information he had gathered. The battle of Pahoa had lasted less than thirty minutes. The clean-up and interrogation had started immediately and continued until Hawthorne sat with Devlin. Included at the meeting was Lieutenant Colonel Sam Weisman.

Hawthorne confirmed everything Devlin already knew.

Sam Kee and an Army Captain named Kingston McWilliams had killed Billy Cranston. Hawthorne also named Lieutenant Colonel George Walker as key in the theft of the Army's weapons. He confirmed that McWilliams and Walker were both dead. Devlin already knew Kee was dead. Devlin had two questions.

"Have you found any of your weapons?"

"Negative."

"Do you have any way of identifying and prosecuting whoever Kee was working for?

Hawthorne answered, "I have another meeting, Mr. Devlin. I've asked Colonel Weisman to speak to you on a related issue."

Hawthorne and Devlin shook hands. Devlin indicated his satisfaction with a nod. Fifteen minutes later, after talking to Sam Weisman Devlin left Schofield with no further questions.

He returned to the North Shore, arranged to meet with Jasper Cranston on Friday night, and continued taking care of Leilani.

During that time, Devlin felt more closeness and intimacy with Leilani than with any woman he'd ever been with. The feelings had emerged as he helped her in and out of bed, changed her dressings, helped her dress, cooked for her, and explained to her how helpful she had been to him and how sorry he was about what had happened to her.

Tuli turned into a gentle giant, running errands, cleaning house, adding his encouragement.

Being near the ocean and in the sun helped impart strength back into Leilani's body, but her emotional state remained dark and subdued.

On Friday morning, Devlin sat with her on the beach. He asked her, "How do you feel?"

"Not great."

Devlin smiled. "Care to be a bit more specific?"

"I can deal with the physical stuff. The goddamn stitches in my scalp are starting to itch. A lot of stuff still hurts. Can't hear through my left ear. Can't breathe through my damn nose with all this packing in it." She shrugged. "But I know in few weeks all that will resolved, one way or another. Trouble is, I don't know if I'm ever going to resolve the feelings I have."

"You will. Over time. It won't ever be like it was. But you will be able to live with it."

"I guess I asked for it. You warned me, didn't you?"

"Yes. And don't forget, you considered what I said and decided to go forward. Don't second guess yourself. And don't ever think I'm not glad you didn't listen to me. Without you, I wouldn't have solved this. Without you, I'd probably be dead."

"But without you, I wouldn't have gone at Kee like that?"

"I'm not sure what that means, but the fact is – you were beaten up, tied up, but you fought back. You knocked that gun away from your head, and you gave me a chance to get to my gun. You went all in. You didn't know I was armed, but you didn't give a shit. You went right at him. No hesitation. No second guessing. That's why you're alive. That's why I'm alive. And that's why he's dead. Don't ever forget that."

Leilani nodded, taking it all in.

Devlin asked, "Do you believe me?"

"Yes."

"And?"

She said, "It makes me feel better. For sure. But I'm still sad."

"Why?" asked Devlin.

Leilani stared out at the rolling blue waves. "It's interesting. I'm not sad about what happened to me." She looked at Devlin with a deep fondness. "You've helped me with that. I'm still sad about Billy."

Devlin said, "So am I. So am I. But not as sad as I would be if we hadn't done something about it."

After a moment, Leilani said, "Yes. I suppose that's right."

"You suppose?"

"He suffered so much for so long."

Devlin nodded. "I know. And yet at the end, he chose to die doing what he believed needed to be done. He was the catalyst. He put a stop to all the misery trafficking in arms creates. He died like the hero he always was."

Leilani nodded. More to herself than to Devlin.

"Okay, so now what?"

"I talked to William Chow. Brought him up to speed on everything. He cleared me to report our findings to your father. I promised Jasper I would do that."

"And what about me?"

Devlin said nothing for a while. He knew he hadn't told Leilani everything, and he knew he never would. He picked his words carefully.

"You know everything I know. What we don't know is what the Army investigation might unearth, or what they'll do about it."

"What do you think the Army will do?"

"I'm going to tell you the truth, and you're going to decide at some point where you stand with it."

"What's the truth?"

"I doubt it will surprise you."

"Go on."

"The Army is going to do everything in its power to make sure nothing like this ever happens again. And then they're going to bury the whole thing as deep as humanly possible."

Leilani nodded. "And we'll never really know what the Army does to make sure nothing like this ever happens again."

"No."

"And what about you, Jack? Are you done now?"

"Not until I talk to your father."

For a moment, Leilani was going to ask him again about that, but she knew Devlin had already given his answer. An answer that let her know this wasn't over yet.

CHAPTER 68

Devlin and Jasper Cranston met on Friday night. Cranston listened to Devlin's report without interruption for a little over an hour. He nursed one drink during the entire time.

"So, you're telling me that everyone who had anything to do with my son's murder is dead."

Devlin hesitated. He knew better than to lie.

Cranston didn't wait.

"You're not telling me that. We both know somebody above all the fools and lowlifes sold the stolen weapons. So, let me make it easier for you, Mr. Devlin. There's only one son of a bitch on these islands who could pull something like that off. Eddie Lihu."

Devlin said nothing.

"You silence confirms it. Next question, sounds like all the human links to Eddie Lihu are dead. Right?"

"Yes."

"What are the Army's chances of discovering who bought the weapons, tracking them down, extraditing them, forcing them to testify against Lihu and making a case Lihu and his lawyers can't shred?"

"There's always a chance."

"Not in my lifetime. And not in yours." Jasper Cranston finished his drink, stood up, and extended a hand to Jack Devlin. "Thank you for everything you accomplished, Mr. Devlin."

Devlin said, "Have a seat, Colonel. I'm not going anywhere."

Cranston sat down. "Stay if you want. Doesn't matter. I'm not going let the bastard responsible for my son's death live to enjoy his profits. No, sir. What's more, we both know as long as Eddie Lihu breathes, my daughter is in danger."

Devlin didn't respond.

"She was a hostage inside Sam Kee's office for hours. Lihu won't know what she saw or heard. He's not going to take the chance. Neither am I."

"What are you going to do?"

"Mr. Devlin, you knew what I was going to do when you walked in here."

"I'm not walking out until I hear it all. I can't let you go out there and ..."

Cranston raised a hand. "Stop. The worst has already happened to me, Devlin. Listen, that rot I told you I picked up in 'Nam. It's not just the stump. I'm riddled with it. Agent Orange, or whatever toxic shit I breathed in over there, I don't have a hell of a lot of time. I'm not saying another word about it. You need plausible deniability. You need to be able to say had no idea a washed up, disabled, elderly, alcoholic retiree had any intention, knowledge or ability to do anything to anybody. That's your response to my daughter, the police, to anybody who goddamn asks. And if I fail, Mr. Devlin, I want you free and clear to find another way. I'm not making you an accomplice. Not in any way. You're going to spend Sunday taking care of my daughter just like you've been doing. I suggest the two of you have lunch in a public place. Use your credit card. And save the receipt."

"Tomorrow lunch?"

"Make it a long one.

Devlin nodded and kept his mouth shut, trying to convince himself there really wasn't anything he could do, and that he hadn't planned on this long before they sat down.

Cranston said, "Good. Now I'm asking one last thing of you,

Mr. Devlin. Convince my daughter to come here for dinner tomorrow night. I have things I want to say to her. Will you do that for me, son?"

"Why didn't you say, 'things I want to say to her before I die'"?

"We're soldiers. It's understood."

CHAPTER 69

Saturday's dinner was a subdued affair. Nobody seemed to have much energy for it except Cranston's mongrel mastiff, Arthur, who wouldn't stop romping around Leilani until she pulled his ears, scratched his big head, and pounded on his chest.

They made small talk throughout a meal Cranston had clearly had taken time preparing: grilled Mahi Mahi and vegetables, buttered baked potato skins, and a crisp, cold Chablis. Dessert was simple: fresh fruit with whipped heavy cream.

Devlin took note that Jasper Cranston didn't drink before dinner and sipped carefully from one glass of wine during the meal. Devlin accepted Cranston's offer of Irish whiskey with his after-dinner coffee and was pleased that Cranston stuck with coffee.

Devlin sat in the living room with his after-dinner drinks. Cranston and Leilani headed to the west wing of the house for their conversation. Devlin sat brooding, chafing at not knowing what Cranston planned to do. At one point, voices were raised, but it didn't last long. Nor did the conversation. After fifteen minutes, Leilani walked into the living room ready to leave. There was no sign of her father.

Devlin asked, "Everything okay?"

"As okay as it will ever be."

He didn't press her for the meaning behind that.

#

The next morning, retired Brigadier General Jasper Cranston drove to Eddie Lihu's ranch situated east of the Waimea Valley. The ranch occupied almost two hundred acres of well-maintained forested areas, pastures, groves, fish ponds, and gardens. Five acres of manicured lawn surrounding the main house where the wedding was to take place.

As Cranston pulled up to the first line of security, he stopped and pointed to his disabled veteran license plates. The guard waived him on toward a parking area near the main house.

When he climbed out of his car, Cranston did not line up at the sign-in tables. He walked around the back of the mansion and onto the front lawn.

Even on a normal day, Jasper Cranston's demeanor kept people at a distance. Dressed in his U.S. Army full-dress blues decorated with a Croix de Guerre lanyard, three inches of battle ribbons, a Bronze Star, two Purple Hearts, and brigadier general's stars made him even more imposing. None of the security guards patrolling the area were inclined to question his presence.

Cranston, of course, realized that some of the guests and guards would remember him, but he didn't care. He only cared about doing what he believed had to be done. He had no concern about what might happen afterward.

The wedding was to take place under a huge red-and-white striped canopy on the lawn behind the mansion. It was early, but over two-hundred guests were already mingling and strolling about the grounds. A dozen serving areas had been set up around the mansion providing drinks and hors-d'oeuvres.

Few of the guests were in the main house, but again, Cranston didn't care. He walked up the front stairs and into a large foyer that was all marble, stone pillars, and furnishings that reflected cost but not taste. The left side of the foyer opened onto a large living room.

To the right, onto a dining area. Facing Cranston were two curving staircases, each a mirror image of the other. There were security guards near both staircases making sure nobody went upstairs.

Cranston walked toward the nearest guard.

"Excuse me, son, but I've got a problem. My stump is slipping around in my socket here, and I need a room or a bathroom where I can take my pants off and secure the damn thing."

The security guard was both intimidated by Cranston and uncomfortable with his stump problem. He walked Cranston through the living room toward a small powder room. He even opened the door for Cranston.

The general thanked him, closed the door, and sat on the toilet seat. He took a soft rubber cup out of his pocket and slipped it over the bottom of his peg leg. He reached under his jacket and extracted his M1911 Colt .45 service gun, which was tucked into his waistband. Anyone looking closely might have spotted the bulge the gun made, but the most people never got past looking at his peg leg. The gun had been with him for many years, and Cranston knew this would be the last time he'd ever use it. He chambered a round, engaged the thumb safety, and replaced the cocked and locked weapon under his belt.

Cranston came out of the powder room and walked through the living room into a huge kitchen/serving area. The catering staff was busy with food prep. Those who noticed Cranston didn't bother to question him.

Cranston quickly found the stairs that led from the kitchen to the upstairs bedrooms. When he came out onto the second-floor landing, Cranston was surprised at how many people were bustling about in the spacious central hallway. Most of the activity involved a photographer and his assistant taking pictures of bridesmaids near the top of the double stairways. He saw people coming in and out of rooms along the hallway. A seamstress, a hair stylist, a woman carrying a case of cosmetics, and another photographer.

Cranston stood in a smaller hallway that intersected with the main hallway. He doubted Eddie Lihu would be anywhere near all that commotion, so he looked to his left and right. It only took a moment to figure out which direction led to Lihu's bedroom. Looking right, Cranston saw Lihu's bodyguard, Charlie, guarding a closed door. The biker wore a dark suit that did little to hide the fact he was a thug.

Cranston headed for the large bodyguard without hesitation. His natural aura of authority made Charlie wait and watch him approach. As Cranston got nearer, Charlie held up a hand and said, "Hold on. Who are you?"

Cranston kept coming.

"I'm here to see Mr. Lihu."

"No, you're not. Nobody called me. Mr. Lihu didn't say anything."

Cranston held up his left hand as if to acknowledge what Charlie said, but he kept closing the distance.

"Hey, I said hold it right there."

Charlie pulled his jacket out of the way and reached for his gun. Two mistakes. He waited too long, and both hands were now occupied.

Jasper was already within striking distance. And he already knew he had only one chance against the much bigger, younger man. His first blow had to be a lethal one.

Jasper Cranston was 74 years old, but still a very strong man. He stepped forward and put all his considerable weight behind a punch that hit the bodyguard directly in the throat, crushing his larynx.

Charlie doubled over, choking, struggling to pull air through his collapsed, rapidly swelling windpipe. Cranston pulled out his Colt and slammed the butt into Charlie's temple, knocking him out. Charlie landed face down, muffling the sound of his dying struggle to breathe.

Cranston didn't wait for the bodyguard to die. He opened the heavy door and quickly closed it behind him. He found himself standing in a sitting room. A half-closed door on his left revealed a large bedroom with a balcony. The sounds of the gathering guests and a string quartet drifted in from outside. Eddie Lihu sat at the foot of a king-size bed trying to fit a cufflink into his starched tuxedo shirt cuff.

A fleeting thought passed through Cranston's mind: Lihu's wife should have been helping him with the cufflink. He concluded that they weren't very close. It didn't surprise him.

The deep pile carpeting in the sitting room completely muffled Cranston's approach, even the usual thump of his peg leg.

When he pushed open the half-closed door and stepped into the bedroom, Lihu did not look up until Cranston was almost within arm's reach. When the fat man finally noticed Cranston, he rose to his feet with surprising speed for a man his size, but not fast enough. Without a moment's hesitation, Cranston shoved the Colt .45 into Lihu's chest and pulled the trigger. Lihu had only managed to get a hand on Cranston's wrist before the .45 caliber bullet obliterated his heart, pulverized his spine, and sent him falling back onto the carpet.

Cranston had been concentrating so intently on killing Lihu that he hadn't really heard the sound of the gun. Perhaps Lihu's bulk had absorbed most of the sound. Cranston looked down at the smoking gun and noticed that his shirt cuff and sleeve were spattered with blood.

The Colt was too hot to place back under his belt, so Cranston simply held on to it, turned, and left the room.

When he emerged into the hallway outside Lihu's bedroom suite, Cranston expected to see people rushing toward him, or perhaps people shouting, asking about the noise. There was nobody except the comatose body of Charlie, the bodyguard.

Cranston didn't even bother to drag Charlie out of view. He walked away from Lihu's bedroom suite heading for the back stairs.

He realized he still held his Colt. He shoved it into his waistband and straightened his dress jacket. Cranston did it carefully, without rushing.

Cranston made his way down the stairs and into the kitchen. This time he walked out a side door, emerging near where the wedding was to take place.

Not caring whether he was caught somehow ensured that Cranston wouldn't be. He walked to the front lawn, aware now how difficult it was on his peg leg. There were even more people mingling. Still no alarm.

Cranston attracted only fleeting attention as he walked back to his car. Nobody noticed the blood on his shirt cuff or dark blue jacket. When he reached his car and opened the door, he thought he heard a faint scream. A woman's voice. Perhaps it was Mrs. Lihu, arriving to see how her husband was doing with his cufflink.

CHAPTER 70

On Tuesday afternoon, following the Sunday death of Eddie Lihu and his bodyguard, Devlin received word from William Chow that he wanted him back on the Mainland as soon as he could get a flight.

Devlin called Leilani who was at her father's house. He told her he was leaving on a 5:05 P.M. flight to San Francisco. She asked him to come over.

It didn't take Devlin long to pack. Tuli drove him to Cranston's and waited in the rental car outside Cranston's house. He insisted his job was not over until Devlin was safely on the plane to San Francisco.

The door to the house was open. Cranston's big mastiff recognized Devlin when he entered and presented himself for a pat on the head.

The house seemed to have lost its neat, well-tended look. Now there were dirty dishes in the sink, a thin veil of dust on the koa wood floors, unopened mail on the dining room table.

Leilani came out from the kitchen where she had been cleaning and met Devlin. Her broken nose was still swollen. There was an ugly little bump at the bridge. Yellowish purple bruises discolored the skin under her eyes. A gauze bandaged still covered the right side of her head where her hair had been shaved off.

They embraced quickly.

"You here to see Jasper?"

"And you."

"He's outside. I'll wait."

Devlin walked out the sliding door and saw Cranston standing about ten feet from the east end of the house. He had set out a metal trash barrel with holes poked in the bottom that made the fire he was tending burn more efficiently. He was feeding the contents of a large cardboard box into the fire: campaign plaques, ribbons, medals, papers the accumulated effects from a lifetime of military service.

Cranston wore only a beat-up pair of corduroy shorts. He hadn't shaved since Sunday. Jasper Cranston looked like he had arrived at some sort of endpoint. The signs of sickness and aging hung on him like a heavy cloak.

When Cranston looked up and saw Devlin he nodded but kept feeding items into the fire.

After a few moments, he asked Devlin, "Do you think my son is at peace finally?"

"I do. What do you think?"

Cranston looked away and poured the last contents of his box into the burning barrel and tossed the box onto the ground.

"I hope so. I don't know. For the last few days, I've been concentrating on ending things. Haven't given much thought to anything else."

Devlin nodded.

Cranston looked out to sea and spoke almost to himself, "I should have never come here. I don't belong in these islands. Lei and her mother and brother deserved better than me."

Devlin said, "You still have time to do something about that."

Cranston turned toward him. "In the time I have left."

"Yes."

Devlin extended his hand and said, "Goodbye, General. I am sorry for your loss."

Cranston shook Devlin's hand and nodded once. They both knew there wasn't much more to say to each other.

As Devlin walked away, Leilani came out of the house and met him.

She said, "I'm heading home. I'm going to walk."

Devlin fell in step with her as she headed toward the ocean. As usual, it wasn't easy for Devlin to keep up with Leilani's long strides, particularly with his right leg still recovering from the bullet wound. But walking on the beach felt good. When Leilani veered south parallel to the water, after a few strides, Devlin stopped. Leilani turned to him.

Devlin said, "I'll leave you here."

"What time's your flight?"

Devlin looked at his watch. "Five. Tuli is parked out front. If I don't go to the damn airport, he won't go home. He's got quite a few people waiting for him."

"That must be nice."

"Yes."

Leilani abruptly asked, "When do you think the police will come for my father?"

Devlin shrugged. "Fairly soon. If they insist on talking to you, tell the truth. You had no idea. If they press you, call your lawyer."

"Is that what you told them?"

"They haven't asked me. If they ever do, I'll say the same thing."

"Is it true?"

"If it's true for you, it's true for me."

Leilani didn't ask Devlin to explain what he meant by that.

"What do you think will happen to him?"

Devlin said, "The clothes he wore are gone. The gun is gone. Nobody saw him commit the crime. They won't arrest him unless they have a solid case. And I doubt anybody is pushing to make an arrest. Even if they do, he'll make bail, and it'll be a couple of years before a trial."

Leilani nodded. "I understand. It'll be what it will be."

"Yes."

"You said, you have to go for now. What does for now mean, Jack?"

"It means that sometime later, this part of the world could be a nice place to come back to. Maybe make a home here. I haven't had one in a long time."

"I'd like to try that with you. You know that, don't you?"

"Yes."

"Will it ever happen?"

"Let's see how we feel about that when you and I heal up a little more."

Leilani nodded. Then she asked, "Where are you flying off to?"

"London. Apparently, a friend of mine there needs some help."

Leilani smiled. "Whoever the friend is, they're lucky." She nodded once, smiled again, then turned, and walked down the beach with a small wave because she didn't want to say goodbye.

Devlin watched her, enjoying the sight of her. When she was about twenty feet away, he called out, "Leilani."

She turned and shaded her eyes. "What?"

"Promise me something."

"What?"

"Promise me the next time we walk on a beach it'll be a little slower."

"I promise. But it's going to be a long walk."